BACKST

THE CHRONICLE OF
GEOFFREY HENDERSON FODEN

The journey from London had been slow and the train had been cold, despite the crush of bodies and the intensity of tobacco smoke. It stopped at all the towns en route where uniformed servicemen and women of various nationalities swarmed about the platforms delaying the passage of the train even more as they argued with station staff about warrants and connections and there seemed to be no attempt to follow a schedule. As he had started his journey from London's Paddington Station he had managed to get a seat but even the First Class compartment did not protect him from the crush of bodies and kitbags.

He was seated next to a major of artillery who had made the journey all the way from Sword Beach to Wiesbaden before he was told he had done enough and a mortar shell had taken a sizeable piece from his arm. They swapped experiences in a polite and unemotional manner, mostly of the strategic and physical challenges they had encountered, seemingly unaware that they were parts in the greatest jigsaw in the history of mankind.

Eventually, after shedding several carriages at some point, the train steamed into Stokesey and he was grateful he could at last relieve his bladder. He had not eaten nor drunk anything since leaving Paddington, knowing that if he vacated his seat someone else would take it. He stepped stiffly down onto the little platform now glowing yellow from the gas lights and glistening in the December mist.

"Mr Geoffrey – or I should now say Captain Geoffrey? How nice to see you. Welcome home, sir."

"Thank you Morris. Mister is fine. Time to bury the war." He was surprised the old station master had recognised him "Has anyone been looking for me?"

"Your father has telephoned two or three times. I rang him when we heard the train had reached Holt Junction so I expect there'll be someone outside waiting for you. Good luck, sir. Thank God you made it back."

Geoffrey Foden took the extended hand and walked out of the station.

"Geoffrey. Geoffrey."

His sister's voice was recognisable and he saw her standing and waving next to the Lanchester and he was surprised that his inside went suddenly limp and he had to take a deep breath to prevent his eyes from watering. She was soon running towards him and he saw his father getting out of the car behind her and then Sheila was in his arms, trying to press the air out of his body. His father reached them and extended a hand.

"Dear chap. How are you?" he said.

"Hello Father. I'm pretty decent thanks. Could do with a beer and something to eat though."

His father laughed and put his arm around his shoulder while Sheila took his bag and held onto his arm as they walked to the car.

His mother cried, the maid cried, Gladys the cook cried and Beryl the housekeeper cried and even Jack, the gardener and general handyman, wiped his eyes. Sheila both cried and laughed at the same time as they fussed around him. There was a fire in the sitting-room and he flopped onto the sofa as his father handed him a tankard of ale.

"Here's to our dear son," his father said after he had

THE GIRL OF DROVERS'S HILL
A NOVEL BY
P K DAVIES

ACKNOWLEDGEMENTS

COVER BACKGROUND
Morning light in a bluebell wood
Alamy Piictures

END PAGE
'Man Thinking' by dreamstime.com

*The author would also like to thank author **James 'Beau' Laidler** for his helpful feedback and support.*

Warning

Procreation is the drive-engine of all animal species. In homo sapiens it has evolved beyond its original purpose and become an instrument of social practice - but is no less powerful. It can be a light in the window or the threat in the shadows. Sexual chemistry dictates ordinary aspects of our lives in our everyday relationships: who we like and who we dislike and what we find attractive or repulsive. In this novel, scenes of a sexual nature are integral to its theme.

Who are we?
Who am I?
I thought I knew
Until
That day
That moment
That second
When a stranger
With my face
Came
From The Dark Beyond
And said
'I am who you are.'

poured drinks for everyone. "Thank God he's safe and with us again."

"Amen to that," his mother said.

"It's only been three years," Geoffrey laughed. "Some poor sods are still out there and they started in forty."

"And may they soon be home, all of them."

"I'm afraid an awful lot won't be," Geoffrey said to himself.

His father tried to lift the mood again. "Let's eat. You must be starving. Is it all ready Gladys?"

"It is. You can start the soup while I prepare the pheasant."

"Pheasant," Geoffrey Foden laughed. "My God! That sounds good."

He fielded many questions over dinner and ran through the places he'd been to as quickly as a Thomas Cooke tour guide."

"What about Berlin?" his father asked. "Would I recognise it still?"

"No, Father. Not much of it. It's terrible. The Allied side is bad enough, they're still finding bodies all over the city, there's very little electricity and water and refugees are still pouring over from the Soviet side. But what is happening in the Russian zone is even worse. Executions are still going on over there."

"Poor devils."

"It's their own fault," Mrs. Foden said decidedly. "Look what they've done to everyone else."

"Just a few men did it, Mother. That's all it takes. Just a few bad men."

He slept in his bed for the first time since he had left for officer training three years before. It was a duck-down mattress and his body seemed to float weightlessly and his organs seemed to press from the inside as though only his bones were immune to the laws of gravity. He wanted to get out and to pull the eiderdown with him onto the floor but he seemed incapable of moving and while his brain considered the problem he fell asleep and slept for twelve hours before he was aware of light and sound. He opened his eyes and attempted to raise himself from the mattress but fell back again feeling that all of his body was tender as though he had been pummelled by an enthusiastic masseur. There was a knock on the door and he managed to groan a response. The door opened and Sheila looked from around it.

"Are you awake?" she asked

"Trying," he replied. "But I don't think I can move." He reached out an arm and she came quickly to his aid.

"Pull me up, Sis."

She heaved on his arm and it was an uneven contest until she dug her heels into the pile carpet and leant backwards like a tug-o-war champion and threatened to pull him sideways off the bed. He suddenly pushed upwards from his elbow and Sheila fell onto the carpet in a fit of giggling. She was two years younger than him and had always been ready to die for him.

"Shall I get you some tea?" she asked

"That would be absolutely splendid, Sis, then I'll have a hot shower, something I haven't had for a few weeks. I presume we have hot-water?"

"We do. Coal is still rationed but we've been using peat on the fires and coal in the furnace." she told him.

"Where do you get the peat?"

"Sir Toby's place. He pays the POW's to cut it for him."

"What POW's?"

" We have a prison camp the other side of Stokesey,"

"What sort of prisoners?"

"Germans. It was all Italians but they've been sent home.

Now we've got Germans."

"And they work outside?

"If they want to. They're really all right. I feel rather sorry for them, actually. They're all officers. Luftwaffe I think."

"Good Heavens. I had no idea."

Later that day he saw the prisoners of war. He had walked up towards the Ridgeway and saw a line of them on the Fender path coming from the marshes. There were eight of them, some with shovels over their shoulders rather like rifles and the back of his neck tingled for a moment. Two of them were pushing wheel barrows laden with what he presumed was peat, probably for their barracks he told himself. They were dressed in dark brown work-dress uniform with distinctive yellow patches on them. He stood and watched them walking along the path towards him and as they got near he could see their faces and he was reminded of the many similar faces he had seen of other prisoners in France and Belgium and the thousands of homeless citizens in Berlin.

"Guten tag," Foden said as they drew level with him. Some of them nodded but one man, bringing up the rear of the column spoke to him in almost perfect English.

"Good afternoon," he said. He was about the same age as himself, and looked even more boy-like in the uniform which was too large for him. He smiled as he spoke and Foden was reminded of the friends he had left behind when he had been taken straight from his boarding school into the army. How many of them might he see again he wondered? That evening he asked his father about the prisoners.

"I've got two of them working for me at the factory," his father told him. "Good chaps. Work hard."

"Doesn't anyone keep an eye on them?"

"What's the point? The war's over. They're not going to

swim the Channel or do any harm are they?"

"I suppose not. But why aren't they going home?"

"I expect they will, eventually. There are thousands of them all over the country. It must be a bit of a nightmare for the chaps at the War Office to arrange it all."

"Will they have a home to go to?"

"That's a good question, Mother" her son answered. "Probably not."

Two days later he felt relaxed enough to want to ride again. He hadn't ridden since his last holiday from school. His sister wanted to join him but Geoffrey said he should ride over to the Henderson's to say hello.

"To Fiona you mean," his sister teased him.

Fiona Henderson was a year younger than him and they had known each other all their lives and it had always been a relationship encouraged by his parents but he had never thought of Fiona as a sexual partner, probably because he had never mentally progressed their friendship from that of children since he had gone away to boarding school.

The Hendersons were pleased to see him and Sir Toby, who had never managed to have a son among his three daughters, was especially enthusiastic. He was older than Geoffrey's father and had been right through the Great War and was keen to hear everything about Geoffrey's experiences. He was given lunch and subjected to two hours questioning before Lady Henderson told her husband that she was sure that Geoffrey hadn't come over to talk about the war.

"We need to forget it," she added.

"You never forget 'em," her husband grumbled but acquiesced by closing his eyes and settling into his armchair and snapping The Times in front of his face.

"Would you like to see my new hunter?" Fiona asked.

"I would love to," Geoffrey lied. She took his arm as they walked to the stables.

"Are you pleased to be back?" she asked.

"I don't know yet," he said. "My mind is still in several places but I suppose it will settle down sometime."

"Soon I hope."

They entered the stables and Geoffrey pulled them up opposite a stall which a young man in dark brown uniform was mucking out.

"Hello again," Geoffrey said. The man stopped shovelling and smiled at him.

"Hello. How are you?"

"I'm quite well, thank you."

"Do you know each other?" Fiona asked and looked cross.

"We spoke the other day." Foden held out his hand to the German. "I'm Geoffrey Foden. Captain Foden." The man wiped his hand on his trousers then took the hand offered.

"Gerhardt," he said. "Hauptmann Gerhardt Muller. How d'you do?"

"You speak very good English. Where did you learn?"

"At school. But I had an English nanny for a while. Do you still say 'Nanny'?

"Yes, we do. What happened to her?"

"She was Jewish." In the silence that followed the two men held each other's eyes.

"Come and look at Hero."

Fiona broke the spell and Geoffrey nodded to the other man and followed obediently to another stall where a chestnut gelding stuck his nose into Fiona's chest and objected to her kissing it.

"He's rather good," Geoffrey said approvingly. "Where did you get him from?"

"From Ireland. One of Daddy's cousins was selling up and

moving to America."

"I think there may be a few more to follow him."

"Are things going to be that bad, Geoffrey?" she asked, a frown pushing her eyelids together.

"Probably. War ruins everyone. It's never going to be the same again. But believe me, we are lucky compared to the rest of Europe. I hate to think what that chap is going back to," he said, nodding towards Gerhardt. Fiona took his arm and pressed her face to his shoulder as they returned to the house. Before he left he promised to join Sir Toby's shooting party that weekend.

"You still have your guns, I hope," Sir Toby asked and Geoffrey confirmed that he had but had been using another type for the past three years.

"Well, if you'd rather use a 303 you are very welcome – but I doubt if even you would bag very much."

"I didn't do very well with bigger targets," Geoffrey acknowledged. "Have you got any beaters?" he asked

"One or two of the old chaps are still around and these POW's are game," Sir Toby told him.

"Then let's hope nobody shoots them," Fiona joked.

The shooting party went by road to the Henderson estate as the gaming area was farther west where the hills curved away and left several hundred acres of rough pasture and woodland. There were some twelve guns assembled from the county families with their retinue of servants and female members. Hot toddies were served before the party set off towards the trees. Sir Toby walked with Geoffrey Foden.

"Haven't you got a loader?" he asked.

Geoffrey thought his sister was going to do it but she chose to talk to Fiona instead. Then he saw that Gerhardt was one of the POW's walking ahead of them.

"That chap can do it," Geoffrey said, pointing. "I met him

in your stables with Fiona. He speaks jolly good English."

The old man looked doubtful. "I think it might be against regulations letting them handle weapons."

"I'm sure they are as sick of killing as we are. I don't think he will murder anyone. Gerhardt," he called. The German stopped and smiled as he recognised the caller. He walked back to them.

"Hello Geoffrey," he said.

"Do you know anything about these things?"

"Yes. I used to shoot with my father."

"Would you like to load for me?"

"It would be my pleasure."

Foden smiled at Sir Toby who scowled but nodded permission.

"You'd better take the left wing," he said and moved away.

Geoffrey gave one of his guns and a pocket of shells to Gerhardt.

"What is the white flash on your jacket for?" Foden asked.

"It means I am the Lagerfuhrer – the one in charge of the prisoners – because I speak English. I relay messages from the Commandant," he explained.

"Do you have guards on the camp?"

"There is a lieutenant Griffiths and a sergeant."

Foden asked him about the camp. He was told there were only eighty prisoners there now since the Italians had gone. They nearly all chose to work outside, mostly on the farms, and were paid for doing so and they had to be back in camp by dusk.

"Otherwise, we can do anything we like. We don't get bored now we can go outside but before it was very hard not doing anything. They did their best to keep us busy; talks and English lessons, that sort of thing."

"How long have you been a prisoner?"

"Almost two years."

"Were you shot down here?"

"No. I was doing photo-reconnaissance. We knew the invasion was going to happen so they sent me to find troop concentrations and to photograph them. I was solo flying a Messerschmitt BF110. The cannons are taken out and replaced by cameras so I had no firepower. I flew in from Holland very low, hopefully under radar, but I met two Mosquitoes, they are very fast. They forced me to land."

"Bad luck."

"Not really. I am alive."

They walked to their positions and heard Sir Toby cry, "Here they come."

"I thought I would never hear that again," Foden said as he raised his gun."

"Did you think you would ever have to kill again?" Gerhardt asked, a smile playing on the side of his mouth.

"It's all right if you eat what you shoot."

"Is that what we should have done; eaten each other, and then it would have been all right?" The two men laughed. "This is a new perspective for me; looking up to the target."

Foden followed the partridge, turning as he released two barrels and saw the birds falling. Gerhardt immediately swapped the guns but Foden was slow to respond and the next pair passed by. "Wake up on the left," Sir Toby yelled towards them.

The second flight of birds turned towards them, probably thinking they stood a better chance. Foden brought down two more but missed with his reload.

"We can eat porridge," Gerhardt suggested.

After the shoot the party and helpers gathered outside the house where Sir Toby's servants brought out drinks and hot sausage rolls. Geoffrey introduced his sister to Gerhardt and left them talking together as Fiona waved for his attention. She was standing with her mother and Geoffrey's mother and two other local people whom he recognised.

"We were wondering what to do about the POW's at Christmas," his mother said. "Sir Toby thinks we should all have one or two of them for lunch – now we are officially allowed to fraternise. What do you think, Geoffrey?"

"I think that's a splendid idea," he said "I don't suppose they've had Christmas at home for a few years and they may not get another one for a long time."

"Mr. Shackleton says the Vicar has asked people in the village to do what they can to help. I think we could have one or two don't you?"

"Yes, I do. I've already made a friend of one of them. Shall I invite him?. He can explain to the others."

"Gerhardt?" Fiona said.

"Yes," Geoffrey answered and from Fiona's expression he saw she did not approve.

"Why don't you do that, Geoffrey," his mother said.

Before he reached them, he saw that Gerhardt had walked away from his sister to answer someone's call for assistance.

"He's so handsome," Sheila said.

"Yes, he is," Geoffrey agreed. "I'm going to invite him over for Christmas lunch. You can flirt with him then."

Geoffrey continued walking to where Gerhardt was translating for Sir Toby's estate manager, Reg Buckley, to two other Germans.

"They can take a brace of birds back with them," Buckley was saying and the German's frowns changed to gratitude when Gerhardt translated.

"Can you cook at the camp?" Geoffrey asked

"Yes. We look after ourselves." Geoffrey told him about the Christmas lunch invitation.

"That would be wonderful. Everyone has been very kind. Last Christmas children came to our camp and sang carols to us. But then we couldn't go out." His mood changed, "Geoffrey, have you been in Germany?"

"For the past eight months. I was with the Control Commission in Berlin."

"What is it like?"

Foden understood the question. Should he tell him what it was really like? Should he tell him about the thousands of prisoners in France and Belgium, of the chaos of what to do with them; of how some were stuffed into trains and sent thousands of miles across Europe with almost no food and little water, some of them Cossacks and East-Europeans who had fought with the Germans and would end up in the Russian zone? Should he tell him of the devastation to the towns and villages, of the destruction of the livestock, of no heating fuel or transport, of the shortage of men to make repairs or clear away the mountains of rubble, of the smell of corpses among the debris? Should he tell him of the rumours of what the Russians were doing to the women and young males?

"It's not very good," he said. "Where are you from, Gerhardt?"

"Cottbus. It's north of Leipzig, near the Polish border."

"That will be occupied by the Russians."

"Yes."

"Have you heard from your family?"

"My father was... He was a panzer commander on the Russian front. We had no news from him for four years. My mother last wrote to me two years ago but I have had no reply to my letters since."

"There is no organisation. Nothing works. In Berlin the allies are getting it together, doing their best. They are reforming civil structures, repairing the infrastructure. But the Russians have no interest in re-building Germany. They only want to get drunk and take revenge for the treatment they suffered. I'm sorry, Gerhardt. I wish I could tell you it was better." .

The other man nodded and started to walk away, then he stopped and looked back at Foden.

"Geoffrey, would you come to our camp and talk to my colleagues. You speak German don't you?"

"A little. I learned at school and learned a lot more while I was in Berlin. What would you want me to say?"

"Just tell them…what you know. What you haven't told me. How it really is. You see, they think things are going to be as they were when they return. Some of them don't understand how bad the war has been for us. They have been only on airfields and most of them have been here for three or four years. I flew from Holland and I know what the bombing was doing there. I think they need to know that. For us, there is another war to be won. The war against ourselves."

"I could try," Geoffrey said.

Lieutenant Griffiths was honoured by a visit from a real soldier even though he was only out-ranked by one grade. The sergeant was less impressed by another kid who could tell him what to do. He was a veteran, a Guardsman who had taken severe shrapnel wounds at Dunkirk. But even he warmed to Foden when he produced a bottle of whisky. Griffiths thought Gerhardt's idea was a good one; "We'll be interested to hear what you have to say."

The sergeant agreed with a warning; "Don't make it too hard, sir or we'll never get rid of the buggers. As it is, some of them are courting local girls so they can stay here."

"Can they do that?" Foden asked.

"It's the only way they might get a permit to return. Don't get me wrong, sir. They've been very useful the last few months; cheap labour, working on the farms. All the land girls left as soon as the war ended."

The camp was the same as many he had lived in, except that the normal wooden huts were prefabricated steel ones. There were only three huts occupied as the rest of the camp had been empty since the Italian prisoners had been repatriated. The men crowded into one of them to listen to him. They listened mostly in silence asking very few questions. He looked at their faces as he finished and knew the despair they all felt.

"But you will make it better," he told them with a sudden insight to their character. "You nearly beat the world so you can mend your country."

He was surprised at the effect the words had on them. He had used them as a placebo but they had the effect of a cure. They voiced agreement and slapped each other on the back and one of them shook Foden's hand and soon they were all trying to do the same. Then they started to sing and the chill returned to his spine. Gerhardt walked to the gate with him.

"Thank you, Geoffrey." Foden said goodnight and went to shake hands but the other man put his arms around him and hugged him.

Three Germans came with Gerhardt for Christmas lunch. They had met the night before as the prisoners had been allowed to attend Christmas Mass at the local church. It was full to the doors. Sir Toby and his family were in the front pews and his rich baritone voice rolled around the arches as he sang with the enthusiasm of a Crusader. Foden had walked to the church and was standing near the back. He saw Gerhardt ahead of him and smiled as the German looked around for him. As they filed out and stood outside, the families talking together, Foden told Gerhardt that he had made a good impression on his sister.

"She told me it is your twenty-first Birthday next month," Gerhardt said. "Is the family making a good party for you?"

"I have no idea. Birthdays haven't been much in my thoughts lately. But I've been pleased to see them. Have you had yours?"

"Yes. Two years ago. We got very drunk and the next day four of my friends were shot down. Geoffrey, I have a favour to ask of you. You know, some of our personal things were confiscated. I have a camera, a Leica, my father gave it to me. I wondered if you could get it back for me. They can't mind me taking pictures now the war is over?"

"I can't see any reason for it. I'll have a word with Griffiths and find out where it is."

"Thank you. I would like to take some pictures of you and your family so I can look at them when we are old and remember that the war wasn't all bad."

Christmas Day was cold but there was no snow. Geoffrey was proud that his family, even his mother, behaved so well to their German guests and had even got small presents, underwear and socks mostly, for them. The Germans had made several decorations carved out of pieces of wood, various animals and objects painted very skilfully which they handed to each of the family and the staff. Gerhardt played up to Sheila and by the time the party ended she thought she was in love.

On Boxing Day, they drove over on invitation to the Henderson's and exchanged presents. In the afternoon, Fiona, Sheila and Geoffrey went riding. They walked the horses up to the top of the hills and watched the sun settling into the blanket of warmer air. They talked vaguely of their individual plans, or lack of them. Fiona wanted to go to

America and work in films and Sheila thought she would like to go to Egypt and write a book like Agatha Christie. They waited expectantly for Geoffrey Foden's ideas.

"I can't make any plans," he told them. "I'm still in the army officially."

"Good Heavens. Why?" Fiona asked.

"Because I'm on some sort of reserve list."

"Don't they know the war is over?" Fiona asked.

"Is it?" Foden answered. "There is a new war coming. The Germans knew that Russia was their biggest threat. Now we will have to deal with them,?

"Geoffrey. I think you're becoming a German lover," Fiona told him.

"No. That's Sheila," he answered and ducked as Sheila aimed several slaps at his head.

They rode back along the Ridgeway Path through Drover's Hill woods and down to Stokesey. There were no fences then, no motorised vehicles to disturb the peace.

His father raised his future later that evening. "I hope you'll soon be coming into the workshop," he said. "The opportunities will be immense now for exporting. We must be ready."

"I was hoping to go to university," Geoffrey told him.

"Good. That's good. Do engineering. Technology is the thing. We have got behind the Americans because of this war. We must catch up."

They sipped their brandies and smoked their cigars and discussed export tariffs until his father suddenly asked about Fiona.

"You like her, don't you?" he said when his son looked surprised at the question.

"Yes. Of course. I mean, she's Fiona."

"Sir Toby is very fond of you, Geoffrey. He has told me

how much he wanted a son. His title will die without one. His name will disappear after four hundred years. He said that whichever of his girls marries first, they will inherit the estate and he will make only one stipulation; that any child will be given the name Henderson, as a suffix to their surname."

"That sounds reasonable,"

"Henderson Foden. I like the sound of that, don't you?"

"Father, I'm not twenty-one yet. My mind is still at war."

"Of course. Of course. But think about it, my boy. It is never too early to think about the future."

Geoffrey's twenty-first was held in the Guildhall in the city. It was a black-tie affair and a local orchestra played the new dance music. Some of his school friends had survived the war and came and stayed with him and one or two regimental colleagues managed to attend, including his old adjutant. Fiona, probably because she had to compete with several pushy females, went out of her way to be atypically affectionate. It was the first time he had become aware that her body, normally shrouded in loose shirts and jumpers, filled a backless dress rather well. They danced the last waltz and her lips played with his ear and before they parted for the waiting cars she drew him under a yew tree and kissed him on the lips. It was two o'clock in the morning when they arrived home. His parents and Sheila went inside while he paid the driver. He was walking towards the house when he heard a noise from the trees on the other side of the drive. "Who's there?" he asked as a figure emerged from them.

"It's me, Gerhardt,"

"Gerhardt. What are you doing here? You should be in camp. It's past your curfew."

"Lieutenant Griffiths gave me permission. I wanted to give

23

you a Birthday present." He held a small parcel towards the other man.

"How very kind. Thank you, Gerhardt. Should I open it?"

"Please," the German answered expectantly.

Geoffrey tore off the paper and opened a small, flat box. He looked at the German.

"This is your Leica," he said.

"Yes. Thank you for getting it back for me. I want you to have it."

"But your father gave it to you."

"Yes. There is a film already in it so you can start taking pictures."

The two men looked at each other and then Geoffrey had made a movement towards the other and their arms were entwined and their cheeks were together and then Gerhardt found the other man's lips and kissed them passionately.

In her bedroom, before she switched on her bedside light, Sheila was about to close the curtains and then her face was against the window as she stared down into the dimly-lit driveway before her breath clouded the picture from her eyes but never from her mind. She closed the curtains quickly; unsure of what she had seen. The next morning, only just, Geoffrey was in his bedroom having dressed. The door was open and as Sheila passed and looked in she saw her brother smiling at something in his hand.

"Good morning," she said, coldly. "What have you got there?"

Her brother turned towards her and held out the camera.

"A Leica. Isn't it a wonderful piece of technology?"

"Is it. Why?"

"Because, dear Sis, it is the finest engineering with the finest lens ever made."

"Did you get it in Berlin?"

"No. I tried. But they were too expensive even now. A month's supply of American cigarettes could get you a decent Mercedes, one packet could get you a Luger and two packets and a tin of coffee could get you the prettiest of girls for the night. But Leicas seemed to disappear like young people."

"Where did you get it then?"

"From Gerhardt. He gave it to me for my Birthday. His father gave it to him. His father is almost certainly dead or in a Siberian prison camp. What do you think of that. Isn't that an incredibly generous thing to do?"

"Yes. He must like you."

"He is just so grateful for what we have done for him. He likes you too."

"Does he?"

"He said you are just as he imagined English girls to be."

"Is that good?"

"Of course. You are the English Rose, Sis."

"Roses are prickly."

"Only when they get up with a bit of a hangover."

He tried to kiss her on her head but she moved away from him.

"Was that Gerhardt in the drive after we got home last night?"

Geoffrey's voice was hesitant. "Yes. He was waiting to give me my present."

"Can he do that, stay out at any time?"

"He had permission. They don't restrict them much now. Some of them are even courting local girls I believe."

"Is Gerhardt?"

"No. I'm sure he isn't."

"Doesn't he like girls?"

"He likes you."

"Would he like to take me out?"

"I'm sure he would. Should I ask him?"

"Why don't you invite him round for tea and we'll see what happens."

"Right-O."

Gerhardt was invited and came to tea. They had it in what had been the nursery. Geoffrey's parents both looked in and stayed for several minutes, asking Gerhardt about his background and family in a polite, unobtrusive manner before excusing themselves to let the young things talk. They played music on the gramophone and Gerhardt got a reluctant Sheila onto her feet and danced her around the floor quite expertly, chasseing and swaying and holding her close around her slim waist so that the colour rose into her cheeks and she bit her lip between giggles and screams until she feigned exhaustion and collapsed onto the settee. Gerhardt was only just into his stride. He held out his arms to Geoffrey.

"May I have the pleasure, sir?"

"Shouldn't it be Madam? Nice girls don't ask," Geoffrey teased.

"Then, dear lady, may I have the pleasure?"

They danced a quick-step, avoiding furniture at a great pace until someone tripped over Sheila's feet and the three of them ended up on the settee laughing.

"Ah. That reminds me of many old friends," Gerhardt said. "We used to get drunk and dance together in the mess after ops. There were no girls. Our airfields were usually miles from anywhere and we weren't allowed to fraternize with the locals anyway."

Sheila was between the two men, she could feel their shoulders against hers as they lay back and smoked Lucky Strikes which Geoffrey had brought back with him from

Berlin. She felt the warmth of their closeness and in the silence of Gerhardt's reverie, she imagined them as one body with one mind and she closed her eyes and smiled to herself until Geoffrey broke the spell.

"Did you like flying?" he asked.

"I love flying," Gerhardt answered. "There is nothing so liberating, so peaceful. It is the essence of Man's genius."

Sheila looked sideways at him but his eyes were half closed and aimed at the ceiling.

"I'm sure it wasn't peaceful," Geoffrey laughed.

"Not always. But taking off in the sunset, rising away from the ground and climbing above the sun – the feeling of peace never left me."

"You must do it," Sheila said with sudden enthusiasm. "You must continue to fly. They will be crying out for pilots soon."

"Sheila's right, you know," Geoffrey agreed. "Every country will be starting up airlines. There will be a shortage of experienced pilots."

Gerhardt turned his eyes towards them like a dog asking to be taken for a walk. "Where would I do this? In a Germany occupied by Russians?"

Neither of his friends could find an answer and he turned his gaze back to the ceiling.

"Will it be bad?" Sheila eventually asked in a hesitant voice.

"Tell her, Geoffrey."

"Gerhardt's home will be in the Russian sector now. They are not treating the German's at all well. What men are left are being sent to Siberia to work in the mines."

"Then you must stay here," Sheila said decisively. "Mustn't he, Geoffrey?"

"I have one or two contacts in the War Office. I could try

to get a permit for you."

"And Sir Toby might help," Sheila added, getting more enthusiastic. "He has many important friends. He was a Brigadier in the last war."

"Do you think there is any hope?" Gerhardt asked.

"I'll certainly give it a try," Geoffrey told him. "If not, you'll just have to marry an English girl."

A quiet smile came to their lips as the two men looked across at each other and then they were both looking at Sheila whose face went very red.

"What about your family," she asked quickly. "Do you have any photographs of them?"

"Yes, I do." He extracted a worn, cotton-backed wallet from his pocket and took out a photograph. "That is my mother and father and little sister."

Sheila studied the picture then handed it to Geoffrey who looked at it and handed it across to Gerhardt. As Gerhardt went to put it back in the wallet another photograph fell out and Sheila retrieved it.

"It's you, in uniform," she smiled. "It's a much better uniform than the one we gave you."

"I think so," Gerhardt laughed.

"Can I keep this?" Sheila asked. "I want to remember you as you were, not as a prisoner."

"Of course. I would be very honoured if you had a photograph of me."

"Sis, why don't you show Gerhardt the rest of our little estate before it gets dark?"

Gerhardt stood up and held out his arm. "Would you do me such an honour, Miss Sheila?" he smiled. Sheila jumped to her feet and took his arm.

"I would be delighted, Herr Gerhardt. But first I need to get a coat or I will freeze out there."

The house was a typical Victorian, eccentric mixture of Gothic and mock-Tudor styles. It had been built for Geoffrey's grandfather. It was situated on an elevated corner sight between Stokesey and Upper Stokesey. It had terraced, landscaped gardens to the front and to one side and an arched entrance to the other side led into a stable and garage yard. The house was partly gabled and on four levels; Beryl and her husband Jack and the maid living in the top layer. Grandfather Foden had expected, as most of his generation did, to have a large family but an operation to his wife caused by a riding accident had limited their offspring to Geoffrey's father. The Grandfather and his wife had both died between the wars soon after Geoffrey's father had married and had moved in with his new wife. It was the only home Geoffrey and his sister had known but Geoffrey, who had been away at boarding school for most of that time, if he'd thought about it, rather hated the house as being too dated, too large and too vulgar. Sheila, as she guided Gerhardt through some of the rooms, told him this and as they entered the stable yard she suddenly asked;

"What sort of home do you have?" He told her it was an old town-house of typical, northern, timber design.

"It is at the top of the hill, like this one, and the street is cobbled so the horses have difficulty getting up in winter so we make straw shoes for them and leave them at the bottom of the hill."

"That sounds nice. I would like to see that," Sheila told him.

"I think it may be a long time before you can do that," he answered. She took his arm and led him into the stables.

"Can you ride?" she asked

"Of course I can ride," he laughed. "Can you ski?"

"No. I've never tried."

29

"Skiing is almost as good as flying. You must come to Germany and I will teach you," and then he remembered and his face changed.

"You will be all right, Gerhardt," she said. "I know you will." Her eyes did their best to persuade him and for a moment they nearly kissed.

"Thank you," he said. "War is a strange thing. It changes what you hate into what you love," and then she did kiss him. Geoffrey interrupted before either of them could react.

"I have to exercise the dogs," he called from the end of the stables. "Should I walk you back to camp, Gerhardt?"

They walked in silence, watching their breath cloud their passage in the freezing air while the dogs ran ahead examining their route.

"She kissed me," Gerhardt said.

It was a moment before Geoffrey responded.

"Did you enjoy it?" he asked. The other man turned to him as he contemplated the question.

"Yes. She has nice lips," he said.

"Nicer than mine?"

Gerhardt stopped and Foden looked back at him, a teasing smile on his lips. The German suddenly stepped forward and then they were kissing, their evening stubble rubbing together.

"Did you see the garage?" Foden asked breathlessly.

"Yes."

"There is a room above it, it was built for a chauffeur but we have never had one, my father likes to drive himself. There is a side-door up to it. No one ever goes there. It isn't locked. But you must be careful no one sees you. Come from behind the gardens, through the trees."

They met in the afternoons. Gerhardt always found an excuse to leave the other men working. He winked when they asked him where he was going and let their imaginations work around the various girls they had seen near their camp.

Foden had put a paraffin heater in the room and had somehow managed to get a straw mattress, blankets and pillows up there too. The windows had been papered over during the war and had not been removed as no one had thought to do it. The paper was not opaque enough to prevent light showing through but the faint glow of the heater and the many Lucky Strikes the two men smoked after their love-making were not sufficient to be noticed from ground-level.

The weeks went by as gently and dreamily as the haze of tobacco smoke which found its way up into the timbered ceiling before settling into the soft pine surfaces of the rafters. They told each other of their childhoods, of their school friends, of their families, of their hopes and dreams and fears. They took pleasure in their physical likeness as though each was a mirror-image of themselves so that their intimacy was almost narcissistic. And they slept a little, like Hansel and Gretel, safe in each other's arms from the bad memories that haunted their sub-conscious minds. There was time too for Gerhardt to play with Sheila's attentions. She accompanied the two men on walks up to the hills and there was an occasion when Fiona joined them and they went to The Badgers and got a little drunk and paired off on the walk home and held hands until they came to the Fender path where they separated, Geoffrey to walk Fiona back to her house and for Gerhardt to see Sheila safely home. The next day the two men exchanged their experiences.

"Sheila likes me," Gerhardt told his friend. "We got a little intimate when we said goodbye. What should I do?"

"Do you like her?" Geoffrey asked.

"Yes. She is very attractive and very nice."

"Could you marry her?"

The German took a deep breath as though his brain needed more oxygen to reply. He kicked the ground as though he was digging up worms and then he looked towards the sky, seeking inspiration.

"I don't know. I don't know. How can I make any plans, Geoffrey?" He looked at the Englishman and the anxiety showed in his eyes. Foden put his arms around him and held him.

"I know," he said. "I know how you feel. Do you want to go home?"

"Yes, and no. I want to see my mother. I want to know what has happened to my father. I want to know how bad things are. I want to find my cousins and my grandparents. But I don't want to be sent to a Siberian labour camp."

"I'll speak to my friend at the War Office. Find out exactly what the situation is. We had a Soviet liaison officer in Berlin, I'll see if I can make contact with her. But it might still be a good idea to marry my sister. It doesn't mean you will never be able to go home does it? It just means you won't be sent home before you know it is safe."

"Even if I don't love her?"

"You only have to love her enough to treat her kindly."

"Is that what you will do with Fiona?"

"Probably. It would mean we could still be together."

Gerhardt took Sheila to the pictures. The girl in the pay-booth was surly and pushed the tickets at him and the usherette made no attempt to show them to their seats. When they came out a group of teenage boys made rude comments and did Nazi salutes as they passed.

"I'm sorry," Sheila apologised.

"Don't be. I can't blame them. It would be the same if you

were walking with me in my town. We are the future, not the past."

Sheila pulled him to a stop and kissed him. "Yes, we are," she said.

Geoffrey made several calls to old colleagues and even managed to speak to Birgit, the translator who had worked with him in Berlin. Birgit was a middle-aged woman who had been married to a Staff officer in the German High Command. She spoke four languages fluently, including Russian as her parentage was Polish. She had done her job efficiently and worked diligently, putting in long hours as they struggled to cope with the constant challenges that the chaos of the ruined and divided city threw at them and she had always maintained a balance between duty and compliance. But Geoffrey had felt that a mutual respect for each other might have hidden warmer feelings and he suspected, although they had never spoken about it, that she had children of his age. He had given her his leather-bound, Folio Edition Shakespeare when he had left and told her it had been his friend from school to Berlin and hoped she would love it too.

She sounded pleased to hear from him and told him she was now in charge of a department evaluating recovered documents from the ruined government buildings. She listened to his story about Gerhardt and was moved to hear of how they had become friends and how many of the POW's were afraid to return. She had no words of comfort about the situation in the Russian occupied territories.

"We are getting no co-operation from them," she told him. "I think there is a big prisoner-exchange being negotiated but they won't give any assurances about their welfare when they are repatriated."

"Is there any chance of Gerhardt staying in the Allied Zone

if he returns?" he asked.

"No. They are being very strict about sending them to their homelands because the Allies do not want to jeopardise the return of their own people from Russian liberated camps."

She promised she would try to find out the situation in Cottbus and whether Gerhardt's family had survived.

She phoned him several days later and told him that Cottbus had been overrun by a Soviet tank division and systematically shelled. Many retreating German forces tried to defend the town but had no chance. Much of the city was destroyed and many people fled before the Russian advance.

"I managed to speak to a German woman in the city administration. She had to speak quickly because they are supervised by Russian military personnel. She didn't have much hope of finding out what might have happened to your friend's family, so many were buried without being identified. It is the usual story I'm afraid Geoffrey."

Foden passed on the news to Gerhardt with careful editing. "It is all chaos. No one has any records. It might be another year before things are organised," he said.

"But the Russians are in control," Gerhardt answered. "I know what my fate will be if I return there. A Luftwaffe pilot, the son of a regular, high ranking German officer."

"You'll just have to marry Sheila – or someone else," Geoffrey advised.

"I don't want to be dishonest.. Pretending to love someone is the worst sort of dishonesty."

"Not if you make them happy. What is love anyway?"

"The passion I feel for you."

"But we would have to be dishonest about that. It is illegal. We would have to hide our feelings. Oh God! I wish we were still children, able to run free and play together without anyone hating us for how we are."

The problem was left to hang over them like a thunder-cloud, unspoken but not ignored and Gerhardt was careful not to be left alone too much with Sheila, unsure of what lay ahead and not wanting their relationship to progress further than the occasional kissing and the holding of hands. But Fiona was less diplomatic. The two girls were riding together.

"Do you like Gerhardt?" Fiona asked.

"Yes. Don't you?"

"Not much."

"Why not. Because he's German?"

"Probably. But I can't be sure of what he's after."

"What do you mean, Fiona. What can he be after? He's a prisoner, a refugee."

"And desperate."

"Desperate to be safe. Is that so bad?"

"I suppose not. But I hear there are local girls going out with them and planning to get married. Why would they do that? Why wouldn't they want to see their families again?"

"Perhaps because they don't think they have any family any more. We have no idea what it must be like in Europe. Geoffrey has told us something of how awful it is. Gerhardt comes from East Germany which is now under Russian control. The Russians are sending the German men to Siberia to work in the mines. They are still prisoners."

"All right. But I hope you are not going to do something stupid like those other girls and marry Gerhardt."

Sheila's thinking had not travelled so far, even after the joke Gerhardt and her brother made about it when they were all having tea, and her silence made Fiona look at her.

"Sheila. You are not, are you?"

"He's very nice. Would it be such a tragedy?"

"Oh God! Sheila. Of course it would be. You know nothing

about him or his family. What would he do here? What would you live on?"

"He's an officer. His father was an officer. He's a pilot. Pilots are going to be needed. Anyway, we are only friends but I don't see why you should be so rotten about him."

"I'm not being rotten. I find him very nice too. But it's not easy to know someone unless you know their background and it's much harder when they are foreign."

Days later, Sheila raised the topic over dinner. "Mama, do you know Rachel Figgis, the girl who works in the bakery?"

"Yes. Her father was killed at El Alemain. What about her?"

"She's getting married to one of the German POW's."

The news could not have had a more surprising effect on her mother than Sheila could have imagined. She brought her knife hand down on the table and made her glass of wine shake as if an earthquake was affecting it.

"How could she do such a thing? Her poor father will be turning in his grave."

"Perhaps she loves the chap," Geoffrey said.

"That is ridiculous. She couldn't have been going out with him more than a few weeks. They've only recently been allowed out of camp," his mother scoffed.

"Perhaps they've been communing through the wire fence for years. Rubbing their noses together and sniffing each other like dogs," Geoffrey suggested and made his sister giggle.

"Don't be vulgar, Geoffrey. Sleeping with the enemy can never be right."

"The SOE wouldn't agree with you, Mother. I believe their spies get their best information between the sheets."

"That is different. We all have to do things we don't like to do for the sake of necessity sometimes."

"Really, Mother? Are you an agent provocateur? Do you know about this, Father?"

"Don't be rude to your mother, Geoffrey."

"What do you think about marrying a German, Father?" Sheila asked.

Her father put down his wine-glass and stroked his moustache. He cleared his throat in the manner he adopted before he told his children or the servants off.

"When I was a young subaltern, at the eleventh hour of the eleventh day of the eleventh month, on three blasts of a whistle, Sir Toby, our Brigade Commander, led us out of that awful labyrinth of mud walls onto No Man's Land where we shook hands with our German foes and exchanged cigarettes. I thought then that we would never again have to go through the hell that the civilised world had just experienced. But here we are again; another No Man's Land. How long before it happens again? And if it does, whose side will these chaps be on, their wives' or their country's?"

"If it happens again, Father. We'll be on the same side. Russia will be the enemy then," his son commented.

As they retired after dinner, Geoffrey took Sheila's arm and whispered in her ear. "The world has changed, Sis. Do what you believe."

But Sheila avoided Gerhardt for several days until she almost bumped into him as she came out of the stable-block. He was as surprised to see her as she was him.

"Hello. Where have you come from?" she asked, looking beyond him towards the garage and seeing Geoffrey walk from it to the back of the house.

"Geoffrey was showing me your father's car," Gerhardt said. "I am very interested in engines."

"Oh!" was all Sheila managed.

"I haven't seen you lately? Have you been avoiding me

since we went to the cinema?"

"No, of course not," she said but could not stop the flow of blood to her face.

"Would you like to go again?" he asked.

"Yes. Why not? But we could go for a walk instead. It's much healthier."

"Yes. That would be better. Shall I call for you on Saturday?"

"No. I'll meet you at the bottom of the Ridgeway. At one o'clock. Is that all right?"

"Yes.Good. Goodnight, Sheila."

"Goodnight Gerhardt."

They met and walked through Drover's Hill Woods and down to The Badgers. Very few people reached the pub in those days as there were not many cars on the road and petrol was still rationed. Sheila sat in a corner near the fire and Gerhardt brought two beers to the table. Before he sat down he searched in his pockets for his cigarettes and pulled out a black leather wallet instead.

"That's rather smart," Sheila commented.

"Yes. Geoffrey gave it to me. He saw mine was falling to pieces. It was very kind of him. You see, he even had my name printed in gold on it."

Sheila examined the wallet.

"It's lovely. Almost as good as the Birthday present you gave him."

"The Leica. Yes, that is very special."

"You must like Geoffrey a lot."

"Yes. Of course. He has been very good to me."

"And he likes you too."

"I hope so. You see, Sheila, there is something between men who have been enemies. Once there was hate and then there was respect, and then…"

"And then there is love?"

"I was going to say friendship. It is a journey we make within ourselves. We find out who we are and who other people are and that really we are the same. We see that hatred is only ignorance. That friendship is much better."

"And love?"

"That is best of all."

"Have you loved someone, I mean, besides your family?"

"Yes. I have loved several people."

It was not the answer Sheila expected and she sat back and looked at him.

"Not girls," he said. "When you live together, fly together, die together, the love between us was a blanket that kept us warm; it stopped us from being afraid. We thought we would die and when one of us did it felt like we had lost part of us. We all died slowly even though we lived."

Sheila saw the intensity, the plea to be understood and she leaned forward across the table and kissed him.

They walked back through the woods, their arms enfolding their backs, and talked of animals they had loved and things they wanted to do and when they reached the house they kissed long and exploringly before Sheila broke away, trying to control the rush of adrenalin that took her breath away. Gerhardt smiled.

"Are you a virgin, Sheila?"

"No. I mean, yes."

"That's good," he said supportively.

"Is it?"

"But of course. You should be proud of it."

"It's just that, well I don't get much chance to meet anyone. Boys of my age are either in the army or away at university and at my secretarial college there are only girls. They talk all the time about their boyfriends but it's easier for them because they live near the city where there are more interesting people. Here we have only farmers and village idiots."

"I understand. So I am the best substitute?"

"No. No. You are…you are a man, a beautiful, lovely man," she finished in a rush. Gerhardt smiled again and kissed her. She pulled away from him.

"Gerhardt. Do you like me?"

"I like you very much."

"If things were normal, if you were just visiting here as a tourist, would you like me so much then?"

"Then I would like you even more."

Sheila opened her little purse and pulled out a ten shilling note.

"I brought this. I wanted to buy you a drink; I know you don't have much money."

"Please, Sheila," he protested.

"Take it, please. You can buy some contraceptives with it. Yes, I want you to make love to me."

The German looked at her face which was straining forward, pleading for him to understand. He took the note from her.

"Sheila, you don't have to do this."

"I want to. Don't you want to?"

"Of course, but…"

"We can do it in the chauffeur's room above the garage. There are plenty of horse-blankets in the stables. Next Saturday would be good because Daddy works at the factory on Saturday mornings and Mummy goes into the city with him for shopping and they have lunch there."

She kissed him almost as quickly as her speech and then she was walking away. "Must go. See you Saturday."

Gerhardt watched her walk towards the house. She turned

as she reached it and waved and then she had jumped up the steps and disappeared through the front door.

The next day, Gerhardt and Geoffrey met for a walk. They walked along the Fender path towards the Henderson estate and Gerhardt told his friend of Sheila's intentions.

"What can I do?" Gerhardt asked. "If I refuse I will offend her and you know what they say about a woman being scorned?"

"Even in German?"

"Much worse in German. A kiss is an engagement and anything more is enforced marriage or else deportation."

"So the Russians aren't the only problem about going home."

"It's serious, Geoffrey. If Sheila gets upset she may cause a big problem between us."

"I know. I think you should do it."

The other man stopped and looked at him.

"You do. You don't mind?"

"I shall be jealous but it will be in a good cause, so I shan't mind."

"What cause?"

Now it was Geoffrey's turn to stop.

"Gerhardt. My friend in the War Office has made enquiries. He said there is no way he could swing a permit for you. He said hundreds of prisoners are wanting them and the Ministry is determined to send everyone home whatever the circumstances – but not yet. Apparently, your chaps are proving too valuable working on the farms and clearing up the mess you made."

"But not officers. They cannot make us work. They won't want to feed us if we don't."

"You're probably right. But that means you will be the first to be repatriated."

"Yes, Geoffrey. I understand."

"Do you? Do you see that marrying my sister may be the only way to keep you here?"

"Or marrying someone else. Someone I don't care about. Someone I can leave once I am allowed to stay."

"I hadn't thought of that," Geoffrey said and they continued their slow walk until they came to the path leading off to Sir Toby's place. They saw Fiona exercising her new horse. She waved to them and cantered up.

"Hello. How is he?" Geoffrey asked.

"Very well mannered. Have you come to see me?"

"We were just getting some fresh air."

"Hello Gerhardt," Fiona said.

"Hello Miss Fiona."

"I haven't seen you around lately. Have you found somewhere else to work?"

"No. I have been on the marsh in the mornings with the other men. Did you want me to do something for you?"

"No, thank you. I wondered if you were still allowed out because Daddy heard they were getting ready to move you all." She watched the reactions on the faces of the two men and they were not dissimilar. "Didn't you know?"

"No."

"How did he hear this?" Geoffrey asked.

"He was talking to some General pal of his at a dinner last evening."

"Do you know when?" Gerhardt said.

"No. He just said it was imminent. They are arranging a big assembly point somewhere in Somerset apparently. Do you want to come in for tea?"

"No, thanks. We don't want to interrupt your work with Hero."

"All right. Will I see you sometime?"

42

"Of course. I could invite myself to supper if you like."

"I would like. Make it Wednesday."

"Right O. Bye."

When she had gone the two men looked at each other.

"You have no choice now, Gerhardt," Geoffrey told him.

"Just close your eyes and think of Germany."

"It's not funny."

"I know. I bloody well know it isn't."

At home. Geoffrey cornered his sister.

"Gerhardt is worried about you," he told her. "He told me what you are going to do."

His sister's reaction was a mixture of anger and embarrassment.

"How could he?" she said.

"Because he doesn't want you to do something you don't want to do."

"Who said I didn't want to? I do and it's none of your business, Geoffrey."

"It is my business. You are my business and Gerhardt is my friend so he is my business too."

"If he doesn't want to do it, that's up to him. I'm not begging him."

"Don't be like that, Sis. It's all right as long as you really think it is all right."

"I do." Her voice was still resentful.

"Would you marry him?"

"I might."

"Do you care what might happen to him?"

"Of course I do."

"I think they are about to send them home."

The reaction on her face was the same as that seen by Fiona when she broke the news to the two men.

"When?" she asked

"We don't know. It could be days, it could be weeks. But no more." He thought she was going to cry. "So, don't do this unless you are serious about him," he told her.

"What would you do?" she asked

He ignored the unintended irony of the question. "If I loved him I would do anything to keep him safe," he said. His sister thought about his reply for some moments.

"Yes," she said. "So would I."

He stepped forward and kissed her head.

"Whatever you want to do, I will support you," he told her.

But events moved faster than either of them thought they might. Gerhardt knocked at their door on the Monday evening. He was shown into the sitting-room where he found Mrs Foden.

"Good evening," she said. "Were you looking for Geoffrey?"

"Yes. I'm sorry to intrude, Mrs Foden but I wanted to tell Geoffrey that we are being sent home this weekend."

"Oh, that's nice for you. I believe he is in town seeing about getting a car for himself. It's such a bore having only the one now that he's home. I'll give him your message when he gets back."

He was walking down the drive when he met Sheila arriving. He told her his news. "We have been told not to make any arrangements after Friday."

"You look frightened," she said. He nodded and she instinctively put her arms around his neck. "I'm frightened too," she told him

She broke the news to Geoffrey when he got home.

"What can we do?" she pleaded.

"It's too soon for you to get married, so that's out," he replied.

"Is that what I should have done?"

"It was the only way he could get permission to stay," and then he saw the reaction in her face. "No, Sis, that's not what he was trying to do. He likes you too much, that's why he didn't want you to make love."

"What a mess," she said. "Can't we do anything?"

"Yes. I'll think of something."

By Thursday, when he was alone with Gerhardt above the garage, he still hadn't thought of something. At supper on the previous evening, Sir Toby had given him more details about the repatriation. Several camps were to be assembled at Wookey Hole, the great cavern in the Somerset Hills, and then they were to be taken by transport to Portsmouth harbour from where the navy was to ship them across the channel to France where reception areas had been organised and from there they would be trained to their various destinations.

"I could desert," Gerhardt said.

"We could hide you here."

"This would be the first place they would look. They know I have been working at Sir Toby's and that we are friends."

"You speak good English. I can give you clothes and money. You could hide out somewhere else," then Geoffrey found the idea he had been seeking. He jumped up. "That's it; clothes. We can exchange clothes. I can go instead of you and you can hide here." His brain was working quickly. "I have my uniform. I can go to your camp and pretend to be you. I will carry your identity papers. I speak German, your friends won't give us away. Then after we have been checked in or whatever they do at Wookey Hole, I can secretly change into my uniform and become one of the military personnel. Yes. By Jove. That's it, Gerhardt. It should work."

"And I would have been ticked off the list as being there.

Do you really think we can do this?"

"I can't see why it shouldn't work. I'll walk back with you and speak to Lieutenant Griffiths and get more info."

The two men hugged each other and jumped up and down. Jack, the handyman-gardener was in the garage below, looking for an axe to chop up firewood. Later that evening he asked Sheila what they were doing with the chauffeur's room and had a sly look on his face. She told him she had no idea but she would find out. It was almost dark when she tried the door and was surprised to find it locked, it had never been locked because the room had never been used. She walked back to the house to look for the key but it wasn't on the key-board in the kitchen where all the keys were hung. She was about to ask Beryl about it when Geoffrey walked through the front door looking worried.

"I've been to the camp," he told her. "They are moving them out on Saturday." Then he took her arm and steered her away from the hearing range of the rooms on either side of the hallway. "But I have a plan," he whispered and told her what he was going to do. His sister looked uncertain and voiced her doubts. "Where will he hide?" she asked. "Here," he told her. "He can stay in the room above the garage. Nobody ever goes in there."

"Is that what you were doing this afternoon, getting it ready?" The expression on Geoffrey's face puzzled her. "Jack heard someone up there, banging about," she explained.

"Ah! Yes. That's what I was doing. Don't tell Father or Mother will you Sheila?"

"No. Do you really think it will work?"

"I can't see anything wrong with the plan."

"How long will he have to hide?"

"If everything works out, not long. Once they think he has

been checked off their lists they won't be looking for him. Then he can just appear and get work and say he has been given a permit or that he has married someone."

"How are you going to get into the camp?"

"That won't be a problem. We are the same size and height and I speak German. I will be wearing Gerhardt's uniform. I only have to spend tomorrow night there and then we will be bundled into lorries I suppose."

"You would get into awful trouble if you were caught," she reminded him, the concern showing in her eyes.

"Don't worry, Sis. This is nothing compared to some of the tricks I've had to pull near enemy lines. It will be a piece of cake."

"Shall I help you prepare the room for him? I was just looking for the key when you arrived."

"No, that's okay. I can manage. I've already put a paraffin heater up there. I'm telling the parents I've got to go to London for the weekend."

"I'll look after him," Sheila said. "I'll take him some food."

"No, Sis. That's too risky, someone might see you."

"You had better tell me where the key is though in case of emergencies."

"Like what?"

"Like the paraffin heater falling over and setting the place on fire," she said.

"I'll give Gerhardt the key. Did you want to go up there with him?"

"I might. At least we could talk in case he's frightened"

"Then I'll tell him you'll knock three times and he can let you in. You can still marry him, you know. Now you can take your time about it." Sheila felt the blood run into her cheeks and the excitement between her legs.

47

On the Friday afternoon Gerhardt and Geoffrey were making love, perhaps aware that it might be the last time they would do so. Unknown to them, Sheila had been given the afternoon off from college and as she walked up the drive she was hoping she would see Gerhardt and Geoffrey before he left. As she entered the stable yard and looked towards the garage she discerned a faint glow beyond the papered window-glass. She walked quietly, almost crept, to the side of the garage and found the door to the upper room unlocked. She opened it and was about to call when she heard a sound, not unlike a muffled cry of pain, from above.

The stairs to the upper floor were not much more than a ladder; they were steep and entered the upper room through a rectangular opening cut into the floor joists. Sheila ascended them with the curiosity of a hunting cat. Her head penetrated the space and then her eyes, just enough to see into the dim light of the room. She almost fell down the steps, the sound of her descent hidden by the now more regular moans coming from above. She opened the door and staggered out to the yard and leant against the wall desperately trying to breathe. Then she bent forward and thought she would be sick. She had never seen a naked man before, that was shock enough, but two naked men enjoined was beyond the capacity of her nervous system not to affect her heart and her stomach and every part of her inner body that needed a sustained mix of oxygen and nitrogen.

Much later, from her bedroom, she saw a dark figure walking around the skirt of trees around the drive towards the gates and disappear beyond them.

When her father arrived home and he and his wife went into the dining-room for dinner he asked Beryl where everybody was.

"Geoffrey has had to go up to London for the weekend,"

his wife said. "But do you know where Sheila is, Beryl?" Beryl said she thought Sheila was in her room. "Then please go and fetch her. Tell her we are waiting to serve dinner."

Beryl returned as Mrs Foden was ladling out the soup. "Sheila says she's not hungry, Madam."

"What nonsense. Tell her she must come down at once, Beryl."

"I'll go to her," her husband said and Mrs. Foden made a sound of exasperation and proceeded to pour the soup back into the tureen. Foden knocked on Sheila's door and was told to please go away.

"It's your father," he told her.

There was a mumbled apology.

"Are you unwell?" he asked.

"I'm all right, Father. I just don't want to eat anything. I'm having a lie down."

Her father returned to the dining-room and told his wife they would eat alone.

"Probably some tiff with a chap," he explained. "We'll see how she is in the morning. It won't do any harm for her to miss one meal."

In the morning Sheila did not appear for breakfast either and her father, now less understanding, went and knocked on her door again.

"Sheila, are you awake?" Sheila said she was but her voice sounded no better than it had the previous night.

"Will you please open the door?" he demanded.

The door was unlocked. Foden pushed it wide and walked in. His daughter was standing with her back to the door.

"Aren't you well?" he asked. Sheila turned and he could see she had been crying.

"Whatever is the matter?" Her father stepped towards her as though to console her but she turned her shoulder towards him. Sheila had always been his darling girl. "Tell me," he pleaded softly. She turned towards him and then the tears returned and she allowed herself to be comforted and then words were stumbling out of her, unconnected, not making sentences. Ashamed. Humiliated. Such a fool. Disgusting. Unbelievable. Behaviour. Immoral. Gradually, her father put some of the words together and made some sense of them. Sheila had freed herself from him as she began to speak and turned back and forth with the increasing spleen of her diction. Her father sat on the bed and asked her to calm down.

"You are trying to tell me that Geoffrey and this German chap are more than friends?"

Sheila confirmed that was what she was trying to convey. The blood left her father's face and his words struggled to get out of his mouth.

"That is a very serious assertion, Sheila," he said.

"I saw them," Sheila almost screamed at him and her face screwed up at the memory. Her father's did the same and even closed his eyes tightly. Eventually he opened them and pulled air deep into his lungs. He stood up and looked towards the window as though seeking an answer from outside.

"Where are they now?" he asked. Sheila revealed the plan to keep Gerhardt in England. "And he is in the room above the garage?" She nodded agreement. "Stay here," he said and walked out of the room.

Sheila, after a moment, followed. She saw her father walk into his bedroom and heard him speak on the telephone. He asked the operator to connect him with the POW camp. After some minutes he thanked someone and put down the phone. Sheila began to retrace her steps quickly but was too late; before she reached her room her father called to her.

"They have left. The camp was vacated in the early hours," he told her.

"What will you do, Father?" Her voice was now hesitant. Already she was beginning to regret the outpouring of her emotions.

"If I reveal what Geoffrey is up to he could be arrested and charged with a serious offence," her father told her. "I hope, for his sake and for ours, his scheme works."

"And what about Gerhardt?" she asked. Her father took some time to answer and he stood and stared at the carpet. Then he looked at her.

"Sheila. Under no circumstances must you tell anyone about this." She nodded agreement. "Not your mother, not Fiona – especially not Fiona – not the servants." She nodded again. "Do you think you could harness one of the horses to the trap for me?" She said she could. "Good. Do that then leave it tethered beside the garage and then come back inside the house and have some breakfast. Understood?"

"Yes, Father. But…"

"Don't ask questions. Don't ever ask questions about this thing from now on. All right?" She nodded again. "Thank you. Off you go then."

He watched Sheila go down the stairs and then he went back into his bedroom and changed from his office clothes into his shooting togs and boots. His wife wanted to know why when she met him at the foot of the stairs.

"I don't feel like going to the office this morning," he told her. "Thought I would try to bag a pigeon or two." He unlocked the gun cabinet and took from it one of his Purdeys. "See you later, my dear."

She watched him walk out with a bemused look on her face.

He took a route around the house to the stable block so as

51

to avoid Sheila on her way back. The pony and trap were waiting patiently beside the garage as he had asked, the reins tossed loosely over an old hay-basket. Foden tried the side-door of the garage and found it locked. He knocked on it three times. There was the sound of shoes descending the steps and then Gerhardt's voice;

"Hello Sheila," and the sound of the key turning in the lock.

Foden pushed open the door forcefully and stepped inside. Gerhardt had fallen back against the stairs and he stared up at Foden, his eyes wide with surprise and then fear.

****

Geoffrey Foden had managed to get into the camp at dusk without being recognised by Griffiths or his sergeant. He had explained to the men of Gerhardt's hut that Gerhardt wanted to marry his sister but had had no time to arrange it so they had had to think of another way for him to avoid being repatriated. The men were mostly supportive, even impressed by his plan. Two of them had courted local girls and were hatching their own plans to return to England. But Foden's scheme appealed almost the same as an escape plan, the idea of which many of them had often entertained, and Foden was accepted as someone on their side. It then occurred to him that he could be considered a spy if he were caught and wondered as he pulled the blankets over himself on the hard bunk whether what he was doing was treasonable. They were wakened at five am and told to breakfast and then to gather all their possessions and be ready to leave in one hour. It was still dark as they assembled for roll-call and then they were marched out of the camp and climbed aboard three three-ton army lorries which were manned by several armed soldiers, two each assigned to travel in the back with the Germans. As it got light, Foden recognised the route they were taking and knew that Wookey Hole would be their destination. When they arrived and climbed down and were fallen-in three abreast, he saw that many lorries were arriving in what had been made into a fenced-off holding area in front of the famous caves. They were separated into files and passed through check-points where their papers were examined and their details transferred to lists then they were allowed to mingle and wander within a wired enclosure. There were armed soldiers around the perimeter. Geoffrey saw that the highest rank among the few officers was a major of the Dorset Regiment and for a moment he feared he might meet someone who knew him. They were given a hot meal served from a canteen wagon about midday and then they were transferred again to lorries which ferried them all throughout the day to Shepton Mallet where they were put onto trains and taken to Portland Naval Dockyard. Geoffrey had several moments when he feared he would not get the opportunity to change into his army uniform and as the train pulled into a siding near to the naval base and he saw only naval personnel he seriously feared his scheme would fail.

They were marched into the dockyard, the army guards then handing over to the navy. There were several hundred men loosely assembled in the yard waiting for instructions. It was then dusk for which Geoffrey was grateful, hoping that it would give him some cover for changing back into his uniform. He filtered his way into the centre of his group and hurriedly stripped out of his POW clothes and hoped that none of the men around him were strangers who would react and attract the attention of the navy personnel who patrolled the perimeter of the groups with their rifles held across their chests. But the men from Gerhardt's hut had remained with him and were quick to explain to their colleagues Geoffrey's scheme to hide Gerhardt. Once he had dressed in his army uniform and put the POW tunic into his case, the group filtered him to the edge of the crowd. He shook many hands and then walked boldly around the perimeter to the dockyard gates. It was almost dark as he saluted two guards and had a cheerful word for the sailor who opened the gate for him and hoped sir had seen the last of the Gerry bastards.

He reached home late on Sunday evening. He took a taxi from the railway station and both Sheila and his father heard it drop him off. Geoffrey looked at the house and waited but when no one appeared to greet him he walked to the side and into the stable yard. He looked into the stables first and then proceeded quickly to the side of the garage. He tried the door and found it locked. He knocked on it three times and waited. He knocked three times more and then called softly; "Gerhardt. It's me, Geoffrey."

"He's not there."

His father's voice made him jump. He turned and looked rather as Gerhardt had looked as Foden forced him back onto the steps the previous day.

"Father," he exclaimed

"I see you are wearing your uniform," his father said. "Did you have military business in London?"

His father's demeanour and tone of voice told him there was no use prolonging his charade. They also told him that Gerhardt's presence had been exposed. Fear and anger drove his protest.

"What have you done with him?" he demanded.

"He has been handed to the police," his father answered coldly.

"Nooooo!" Geofrey's voice rose into the cold air like the cry of an animal and he shook his head as though to eject the reality of the information. He started to walk quickly, almost breaking into a run.

"I must go to him," he said.

"The Military Police, Geoffrey." His father's voice stopped him mid-stride. "If you go to them they will arrest you. What is the punishment for treason now the war has ended?"

His son's shoulders slumped and his stomach folded inwards and his voice reflected the physical weakness he now felt.

"Why Father. Why?"

"To exorcise the deviant evil that possessed you both."

Geoffrey Foden's body then collapsed. He sank to his knees on the gravel and his head fell forward onto his chest as though he was preparing himself for a guillotine. He began to weep quietly.

"You will marry Fiona, Geoffrey. You may go to university but then you will come into the business and assume your responsibilities like a man," his father told him and then he turned and walked away to the rear of the house from where he had emerged.

Geoffrey gradually got to his feet and walked out of the yard and up the steps and through the front-door. His mother met him in the hallway and smiled her surprise.

"Geoffrey. We weren't expecting you so soon. You look so nice in your uniform."

He allowed himself to be kissed and mumbled a greeting but hardly checked his progress through the hall and up the winding staircase. He almost fell into his room. He opened the small suitcase he had carried and took from it Gerhardt's uniform jacket. He held it to his face and began to cry loudly.

His sister, who's bedroom was next to his, had witnessed his arrival home and had seen him proceed to the side of the house. She had then run up to the servant's level and opened a small corridor window under the gabled wing which overlooked the stable yard and from there she had seen the confrontation between her brother and her father. She now heard the sobs and cries of anguish from her brother's room and crept onto the landing. His door was ajar. She pushed it further inwards and the creaking of the hinges made Geoffrey drop the tunic jacket and turn towards her. The expressions and feelings flowed between them.

"How did Father know?" he asked. "How did he know how to make Gerhardt open the door.?"

Sheila could not answer and tears, already well rehearsed, flowed again into her eyes. The meaning of them hit Geoffrey with the impact of an ice-storm.

"You told him? God, Sheila. You told him."

Sheila's emotions erupted angrily. "I saw you," she cried. "I saw you with him," and her face screwed up again at the memory. "I came back early on Friday and saw you," she said.

Her brother looked at her as though he was seeing her for the first time.

"You have killed him," he told her. "He will be sent to a Soviet labour camp where he will slowly die of fatigue and malnutrition, and however many years that will take, every day, every night, every minute, he will think of who it was who betrayed him."

His sister turned and ran from the room and her sobs echoed around the landing.

THE RECENT PAST

She had slept as only a seventeen-year-old can. The physical pleasure of her naked body immersed in the duvet was a catalyst for the sexual fantasies that were soon relieved, prefacing a dreamless sleep, a sleep without conflict, sadness or regrets; the sleep of a child.

As the spring sunshine rose above Drovers' Hill and shafted through the tiny window onto her bed, Katy Rose Lewis had flung the duvet behind her and lay on her stomach, one half of her body exposed to the air, an arm hanging to the floor, a breast squeezed sideways past her ribs, a perfectly shaped leg stretched the length of the bed and a mass of auburn curls glowing in the sunlight.

"Kat, you awake?"

Her mother's voice abused her flickering consciousness. She had been aware of the constant pleading of the Martin chicks under the thatch since dawn. That was a sound she had heard from that same room every spring for all of her life and was more of a lullaby than an irritant. The sun too was more soothing than disturbing, but her mother's voice could not be ignored

"Dad wants you to go to market to collect the meat. Frank's van is poorly."

Now she was awake. She raised her face a few inches.

"Can I go to Nan's?"

As long as you're back by twelve. We want the meat for the lunches. An' you put some knickers on. I don't care how hot you think it is.

"Yes, Ma." She turned on her back and smiled at the wall.

"Like what you see, d'you Damon? You naughty boy."

Damon Albarn looked wistfully back at her.

She jumped from the bed and paused as she passed the window which was now at knee-height. He was there, pretending to brush the terrace of the pub but staring expectantly towards the window. Katy turned quickly sideways and back before moving away, smiling to herself and putting on her robe. She was in the bathroom when her mother called up again.

"Mrs Challis wants you to look after Jenny. She has to go into the city for a meeting. I said you would."

Her daughter unlatched the door and peered down the old staircase.

"How can I do that if I have to go into the village?"

"You can take the pushchair on the bus."

Kat was not pleased. She loved little Jenny like a puppy but Nan was fib-speak for Bobby Paget and she knew he was working on a house near her Nan's.

"I don't know," she tried.

"What don't you know?" her mother responded. "You need the money. When you get yourself a job you can start to get picky. Till then you have to take what's goin' m'gal. An' hurry up. Mrs Challis will be here before you've had breakfast."

The Challis' had bought the Mill House two years previously. Ian Challis was a graphics designer and was often away working for film and television companies. His wife, Virginia, was an accountant and worked mostly from home but sometimes had to see clients in the city and she had been able to rely on Katy Rose to baby-sit Jenny since she was born.

The Challis' were one of only three families to have moved into the hamlet in many years – mostly because it was almost twenty miles from the city and seven miles from Stokesey, the nearest town and it was not conducive for commuting nor for the holiday renters who favoured the areas nearer the coast.

The traditional thatched cottages had been occupied by members of the same families for generations and even The Badgers had been bought by Katy's great grandfather when he retired as a sea-captain, and his son and then Katy's father had kept it in the family since he had drunk most of the profits and died at the age of ninety some fifty years previously.

The inn was opposite Drovers' Hill and was a popular stop for walkers, cyclists and motorists in a picturesque part of the county. It was set back from the A road that followed the contour of the crescent-shaped hill and was the route between the various hamlets and farms in the narrow Fender valley and Upper Stokesey, the nearest village, which was some four miles away by road but much less to the walkers who traversed the spine of which Drovers' Hill was part.

For those walkers who started from Upper Stokesey – or even farther afield from the town of Stokesey – and looked back from Drovers Hill they had an uninterrupted view across a patchwork of grazing fields to the estuary where the little river emptied into the tidal basin and for them, and the many motorised tourists, the Badgers was perfectly placed to renew their energy as it had once been for the drovers and shepherds before them.

Katy put on her favourite cotton dress; it was bright with a pattern of tiny flowers and had a loose bodice and scooped neckline that drew the eyes to the sand-white perfection of her skin and the movement of her breasts beneath the cotton and was a perfect hook for the likes of Bobby Paget. After a moment's reflection she chose not to wear pants.

Her brother, Thomas was about to depart for school as Katy entered the kitchen. He took the piece of toast from his mouth.

"Bloody 'ell!" was his comment and ducked as his mother

59

aimed a slap at his head. "She's got a date. Kat's got a date," he parroted.

"Try to act your age," Katy told him haughtily. "An' wipe that butter from your face before you get on the bus otherwise little Annie Davis will know what a slovenly little pig you are."

Thomas was about to muster a response when the horn of the school bus and his mother thrusting a lunch box into his hands and pushing him towards the door interrupted the idea.

"Go on. Get," his mother told him but was unable to prevent him aiming the remains of the toast at his sister before his departure.

"Why do you wind 'im up?" her mother asked as Katy poured herself some tea. "And why are you wearing that dress just to go into the village?"

"You know Nan always wants me to look nice."

"Nan doesn't have to buy your clothes does she?"

"You look nice," Katy's father told her as he came in from the bar.

"Mornin, Dad," she said, hugging him. Her mother raised her eyebrows as she watched them and knew any other admonishments would be a waste of time: Katy could eat up any man just by looking at him and her father was no exception.

"That's Mrs Challis," she said as a car was heard driving up to the back of the pub. "Hurry up, gal."

She opened the kitchen door and watched Virginia Challis unfolding the pushchair and lifting Jenny from the child-seat and felt that surge of emotion that mothers feel when their children have grown up and they haven't yet got a grandchild to compensate for their loss.

Jenny was a child to bring out the best in any woman;

60

twenty months old with a ready smile and a head of blond curls. She smiled at everyone but giggled uncontrollable as Katy took her from the pushchair and blew raspberries into her neck. Mrs Challis waved goodbye, knowing her child was in safe hands.

Jenny played with a piece of Katy's toast until Katy's mother told her to get a move on or she'd miss the bus. Jenny was put back in the pushchair and they set off up the side of the pub towards the road. Jack, the aged cleaner, looked slyly towards them.

"Seen enough, did you, Jack?" Katy asked as she passed

"I don't know what you mean, Kat."

"Course you don't. You've forgotten what it looks like," she laughed and walked on.

She reached the road and pushed Jenny along the pavement singing 'Lay Your Hands on Me,' to Jenny's giggling appreciation. Just before she reached the point where a pull-in had been cut into a meadow on the opposite side of the road for a bus stop, the bus overtook her and went by without stopping despite Katy's despairing yells. She cursed loudly and shouted abuse after the departing vehicle. Jenny reflected her concern by puckering her face upwards at her. Katy smiled down at her,

"Sorry m'darlin. Don't you worry. We'll think of something."

She crossed over the road, still thinking of what to do.

****

Jenny had been found three hours later, strapped into her pushchair, at a bus-stop just before Upper Stokesey on the return side of the road. A bus driver had raised the alarm. He had stopped, expecting Jenny's mother to appear from behind the advertisement-wrapped shelter as he opened the doors but Jenny's distressed crying soon alerted him and his passengers to a serious incident.

Constable Steve Jennings was there in less than ten minutes from Stokesey police station by which time Jenny had been taken from the pushchair and was being comforted by several elderly women and had soon recovered her delightful demeanour by the time constable Jennings arrived. One of the women knew who Jenny was and that Katy Lewis from The Badgers often baby-sat for her mother. The woman, the pushchair and Jenny were taken into the police car and driven to the inn.

Katy's parents immediately abandoned their anger and frustration at their daughter's irresponsible absence and were soon overwhelmed by the ice-cold grip of fear for her safety.

Jennings' sergeant, Alec Faye, was quickly on the scene with a WPC after the constable had called-in the incident. Faye made a speedy assessment of the possible situation. He obtained from her mother, a strip of three photographs of Katy taken during her last term at school and had it photo-copied at the station. With the two police cars, he then set-up a road block chicane between the spot where Jenny had been found and Upper Stokesey, making a single lane. Cars from both directions were stopped and their drivers questioned until a large team of officers were sent from the city in the afternoon by which time Mrs Challis had returned to take charge of her daughter.

A CID team was led by Detective Sergeant Colin Laxton who assumed command of the operation as it was then realised that a criminal investigation was likely. Uniformed enforcements were sent to Upper Stokesey with copies of the grainy image of Katy Rose and every retail establishment and pedestrian were questioned. Katy had not arrived at her Grandmother's house and Bobby Paget and his building mates were among the many people who said they had not seen the girl that day.

The temporary road blocks were reinforced and every driver moving through Upper Stokesey and beyond continued to be stopped and questioned.

It took until the next morning for the bus company to admit that the bus Katy Rose had intended catching had been running early because the driver's mother had been taken into hospital and he wanted to get back to the city to find out how she was. After robust questioning the driver admitted he had seen Katy Rose and Jenny about to cross the road to the bus-stop as he passed.

The assumption that Katy had started to walk to Upper Stokesey was an obvious one for the officers to make. But it did not explain how Jenny Challis could have been left at a bus-stop just before Upper Stokesey on the return side of the road. The buses ran every forty-five minutes and that would not have been sufficient time for Katy to have reached the spot where Jenny was left before the next bus had caught up with her – and none of the other drivers had seen her. It was unlikely, almost impossible, for a driver not to notice a girl pushing a wheelchair along the narrow, twisting road.

DS Colin Laxton, soon concluded that Katy Rose must have accepted a lift and at some stage before reaching Upper Stokesey, Katy's potent allure had intoxicated the driver to ideas beyond those of being a Good Samaritan.

"How would he have got Jenny out of the car and into her pushchair without Katy stopping him?" one of his team enquired.

"He immobilised Katy first," the DS said.

"In a car? Katy was not little. She would put up a fight – especially if she thought Jenny might be harmed," a female detective said with experience.

"We don't know how he did it. He could have had a van couldn't he?" Laxton responded irritably, inwardly aware of the seriousness of the case that had been dumped on his relatively inexperienced shoulders because his DCI was ill.

"What other explanation is there? Perhaps the driver knew Katy – that's very likely. Her Dad says she would never have accepted a lift from a stranger. Let's question everyone Katy ever met. I don't care how long it takes. And let's check every damn traffic camera in the county."

To that end a better photograph was obtained for media release that evening. Katy's parents had said that Katy had told them a local amateur photographer, Charles Foden, had taken pictures of her at the recent agricultural fair. Foden was contacted and supplied a full-face professional image which was then circulated to the wire services and the local television network.

After a week the search had gone nationwide. All the media outlets covered Katy's disappearance and many false reports did nothing to assist the investigation. All her known acquaintances, including the many school friends who had left with her the previous summer, were questioned but their opinions about Katy's preferences and inclinations were typically contradictory to be useful: she was a flirt, but wasn't dating anyone; she had a thing about Bobby Paget but only because he ignored her; she was popular with the teachers but never played up to them; she was loyal to her friends but could be sharp-tongued if they did anything to upset her; she was brazen but shy; she was the best swimmer and runner in the school but was not competitive and she loved babies but didn't want to get married. To her parents it was simple: she was just a lovely, warm, funny, helpful girl. To her brother; well, he couldn't think of anything to say about her; he was too upset.

CCTV and Traffic cameras failed to reveal any trace of her. Petrol stations onto the motorway links were questioned but no one could recall seeing her, or any drivers acting suspiciously. There were two hundred 'sightings' investigated but none had any credibility.

The Press had been used extensively in efforts to broadcast Katy's disappearance nation-wide and one of the negative results of that was that the publicity attracted many people soon regarded as 'cranks' by the investigating team. One of those was a psychoanalyst called Ivana Katowice. She was interviewed by a journalist from the local newspaper and in that interview declared that little Jenny Challis would know what happened to Katy Rose and at a later date could be induced to recall the event by regressive hypnotherapy. The idea caught the imaginations of readers and the general media and Ivana Katowice was soon expounding her ideas in radio and television interviews and claiming that regressive hypnotherapy was a proven technique and did work. The last thing the police wanted was another 'crank' posing as an authority.

If the officers had been less involved with the mechanics of their investigation they might not have dismissed Ivana Katowice so lightly and would have foreseen the possible consequences of her claims and counteracted them quickly with a denial from a medical expert. But they acted too late for little Jenny Challis's safety.

The Mill House was a small building which sat prettily where the narrow river babbled down a series of natural steps and settled into a deeper pool just beyond the mill before continuing its journey to Upper Stokesey and Stokesey before it emptied into the estuary. It was on the other side of the stream from the Badgers and the cottages and accessed only by a footbridge which was once used for the grain carts to be backed up to the mill for the sacks to be winched to the first-floor loading hatch. But the old oak was not strong enough for modern vehicles and the loading floor had become the Challis' bedroom and the hatch a full length window.

It was a week after Ivana Katowice's several interviews that Ian Challis wakened in the early hours of a moonlit morning and realised his wife was not next to him. He was about to turn over having decided she had gone to the toilet when he heard her scream. He was awake and out of bed in an instant as his wife's voice yelled up to him.

"He's got Jenny. Stop. Stop."

Ian Challis was quickly at the open window. He saw a figure moving across the bridge away from the mill and he called aggressively to the intruder. The figure hesitated, looked upwards for a second and then threw a dark bundle into the mill pool and continued his journey across the bridge, running at speed towards the trees on the other side. His wife screamed again and he saw her run onto the bridge and look towards the water. Ian Challis sprang onto the window-ledge then launched himself out and sideways over the bridge towards the pool. He hit the water and quickly came to the surface and saw the dark bundle the man had thrown into the water drifting on the current and slowly sinking. He struck out and enfolded it in his arms and felt Jenny's face against his own and her breath warm against his mouth.

The Challis' moved away even before they sold the Mill House and nobody in the local area heard from them again.

After six months the police pulled all but routine officers from the case and Katy Rose's file was moved to the 'Non Active' folder but not yet to the 'Cold Case' archive.

THE PRESENT
1

Penny Featherstone surveyed the model in front of her for the umpteenth time. She groaned to herself, still unhappy at what she was surveying.

There was a knock on the room door.

"Not now, Gerry," she yelled at it.

"It's Graham," came a reticent voice. Penny closed her eyes and sighed. She opened the door.

"Sorry," she apologised. She stood back and Graham entered. He looked at the model laid out on the table.

"Wow! That's fantastic," he said.

"No it's not. It's awful," she corrected him.

Graham contoured the table.

"How can you say that? It's terrific," he argued. "It's amazing the way you've married the rectangular shapes to the circular interiors." Penny softened.

"It's so I can graduate the rise to the upper floor without using stairs," she explained.

"I can see that. It's a great idea. It gives old people the use of the upper floors without the danger of falling down any stairs."

"It exercises them without having to go outside – and one member of staff at that central desk can see all of the elevation without moving."

"Ingenious," Graham decided. Penny kissed his head.

"Do you want some tea?" she asked.

"No, thanks. I've got a band rehearsal. I just wondered if Noel had mentioned anything about going to his place for Easter."

"No. I haven't seen him since the Union debate the other night. Are you going?"

"I'm tempted. Apparently his parents have got quite a

place – and there's a gig near there on the Sunday. Cold Play and a few other bands are appearing."

"Where does he live?"

"Near a place called Stokesey. It's not a huge drive from here and he's got the car. Are you going home?"

"No. It's too awkward by train – and I should finish this project. I've got to hand it in next term."

"You can't stay here alone, Pen."

"I'll be okay. Anyway, I'm not so keen on Noel."

"I know – but he likes you. He's not so bad. He's a bit gross sometimes but he's harmless enough."

"He's dangerous."

Graham looked at her and his look required an explanation.

"I don't trust him. I think it's because he doesn't trust himself."

"That's a bit incisive, Pen – but I know what you mean. Harry is supposed to be coming too – and Caroline. You like them don't you?"

"Yes, they're okay. Listen to me. I sound like a bloody prig."

Before Graham could answer there was a sort of knock before the door crashed open and a large Noel burst in. He wound his college scarf around Penny's neck and pulled her into him. She pushed him away and untangled herself.

"Come in, Noel. I might have been naked."

"Course not. You don't do naked."

"No. I shower in a wet suit," she answered.

"Well, have you asked her?" Noel said as he locked his great arms around Graham's neck.

"I just mentioned it," Graham answered. Noel turned to Penny

"What d'you think, Pen. It's a great concert – and the weather forecast is good."

"Are Harry and Caroline going?"

"Yes. And we're meeting a few others there; Goring and Phillips and Chivers. I think Goring's brother lives that way."

"Won't your parents mind?"

"Course not. Anyway, I think they're still away and won't get back until the Monday. You'll love it. There are burial mounds and a castle nearby for you to photograph. You'll be in your element. And you can see Dad's pictures."

"He's a painter?"

"No. He's really into photography, has been since he was a boy."

"What about it, Pen?" Graham asked. "You need a break. It might help to get away and clear your mind."

"All right – as long as I don't have to sleep in a tent or on a bloody floor," she said.

Noel laughed and hugged her before she could resist.

"You won't have to do that, Pen. You can choose any of nine beds."

It was a large Georgian house set in an elevated position between the town of Stokesey and the village of Upper Stokesey and had an uninterrupted view to the south towards the estuary and the city beyond and to Drovers' Hill to the north. It was dark when Noel and his companions drove onto the drive and stopped outside the porticoed entrance but spot-lights illuminated the building and various sounds of appreciation from his passengers pleased the driver.

"Knew you'd like it," he said. "It's too bloody big though. It'll be great to have a few bodies around the place."

They were greeted by the housekeeper.

"This is Betsy," Noel told them as he lifted the middle-aged Betsy off her feet and twirled her round.

"Anyone else about?" he asked her.

She told him Phillipa was staying in London with friends for the holiday, Grant was on a tour with the school and Edmund wasn't sure if he'd get home because they were on stand-by.

"Poor sod's in the army," Noel explained to his companions. "What about Ma and Pa?" he asked of Betsy.

She explained his father had phoned from Nice and left a message for him not to wreck the house and to drink only the wine that he'd left in the larder.

"And he's hidden the cellar key anyway," she added with a hint of triumphalism in her voice.

"What's to eat, Bets?" Noel asked and was told she had made two steak pies.

"And that's another message from your father; don't use the dining-room. I've set five places in the kitchen for you."

Noel made a tour of the upper floors and pointed to the four guest bedrooms available. Penny had had a secret word with Caroline and they had both agreed they would share a room as Caroline didn't want to get too heavy with Harry. Noel and Harry looked disappointed at the news.

They enjoyed Betsy's steak pies and two bottles of decent Burgundy then the boys played snooker in the games-room while the girls sipped their wine and developed their acquaintance as they had chosen to share a bed together.

Penny was the first to wake. She parted the curtains and blinked at the sunlight. The grounds were not excessive. A lawn was divided by the short drive that led off a lane and there were two meadows beyond, which seemed to be part of the grounds. The bedroom was facing west and Penny could see the hills to her left. Scrub land on their lower slopes gave way to open grazing land and an area of wetlands fed by several streams from the hills and stretching to the river. She was pleased she had let herself be persuaded by Graham to join the house-party and she was even more pleased she had packed her beloved camera. Caroline stirred and blinked at the light. She took a few moments to remember where she was. She smiled at Penny.

"Did I wake you?" Penny asked.

"No." Caroline sat up and stretched. She wore only her knickers and Penny's artistic eye appreciated the way her breasts stretched and her hair fell about her shoulders.

"You slept well," Penny said.

"Didn't you – did I snore?"

"No. I slept great, the best sleep I've had for ages."

Caroline got out of bed and put her arms around her room-mate.

"Good morning," she said.

Penny was surprised by the physical pleasure she felt from the greeting.

"Have you showered?" Caroline asked, moving towards the en-suite bathroom.

"Not yet. You go first."

There was a cry of appreciation from inside the bathroom.

"Have you seen the size of the shower?" Caroline called. "We can share it."

Betsy was busy in the kitchen and Graham was already sitting at the table drinking coffee when the girls joined him.

"Full breakfast or toast and cereal. Coffee or tea?" Betsy asked. They chose tea and toast. Harry and Noel, neither of whom looked or smelled as though they had washed, chose a full breakfast.

"What should we do today?" Graham asked. What is there to see in this part of the country?"

"Look out of the window," Noel told him. "That's it."

"I thought you said there was a medieval barn and a castle and an old monastery nearby," Penny challenged.

71

"Yeah. Yeah. If you like that sort of thing," Noel responded, not yet looking or sounding as if he was properly awake.

"The Castle is on the other side of the valley," Betsy said helpfully. "Why don't you walk over Drover's Hill and have lunch at The Badgers then go on to the castle?" she suggested.

"That sounds good," Graham agreed and the girls supported the idea.

By the time they set-off, Noel was in a better mood and he and the boys amused themselves with a rugby ball while Penny and Caroline progressed their relationship. Caroline was a second-year psychology student and had a natural interest in behavioural patterns while Penny wanted to use her architect degree for social developments and especially for the aged and disabled, so they easily found subjects of mutual interest.

The Ridgeway path up to the hills skirted the village of Upper Stokesey and climbed steadily, curving up the inclines towards Drovers' Hill. The Hill was the apex of a ridge which ended suddenly and swept down to Upper Stokesey. Below the high point a trough had been worn by thousands of years of erosion and now supported a substantial area of mixed woodland which started half-way up the climb. The boys were some way off the path as the girls reached the woods and Noel kicked the ball towards them, shouting for them to return it. Caroline attempted to catch it but it hit a tree and bounced away from her. She chased it down the slope and had several attempts to connect with her foot as the boys shouted abuse at her.

Penny had walked on into the trees. She stopped in a particularly pretty glade. The trees on one side were thick woodland but were sparser on the other side of the path.

Penny had no idea why she had stopped but as she looked around, she was suddenly surprised to see a young woman standing behind a clump of gorse. The woman smiled and waved her fingers at her then bent down behind the gorse.

Penny turned as the boys entered the trees, chasing Caroline in a concerted effort to retrieve the ball from her which she had decided to retain because of their rude comments about her footballing ability. They rushed past Penny who was pleased as she had a good idea what the woman was doing behind the gorse. She smiled to herself and followed slowly after them, looking back but not seeing the woman appear again.

She caught up with the group who were enjoying trying to prise the ball from Caroline's bosom and Caroline, in turn, seemed to be enjoying the contest as much as them. When Noel had finally retrieved the ball and kicked it skilfully ahead in a straight line between the trees, a breathless Caroline took Penny's arm and rested her head on her shoulder.

"What kept you?" she asked and Penny told her about the woman she had seen. They both looked back but there was no sign of the stranger.

When they cleared the trees and reached the apex of the hill and looked back the view was as good as Betsy had told them it would be. Noel pointed out the geographical locations. It was a clear day and they could see beyond the estuary as far as the city where a haze marked its presence in the cool April air.

They reached the top and started down towards The Badgers. Penny took several pictures of the hamlet and wished only that the thatched cottages had wood smoke spiralling from their chimneys to perfect a timeless view of an England almost gone. By the time she caught up with the group they were already in the inn and ordering beer.

"That's her," Penny squealed, pointing to a large photograph of Katy Rose set in a frame behind the bar." The woman I saw."

"She's gorgeous," Caroline commented.

The middle-aged man pulling their beers scowled at Penny.

"What d'you mean, *that's her*?" he said.

"I just saw her, in the woods," Penny answered and gestured outwards and upwards in the general direction of Drover's Hill. The man slammed a pint on the beer-mat, spilling much of its contents and turned away.

"Serve em," he growled at a barmaid and disappeared into a back room.

"What's up with him?" Noel asked the barmaid. The woman looked at Penny.

"Her," she said as though the one word explained the situation

"What did I do?" Penny asked with amusement in her voice

The woman finished filling the glass and looked at Penny with the cold eyes of damnation.

"You just said you had seen Katy Rose, who disappeared twenty years ago."

There was a silent transmission of varying thoughts. They looked from the barmaid to the photograph and then to Penny but the barmaid looked only at Penny who crumpled under the scrutiny and tucked her chin into her chest. Caroline put a protective arm around her.

"Let's go outside," Graham said and they followed him onto the terrace.

"I saw her," Penny broke the silence defiantly.

"She did. She told me," Caroline supported her.

The boys made no comment and they sat sipping their

beers in silence until Noel attempted to break the spell.

"What the hell! You saw someone like her having a pee. What's so weird about that? Doesn't give that jerk an excuse to be so bloody rude."

They all agreed but Penny stared up to Drovers' Hill with a deep frown on her pretty face.

It was dusk by the time they felt the chill of the late April evening and left the pub and they were relieved when they saw a bus approaching. They waved it down as they charged towards the same stop where Katy Rose had fatally been less successful many years before.

Betsy had cooked a ham which they ate with new potatoes and salad and by the time they had eaten and sat around the comfortable sitting-room listening to music, the Badgers incident had been forgotten and they were looking forward to the gig the following day.

Harry had tried unsuccessfully to persuade Caroline to sleep with him and Noel had made several attempts to be intimate with Penny to such an extent that Graham uncharacteristically told him not to be such an immature shit and the outburst was like a stopper to the day and Noel petulantly declared he was going to bed.

The girls did together what girls do in bathrooms and giggled at the antics of Harry and Noel and dissected the boys' personalities with the expertise of their instincts and climbed into bed wearing only their knickers.

The next morning Penny was again the first to wake. She washed and dressed and left Caroline still sleeping. Betsy wasn't to be seen in the kitchen but a coffee pot was full and warming on the Aga. Penny decided to explore the parts of the house she had not seen.

There was a morning-room off the sitting-room and Penny was drawn to the many framed photographs on the walls.

They were mostly landscapes but were of a very high standard and she assumed they had been taken by Noel's father. She was still studying them when Betsy entered and spoke behind her.

"I thought I heard someone walking about," she smiled. "You are always the early one."

Penny asked about the photographs.

"Noel's father has always been keen on photography," Betsy explained. "He's got hundreds of pictures, Have a look at those albums," and she pointed to a bookshelf. Penny took down an album and studied it.

"I'll go and get the breakfast ready," Betsy said.

Penny was still sitting with the albums when Caroline found her.

"You deserted me," she said, kissing Penny. "What have you found that's so interesting?"

Penny showed her the albums.

"He's really good. Portraits or landscapes and so many in black and white which is a bit odd these days. I wonder if he develops them himself."

She didn't have long to wait for the answer as the boys arrived and told the girls that Betsy was waiting to serve breakfast.

"We'd better have a good one," Noel told them. "There's only shit burgers at the concert." He seemed to have recovered his spirit. "Those are Dad's albums," he said to Penny, almost accusingly.

"I'm impressed," Penny told him. "Does he process them himself?"

"God! I should say. He's even got his own laboratory.

"I'd love to see it."

"Bit difficult that. It's at the other house and he doesn't let anyone in there without him What about breakfast? Come

76

on. I'm bloody starving."

He led the way back to the kitchen.

The concert was what was expected; noisy, crowded and soon muddy under feet despite there not having been any rain for several days. They had met the other party from their university in a pub and consumed several beers and Noel had bought a bottle of vodka which was regularly handed between them and by the time the concert had finished and the huge crowd had filtered onto the narrow access road it was past midnight and by the time they had walked, in an increasingly difficult manner, the four miles home it was two o'clock in the morning.

Penny was only a social drinker and had taken sips of the vodka only as the April night temperature defeated the body-heat around her so she was in a better physical and mental condition than her companions when they fell into their beds. She lay awake for some time listening to Caroline puffing and when she eventually fell asleep it was with an image of Katy Rose in her head.

It was past nine when she awakened. Caroline was still sleeping deeply. Penny showered and dressed without attempting to be quiet but Caroline did not stir. Penny went down to the kitchen where Betsy was alone.

"I think the others might be a bit hung-over today," Penny told her.

They sat and talked. Betsy explained she had become the housekeeper because of Noel's mother.

"I was married to a soldier. He was killed in a helicopter crash in Iraq. Mrs Foden is from a military family and runs a branch of the Heroes charity. She knew I was in financial difficulties and suggested I came to them as their housekeeper. The children had a nanny but she had just died. It was marvellous for me because I have the old orangery

77

which they converted into a self-contained annex. I don't know what I would have done only for them."

"What does Noel's father do?" Penny asked

"He runs the family engineering business. It was started by his Great Grandfather who invented some agricultural tool. They sell agricultural machinery all over the world. Charles, that's Noel's father, really made it an international business but he would rather take photographs," she laughed.

"Is that the family?" Penny asked, pointing to a large photograph of a shooting party on the wall. "It looks very old."

"Yes. That's Noel's Great Grandfather. That's his Great Grandmother. Then Noel's Grandfather and I think that lady is his grandfather's sister.

"Who is the important-looking man in the middle?"

"I believe that is Sir Toby Henderson, he owned what is now the Bishop's estate. It was in his family for four hundred years. The estate was sold when he died. His daughter, Fiona, that's her bending down with the dogs, was married to Noel's grandfather.

Penny was standing, studying the photograph with the fascination people have for the past.

"They all look very elegant – even for shooting," she said. "So that's Noel's grandfather: Charles' father; he's very handsome."

"Yes he was. Charles once said he must have got his grandfather's genes."

"It was another world then wasn't it?"

"It was. Charles once said that's when they were happy."

"What did he mean?"

"I don't know. The way he said it I didn't like to ask."

"And who are the men in some sort of uniform?

"They were German prisoners of war. There was a prisoner

of war camp at Stokesey."

"What are they doing?"

"Some of them worked locally, mostly on the farms."

"Really? That's amazing. Were they free to walk about?"

"Only when the war had ended – while they were waiting to be repatriated."

"That's so interesting. It's a historic time-capsule. Where was the photograph taken, it looks a very big house?"

"On the Henderson estate. It's just the other side of that hill." She pointed through the window where a promontory swept down beyond Drover's Hill. "The estate takes in that part of the marshes by the estuary. They shoot wildfowl out there in the winter. I can see you don't approve by your face."

"I'm with Noel's father on that one. I would rather photograph them than kill them. What happened to the Hendersons?"

"I think the family went their separate ways when the estate was sold after Sir Toby died."

"I was thinking of exploring a bit and taking some photographs. Noel said there was an old monastery near here. I wondered if you knew about buses."

"Take the Mini," Betsy told her. "It's what I use for shopping. I won't need to go anywhere today and if the boys are going to be hung-over I'd better be here to look after them. I'll find you a local map."

Penny found the ruins of the monastery. The arches and towering walls displayed the grandeur of the masons' craft, silhouetted against the open landscape and sparkling sky, and Penny dropped the aperture to emphasise the stark shapes and dramatic images. She then went to the castle which they had failed to visit after the confrontation in The Badgers had blunted their enthusiasm for sightseeing. It was in a good position to command the river valley but had been mostly destroyed by the Parliamentary forces in the civil war and was of no photographic interest. She descended the hill into the hamlet and took pictures of the thatched cottages, conscious that she might be creating an important archive for future generations. She moved past them and saw the mill-house. She approached it slowly, looking right and left as though expecting to see someone but it was not until she had reached the footbridge that a woman opened the door and smiled at her.

"I'm sorry," Penny apologised. "I'm being a nosy tourist and taking pictures. Do you mind?"

The woman crossed the bridge and smiled at her. Penny supposed she was in her thirties and seemed pleased to have someone to talk to. She told Penny how they had bought the mill twenty years ago and loved it.

"Do you want to come in?" she asked. Penny declined politely but had no reason to refuse the invitation beyond a feeling that she didn't want to cross the bridge.

She took pictures of the mill and the river and then moved up to The Badgers. It was lunchtime and several cars were parked behind the pub. Penny hesitated before deciding to brave the bar staff again, but she was hungry and needed to use the toilet. A middle-aged woman was serving and Penny was relieved neither of the two staff who had been so rude to her were to be seen. She ordered a pie and a glass of beer then went to the toilet as she was waiting.

When she returned she was able to study the photograph of Katy Rose and tried to analyse its vibrant appeal. It was a full-on portrait of a beautiful face. Katy was looking straight into the lens, her eyes wide and her mouth was open and half-smiling. The picture had been expertly processed. The area around the face and neck had been bleached out so that the outline of the face and the features, the mouth, the nose and the eyes looked as though they had been line-painted with black ink but Katy's deep auburn hair surrounded the top half of the picture in shocking contrast, emphasising the perfection of her features. Penny looked sideways and saw the man who had been so unpleasant to her, looking towards her from the other bar and she took her beer and pie and sat outside.

The pie was very good and she had almost finished it when the man from behind the bar came out. He studied her from the doorway before moving towards her. Penny avoided his gaze by raising the glass to her lips. The man was at the table, looking down at her.

"What do you want?" he demanded.

"Excuse me?"

"What do you want?" he repeated. "Are you a journalist?"

"No. I'm a student," Penny answered aggressively.

The man pulled out a chair and sat down and continued to look at her intensely.

"I didn't invite you to sit down. Leave me alone and please go away."

It was not the reaction the man was expecting.

"I'm sorry," he said. "I'm sorry I was rude to you on Saturday. It's just that we have had so many people saying they have seen Kat over the years."

"Kat?" Penny queried

"Katy Rose; my sister."

"I'm sorry," Penny said.

"You think you saw her?"

Penny didn't answer. She didn't want to remember or talk about it any more.

"Are you a photographer?" the man asked.

"I told you; I'm a student. Architecture."

"It's a fancy camera you've got."

"Architects take pictures," she explained.

"So you have a good eye for faces?" he said

"Yes," She answered defiantly.

"Where did you see this person?"

"Up there. On the other side of the hill, just into the trees."

The man looked up to Drovers' Hill and held his gaze for some moments. Then he stood up.

"Show me," he said.

"What?"

"Show me where you saw her."

"I'm not climbing up there just to please you."

"No need. Wait a moment."

He strode away towards the back of the building. A few minutes later he appeared noisily on a quad-bike.

"Come on," he called up to her. Penny didn't move.

"Please?" he said and his voice matched the plea. She rose and went down off the terrace to him.

"Why?"

"Because I believe you. What's your name?" She told him.

"Then please, Penny. For twenty years I have dreamt that Kat will show up one day. I could never sleep again if I ignored you and didn't give you the benefit of the doubt."

He gestured towards the seat behind him. Penny climbed onto it. They crossed the road near to the bus-stop where Katy and Jenny had crossed twenty years before. The man drove onto the grass verge to a gate beside which was a style and a signpost marking it out as the footpath on which Penny and her companions had reached The Badgers two days previously. The man got down and opened the gate then drove through it onto a field. He got down again and closed the gate behind them. They bumped up the field beside the footpath, bouncing and swerving between the clumps of rough pasture so that Penny had to grip hard to the edge of the seat to stay on it. They cleared the field and entered the trees and followed the ridge path between them, driving slower, the man inclining his head backwards, waiting for her instructions to stop. They could see the open sky ahead as they neared the end of the woods and had almost passed the spot before Penny recognised it and yelled for the man to stop.

"There." She pointed. "Just behind that clump of gorse."

She explained how the woman had smiled and waved at her before bending out of sight.

The man stepped down. He stood on the path looking towards the spot she indicated. He then looked around to the other side of the path before he moved forward to the clump of gorse. He carefully stepped behind it as if he were expecting to find someone hiding there. Penny watched him. She could see him only from his waist up as she had seen the woman. He seemed to be kicking the ground, looking down all the time and moving around behind the gorse. He bent down out of her sight and was several minutes. She could hear him breathing heavily. Then he stood up and looked towards her.

"Would you come here and take a photograph please," he said in a strange voice. Penny got down and crossed the path and went behind the gorse bush. He was bending down with one knee on the ground and was holding something just above the grass.

"What do you want me to photograph?" she asked him.

"Me. Just like this – and all of this area so I can identify it again."

Penny obediently took a close-up of him and the object he was holding and then moved back and took several location shots. When she had finished he held the object towards her.

"What is it?" she asked. He was rubbing it with the elbow of his shirt.

"It's Kat's shoe," he said. "The ones she was wearing when she disappeared."

He stared at her and Penny stared back. Her spine had gone cold, right up into the nape of her neck. The blood had disappeared from the man's face. Eventually he spoke, but his voice was not much more than a whimper.

"Are you psychic?" he asked. His eyes studied her with a desperate expression in them.

"No. No. of course not."

He continued to stare at her.

"Please. I want to go back," she said and her voice reflected the fear in her body. He nodded like a toy dog and they walked back to the quad bike and climbed onto the vehicle. He turned it round and they drove back in silence. At The Badgers he parked and held his hand to help her down.

"Thank you," he said. "Thank you." He kissed her hand and held it to his face.

She pulled away and ran to where she'd parked the Mini. He was standing in the drive when she drove up. He held out his arms in an attempt to stop her but Penny swerved around him and drove onto the road and accelerated away.

****

Penny's companions were experiencing various stages of alcohol poisoning. None of them had attempted to get out of bed until lunchtime and even then only Harry and Graham managed to reach the kitchen in any state of mental and physical cohesion. They both sipped black coffee and mumbled to each other incomprehensibly. They had started on their third cups when Noel emerged looking more than ever like an Old English sheepdog, his hair covering his face and his hunched shoulders pressing his chin into his chest. He wore only a pair of cotton shorts and Betsy was repulsed enough to find something to do elsewhere. Shortly after, Caroline joined them. She was wearing a long T-shirt under which her breasts swung and bobbled freely and as she sat down the shirt rose high on her thighs.

It was not surprising that Noel was the worst affected as he had consumed the most of the vodka and they had all had several beers before going to the concert when they had met their university chums in a pub as arranged. But Caroline had less excuse as she had had only one glass of wine beforehand and had not indulged heavily of the vodka. But whatever the cause, her legs were heavy and her head still throbbed and she carried her coffee unsteadily back to her bedroom. After nibbling several biscuits and emptying the large percolator, the boys separately made their way back upstairs to their respective rooms, hoping to get themselves together before Betsy served the evening meal which she had commanded they all would eat and not waste.

Caroline sat on the edge of the bed and took several draughts of the coffee before feeling again the nausea return. She was suddenly hot and she pulled off the T-shirt. She tried several more sips of the coffee before collapsing backwards and closing her eyes to calm the throbbing in her head.

Noel was the last to return upstairs. As he reached the rectangular landing above the stairwell, he noticed that Caroline's door was not properly closed as a sliver of daylight leaked in a thin line across the oak-planked floor. He looked about him. The other guest rooms were directly opposite on the other side of the stairwell while the family rooms were off the long corridor leading from it. The doors to the other guest rooms were shut. Noel crept forward and pushed Caroline's door gently inwards. He peered round it. Caroline was lying on top of the duvet, half on her side, her legs splayed as though she were running in her dreams, her breasts flopping heavily sideways and one arm bent under her head. Noel closed the door behind him and crept towards the bed. He looked down at the semi-naked figure and took off his shorts. As his weight went onto the bed Caroline turned towards him so that she was almost lying on her back. She opened her eyes and panic shone from them.

"Hello Caroline," Noel leered at her and hoisted a leg to the other side of hers. She attempted to say something and reached up to push him away but his left hand gripped her outstretched right wrist and held it down onto the bed while his right hand tore at her pants and shredded them. She attempted to yell but his right hand came up quickly and went over her mouth. She swung a punch at his head with her left fist but he countered it by bending his right elbow forcefully into her biceps. He was now holding both her arms down while his hand still closed over her mouth. His knees dug into her thighs forcing her legs apart which were fighting desperately against his weight. She managed to bite into the palm of his hand and as he took a stronger grip on her mouth her voice found an outlet before his fingers closed her lips painfully together.

Harry had decided to take a shower and get himself together. He had left his bedroom to walk to the communal bathroom which was situated between his side of the stairwell and that of Caroline's bedroom when he thought he heard Caroline cry out. He waited, listening for a further sound but when none came he went and listened at her door. The sounds he heard were not explicable. He knocked gently and called her name.

"Go away, Harry,"

Noel's voice came back to him.

If he had been Graham he might have stopped to consider the various possibilities that might have caused Noel to be in Caroline's room but Harry had no doubt as to the reason. He opened the door and rushed inside and quickly analysed the situation. Almost without breaking his stride he swept up a chair and smashed it against the side of Noel's head. Noel fell from the bed and crashed to the floor and lay there unconscious, blood running from a wound on the side of his head, his genitalia obscenely of a similar colour.

****

Penny drove in a state of impaired awareness. There was a part of her brain working sufficiently to read the road signs and to recognise the route back to the house but mostly it was closed to any other processes beyond an image of the face of Katy Rose. It was only as she turned off the lane onto the drive and saw the flashing light of an ambulance that it began to reason. Who was ill? Had there been an accident?

The ambulance drove away as she pulled up behind it and she was met by Betsy and Graham

"Who?" she asked and surprised herself by feeling relief that it was Noel.

Reluctantly, slowly, in unconnected sentences the story was revealed. She immediately rushed upstairs to Caroline. She had to call out to her as the bedroom door was locked. Caroline met her and sobbed in her arms. They sat on the bed together and it was some time before Penny could ask the important questions.

"Did he come inside you? There was some confusion with first a Yes and then a No before they clarified the meaning of "come".

"He penetrated," Caroline explained. She was now wearing the T-shirt again and a pair of shorts. Penny had seen the torn panties on the bed.

"Show me," Penny told her. Caroline obediently stripped and Penny saw the bruises on her arm, her wrist and her thighs. Her lip was already swollen.

"Wait here," Penny told her and left. She was soon back, carrying a newspaper she had picked-up from the table at The Badgers. First she photographed Caroline's mouth and then told her to lie on the bed and stretch her arms outwards. She placed the newspaper across Caroline's chest then stood over her, framing her torso and arms and took several photographs. Then she got Caroline to sit on the edge of the bed while she photographed the bruises on her thighs. When they had finished she took her friend and put her in the shower then dried her gently and helped her dress.

"What do you want to do?" Penny asked her. "Do you want to bring rape charges against him?"

Caroline began to weep again and went through several emotions: anger, fear, self-loathing, helplessness then anger again and Penny held her hands and listened.

It was two hours before Caroline felt strong enough to allow Penny to take her downstairs. Betsy was motherly and said she would find some arnica for her face. Graham and Harry were mostly silent and helpless like expectant fathers at a birth.

"How is he?" Caroline eventually asked, looking gratefully at Harry.

"The medics stitched him up but they said he will need a brain scan," Graham told her.

"Was he conscious?" Caroline asked and as the boys looked bemused Betsy told her he was semi-conscious in the ambulance.

Asking the questions and listening to the answers helped Caroline focus and in the silence she told the others they could talk about the situation. Harry was frightened by what he had done and needed assuring that he did the right thing.

"What if he dies or is brain-damaged?" he asked.

Surprisingly it was Betsy who was the first to assure him. She took him by the shoulders and looked into his face.

"You did the right thing," she said forcefully. "If you hadn't interfered God knows what the outcome might have been. So don't feel guilty."

"How do we get back to uni?" Penny asked.

"How do we let his parents know what happened?" Harry wanted to know. Betsy told them she had already spoken to Noel's father.

"I just said there had been an accident. They were coming home tomorrow but now they are catching a flight this evening. It will be late by the time they're here. I suggest you have an early night and leave everything till morning when Mr. Foden can sort everything out."

Penny did not sleep very well, mostly because Caroline, understandably, wavered between draughts of deep unconsciousness and semi-consciousness when she mumbled and squealed like a dreaming dog and when she involuntarily groped for Penny's hand or turned and hugged her as though for warmth. But her own efforts were no better. After the first two hours when they both surrendered to their separate exhaustions, images of Katy Rose and her brother stabbed at her mind and forced her to open her eyes to reconnect with reality. It was during one such interruption that she heard a vehicle arriving noisily on the gravelled driveway and assumed, correctly, that it would be Noel's parents. She had no idea how long she had slept or of the time but thought vaguely that it had taken the parents longer than the time Betsy had proposed for their arrival. Penny was not then to know that Charles and Arabella Foden had called in at the hospital in the hope of being allowed to see their son as the hospital was on their way from the airport. They had found the night-staff sympathetic to their concerns and they had been allowed to see Noel but not to wake him from his sedated condition. They were told his head-wound had been stitched and they had checked for possible internal bleeding but they would not know the exact prognosis of the brain-scan until a consultant saw him in the morning.

Betsy had told them that Noel had been involved in an accident and when questioned further as to its cause she had revealed only that it had been from a confrontation with one of his friends over a young lady, so when Penny ventured downstairs at first-light to make herself some tea, it was not surprising that she heard the voices of the Fodens discussing the incident before she reached the kitchen. Arabella's voice was sharp and authoritative.

"Bloody impertinence," she was saying. "They come here, eat our food, drink our wine, sleep in our beds and fight like tomcats. I thought it was supposed to be a decent university for decent people, not for riff-raff from comprehensives."

Penny had stopped in the passageway leading into the kitchen upon hearing the voice. She now turned to retrace her steps but Charles Foden, crossing the doorway to get to the refrigerator, turned and saw her.

"You are?" he demanded to know.

Penny turned. "Penny Featherstone," she told him.

Arabella Foden joined her husband to peer through the

doorway at the subject of his question.

"What do you want?" she demanded with all the ire of someone who has been overheard.

"I was going to make some tea."

"Are you the girl…" Arabella began but Penny interrupted her.

"No. I'm not the girl your son raped."

Her response had the effect she expected of it. Arabella Foden's mouth remained open mid-sentence and got wider. Her husband dropped the plastic milk container he had just taken from the refrigerator.

"How dare you?" Arabella said, finding her voice. "How dare you? In our house."

"Be quiet," her husband told her. He gestured for Penny to enter the kitchen. "Please?" he said.

His wife gasped angrily and disappeared from Penny's view.

"Please?" Charles Foden tried again and Penny reluctantly obeyed. Foden picked the milk container off the floor.

"We've just made some tea," he said. "How do you like it?

Penny told him with milk only. Arabella was standing by the Aga with her back to them, seemingly hugging herself for comfort. Foden gestured for Penny to sit and handed her a mug of tea. He sat opposite, on the other side of the table.

"Tell me what you think happened," he asked her.

Penny told him.

"Ridiculous," Mrs. Foden turned and snapped at Penny.

"Be quiet, Arabella," her husband snapped back without taking his eyes off Penny. "Please continue," he told her.

"Harry heard Caroline trying to scream and knocked and asked if she was all right. Noel told him to go away. So Harry rushed into the room, saw what was happening and he hit Noel with a chair."

"Why did he do that?"

"Because he was fucking Caroline and holding her down and holding her mouth so she could not scream."

Her eyes challenged Foden and then his wife who seemed about to hit her.

"Were you present?" Foden asked.

"Of course I wasn't. I had been out. I returned just as the ambulance was taking Noel away."

"So you do not know what happened?"

"I do know what happened."

"How? From what your friends told you? How do you know Noel and this girl were not having consensual sex and this, *Harry* fellow was not jealous and nearly killed my son?"

Penny looked from him to his wife, who was now almost sneering at her. She got up and walked out of the kitchen.

"Where are you…" Foden began to ask.

"Well done, Charles. That's put her in her place," his wife said.

Penny went upstairs and gently shook Caroline awake.

"Caroline. I want you to come downstairs with me."

Caroline allowed herself to be pulled into a sitting position and then to have her feet swung onto the floor. She was wearing the same long T-shirt she had worn before. Penny pulled her to her feet and led her across the bedroom.

"Where are we going?" Caroline wanted to know but Penny held her hand and guided her downstairs and into the kitchen where Caroline blinked at the sudden assault of electric light. Her mouth was still swollen and the bruising around it was now purple.

"This is Caroline," Penny told the Fodens. "This is where Noel gripped her mouth to stop her screaming. This is where his elbow held one arm to the bed and this is where he

gripped her wrist to hold the other arm down. And these…"
She lifted Caroline's T-shirt to reveal the bruises on her
thighs "Is where your son's fourteen stone forced her legs
apart while he penetrated her."

The two girls stared back at the speechless Fodens with
diverse emotions until Penny put her arm around her friend
and led her from the kitchen and back to their bed where
Caroline snuggled up to Penny and whispered her thanks.
The two girls then managed to sleep and it was light when
they opened their eyes and remembered what Penny had
done.

"If you want to take this further, I've got evidence," Penny
told Caroline and still felt the controlled anger she had
displayed two hours earlier.

"I don't know what I should do," Caroline said. "What do
you think, Penny?"

"It's what you feel that matters, not what anyone thinks."

"I just want it to go away."

"I know. But I don't know how long that will take."

They washed and dressed and packed and when they
returned to the kitchen Harry and Graham were drinking
coffee and eating toast and Betsy was tending to them.
Penny told them of her confrontation with Noel's parents
and what she had done. Graham was a law student and was
immediately supportive.

"Well done, Pen," he said. "Thank God you had your
camera. We've no idea how the local police would handle it.
Not many forces have Rape Units."

"Will you bring charges against him?" Betsy asked
Caroline and looked concerned.

"Caroline doesn't know what she'll do. She's still in
turmoil," Penny explained.

"Of course you are, poor girl," but Betsy looked

uncomfortable and the sympathy did not sound genuine.

"What's the matter, Betsy? You know what happened. Don't you think Noel deserves to be punished for what he did?" Penny asked with her recently kindled assertiveness.

Betsy stepped towards them and almost whispered. "I do. But just be careful. You don't want to do anything to make it worse for yourselves. Mr Foden's got influence around here. Even with the police."

She suddenly stood upright and noticeably pressed her lips together and busied herself at the Aga and before anyone could question her, Charles Foden entered.

"Good morning," he said as the boys got to their feet. "I'm Charles Foden."

The boys introduced themselves as they shook hands. Foden held Harry's hand tightly. "You're the chap who hit my son with a chair," he said. Harry avoided his stare and retracted his hand.

"To stop him raping Caroline," Graham interjected.

Foden turned his eyes onto Graham but Graham stared back.

"That is a matter of opinion," Foden told him.

"No. It is a matter of fact," Graham answered and Penny began to like the steel she suddenly saw in her friend.

"And how would you know that?"

"By the physical evidence of your son's assault on Caroline, which demonstrates his determination to rape her. And his denial by force of any means by her to protect herself."

"You sound litigious Mr...?"

"That is the way it will sound if Caroline chooses to bring charges against Noel."

Foden was aware of eight eyes watching him. He suddenly smiled. "I thought you were Noel's friends," he said.

"Surely you don't want to let the police and lawyers into your lives. You are all so young. It is so easy to do the wrong thing at your age that might affect the rest of your lives."

"The wrong thing is already done," Harry said.

It was the first time he had spoken and his voice was stronger than expected

"Two wrong things," Foden reminded him.

"My son might be brain damaged. He might not be able to defend himself from any charges made against him. But you, Harry... " He let the sentence hang in their minds.

The telephone rang and Foden strode across the kitchen to answer it. From his questions and replies it was obviously from the hospital. When he had finished he returned to the table.

"Noel is conscious," he told them. "He has spoken so they do not think he has any permanent damage but the surgeon hasn't seen him yet so we don't know the result of the brain-scan. A police officer wants to come and see me." He waited long enough for them to consider the implications before continuing. "It's routine for them to check on violent injuries. I could tell them you all had to get back to the university?"

The group looked at each other and then they were all looking at Caroline, waiting. She nodded without speaking.

"Harry?" Graham asked. He too nodded agreement.

"I can drive you into the city. There's a direct train from there you can catch," Foden told them.

They were assembled in the entrance-hall fifteen minutes later. Foden joined them, carrying boxes of Easter eggs. He handed a box to each of them, explaining that he had got them at the airport for the children but thought they should have them instead.

"You'll be hungry before you get back to the university."

They thanked Betsy for her hospitality then climbed into Foden's large SUV. They drove most of the way in silence except for when Foden commented on Penny's camera. She explained she was reading architecture.

"I do a bit of photography myself," Foden told her.

"Yes. I saw your albums. You are very good," she said.

They talked politely about photography and then penny suddenly asked:

"Did you take the picture of that girl who went missing a long time ago? The one in The Badgers?"

"Yes. Yes, I did. How did you know that?"

"It was just a thought. It was a similar style to other portraits I saw in your albums."

Foden laughed. "I didn't realise I had a particular style. Awful business that. Delightful girl."

"Did you know her well?"

"Only as one gets to know one's neighbours. I have taken many pictures of the locals over the years."

"It's a strong portrait."

"Thank you. It's what the police used to publicise her disappearance. I think I took it at the local agricultural fair. We have one every year."

"What do you think happened to her?" Penny asked.

"Almost certainly abducted by some deranged motorist. That's what the police thought anyway."

"She was a lovely girl."

"Yes. She was. Delightful. Awful tragedy."

On the train, Graham decided he was hungry and opened his egg-box. They were large eggs made of chocolate and were in two halves and were supposed to contain other sweets but when Graham split the two halves apart he shot back in his seat and they all stared at the egg that was filled with a roll of bank-notes. Graham took out the roll and counted two hundred pounds. They all opened their boxes with similar results except that Caroline's contained twenty fifty-pound notes.

"Bribery," Penny said.

"Evidence of guilt," Graham added

"Useful though," Harry conceded.

Caroline only smiled uncertainly.

"Take a picture of the haul, Pen," Graham told her.

Penny arranged the egg halves on the table with the money inside and took several pictures. She then stacked the notes outside each box and took more pictures.

****

After Penny's hasty retreat from The Badgers, Tom Lewis did not rush to a telephone to inform the police of his discovery of his sister's shoe. Nor did he tell his wife about it. He did not even go to his mother's nearby cottage and tell her, even knowing that it was news she had awaited every day for twenty years to hear. Instead, he went down into the cellar of the pub and sat on a steel keg and held the shoe to his face and cried as he had failed to cry since the day his sister had disappeared from their lives like a passing cloud.

Twenty years of suppressed grief took some time to weep from his body and when it had done so it had the effect of a breached dam with all the detriment expelled, leaving behind an empty container ready for refuelling with new energy. His brain was the first part of his body to benefit from the cleansing process and it quickly recognised that while the discovery of the shoe was a marker for obvious progress in the search for Katy Rose, it was also a marker of the failure in the original police investigation.

It had been assumed by everyone – force-fed by the police themselves – that Katy Rose had been abducted by someone in a vehicle. Why, oh why, had he or his parents not thought that Kat might have decided to walk to Upper Stokesey via Drovers' Hill when she realised she had missed the bus? It was the sort of thing she would do. It was in her nature to find the easiest way out of a problem. There was nothing sophisticated about her. She was the most uncomplicated person he had known. Some people might say 'naïve' but that would be to mistake her uncompromising simplicity for stupidity. The very act of deciding to walk over Drovers' Hill to Upper Stokesey was a good example and Tom Lewis now saw the reasons why no one, not even his parents, had considered the possibility. The footpath from the road up to the main ridge-path was steep and the footpath itself narrow and cobbled from hundreds of years of wear on the sandstone and the only access to it then was over the style as the gate had only recently been added when the landowner decided to cultivate the adjoining meadow.

Katy Rose had been wearing her favourite dress and she was particular about her looks. She had been wearing her best shoes and Jenny was in a pushchair. It was easy to see why adults would consider such things impediments to doing what she had obviously done. But Kat was not an adult. Underneath the burgeoning gifts of womanhood she was still a child as nature had made her. That is why she hated wearing knickers. That is why she flaunted her sexuality because she was unaware of its effect on other people. That is why she would never refuse a physical challenge.

Tom could see it clearly now: she would lift Jenny from the pushchair and carry her over the style and sit her on the grass while she folded the pushchair and carried that across.

Then she would carry them both up the steep path and onto the ridge path where she would reassemble them and continue the now easy journey to Upper Stokesey, probably singing as she went. But it was not all the way, it was only as far as the spot where he had found her shoe; there his vision ended. What happened after that was unknown and should not be imagined. But of one thing more he was sure: she was not miles away. She was near, somewhere up there on Drovers' Hill.

Despite the clarity of his mind, he was not confident of what he should do with the new evidence. He realised that he had to take it to the police but he was uneasy with the thought. The discovery of the shoe was a massive indictment of the original investigation and some of the officers who worked on the case were still in office and two of them were now in senior positions. What would be their reaction to the sudden exposure of their failures? He saw the arguments they would muster: how could he be sure it was Kat's shoe after twenty years in the undergrowth? And how did he find the shoe? What made him look there for it? That, he quickly knew, was his main problem; a girl called Penny had seen Katy Rose and led him to the spot.

The problem became larger when he realised he did not know her second name. He knew nothing about her, who she was, where she was from or from where she came.

She had denied being psychic, and from her reaction to the thought, he believed she had no idea that she might be. There had been such people offering their services in the original investigation but DS Colin Laxton, who had been the lead detective, was not interested in hearing other ideas beside his own or those of his chosen team.

Laxton was now a detective superintendent and was likely to head-up any new investigation. Steve Jennings was still local. He had been the constable who had been called by the bus driver when they had found young Jenny. He was now a sergeant and still based in Stokesey which had managed to retain its small police station despite the cuts to the service. Steve was the governor, with a constable and a WPC in his team. He would be a good man to talk to. He was a local boy and had known Katy who had been only three years below him at school. He had also been very supportive of their parents as he often drank in The Badgers. Yes, Steve would be the man to talk to. But first, he had to see his mother.

Mrs Lewis was now in her seventies and lived alone since her husband had died ten years previously. They had said the cause of death was coronary pneumonia but she knew, and Tom knew, that the cause had been coronary stress from years of waiting for Katy Rose to be found. He had not taken to drink or become violent or even bad tempered. He had stopped talking to customers about the weather or politics or their health. He had stopped asking how their wives or children were. He had stopped enquiring of walkers how far they had travelled and didn't offer his usual advice on routes they should take or monuments they should see and as soon as Tom was old enough to help his mother run the pub, Mr. Lewis was content to sit in a chair and stare at the television. He had just seen Tom married and had held the photograph of Katy Rose which Tom had insisted be put on the wedding-table, and then he had gone outside and fallen in the churchyard and had died two days later.

Mrs Lewis was surprised to see her son at that time in the afternoon. He often called in just after breakfast once he had organised the bar and helped his wife in the kitchen to prepare the lunches and then he would visit again when the pub had closed, often just to check on her even though she had gone to bed. She knew straight away that something had happened. He sat down and didn't speak.

"What you got there?" his mother asked.

Tom put the shoe on the table in front of them.

"What's that dirty old thing?" she asked again.

"Look at it, Ma."

"Why would I want to touch that?"

"Look at it, Ma," he repeated.

Reluctantly, she picked the shoe off the table using only her thumb and a finger. The leather was green and broken-down, looking more like blotting-paper but the structured cork of the wedge-shaped heel had survived without any alteration apart from its colour. Parts of the leather had been nibbled by mice or insects but where Tom had cleaned the toe of the shoe and inside the laced tongue the original red colour could still be seen. Mrs Lewis still showed some reluctance to handle it but when she peered inside, where Tom had cleaned the leather, and read the name etched into the hide, *Pagan*, she dropped the shoe as though it were suddenly hot and sat back and gasped for breath.

Tom hurried over to her but she soon recovered, taking in draughts of air. Pagan had been a shop in Stokesey, popular with the youngsters, but had closed-down some years previously. She remembered when Kat had spent all her Birthday and Christmas money on the shoes. Mrs. Lewis regained some composure, the grim toughness she had developed to keep living without Katy Rose.

"They must have sold a lot of those," she said.

Tom told her where he'd found it and the thought processes his brain had undergone in the cellar were absorbed much faster in his mother's head. She stared at the shoe, then, much as he had done, picked it up and held it to her bosom. Neither of them spoke for some time until Mrs.

101

Lewis mimicked her son.

"Why. Oh, why didn't we think that's what she would do?"

And then she began to cry. Their grief was disturbed by his mobile ringing. It was his wife, Doreen, wondering where the hell he was and what was he doing gallivanting around on the quad-bike with some tart and did he know they had customers waiting to be served? He kissed his mother and told her they would have to talk later.

They had a family meeting that evening: him, Doreen and his mother. Monday evening was never busy and their barmaid could cope alone. The conversation went much the same way as his own thoughts had taken him earlier. They doubted whether the police would be enthusiastic about reopening the case but they agreed a search of the woods was needed and only the police could do that properly. Both the women wanted to know more about Penny and were almost angry that Tom had let her go without finding out who she was. Doreen was even ready to accuse her of some complicity in Katy's disappearance but Tom emphasised how frightened she had been by her experience and, besides, she was much too young to know anything about the original case.

"We've got to find her." Doreen said. "She might be able to tell us where Kat is."

The thought of where Kat might be sobered their enthusiasm and Tom saw the effect on his mother.

"The police will have to find her," he said quickly.

"The girl was with a group and one of them was Charlie Foden's son."

"Which one?" his mother asked. "He's got three."

"I don't know, but he looked like a younger version of his old-man," Tom answered.

"That would be Noel," his mother said. "He was always

his father's boy. The others are like their mother."

Mrs Lewis agreed that the best approach to the police would be through Steve Jennings. "He'll know what to do for the best."

Steve Jennings called at The Badgers the next day and Tom explained everything: from Penny's first reaction to the picture of Katy Rose to her hasty departure two days later. The policeman had listened in silence without interrupting and when Tom had finished his reaction was typical.

"Well, Tom, I don't suppose it matters now that you might have disturbed a possible crime scene."

He had always been a careful man, slow, was how most people described him. But he had a reputation for getting there, rather like the astonishing slug. He also had a similar sense of smell. He could sniff out trouble better than a spaniel according to one detective. It was a combination of such qualities and personality that had kept him in Stokesey and prevented him being promoted so that he would have to be moved somewhere else. He worked for Stokesey and Stokesey worked for him. He was married to a local girl, all his relations lived there and he already had two grandchildren, even though he was barely older than Katy would have been.

He showed no enthusiasm for Tom's evidence.

Like Mrs Lewis' first reaction, he speculated that the shoe could have belonged to any of several teenagers who went up to Drovers' Hill for hanky-panky. But he was disturbed by the girl Penny.

"She might be psychic," he said. "I've always kept an open mind about that sort of thing. I have no experience of it so I can't say I have an opinion but I do know there have been cases where psychics have been useful."

"Steve, it's the only answer. Kat took the short-cut when

she missed the bus. It's obvious."

"It weren't obvious to a CID team," Steve commented and Tom shrugged.

"Why don't you take me up there, Tom an' I'll see what to make of it."

They took the quad-bike and drove to the spot where Tom had found the shoe. Steve Jennings looked around carefully as though not to disturb the scene too much. He then crossed the path and went into the trees on the other side. Tom followed him like an expectant servant. The trees on that side of the path were in a narrow strip and they soon emerged beyond them to the edge of a golf-course. Steve surveyed the scene and then led the way back to the quad-bike. They drove back in silence.

"Well, what do you think?" Tom asked

"I think we'll have to conduct a proper search of the area."

****

Sergeant Steve Jennings brooded over Tom Lewis' discovery all that evening and part of the next morning. He did not tell either of his constables about it and it was lunch-time when he called HQ and requested a meeting with the Chief Constable. Despite refusing to disclose the reason he was eventually rung and told the Chief Constable would see him for five minutes at six o'clock.

"Why did you need to come directly to me about this?" the Chief Constable asked when he had heard what Steve Jennings had to say. Steve had his answer ready.

"Because, sir, I thought you would not want this being handed to CID considering the publicity that will be generated if we reopen the Katy Rose case. I thought you would want to consider the possible fall-out first before other people get involved."

"Because the first investigation might prove to be a costly cock-up?"

"Yes, sir."

The Chief Constable nodded acceptance of the judgement and then asked many questions. He had come from another force and knew only of the case from the publicity it had generated. Jennings quickly gave him the full picture, even the names of the CID officers involved and the effect the case had had on the local community. He then explained how the girl Penny had led Tom Lewis to the scene and why Tom thought Katy would have decided to walk to Upper Stokesey across Drovers's Hill.

"It's only a couple of miles from The Badgers, using that route," he explained.

"It was a huge oversight not to consider that possibility then," the Chief Constable commented when he had finished.

"That's why I came to you, sir," Jennings replied.

After some thought the Chief Constable was decisive.

"You did the right thing, Jennings. Thank you."

Steve Jennings thought he was being dismissed and rose to go but the other officer continued.

"We will have to do a search of the area. That will make a hole in my budget but it has to be done. That comes under Uniform Branch so there's no need to have CID involved at this stage – we can smooth their feathers later. I'll put one of my personal staff, Inspector Morrison, in charge and ask her to liaise with you as you are the man with local knowledge. We'll need a lot of that. Well done, Jennings."

Inspector Daphne Morrison was a good ten years younger than Steve Jennings but he was used to that and he bore no resentment; he knew his worth and his limitations. She arrived at his station the next day and gave permission for his two constables to know what they were up to. A large ordnance map of the Stokesey area was framed on one wall and Morrison studied it carefully with the local officers standing behind her answering her questions.

"First I will have to leg it up there and have a look round myself," she told them. "What's the best way of doing that?"

"We could drive to The Badgers and borrow Tom Lewis' quad-bike or take the car to Upper Stokesey and walk from there," Jennings said.

"Walking sounds like the best thing to do. It will give me a good chance to see the whole area."

The two officers set-off on a dull, cloudy day but without rain. Daphne Morrison was easy to like, uncomplicated and not protective of her authority. She told Steve Jennings that, although she was based in the city and enjoyed the urban environment, she was a country girl and proved it by the way she strode strongly up the steady climb to Drovers' Hill, leaving Jennings wishing he did more walking himself. She pointed to various areas, some quite distant, and wanted to know where they were, was it private or common land and whether there were public Rights of Way. As they approached the wooded area of the Ridgeway Path she asked who owned the woods.

"It was always common-land but I believe the National Trust is the guardian as it's a conservation area," Steve Jennings told her.

"Then we'll have to get their permission if we're going to dig it up," Morrison replied. The sergeant looked at her enquiringly.

"Well, Steve, if Tom Lewis is right about this we're going to have to be looking for a grave aren't we?

When they reached the spot where Lewis had found the

shoe, Morrison walked carefully around the area as Jennings had done on the previous day.

"We'll need a forensic search of this area first," she said. "I can't imagine it will do much good this long after the event but we'll give it a go. Do you know if the girl was wearing any jewellery?" Jennings didn't know. "I think it's a waste of time but we'll have to go through the motions. How many people use this path and these woods?"

"In the summer, hundreds. It's a favourite walk for hikers and Stokesey people get up here with their dogs," Jennings said.

"That's what I was afraid you would say. Okay, we'll contact the local Ramblers Association and see if anyone has ever found anything up here. Let's walk the whole route Katy would have taken."

She even insisted on going down to The Badgers and meeting Tom Lewis. She was studying the photograph of Katy Rose when Tom came through to the bar and was introduced to her.

"She was a lovely girl," Morrison said.

"She is," Tom replied.

"Who took the photograph?"

"Charles Foden. He does a lot of photography."

"Of Foden's Agricultural Machinery?"

" Yes. Do you know him?"

"I know of him. Everyone does in the city. He's a pal of the Chief Constable I believe."

"When Kat went missing and the police wanted a good publicity photo we only had school ones. But Kat had told Mum and Dad that Foden had taken pictures of her at the agricultural faire. Foden provided the police with a picture. It was like that one but not as special. A little while afterwards, Foden brought that one, framed and all, and some flowers for my parents. He said he'd taken the pictures of Kat and her friends at the faire.

"Mmm," Morrison commented thoughtfully.

Tom wanted to relate everything about the case from the time of Katy's disappearance but Daphne Morrison told him she would be reading the files and just wanted to know about the girl Penny and how she came to lead him to the spot where they found the shoe.

It was dusk when they left the pub and Steve Jennings was relieved when the inspector asked him to phone the station for someone to collect them. By the time they had returned to Stokesey, Steve Jennings felt old but Daphne Morrison looked as though she could have walked back and he suspected she had arranged the lift for his sake rather than her own.

The Chief Constable authorised a forensic examination of the area around where the shoe had been located

Several officers were drafted in under Morrison's supervision and two forensic officers carefully cut-back the undergrowth and went over it on hands and knees without results. But then, one of the officers with a metal-detector found an earring which was later identified by Mrs. Lewis as one of a pair that Katy had got from her Nan for her seventeenth Birthday. It had been farther into the wood from where the shoe was found and Morrison thought it likely that Katy had been dragged and hidden where the undergrowth was thicker.

The further evidence of Katy's presence at the spot was enough to authorise a complete search of the woods.

"If she's up there she has to be in the woods, everywhere else is too open," Morrison had said.

Twenty five officers were organised in a grid-system. GPR, Ground Penetration Radar, equipment was used; using electromagnetic radiation it fires vertical signals into the earth and can detect any changes in the ground strata including layering as when a grave is dug and refilled. It was difficult as the radiating box needed to be used close to the ground and that meant most of the ground cover had to be cut down to earth level, much to the consternation of the National Trust representative because a lot of the area was then covered by bluebells.

After two weeks the area had been covered but nothing found and the officers returned to their various units. The disappointment was felt by everyone in the team but to Tom Lewis and his mother the failure was physically painful.

As the search team abandoned their work and trudged back towards Upper Stokesey, Daphne Morrison and Steve Jennings were walking together behind the last of the police officers. As they cleared the trees Morrison's eyes made a wide arc of the landscape.

"We know whatever happened to the girl happened back there in the woods," she said. "But why wasn't she buried there if she was killed. How would anyone take her somewhere else and if they did, where to?"

"And how did someone get little Jenny down onto the road from here and leave her at a bus-stop?" Jennings added.

As the Ridgeway turned left and started its descent to Upper Stokesey, Morrison left the path and crossed the rough terrain to their right as though to answer Jennings' question. The trees on that side of the path had not been very deep but had been sufficient to screen their view and as they had now cleared the woods they had a clear view of that part of the hill. There was a high wire-mesh fence with a ditch running along the inside of it and they were looking across a golf course. The course was plateaued and descended downhill to where they could see the clubhouse and car park and beyond it the road. The seventeenth tee was near to where they were now standing. It was a short hole to a raised green in the top corner of the course and the eighteenth led downhill to the clubhouse and was bordered all the way on its left side by a boundary fence marked with white posts. Morrison led the way along the wire-mesh fence until they came to the end of the course where it turned downwards towards the road A rough footpath skirted it separating the course from wooded land which was fenced and was part of the properties on the outskirts of Upper Stokesey.

"There," Morrison said pointing to the path. "That's how Jenny was taken down to the road."

"And Katy?" Jennings asked

"That's a good question."

She had already led the way to where the footpath skirted the end of the golf-course. It was a narrow, twisting path overhung by brambles and wild shrubs.

"Not wide enough for any sort of vehicle," Jennings said.

"No," Morrison agreed. "But wide enough for a pushchair. It might not have been so overgrown then."

"Perhaps Katy Rose did meet someone up here, someone she knew who offered her a lift into Upper Stokesey. She could have gone down to the road with him along this path," Jennings suggested.

"Why would she do that? She only had to walk less than a mile on the Ridgeway and she was in Upper Stokesey?"

"Perhaps it was someone she liked.

"Where would he have left his car? The road is narrow down there and winding. There's nowhere to park it."

Jennings made no reply and the questions were left unanswered as they walked on towards the village.

"We have to find the girl Penny," Daphne Morrison told

Steve Jennings later as they drank tea and ate sponge-cake Jennings' wife had made. "If she was right about where Katy disappeared she could be right about other things."

"Do you believe that psychic stuff?" Jennings asked. Morrison shrugged.

"How else would she know?"

"It's a bit weird. Actually seeing Katy as though she was real according to Tom."

"Yes. That's a bit scary. You said she was with someone from around here."

"Noel Foden."

"The same Foden who took Katy's picture?" Morrison exclaimed.

"One of his sons, apparently. Tom said the lad looked just like Charlie Foden and Tom's mother said it would have to be Noel because the other kids look like their mother."

"Then we'll have to have a word with them and see if they know this Penny."

****

Arabella Foden was planting garden pots when the police car drove onto the drive and Daphne Morrison got out of it. Arabella froze mid-trowel. She saw the smile on Morrison's face as she approached but it did nothing to alleviate the fear that had spread from her stomach to her throat.

"Good morning, Madam. I'm Inspector Daphne Morrison. Would you be Mrs. Foden?"

Arabella nodded but could not find her voice. She was vividly conscious that Noel's elder brother and sister were now at home and knew nothing about the ghastly, unpleasant incident of the Easter weekend.

"Can I help you?"

"We were told that one of your children, Noel, visited The Badgers three weeks ago with some friends."

Arabella's brain was soon confused. Why did they want to know about The Badgers? She didn't know anything about The Badgers. What else had Noel got up to that weekend?

"I'm afraid I couldn't tell you that. We were away that weekend."

"I'm sorry. Which weekend?"

Arabella's brain was now in gear. "I presume you meant the Easter Holiday weekend, that was the only time Noel was here. He's gone back to university."

"Then it must have been that weekend. He was with a girl wasn't he?"

The fear returned to her stomach. "I believe he was with a few friends. I think there were two girls."

"It's someone called Penny we are interested to find?"

Arabella almost sighed audibly.

"Penny. Yes, I think there was someone of that name. What has she done?"

"Nothing, so far as I know. She left a camera in The Badgers. Tom Lewis reported it to us because he didn't know how to contact her."

Now Arabella was smiling. "Really? She must have had two cameras because she had one here with her."

"Then you did see her, you weren't away?"

The doubt returned. Was she being interrogated? She explained they had returned before the friends had gone back to university.

"Do you know her other name?"

She did know it, she had taken an immediate dislike to the girl and she always remembered the names of females she did not like. "Featherstone, I believe."

"Would you or Noel happen to have a number for her?"

"No. You could get in touch with her at the university. I believe she said she was doing architecture."

"Thank you, most helpful. I don't suppose your husband is home?"

"No. Did you want him for something?"

"I was only going to ask him about a photograph he took. Not to worry. I'll call and see him sometime."

Mrs Foden experienced different emotions as the officer got into her car and drove away. Was it about a camera or had Penny contacted the police? And if they start asking questions at the university what else will they discover?

Her husband was equally concerned when she told him of Morrison's visit and after dinner he telephoned Noel.

Noel Foden had reluctantly returned to university, dreading the experience. Charles Foden had called at the hospital after he had dropped Noel's university colleagues at the railway station. He had spoken to a consultant who had told him that a scan had shown no damage to Noel's brain and that he could take his son home. Noel was relieved he could go home and they were soon in the SUV after calling his mother and telling her they were on the way.

"How is the head?" his father had asked

"Sore, but no problem," Noel replied.

"You were lucky."

"Lucky? I don't think it was lucky to be whacked with a chair by that maniac, Harry."

"I meant you were lucky Caroline won't be bringing rape charges." his father said.

He had waited some moments before turning and looking at Noel who was staring at him open-mouthed.

"Father, you don't think…"

"I saw her bruises."

Noel closed his eyes and pressed back into the seat as though he had been stabbed in the stomach. Suddenly there were tears running down his face.

"I don't know…It must have been the drink…She wore this loose T-shirt…It showed all her thighs…"

"You must apologise to her," his father had told him. Noel turned, panic on his face.

"I can't go back. I can't go to university."

"You will go back. You will finish your degree."

"Father, I can't. Everyone will know about it from the others. It will probably be all over Facebook."

His father had pulled into the side of the road and stopped the car. He turned again and leaned close to his son.

"Noel, you will go back to university. You will get your degree and you will face up to everyone. You made a mistake, we all make mistakes. But we can't let mistakes ruin our lives. We apologise, eat humble pie, learn our lesson and move on. You will regard the incident as a failure and there is only one way to mend a failure and that is to be successful. You will be stronger and you will be successful. Is that understood?"

So Noel had obeyed. Now, three weeks later, he had had no painful encounters with any of his friends. On his father's advice he had written letters of apology to everyone who was in his house-party. As he was doing Politics, Economics and Philosophy he was capable of writing eloquently even though apologies did not come naturally to him. He blamed drink and being an "immature shit" for his behaviour. Quoting Graham's opinion was an instinctive ploy to soften the hard feelings against him and was the reason why his father had suggested he should read politics. His task was made easier in that he did not room with any of the group nor did he share lectures with them as they were all on different courses and he deliberately kept a low profile by not frequenting the student bar so as not to have to face them until emotions were less raw.

Neither Harry nor Graham were particular pals as their association was mostly that they played rugby together but as the season was ended he had no cause to see them unless it was arranged.

Caroline presented a greater challenge to his ingenuity and he plundered several writers to express his remorse: *I have plunged into the valley of humiliation and see no light beyond your forgiveness,* and sent the letter by messenger with a large bouquet of roses.

"Did that girl Penny have two cameras with her when she came here?" Foden asked his son.

"I only saw her with one," Noel replied. "She takes it everywhere with her, it's the love of her life. I don't think she has another. Why do you want to know about her camera?"

He was told of his mother's encounter with Inspector Morrison.

"That girl might be a problem," his father added. "It would not surprise me if she had taken photographs of the bruises on the other girl."

The reminder of his brutality made Noel cringe but the information made him feel much worse.

"I don't think Pen would do anything unless Caroline wanted her to," Noel replied hopefully. He had liked Penny a lot and facing her would be harder than facing Caroline.

"Then why would the police want to see her and lie about the reason?" his father asked.

"Perhaps it has something to do with what happened at The Badgers," Noel suggested and explained the strange coincidence Penny had experienced.

"She said she saw Katy Rose?"

His father's voice sounded as incredulous as the incident had been.

"She obviously saw someone like her having a pee behind a bush but Tom Lewis was not happy and refused to serve us."

"Where did she see this?" Charles Foden's voice was now calmer

"Up on Drovers' Hill."

****

The failure of the police search was as disappointing for the Chief Constable as much as it was for Daphne Morrison and Steve Jennings. It had blown a considerable hole in the annual budget and had failed to find Katy Rose.

The search had also attracted rumours and renewed interest in the case and the local media had been told only that new evidence had opened a fresh line of enquiry into Katy Rose's disappearance, but no reference as to the source of the new evidence was given, not even to the CID branch who were just as keen to know more about the new evidence as were the media.

Detective Superintendent Colin Laxton, who had led the original investigation as a detective sergeant, was particularly persistent to find more about it and when his peer from the uniform branch told him the Chief Constable had taken a personal interest and given Daphne Morrison the job of investigating the new evidence, Laxton did his best, including a bit of furtive bullying, to get the inspector to reveal all. But Daphne Morrison had been chosen by the Chief Constable for his personal staff because of her character as well as her intelligence and she had no problem in dealing with domineering males like Laxton. But she realised that giving the impression that her chief had deliberately withheld information from the CID would only make Laxton more inquisitive and assertive.

"An item of clothing Tom Lewis thought could have belonged to Katy Rose was found on Drovers's Hill. We had to follow it up otherwise Tom would have made a fuss. It looks like we wasted our time."

"And money," Laxton said and Morrison laughingly agreed.

The Chief Constable had insisted that no one outside of herself, Steve Jennings and the Lewis family should know that Penny Featherstone had been the source of the information that had led to the discovery of the new evidence. Mention of psychics would reopen old follies and another media storm and would give Colin Laxton reason to pour scorn on the evidence as he would not welcome a new investigation that might damage his reputation.

As she faced her chief to be debriefed on the relative failure of their search, Daphne Morrison was acutely aware of how he would probably read the situation.

"Tom Lewis and his mother are taking it very badly," she told him. "They were desperate for us to find Katy."

"I can understand that. So were we all," the Chief constable responded and by his tone Morrison guessed his disappointment might be terminal. "Do you think this shoe and the earring are genuine? Could Tom and his mother just be saying they were Katy's to get us interested again?"

"I don't think so, sir. I know it's a possibility but Jennings said Tom was really shocked by the discovery. And we have to admit that the way he found the shoe was a bit strange."

"Yes. What about this girl, Penny. Is she psychic?"

"I don't know. She must be something; a complete stranger

who couldn't have known about Katy, seeing her like that? And it is possible, according to Tom, that Katy could have climbed up to Drovers' Hill. We had to do what we did."

The Chief Constable nodded thoughtfully. "Yes, but it's going to be bloody difficult to explain it to the police committee."

Morrison felt the axe was about to fall.

"Perhaps I should talk to this Penny – just to get a feeling of who she is; see if she has any other ideas?"

The Chief Constable recognised that despite the failure of the search and the probability of clashing with Laxton and his team, Penny Featherstone would have to be questioned.

"Then do it informally: woman to woman. You will be able to tell whether she's genuine or just another nutcase."

****

Penny was both anxious and relieved when Morrison introduced herself over the telephone. Her immediate reaction was to think it was about the attempted rape incident but when she learned the reason for the call, the anxiety returned after a moment of relief . She had buried within herself the incident on Drovers' Hill but it had always been there, nagging away at her sub-conscious. The event had been as dramatic to her as it had been to Tom Lewis and had been as inexplicable as a miracle. She had been unable, and probably unwilling, to tell anyone about the shoe. Caroline's emotional state had not been conducive to listening to someone else's problems and the only other person she considered talking to about it had been Graham – but they had both been busy since their return to university and had seen very little of each other and when they had it had been with other friends present.

118

She agreed to meet Daphne Morrison when the officer was gently persistent but emphasised that she could see no way that she could be of further help.

They met in a café near the railway station on Penny's suggestion. Morrison had hoped she might have been invited to Penny's rooms where she could get an idea of the girl's character but Penny had decided their meeting should not be publicised. She had expected to see a uniformed officer as Morrison had not introduced herself as a detective inspector, and was surprised to see an attractive woman wearing a casual jacket and high-heels smiling at her, holding up a copy of the Financial Times as she had arranged. Daphne Morrison ordered coffees and tea-cakes and asked about Penny's course and seemed interested in the care-home project that was the major module for her degree and then she wanted to know about her interest in photography which led easily into the pictures Tom Lewis had asked her to take of Drovers' Hill.

"I haven't downloaded them from the camera yet," Penny told her. "Is that what you wanted?"

Morrison told her the pictures were not important as their Forensic people had taken plenty themselves. She then told her about the earring find and of the systematic search of the woods. When she'd finished Penny only stared at her helplessly.

"So I wanted to thank you for what you did," Morrison told her.

"I didn't do anything. I don't know what I did."

Morrison could see the confusion in Penny's face.

"You have given the Lewis family hope that they will find Katy and be able to mourn her properly. You've also blown huge holes in the original investigation."

The confusion in Penny's mind spilt out in incoherent

denials and apologies.

"I didn't. I don't. I can't…"

"Have you ever had a similar experience like seeing someone or something you couldn't explain?"

"No," Penny protested

"It does happen. People do have such inexplicable experiences. A friend of mine once told me how he was driving along the road through a village in the autumn. He saw a woman with a child coming towards him on the pavement. The child was picking up the fallen leaves off the pavement and for no reason that he could explain, he slowed almost to a stop as he neared them. The child was on the inside of the pavement but as his car drew level, she suddenly rushed out into the middle of the road to pick up a leaf, right in front of his car, but because he was going so slow he was able to stop without touching her. He could not explain why he had slowed down like that. Some people have this ability to know when things are going to happen. We don't know the limits of our senses because we don't have to use them."

"That's not the same as seeing things that happened," Penny said.

"No. But it's all part of the great mystery of who we are."

She saw that Penny was in a calmer, more receptive mood.

"I would like you to come to Stokesey and walk the area with me."

The anxiety returned to Penny's eyes.

"You don't have to do anything except that: just walk around and tell me what you feel or think. You could come one weekend and stay at my place. Think of it as a weekend in the country."

The anxiety left Penny's face and was replaced with doubt.

"Please, Penny. It might help a lot of people. Bring your

camera. Take pictures."

"I'll think about it," Penny promised. Daphne Morrison put her hand over hers.

"Thank you." She gave her a card. "Phone me. I'll meet you at the station – and don't worry about the train fare, we'll organise that."

They said goodbye and Penny started to walk home, still unsure of what she would do. As she entered the High Street she almost bumped into Graham coming out of a music store.

Her relationship with Graham was careful. She knew he liked her and wanted to make more of it and they had used each other for several social occasions but she had always resisted the temptation to let it go further even though she liked him. She did not want to be distracted from her work; it was part of her nature to put maximum effort into what she did and, if she had consciously thought about it, the same would apply to a sexual relationship. She sensed that Graham was the same and she was not ready for such a commitment. She told him about Daphne Morrison and what she wanted her to do.

"That's amazing. You really saw someone who is dead?"

"I know. It's really scary."

"Perhaps she's not dead. Perhaps she was just looking for her shoe."

"Looking the same as she did twenty years ago? I don't know what to do, Graham."

"It can't do any harm to go back and see if you have any other ideas."

"God! I don't need this, Graham. I hate that place after what happened to Caroline."

He put his arm around her and hugged her gently. "You worry about other people too much. Just treat it as a project.

Don't let anything but your head get involved."

"So you think I should go?"

"Why not? You've already done something amazing. Who knows what you might find. If you have some special ability it's better that you find out about it than if it jumps up at you as it did at Drovers' Hill."

They talked about other things and Graham asked about Caroline.

"She's still suffering," Penny told him. "Who would have thought Noel would do a thing like that?"

"You would. Don't you remember what you said? You said he was dangerous because he didn't trust himself."

She had forgotten.

"Maybe it wasn't just female intuition," he added.

"Oh, don't, Graham. It was intuition. We all have unexplained feelings about other people. I just felt Noel was always playing a part. All that jolly bonhomie was a cover for what he's really like."

"What is he really like?"

"His father's a cold, calculating so and so and his mother is a bitch. What do you expect with those genes?"

Graham laughed and hugged her again. "Shall we go to a film tonight?" he asked.

"All right," she agreed. "Did you keep the Easter Egg money?"

"No. I sent it back."

"So did I." She took his hand as they walked.

She rang Daphne Morrison that evening and told her she would come the following weekend.

The inspector met her as promised at the railway station. She had a small cottage just across the estuary near Stokesey. It was old and pretty with low ceilings and Penny loved it. Daphne had made a fish pasta for lunch which they had early as Daphne explained their plans.

"I hope you've brought some walking shoes," she said. "The weather's been a bit iffy lately so the ground will be wet."

"I've got my boots," Penny told her. "My Dad bought them for my eighteenth. He's a great walker and we do the Peak District a lot."

"Good, then I needn't worry about you. I thought we could start by doing a big circle of the area, starting down here and working our way round and on to Drovers' Hill."

When they started, heading west parallel with the little Fender River before it ran into the estuary, they followed a decent path with Daphne reading an Ordnance Survey map as they went.

"Somehow, we've got to find a way up to the hills. It all looks a bit soggy ahead but there is a path marked on the map, climbing up past Hill Farm."

"It must be okay because they go duck shooting further out than this," Penny told her.

"How do you know that?"

Penny explained about their stay at the Foden's and the picture of the shooting party and Betsy telling her how the Bishops owned the shooting land."

"You know more than I do," Daphne said. "I've heard of the Bishops but I've never met them. So we might be trespassing. Well that's one good thing about being a copper; we can go anywhere."

They got into trouble as they started to head inland towards the rising ground. The ground was soft with hill streams forming pools of brackish water and they had to do a lot of jumping between clumps of solid turf to make their way before they picked up a firmer path leading upwards. As they neared the foot of a protrusion from the hills which formed a crescent from Upper Stokesey with Drovers' Hill in the centre, and started to climb they looked down and westwards towards the mouth of the estuary. A small farmhouse nestled in what was a stretch of fertile area between the high ground and the marshes and beyond it was a large, timbered mansion.

"That must be the Bishop's place," Morrison said.

Penny took out her camera and was taking photographs when she saw a Land Rover leave the house and head towards them. They continued walking uphill but realised the Land Rover was following them. Daphne Morrison stopped and waited for the vehicle to catch-up.

"You're trespassing," a middle-aged man barked down at them.

"We are following a path marked as Right of Way on the Ordnance Survey," Morrison told him.

"That's an old shepherd's path, went out of use years ago," the man said.

"You came from the big house But this path goes to Hill Farm," she argued.

"Mr. Bishop bought Hill Farm when old Fogget died. Who are you?" the man asked, not liking Daphne Morrison's authoritative manner. She told him.

"Oh!" he said.

"Who are you?" she asked. He told her he was Ken Hewlett, Mr. Bishop's Estate Manager.

"Are you on official business?" he asked suspiciously.

"Sort of. We are investigating the disappearance of a girl in this area a few years ago."

"Katy Lewis?"

"Yes. Did you know her?"

"Course I did. I was born just the other side of her place. She was a lovely girl."

"That's what everyone says. But someone didn't think she was too lovely to murder."

"So you think she was murdered?"

"Don't you. Don't you think she would have come home by now if she hadn't been?"

"I dunno. You never know with young women. They want to be famous. They want to go to London. They want to be rich. They're never happy where they are."

"You sound like an authority."

"Course not. But I 'ave got two girls an' I know what they're like."

"Was Katy like that?"

"Let me put it this way; she was quite a beauty. She could 'ave been a model for one of them magazines, no problem, an she knew it. Have you any reason to be looking down here for her?"

"No. We think she disappeared from Drovers' Hill woods."

"Yes. I 'eard about that."

"But we didn't find her so we're investigating other possible sites where she might be buried. Perhaps you can help us?"

"Well it won't be down 'ere. The ground's too shallow on this sandstone and down there," he pointed towards the river from where they'd come, "It's too dangerous unless you know the ground. There are a few bogs down there."

"I know. We had a job picking our way around them."

"You were lucky. Well, mind how you go."

He touched his cap and turned the Land Rover round and headed back towards the house.

"Is it possible Katy could have chosen to go off with someone?" Penny asked

"It's possible. It happens. But I don't think she did. From all we know about her she was a happy, family girl. Only the unhappy ones do that sort of thing."

They continued up to the top and then turned east along the Ridgeway path back towards Drovers' Hill.

"Shall we go down to The Badgers and have a drink?" Morrison suggested.

Tom Lewis was almost ecstatic to see Penny again and thanked her profusely for helping them and introduced her to his wife.

"You must come and meet my Mum," he said but Daphne Morrison said they would just have a drink and crack on or they wouldn't get back before dark. They were sitting opposite Katy's photograph and Penny had been staring at it.

"It's a striking portrait isn't it?" Morrison suggested

Penny agreed. "It's a bit old-fashioned – all that bleaching-out. It was used a lot in the sixties. But it's very effective."

"You know a lot about it, obviously," Morrison laughed.

"Did you know Noel Foden's father took the picture?"

"Yes. I saw his albums when we were staying with Noel and I asked him if he'd taken this picture; I recognised the processing style from some of his other portraits."

"So he's a serious photographer?"

"I think so. I wanted to see his studio but Noel said it was at their other house and he didn't let anyone in there."

They finished their drinks and Tom embarrassed Penny by hugging her as they left. They climbed back up to Drovers' Hill and followed the path through the woods and down to Upper Stokesey but Penny didn't have any other visions or feelings.

They got back exhausted. Daphne took her to a little restaurant where they shared a bottle of wine over dinner and then they were both pleased to get into bed where Penny slept heavily until the morning. The policewoman kissed her goodbye and said she would keep in touch. As she left the station, Daphne Morrison felt empty and depressed but on the train Penny felt better, much better. Perhaps she wasn't weird after all.

****

Daphne Morrison had mixed feelings about her weekend with Penny. On a personal level she had found it pleasant and had enjoyed her company, so much so that she had realised she did not have enough of a social life and should do something about it. But from a professional perspective she had to admit it was disappointing. She had not expected much from the visit. She had no experience of psychics and had never been convinced of their abilities, but the fact that Penny had had some sort of visionary experience and that it had led to a break-through in the Katy Rose case was indisputable and she had hoped that her visit might have created another lead. She also hadn't felt that Penny had any extraordinary qualities. On the contrary, she had found her factual and practical, rather like herself, and she had even thought that she would make a very good copper. So she was left with one clue: that Katy Rose had been on Drovers' Hill before she disappeared – and a blank sheet after that; and a feeling that her report back to her chief could be the end of the investigation.

After seeing Penny onto her train she went to her office and spent most of the night flitting through the files, subconsciously desperate to find something to keep the case alive. Sitting down and reading for hours on end was not her preference and that was why she had chosen to stay in uniform rather than move to the CID, so she searched with imagination rather than diligence, concentrating on the statements from local people. Most of the statements were nothing more than brief answers to questions asked by the many officers who had hawked Katy Rose's photograph around Stokesey and the local area, and many similar statements from motorists who had been questioned when road blocks had been established: name, registration, destination, address, schedule from start of journey. All the local people seemed to know Katy, from her school friends and their families to shopkeepers and farmers.

She was struggling to stay awake when she found something that snapped her alert. It was a comment made by The Badgers aged cleaner, Jack. 'The girl was dirty,' he had said. It was the first criticism she had read of Katy. When asked to explain, Jack had said she paraded herself in the window 'Like a harlot.'

"Was that the window of her bedroom?" the questioner had asked and apparently Jack had failed to answer. It was an obvious scenario; an old man spying on a young girl. What would that do to an old man's mind? Unfortunately, it was not recorded, but Jack's alibi was sound; he was working at The Badgers for all of the morning of Katy Rose's disappearance.

But then Morrison had noted Jack's address. He lived in one of the cottages of the hamlet of which The Badgers was part and that his next-door neighbour was a Mr and Mrs Hewlett.

She remembered Bishop's estate manager. He had said he came from near The Badgers. She guessed he was about sixty years of age and would then have been forty. "Did he still live at home?" she wondered. "Would Jack have told him how dirty Katy was?"

After three hours sleep she rang The Badgers and spoke to Tom Lewis. She asked him first about Jack.

"He's long dead."

"Did you know what he'd said about Katy?"

Tom did know. "When we heard, Dad sacked him right away. He was past it anyway so Dad used it as an excuse."

"But was it true what he said about Katy. Did she flaunt herself?"

The question provoked an angry response. "Why do you want to take any notice of what Jack said? He was a sly old bugger and I dare say he spied on Katy."

"In an upstairs bedroom?"

A cry of frustration and anger was the only answer.

"Tom. I'm sorry we have to ask these questions. But I have to try to get a true picture of who Katy was?"

"You won't get a true picture by listening to what someone like Jack said about her."

"Would you say Katy was a flirt?"

The sounds were more conciliatory.

"She might have teased people a bit – but she wouldn't have done anything wrong."

"Thank you, Tom. What can you tell me about Ken Hewlett?"

Tom told her quite a lot. He was always complaining about Tom and Kat when they were kids, accusing them of throwing stones at their hens and breaking their fence among other things. He didn't marry until he was about forty. Then he married a girl younger than himself who's father owned the fish and chip shop in Upper Stokesey.

'Everyone was surprised when he got married and suddenly had three kids. He never seemed interested in girls, always out with his guns and if he wasn't shooting he was doing that motocross thing.'

"You mean, cross-country biking?"

"That's right. He gave it up when he had an accident and

hurt his back."

"When was that?"

"Oh, must be about ten or fifteen years ago, soon after he was married. Everyone joked his wife had arranged it, the wheel came off apparently."

"So he knows the country pretty well?" she asked

"Every inch," Tom said. "He was the gamekeeper for an estate out at Bredon. Bred birds and organised shooting parties. When the Bishops came he went to them as their Estate Manager. Done all right for himself."

"Was he a friend of Jack's" she asked.

"Course he was, they lived next door to each other for a few years."

"Do you like him?"

"Not much. He's better now since he's been married but he was always a surly old sod."

When she put down the phone she thought about trail-bikes.

'Apart from a tractor that's about the only vehicle that could move someone across rough terrain,' she told herself. And Ken Hewlett knew every inch of the countryside – including the marshes. She searched through the interviews but failed to find one with Ken Hewlett.

The only way to get to the Bishop's estate by road was a journey of fifteen miles from the city; through Stokesey, Upper Stokesey past The Badgers and four miles further on where an access road led back to the estate, the journey being more than a half-circle from Stokesey. The house was a rambling affair of several periods, mostly of timber and brick construction but a stone front had been built on at a later period. There were barns and other outbuildings and farther away there was Hill Farm where, Morrison later discovered, Hewlett lived with his wife and one of his children. When she pulled up to the front of the house she was met by a young woman who was leading a horse from one of the paddocks. Morrison introduced herself and said she wanted to speak to Ken Hewlett.

"I think he's out on the estate," the woman said. "Would you like to speak to my father?"

Mr Bishop was an affable man who looked as though he enjoyed eating more than riding or other country pursuits.

"I heard from George Sanderson that you were reopening the Katy Lewis case," he said, using the Chief Constable's name and causing Daphne Morrison to wonder if her boss was capable of keeping his mouth shut.

"We're not actually reopening it yet," she corrected him. "There has been a development which I am investigating in order to ascertain whether a full investigation would be appropriate."

"Well said. I do appreciate diplomacy," Bishop smiled.

"Are you a diplomat sir?"

"Only when I have to be. I'm a boring old business man I'm afraid: commodities trading, that sort of thing. What do you want with Ken?"

Morrison explained that he had not been interviewed in the original investigation.

"I just want to find out how he escaped."

Bishop knew very little about Katy Rose Lewis, only what locals had told him. He and his family had moved there after she had disappeared.

"Who owned the estate before you?" she asked

"I believe it was empty for some time. Then a Swedish chap bought it off the Fodens – but he hardly used it, he was mostly overseas. "

"You said, 'off the Fodens.' I thought a family called Henderson owned it."

Bishop explained the relationship between the Hendersons and the Fodens.

"The Hendersons had been there hundreds of years, very respected by all accounts. I could never understand why not working for a living gets more respect than earning it," he smiled. "I believe Charles' father married the eldest Henderson girl and inherited the estate. That's why he uses Henderson Foden in his name."

But Morrison was noting again how Foden's name kept coming into the picture.

"You used his first name, do you know him well?"

"Yes, our paths cross quite a bit. He's very active in the city and we are both members of the same golf club."

"With the Chief Constable

"That's right. It's a small world isn't it?"

"I heard the Henderson's used to shoot on the marshes. Do you do any shooting?" she asked

"Yes. That was one of the reasons why I bought the place. Ken has a breeding programme in our woods but in the winter we do some wildfowling – much the best.

"On the marshes?"

"By the estuary, beyond the moss. They fly in to the feeding grounds off Great Marsh Head. Just a nice height when they get over here. Hard targets. Good challenge. Do you shoot?"

Morrison said she didn't. "Isn't it a bit risky going out on the marshes," she asked.

"Can be if you don't know what you're doing. That's why I engaged Ken, he knows every inch of ground out there. That's his Land Rover now."

Ken Hewlett scowled when he climbed down and saw Daphne Morrison standing with Bishop. He scowled even more when Bishop shook hands with the inspector and told her to pop in any time as it was a pleasure to meet her.

They walked towards one of the barns."I don't know why you want to talk to me," he protested.

Morrison explained she was just clearing up omissions in the original investigation.

"I was going through the interviews with all the people Katy might have known and realised your name wasn't on the list," she said.

"That would be because I weren't here at that time; I was workin' over at Bredon. That's on the other side of the hills towards Shirley."

"Yes, I realise that. But you did know Katy. You lived near her for all of her life."

"But she must have been only twelve or so when I got the job at Bredon. I was livin' in there."

"Didn't you ever visit your parents while you were working there?"

"I suppose I must 'ave. But I don't remember seein' much of the girl if I did."

"Do you remember where you were when Katy disappeared? What you were doing?"

"I do. I remember very well. I was delivering some venison to the butchers in Stokesey. It was market day, you see. Everyone there was talking about the police asking questions in Upper Stokesey. On the way back I was stopped in Upper Stokesey. It were swarmin' with police. They were showin' this picture of young Katy. I was damned shocked, I was."

"Why was that?"

"Why was I shocked? That's an odd question. Everyone was shocked. We'd never 'ad anything like that 'appen. Never 'ave since."

"You knew Jack who was once your neighbour and worked

at The Badgers at the time?"

"Course I did."

"Did he talk about Katy to you?"

Hewlett looked doubtful

"Jack liked to gossip."

"He told the police Katy was dirty. What do you think he meant by that?"

"He said she used to undress in front of the window – but he shouldn't 'ave been lookin' should ee?"

"Wouldn't you if a young woman undressed in front of you?"

"No. I'd tell 'er not to demean herself. If one of my girls were like that I'd give 'er a right old slap."

"Would you Ken? May I call you Ken?"

"Be my guest, that's my name."

"Ken. You know this land back to front don't you?"

"Guess I do."

"Would you take me to that point where you met us the other weekend and show me the terrain and where it's safe to walk?"

"What? Now?"

"If you don't mind. It's a long drive here so while I'm here I might as well take advantage of your local knowledge. I can ask Mr. Bishop for permission if you like."

"He won't mind. Lets me get on with my job. "

They drove away from the house past Hill Farm towards the promontory which Morrison and Penny were climbing when Hewlett had caught up with them. The track was no more than the width of the vehicle, worn by use into the stone base and Morrison wondered if she would be sick before she got back. The Land Rover negotiated the incline up the promontory and they stopped and climbed out for which Morrison was grateful.

"Now, what d'you want to know?" Hewlett asked

"Do you know if anyone lived here between the Swede moving and the Bishop's buying?

"Old Fogget rented Hill Farm."

"When was that?"

"While the Hendersons were still here – until Sir Toby died and his grandson sold the place."

"That would be one of the Fodens?"

"Charlie's father inherited the estate, married one of the Henderson girls. But Charlie sold it. Took a few years an' it got a bit run down. Mr. Bishop has spent a fortune on it."

"So there was no one here when Katy Rose disappeared?"

"The Swede owned it then – but he was never here, so I suppose there weren't anyone here when poor Katy went missing.

"You called Foden 'Charlie'. Isn't that a bit familiar? He didn't give me the impression he would like to be a Charlie."

Hewlett laughed. "Probably not. But we knew each other, sort of, when we were kids. We played cricket for Stokesey Juniors until he went off to that posh school."

"Do you keep in touch?"

"No. We bump into each other from time to time. When he was home from school he did a bit of shooting with his grandpa an' I used to 'elp my dad organise the shoots."

The inspector looked outwards towards the estuary.

"Where do they do the duck-shooting," she asked. Hewlett pointed.

"See that thin track going towards the river. That follows the Fender until it opens out onto the mud-flats. I built hides near there."

"But that path goes from the house. How would you get there from here?"

135

"I don't know why anyone would want to. But that track you followed up here would take you down to the Fender and then you could follow the Fender path. It gets very narrow once you get past the house. It used to be wide enough for horse carts all the way to the Estuary when they used the peat but now it's no more than a footpath once you get out there."

"Is the ground safe?"

"As long as you stayed on grass. If you strayed off that you could be in trouble."

Morrison hadn't thought of a horse. "Does anyone ride much around here?"

"Only Mr. Bishop's youngest, that was her in the yard. There are bridal ways on the hills but down here you could only ride on Mr. Bishop's land."

"What about a motor-bike?"

"A motor-bike? Well, I suppose a trail-bike could get down there easy enough."

"Have you ever done any biking, Ken?"

"Yes. I used to do a bit before I got married."

"Cross country stuff?"

"Yes."

"Where did you do that?"

"Over at Shirley. There was plenty of good track there. All the motocross boys used to go there on a Sunday. We had great times, we did."

"Ken. If you wanted to hide a body out here, where would you put it?"

The question stopped the smile of remembrance that had begun to appear on Hewlett's face. He scowled again.

"You really think Katy Rose is buried somewhere here?"

"Yes, Ken. I think I do."

He put his hand to his mouth and frowned at the landscape.

"Well, anywhere down there I suppose. It's all boggy ground. But how would anyone get her down there?"

"That I don't yet know."

"And if they did, they would 'ave to know where they was treadin'."

On the drive back, that was not the only question Daphne Morrison pondered. Hewlett had said something else that she was surprised she had not checked. He had said there had been no such thing as Katy's disappearance before or since.

As she drove into Upper Stokesey she realised it was Saturday and Charles Foden would probably be at home. Instinctively she turned towards his house. As she drove up the drive she saw a man inside the open, three-car garage. He turned as she got out of the car and she walked into the garage and asked if he was Charles Foden and introduced herself. Foden was not pleased.

"I heard you had called before and spoken to my wife. Do you not have telephones?"

"We do, but sometimes we like to surprise people," she smiled.

"Well, I don't like to be surprised, Inspector. Please phone and make an appointment."

"I don't have your number, sir. Aren't you ex-directory?" she guessed and knew it was accurate by Foden's change of manner.

"I thought you could get anyone's number," he argued unconvincingly.

"Only if we can convince a magistrate it is necessary," she said. "I'm sorry, Mr. Foden. I happened to be passing through Upper Stokesey and I remembered I had told your wife I would call and see you. I wanted your help, sir."

Foden relented. "Is it about that girl who stayed here?

Something about a camera?"

"No. We sorted that. I wanted to ask you about the picture you took of the girl who disappeared: Katy Rose Lewis?"

"Good Heavens! That was years ago."

"Yes but we are looking again at the case."

"Are you? Has there been a new development?"

"We now think she was abducted from Drovers' Hill."

"Do you? I thought she was supposed to have been taken by a motorist. Why have you decided she wasn't?"

"We don't want to disclose the reason at this stage. About the photo, sir. The one in The Badgers. Did you take the picture?"

"Yes, I did. When the police were searching for her and asked her father for a picture he realised he didn't have a good one and suggested I might have one. You see, Inspector, I have always been a keen photographer and I was well-known for taking pictures at the local events."

"And you had one of Katy?"

"Yes. I believe it was taken at the agriculture fair."

"For any special reason?"

"I don't believe so. I used to enjoy snapping people when they weren't expecting it. That way, one gets a better photograph."

"The photograph of Katy looks better than a snap to me."

"I do take other photographs. I used the word snap because I usually carry my little Leica around with me. It's small enough to keep in a pocket, that way it's always there if I see something interesting. I have other cameras which I use for colour, but they're too big to use casually.

"The picture looks a bit special from the processing."

"I try to make something extra of my pictures in the processing. the best part of photography."

"And it shows in the portrait. Was she a willing subject?"

"So far as I remember. Yes, she seemed to enjoy being photographed."

"Have you got other pictures of her?"

"I'm sure I must have taken more than one. She was a very attractive girl. But I can't say I would still have them. It was so long ago. I have taken thousands of photographs since then."

"I appreciate that – but Katy was not someone you could easily forget, I imagine."

"No. She was a bit exceptional. But when I took the picture she was with a group of other girls from the school and they all wanted their pictures taken. So I couldn't just make an exception of Katy, could I? The other girls were probably jealous of her as it was."

"Do you think she made people jealous?"

"I can't be sure, I hardly knew her. But beauty does have its enemies."

"And some people might want to destroy it?"

Surprisingly, Foden laughed.

"Only religious fundamentalists I would imagine,"

"And people who are threatened by it,"

"Who can be threatened by beauty?"

"People who have no control over their sexual desires."

"Well, I wouldn't know about that, Inspector. That sort of thing is more your sort of world."

"It's everyone's sort of world. We just have to deal with it."

"And I don't envy you doing so. Is there anything else I can help you with?"

"If you can find any other pictures of Katy, especially with other people, I should like to see them. Sometimes, background information can be very useful."

"I'll see if I still have any."

"Thank you, sir. I'm sure you know where to find me."

Morrison began to walk away.

"Inspector, who told you I took the picture of Katy. Was it Penny Featherstone by any chance?"

"Yes it was. Do you know her?"

"Only briefly. She and some friends stayed here on the Easter weekend. I know she is keen on photography. How did you come to discuss the picture with her?"

Daphne Morrison realised she had made a mistake.

"When we returned her camera we talked about The Badgers and she wanted to know more about Katy Rose, she was curious about the picture. We talked about photography and she told me you had taken the picture."

Foden looked unconvinced, more than likely because he knew that Penny had not left a camera in The Badgers. But later, he wondered how Penny Featherstone could have told Morrison he had taken the picture as he only admitted doing so as she was returning to university. Had she seen or spoken to Morrison since and if that was the case, for what reason? Noel had said she had seen someone like Katy Rose in Drovers' Hill woods. Was Penny Featherstone psychic and would the police be interested if she were?

"She did ask me about the picture. I believe she saw my albums and recognised some similarity to my work. But I can't think why she should be obsessed with that one photograph."

"I don't think she is obsessed with it. She was more interested as to why it was there in The Badgers – like most people would be I imagine."

"Did she say anything else about the girl?"

"Such as?"

"That she had seen her before? My son mentioned something about her recognising the girl?"

Morrison was now uncomfortable. "I think that was a

mistake. She thought she saw someone like her."

"And is that why you have reopened the investigation?"

"Did I say we had done that? We are just making further inquiries due to possible new evidence."

"What sort of new evidence?"

"I'm afraid I can't discuss that, Mr. Foden. Thank you for your time – and please have a look for any other pictures you might have of Katy Rose."

"Yes. I'll see what I can find."

As Morrison turned towards her car she saw a golf trolley in the corner of the garage.

"I see you are a golfer, sir."

"Yes. Not so much now. I used to be rather keen. Do you play?"

"No. The Chief Constable does."

"Yes. We're members of the same club."

Foden watched the inspector get into her car and drive away. He stood as though looking after her but saw only Katy Rose Lewis and the visual memory of their first meeting was still as bright and sunny as the day:

There is probably nothing more provocative to a man's sexual and emotional fantasies than the sight of a sixteen year old girl's burgeoning body inadequately contained in a school uniform. So it was when he first saw Katy Rose. She was with five other girls and they were working a swing-boat at the autumn agricultural fair. Katy was on one of the ropes, standing, legs braced against the movement of the boat, her skirt stretched high against her thighs. Each time she pulled on the thick rope her body bent forward and her breasts bulged inside her shirt and as the boat went upwards the rope stretched her onto her toes and her hands went high, stretching the shirt across her breasts

141

and challenging the security of the buttons. The girls were screaming and Katy Rose was laughing, her auburn hair flying around her face like a mare's mane, her mouth wide enough to show her perfect teeth, catching the sun like diamonds with each ascent. He was transfixed for a moment, then he was aiming the Nikon and firing off frames like a machine gun.

Despite her apparent engrossment with the mechanics of her duties, Katy Rose was not oblivious to the gathering audience of male admirers but when she saw him wielding a serious camera like a professional, she became strangely self-conscious and abandoned her teenage exuberance in an attempt to look more sophisticated. The result was an uneven rhythm as her companion on the other rope continued to pull as hard as she could. The boat rocked sideways and spilled two girls from their seats onto the floor and the attendant came and yelled at them to stop messing about and told them their time was up anyway.

The girls tumbled out, screaming and laughing and pulling at their knickers under their skirts but Katy Rose alighted carefully, watching the man with the camera out of the sides of her eyes.

"Kat. Come on. Let's get an ice-cream," one of the girls called to her as they staggered across the grass.

"You go on. I'm going to the loo," she called back. She turned and smiled at him; he was now only three yards from her. "Are you a photographer?" she asked.

"Yes, I suppose I am," he laughed.

She felt the flow of blood to her cheeks. "I meant a proper photographer?"

"I'm not a professional, if that's what you mean," he answered.

"Not for a paper or a magazine?" she made the question

sound like an accusation.

"No. But I've had one or two exhibitions," he defended himself. "Did you mind me taking your picture?"

"No," she answered. "Could you take some more pictures of me?"

"I'd like that. Let's walk around the fair. What's your name?"

They introduced each other and talked as they walked and he learned that Katy Rose would like to be a model.

He took many pictures of her. Against moving hobby-horses. In the Hall of Mirrors. shying at a target of cans and trying to lift the sledge hammer to register her strength. He bought ice- creams and they were at the edge of the show-ground under a chestnut tree when she asked;

"Mr Foden," he told her to call him Charles. "Charles, would you take another picture of me. Sort of private like?"

"You mean, nude?" he asked.

The blood rushed to her cheeks again.

"Not the whole thing. Just my boobs. I thought I could be a Page Three Girl."

She looked nervous as he didn't answer and began to bite her thumb, leaving the ice-cream cone to drip onto the grass.

"Why do you want to be that sort of model?" he asked. "You're a beautiful girl, Katy Rose. You could be a photographic model. You could get work in advertising, but you would have to go to an agency and learn your trade."

"Wouldn't that take a long time?"

"Two or three years. I could take the pictures for you, build up a portfolio. But there is more to modelling than just looking pretty. You will have to learn about make-up and angles and posture. When do you leave school?" She told him the next spring. "Then call me and we'll see what we can do." He gave her a card and started to walk away.

She took the card and her brows puckered together. "Don't you like me?"

"Yes. Of course I like you."

"Then why don't you want to see my boobs?"

He made a helpless gesture. "It's not that I don't want to see them, Katy. It just wouldn't be right for me to take that sort of picture. I'm not a professional photographer. It wouldn't be right. I might get into trouble."

"How?" she asked, her puzzlement increasing.

"I'm well-known in the city. I'm a married man. How would it look if it got known that I had taken nude photos of a sixteen year-old girl?"

"I wouldn't tell anyone," she said, her anxiety increasing as he backed away.

"Look, Charles," she quickly unfastened two more buttons on her blouse and pulled down a cup of her brassiere revealing a large brown nipple in a pink whorl, the white of her flesh bulging against her hand. He looked quickly behind him then realised she had manoeuvred herself so that he shielded her from any distant strollers.

" You can touch me if you'd like to."

He snarled at her.

"Dress yourself," he snapped.

He thought she was going to cry as she clumsily fastened her blouse.

"Look, I'm sorry Katy. I must go. I'm late already. I know where to find you at The Badgers. I'll pop the pictures over there when I've developed them. I'm sorry."

She watched him walk quickly away across the grass and her threatened tears turned to anger.

"Don't bother," she yelled after him.

There, Foden's memories became less bright and sunny as though thunder clouds had darkened the sky and day had become night. He walked into the house but his past followed him for the rest of the day.

THE PRESENT
2

Unlike Penny, whose course work involved her in physical activity, Caroline's subject of psychology was not the best companion for someone trying to recover from a traumatic experience and her emotions had become less predictable after her return to university.

It had helped that she had been able to move into Penny's house as the dreaded Gerry, who had been a constant nuisance to Penny by seeking her company with the most trivial excuses, had moved out because his tutors had advised him that he needed to change courses to remain at university as he was almost certainly heading for a failure of the one he was reading.

Caroline had accepted the letter of apology and roses from Noel without responding to them – as had her friends to their letters – and it helped that her friends still talked about Noel referring to him by adjectives such as Wanker, or by Graham's inspired, Conan, which was healthier than not referring to him at all. But there were moments when Penny found her looking depressed and she confessed to not sleeping well and still waking with Noel on top of her.

It was after an incident in the local bookshop that Caroline's defences crumbled. She was browsing among the shelves when, out of the corner of her eye, she saw Noel enter the shop. Her first reaction was to hide her face behind a book and turn quickly into the shelves and it took her some moments to find the courage to turn back and peep around the book to look for him and when she saw him walk boldly farther into the shop she felt herself shaking and she replaced the book she had been holding and almost ran back to her rooms.

"Talk to Nicola," Penny suggested as Caroline tearfully

recalled the experience. Professor Nicola Bevin was Caroline's tutor.

"I can't do that," Caroline answered.

"Why? She's a clinical psychologist. Who better to help/"

"She's my supervisor."

"You always said she was more like a friend. You should talk to someone, Caroline. I'm not much help. Perhaps you should bring charges against him if it will help you."

"It would ruin his life," Caroline said.

"Better that than he ruins yours. Perhaps you need revenge."

"No. I just need not to be such a bloody wet blanket about it."

"Talk to Nicola. Please?"

Nicola Bevin was easily approachable and was idolised by her students. She had published several books, one of which had become a standard work, and loved what she did so when Caroline told her she would like to see her about a personal matter she immediately arranged the meeting in her comfortable flat and asked Caroline if she would like alcohol, tea or coffee after she had ushered her onto the settee. Caroline chose a glass of wine and the bottle was put between them on a coffee-table.

After Caroline had told her the sequence of events of their Easter weekend and its damaging conclusion, Nicola considered the tale with her legs folded under her on the worn armchair and regarded Caroline over the top of her glass.

"Do you want me to talk to you as a friend or as a counsellor?" she eventually asked.

"A bit of both." Caroline replied.

"Then as a counsellor can I ask you about your sex-life? Are you a virgin?"

Caroline smiled at the idea. "No."

"How far did he get?" Caroline told her and was then asked for a graphic explanation of the physics involved. The bruises had now almost gone but Caroline pointed to where they had been and told Angela about her lip and watched the distaste in the other woman's eyes.

"That is criminal assault. It is sexual violence. Do you think he could do it again?"

It was not a question Caroline had asked herself nor had Penny done so.

She thought about it but was unable to offer a truthful answer. She told Nicola about the letters and the flowers, and then she asked a good question herself.

"I don't know. But if I brought charges against him do you think that would stop him from doing it again?"

"It's impossible for me to judge. Most sex offenders re-offend but I don't believe there are any statistics available to know how many sex offenders learn from their experiences if they are not charged. Sex-violence is common in marriage and one of the main reasons many of those male offenders are not charged is financial. Most of those victims would feel no remorse if their husbands were punished. Do you want to punish him?"

"I just want to get him out of my mind."

"Then I'll now talk as a friend. How many sexual relationships have you had?"

Caroline explained there had been two 'experiences' as a teenager. "They were messy and clumsy and minor disasters." Then there had been a serious relationship with a boy for two years and two one-nighters since.

"Have any of them been sexually pleasing?" Nicola asked.

A hesitant smile came to Caroline's face. "Well, one of the one-nighters was a bit special. But he was married."

"So how would you sum-up your sex-life so far?"

Terrible. Terrible. Nice but unsatisfactory. Shaming. Amazing."

"And the rape?"

"How d'you mean?"

"How would you describe it; one word?"

"Frightening."

"Because of the violence?"

"Because…it was imposed."

"And now you feel vulnerable?"

"Yes."

"Because this person didn't play by the rules."

"The rules?"

"He didn't date you. He didn't take you to dinner. He didn't try to kiss you. He didn't hold your hand. He didn't even ask to fuck you. They are the rules. Without them we are vulnerable, we are weak. He did what males do in the animal world. He used his strength to get what he wanted."

"Yes." There was a touch of anger in Caroline's response.

"How would you feel if you had done what this other boy did: hit him with a chair?"

Caroline thought about the question but then answered decisively.

"Good. Really good."

"Then that is what you have to do?"

"Hit him with a chair?"

"No, because that would be assault and you could be in trouble with the law. The law doesn't allow us to take revenge – not physically anyway. But you need to be positive,"

"How?"

"You will think of something. There are three irresistible positives in the gene pool: sex, revenge and love. You're one of my best students, Caroline. Use your brain – find a positive from those three and be clever how you use it. And for now, just think of the incident as bad sex. Very bad sex."

****

Caroline and Penny were preparing a meal when Harry called. They hadn't seen much of him since the incident at the Foden's and Caroline had been sure he had been avoiding her. "Thinks I'm ruined goods," she had said. So they were both pleased to see him and gave him a glass of wine. They avoided talking about Noel until Harry asked if they were going to the Union debate.

"The bastard's speaking in it," he explained. "I don't want to go on my own."

He told them the subject of the debate was 'Is capitalism dead.'

"You don't have to tell me which side Conan will be on," Penny said.

"The thing is, as I'm doing economics my tutor expects me to be there but I can't stand the idea of seeing Foden again – and especially not holding forth on a platform. I wondered if you chaps would come too to stop me doing something stupid."

Penny looked at Caroline.

"Why not?" Caroline said.

Penny was pleased; it was progress. "I'll ask Graham as well," she said.

"Too late. I've already asked him," Harry told them. "He's agreed. I think it will be a bit of a shock for Foden to see us all there together. What do you think?"

They thought it was a good idea.

The hall was full and the debate got noisy and threatened

to get out of hand. Noel Foden was sitting on the platform with the other speakers but was behind the dais and was partly hidden. Someone from the Socialist Alliance was being heckled and cheered at the same time and the Speaker had to intervene and ask for quiet before he could finish. And then Foden was called to reply. He stepped up to the dais and cleared his throat nervously and shuffled his notes.

"Maynard Keynes said," he began but was soon shouted down.

"An old fart for old times," someone shouted. Foden was suddenly aggressive.

"No, my friend. That just shows the paucity of your knowledge. Keynes' ideas are very much pertinent to where we are today."

"Where's that? In the shit up to our necks, thanks to people like him and you," someone responded and was loudly applauded and the Speaker had to intervene again.

"All those people around the world, and yes, people like you, who are demonstrating against capitalism are not accepting that their wages, their pensions, their jobs and their education, all depend on capitalism and the only alternative answers they have are more state control, nationalising the banks, higher taxation on profits, more state spending to create jobs that have no profit motive. Those things will immediately increase private debt and will kill off what we have. We need more capital creation. We need to cut taxes, cut government spending and interference with markets. We need to create more millionaires..." the response was a volley of abuse and cheers from the floor and Noel Foden stood defiantly and shouted back more aggressively than anyone opposing him.

Penny looked sideways and saw that Caroline had her eyes closed. The Speaker eventually restored order and brought the debate to a close When the furore had calmed down he thanked the speakers and someone stood up and said, "Noel Foden; our future Prime Minister," and was promptly pulled down and shouted at. But Noel Foden smiled indulgently and Penny cringed inside as much as she knew Caroline was doing. As they filed out Harry broke the silence between them.

"God help us if that bastard ever becomes Prime Minister."

"If his father has anything to do with it, it might happen," Graham added.

In the street Graham said he had an extra tutorial and Harry asked the girls if they wanted to go for a drink but neither of them seemed enthusiastic and chose to go back to their rooms. They felt each other's depression as they walked.

"How do you feel?" Penny asked, putting her arm through Caroline's and feeling her friend shiver involuntary.

"Terrible," she answered. "I thought I was getting better. But the way he looked, that sneer, so aggressive..." she shuddered and Penny squeezed her shoulder.

"Princess," a voice made them turn. A tall, thin young man was bouncing towards them. Caroline squeaked excitedly and the man swept her up and swung her round.

"Penny, this is Camp Ronnie," she said.

Penny knew the soubriquet was appropriate, even in the street lighting. She could see he was wearing make-up and carried a shoulder purse and his trousers were tight and yellow and he was wearing a suede cowboy jacket with a flowered vest beneath it. Ronnie kissed her on both cheeks.

"Are you two an item?" he asked, puckering his lips.

"No. Of course not," Penny laughed.

"Don't be offended luvvy. We all come in different packages." he said. "And you make a lovely couple."

"Ronnie and I did the pantomime together," Caroline explained. "You didn't come did you?"

Penny said she had gone home with a bug and missed it. She knew Caroline was in the drama group.

"And you were the best princess we've ever had," Ronnie said.

"Are you at university?" Penny asked him.

"Aren't you lovely," Ronnie said. "Do I really look that young? No, sweetie. I'm afraid I have to work for a living."

"Ronnie's the stage manager at the Royal," Caroline explained. "And he's the best."

"Where are you two lovely ladies going?" he asked and was told they were going home.

"On a Friday evening? Don't be so ridiculous. You cannot go home on a Friday evening. Come with me and I'll show you a good time."

"I've heard that before," Caroline laughed

"Such filth. I don't wish to know about your indiscretions," he said. "Come and have a nice dwinky winky at the Hussar."

The Gay Hussar was well known as the gay bar for both genders.

"We can't do that, we're not gay," Caroline said.

"You can pretend. You look convincing to me. No, darlings, you will have a nice time and meet some nice friends of mine and I think you need cheering up."

Caroline looked at Penny enquiringly.

"Why not?" Penny laughed. "After that debate I think we do need cheering up."

It was a huge pub and was packed. A clover-leaf bar was in the middle and there were stall tables around the sides and a disco at the far end. They pushed their way towards the bars with Ronnie swapping banter with people as they passed. He was obviously well-known and popular. After they had been served they found a corner stall near the entrance as most people seemed to prefer to stand in the crush. Ronnie was in good form and kept them amused gossiping about various couples or individuals but his face suddenly froze and he turned it away from the entrance. The girls looked towards it and saw four men moving inwards with most people getting out of their way and those that didn't were moved physically aside. They were dressed in leathers with white vests beneath showing heavy pectorals. They were shaven-headed and wore prominent earrings pierced into their lobes. Ronnie continued to look down until they had passed.

"Who are they?" Caroline asked.

"Doggers," Ronnie told them and had to explain what dogging was.

"But they don't just like it al fresco, they're sadists. The other doggers post lookouts like meerkats because Warren and Elvis and their crew don't ask for what they want, they just take it."

"Warren and Elvis?" Caroline said.

"Batley. They own a garage in Hall Street. They're twins. The other two are their cousins."

The group selected a stall and the inhabitants vacated it without being asked.

"They're horrible," Penny said.

"They don't come nastier, darling," Ronnie assured her.

They stayed some time, even joining the dancers at the disco. They left when Camp Ronnie was getting particularly involved with a new friend and they pushed their way to the entrance.

They stood in the shock of the cool air for a moment before walking a little unsteadily towards their rooms. They both felt better and Caroline continued to sing one of the songs from the disco.

"You seem much happier," Penny laughed

"I am. That was a great idea of Ronnie's," Caroline replied and continued humming to herself as she slid her arm through Penny's.

THE PRESENT
3

Daphne Morrison was reluctant to report the failure of Penny's visit to the Chief Constable. His response could only be a negative one. The thought of what that would do to Tom Lewis and his mother caused a nauseous pain in her stomach and she also felt the failure was personal. She rethought all aspects of the investigation and saw no logical reason for blaming herself but she could not dispel the idea that she might have done something different or that she had missed something important.

Despite the relative failure of the search she still believed vehemently that she was right, that Katy Rose had been abducted from Drovers' Hill, and beneath all the other emotions a quiet anger seethed that she might not be allowed to prove it. Above all else, no one could deny the extraordinary experience of Penny Featherstone's vision. But she had nothing to give her chief to justify continuing the search for Katy Rose.

She was not expected into the office since she had been assigned the investigation, she was always at the end of her mobile if the Chief Constable needed her. She had written up a report of Penny's visit and her interview with Ken Hewlett but as she had received no summons from her chief, she delayed the unwelcome meeting by calling in at Stokesey police station to have tea and cake with Steve Jennings and to bring him up to date with the case. He was supportive but whether it was to alleviate her obvious depression or that he really believed they should continue the investigation she did not know.

"What about Ken Hewlett?" he asked encouragingly. "Is he a reason to keep the investigation going."

"Do you know him?"

"Certainly. He's a local lad. I haven't had much to do with him because he's older than me but he's well-known in the area."

"He says he has an alibi for the day Katy disappeared. He said he was delivering venison to the butchers in Stokesey at the time. "

"Well, old man Pethick is still workin' and his son Alfred runs the shop."

"I'll have a word with them," Morrison responded without enthusiasm. "Did you have any luck with the request for items found on Drovers' Hill?"

"Aye. I did. There's a list. Not much I'm afraid."

Morrison studied the sheet of paper. Several scarves, two hats, dog-leads, a wallet, keys, a walking-stick and a golf club.

"What have you done with them?"

Jennings told her some of the items, the wallet, two scarves and one set of keys had only been reported from memory and the finders had no idea what they had done with them. The other two sets of keys had been handed into the City Police and the golf-club and walking stick and the other items had been bagged up and were waiting for Morrison's instructions.

"Aren't people amazing," the Inspector noted. "Twenty years and they have still kept them."

"I've had things in my shed for that long," Jennings replied.

Morrison had been shown the items; the small ones in issue-bags and the walking-stick and golf-club wrapped in plastic. She examined the two large items through their wrappers. The walking-stick was clean but the golf-club still had what looked like mud on the face and the shaft was covered in cob-webs.

"The woman who found the walking-stick admitted her son had used it quite a lot until he left home," Jennings said.

"And the golf-club?"

"That was handed in by a nice old-boy. He was the local organiser for the Ramblers. Said he'd had it for many years. He'd rung the golf-club at the time and told them about it but nobody bothered to get back to him. It's been lying in his garage since then. He saw our request for info in the Rambler's newsletter."

Morrison continued to examine the club. "The small items are not worth the cost of putting through Forensics," she said. "The walking-stick neither, that has been used a lot. But the golf-club might be worth a try."

She put the club beside her chair and continued to look at it as she drank her tea. "How would a golf-club get into the woods?" she asked.

"Someone looking for a ball probably," Jennings replied.

Morrison's eyes swivelled towards him.

"How? There's a mesh fence all round the course."

"Never used to be. They only put that up a few years ago. Someone got hit with a ball and threatened to sue the club."

Morrison stared at the man and wondered if complacency of being a local copper had warped his brain after all. She sat forward to get his attention.

"Steve, are you telling me that the top part of the course, the part adjoining Drovers' Hill Woods, used to be open?"

"That's right," he agreed.

She wanted to yell at him, *why didn't you tell me that a long time ago* but she only said; "Have you got the details for the person who handed the club in?" Jennings found them and gave them to her. "Thank you," she said. She picked up the golf-club and left without another word.

The ex-rambler was a Mr. Arnold and lived in Upper

Stokesey. Morrison rang him on her mobile and asked if she could come and speak with him. He opened the door of a small bungalow to her. He looked old but fit, sparkling eyes in a gnarled face. He offered to make her tea which she would have declined until she sensed there was no one else in the house and he was probably pleased to have company, so she allowed herself to be shown into a small sitting-room dominated by a large television and she sat on one of two sofas. They exchanged local experiences and knowledge, Mr. Arnold seeming to be a keen historian, before Daphne Morrison had the chance to mention the golf-club.

"Queer business that, "Arnold said. "I rang the club as soon as I got home with it. I gave them the make and said it was a number nine iron and told them where I'd found it. The Secretary said he would ask the members about it and get back to me when someone claimed it. He never did. So I just put it in my shed after it had been in the hall-stand for a week or so and forgot all about it – until I saw your appeal in the Rambler's Newsletter."

"How long ago was that?" Morrison askcd.

Arnold said his kids were still at school then. "So it was a long time ago. "Our youngest is thirty two now."

"Do you remember where you found it?" Morrison asked.

"I know exactly where I found it. But I couldn't show you I'm afraid, my walking days are over; bad knees."

"Do you think you could show me on a map – we had some detailed ones made of the woods when we searched the area?

"I could. I know those woods like my own teeth. But don't bother going out, I have a map here."

"That won't be detailed enough. I've got one in my car."

The area of the woods had been mapped, showing each tree, and printed on plastic sheet when the ground search for

Katy Rose had been done. She unrolled the map on a coffee table that Arnold had cleared.

"If you think you can show me where you found the club, point to the spot with your finger and I will mark it," she told him. "But don't touch it until you're sure, so we don't get confused."

Arnold pored over the table, his finger hovering expectantly. "Let me see; that's the Ridgeway, Dingle Dell...Yes. That's the big oak on the golf course. There. Right there." His finger went down emphatically.

"You are sure?" Morrison asked and felt a surge of excitement; it was on the other side of the path from where the shoe had been found.

"Absolutely. I walked the dog up there every morning and I used to go to the edge of the course to see if anyone I knew was on that hole."

Morrison had pencilled a circle around the spot his finger had detailed.

She thanked Mr. Arnold enthusiastically. "How did you come to find the club?" she asked. "It's a little way off the path."

Arnold gave her a mischievous smile. "Call of nature," he said. "I was doing what I had to do and then I saw the club, it was just propped up against a tree. I think what might have happened is they took two clubs into the trees not knowing which one they would need and forgot to pick the other one up after they'd played the shot. I've done the same in a bunker when I've taken a sand-wedge and another wedge with me. Mind you, I was always leaving a club somewhere and having to walk back for it. I think, sub-consciously I was telling myself I was no damn good at the game and I should give it up. I did in the end."

"Were you a member at Stokesey?" she asked. He said he

wasn't, that he played when he was young with his father, before he married and moved into the area.

She thanked him again and promised to call in when she was passing.

She checked her watch and decided she could just get to the laboratories in the city before they closed. She booked-in the golf-club and the map and then she drove home and poured herself a large drink.

The next morning she was up early. She reported into the office and told them where she would be and then drove to Stokesey Golf Club.

Even before nine am the car park was busy. She watched the scene from her car: golfers coming and going, some sitting on the open boots of their cars changing into golf-shoes, the struggle to get golf-trolleys and bags from the cars, the cheerful banter between the players – then something else: an electric buggy appeared from behind the clubhouse and buzzed towards the first tee. Another one joined it and four elderly players got stiffly out of the buggies and prepared themselves for teeing-off.

Morrison walked into the clubhouse. There were people hustling each other in the corridor and spilling out of the equipment shop and the locker-rooms. She asked a young woman, who was dressed like a waitress, for the secretary and was pointed in the direction of an office at the rear of the building. She knocked on the door and found a man with his mouth full of croissant and holding a mug of coffee in his hand. She introduced herself. Ronald Baxter quickly emptied his mouth and looked concerned.

"You seem very busy this morning," she said. Baxter explained there was a monthly medal tournament that day. Morrison told him she was supervising new enquiries into the Katy Rose Lewis disappearance.

"I was told all about the case," Baxter said. "It was well before my time so when there was all that activity up on Drover's Hill the Committee asked me to look into it. They thought the Trust might be going to cut down some of the trees or something."

Morrison asked about the fencing and was told it was put up seven years previously after someone was badly injured in the face by a stray ball.

"Why they were on the edge of the course I've no idea," he added. "But the Club felt they had to find the money for the fencing to ward off any legal proceeding."

"Did people often stray onto the course before it was fenced-off?" she asked. Baxter said not, that the accident was the only incident he could remember.

"Who was the person hit by the ball, do you know?"

"A woman. I could find the name from our committee minutes if it's important."

"It's not important. I notice you have electric buggies."

Baxter sighed. "They are still a bone of contention," he admitted and explained that they lost a lot of members as they got elderly because the top half of the course was steep and hard work. "So it was decided to get some buggies to keep the membership alive – but many of the younger members objected, thought mechanical aids should not be part of a physical sport."

"So they are quite recent then?"

"About ten years. But some of the better-off players did have their own before the committee decided to get some. It all caused a lot of unpleasantness at the time. The committee felt it was an unfair advantage for some members to have them. They tried to ban them. Quite a few members left and the row unfortunately coincided with the new Mountfield course opening on the other side of the estuary. Some of the older members could tell you more about it than I can."

"Would it be possible to get a copy of your membership list at the time of Katy Lewis' disappearance?" Morrison asked.

Baxter smiled to lessen his astonishment. "Inspector, you can't possibly think that one of our members..." but Morrison interrupted him.

"What I think does not matter. Can you get me that list?"

Baxter's smile and astonishment disappeared. "We do keep such records, of course. But you should realise the course is not just for members, it is open to green-fees three days a week," and he enjoyed the doubt in Morrison's face.

"You mean anyone can play?" she asked.

Baxter said that was exactly what he meant and did not keep the satisfaction from his voice.

"Never-the-less, I would still like to see that list."

"I'll ask the committee for permission to release it."

"Thank you, Mr. Baxter. That would be very helpful. And do you think you could mark on the list those members who used golf-buggies at that time?" she added. Baxter thought there probably wouldn't be a record of that. "But our President, Mr. Farringdon, might remember them, he was Captain at the time."

She had decided to give Steve Jennings the task of reviewing the interviews with golf club members in her anger at his negligence for not telling her about the boundary fence. She called in on her way back from the club and dumped a box-file on his desk. She told him she had sent the golf-club for forensic analysis and had requested a members list for the time of Katy's disappearance.

"But what I would like you to do, Steve, is to go over the statements given by the golf club members at the time and those people living in the houses opposite."

"Are you thinking it was someone from the golf-club.?"

She ignored the hint of sarcasm in his voice.

"It's a possibility – now that we know there was no barrier between the course and the woods."

Jennings acknowledged the touché with a frown.

"Because someone found a golf-club in the woods?"

"No, Steve. Not just because of that. Golfers use electric golf carts. What could be more convenient to take Jenny down to the road and possibly move Katy Lewis' body somewhere else?"

The logic of the idea shone briefly from Jennings' face until it was gone in another frown of concentration.

"How would someone carry a body from the woods to the Club car park without being seen" he asked.

"Those golf buggies are made to hold two sets of clubs on the back. That would be enough space to hold a body. Katy could have been hidden in the woods until her assailant was able to move her down to the club car park and transfer her body to a car." She waited for Jennings' reaction; it was slow in coming.

"That would be difficult," he said. "There's always someone around at golf clubs. Even if the man waited until it was dark there would be lots of people around to notice or hear an electric golf buggy driving about. Social members use the bar and go there for dinner. And the golf pro lives above the clubhouse."

Morrison felt an irritation by the sergeant's negative reaction. "Perhaps they didn't wait. Perhaps they did it during the day when there were people about. They could have covered the body up with something, a golf-jacket or their waterproofs – and put the golf-clubs on top."

"If a golf-buggy was used it could just as easily have

164

moved the body almost anywhere," Jennings responded. "Even down the Ridgeway to Upper Stokesey or even to Stokesey."

Morrison wondered if he was just playing devils advocate or still reacting to her obvious annoyance with him for not telling her about the fencing.

"Access from the path into both those places is fenced off except for a pedestrian gate – or are you now going to tell me they were only put there recently?"

"If a golfer was responsible why would he risk what you're suggesting? Why wouldn't he just come back after dark and bury Katy under one of them bunkers. Wouldn't that be easier?"

Morrison hadn't considered that possibility and began to question whether she was falling into a policeman's trap of pushing one idea at the expense of others.

"You might be right," she said. "If that club comes back with positive DNA to one of the Stokesey members we'll dig up the whole bloody course. But meantime I want to know where every member was on the day Katy disappeared. Do you think you could find that out from those files, please?" Her voice was firm enough for him not to argue with her any more.

"I will," he answered just as firmly.

"Thank you. I saw there was another batch there which was done by uniform marked, *Traffic Specs*. I presume they are the drivers who were questioned. You were probably doing that yourself?"

Jennings ignored the question. "What am I supposed to look for?" he asked.

"Make a note of anyone who said they were playing that day then get one of your team to follow it up and find out who is still around and where they are now. Anything, any little thing that strikes you as odd or not watertight I want to know about it. You said the pro lived over the clubhouse. Do you know who the pro was at the time of Katy's disappearance?" The question was asked more in hope than expectation.

"Julie Norris," he answered.

Morrison's surprise was twofold.

"A woman?" she said.

"They were lucky to have her. She was English National Match-Play Champion."

"Is she still alive?"

Jennings said she was the senior pro at the Mountfield Club. Morrison recognised the club in the city of which her Chief Constable and Charles Foden were members. But she was surprised that Jennings would know that. "Do you play golf?" she asked?"

"I tried a bit before I was married. But I was no good at it."

"Did you play at Sokesey?"

"I played a few times at Stokesey on the pay-and-play days but even then it was a bit pricey for me. When the Mountfield club opened a pay-and-play course I went there, it was quite a bit cheaper. That's the other thing; the files won't tell you about the non-members who played that day."

"I know. But those players wouldn't be using golf buggies. By the way, if Katy had been buried in a bunker I think a fox or something would have soon dug her up again," Morrison said as she walked out.

She rang the Mountfield Club to arrange a meeting with Julie Norris. She had not been to the Club before and was surprised by the size of the complex. There were three courses, Julie Norris explained, only one of which was for private members. She was a fit looking woman in her forties and had a business-like, no-nonsense style developed over years of competition and dealing with a predominately male environment.

"Do you play?" she asked Morrison.

"No. I like walking," Morrison replied.

"I know. Someone said that golf spoilt a good walk," Norris anticipated. "What can I do for you, Inspector?"

Morrison explained she was investigating the Katy Lewis disappearance. Norris' impatient attitude changed quickly to one of sympathy.

"That was so awful," she said. "I knew the Lewis family well. I used to drink in The Badgers quite often. I heard a rumour or two that you were re-examining the case."

Morrison hoped she hadn't heard via one of her particular members. She asked if she knew whether any of the members of her previous club had been questioned at the time.

"Oh, Lord. Yes. We all were. We had to give our car registrations to the police. They checked who was at the club that day, what time they arrived and when they left. It upset a few members I can tell you."

"Why?" Morrison asked.

"Because some of them were pompous arse-holes. They objected to anything or anyone who interfered with their routine or disagreed with their opinions."

"Is that why you left?

"Partly. The final straw was when Nigel Farringdon became Captain. He was the worst of the lot," Norris answered.

"When was that?"

"About that time. Just after Katy disappeared. I hoped Charles would have got it but Farringdon won the Harlequin Trophy and it was more or less accepted that if he or Charles won they would get the captaincy."

"Would that be Charles Foden?" Morrison said. Norris confirmed it was.

"Lovely chap. I was really surprised when he decided not to compete for the trophy, knowing that the winner would get the captaincy. He left as soon as this place opened. He was a much better player than Farringdon and they didn't like each other at all so I can understand why he left."

"Julie. I'm interested in who had electric buggies at the time. I've asked Stokesey for a list but I thought you might remember."

"A bit of a sore point with some members," Norris confirmed. "In a way I saw their view. It was unfair that a few richer members could use them. But now almost everyone uses them; saves time, I use one myself – but I'm getting a bit creaky now. Let me think: Farringdon and Foden, definitely. Then there was Levy, he's long dead, and Ben Thomas – I think that was about it at that time. Why the interest in the Club and buggies?"

"I understand there was no fence between the woods and the course then. We're now working on the possibility that Katy Rose and Jenny Challis were abducted off Drovers' Hill."

Julie Norris looked at the inspector shrewdly and made no comment for some time. Morrison waited, hoping her deliberation would be helpful.

"And you're thinking that someone removed them from there in a golf buggy?" she eventually said. "Levy was a very small man, in his seventies even then. Ben Thomas never played alone, he just liked playing for the company. Which leaves Nigel Farringdon and Charles Foden. To be perfectly honest, I couldn't imagine either of them doing anything sexual outside of their marriages. We had some very pretty waitresses and staff at the Club but neither of those guys made the slightest pass at them. They are both too up their own arses to do that sort of thing."

"In what way?"

"Too straight. Too moral," Norris answered.

"Why didn't they get on?" Morrison queried.

"They are both very competitive. They couldn't stand being beaten."

Morrison thanked her and was about to leave when Norris stopped her.

"There's another possibility," she said. "The greenkeeper and his assistant used an electric buggy to get about. They work early in the morning before most people started playing and in the summer evenings too."

Morrison turned back into the room. "Tell me about them," she said.

Norris told her the head groundsman was Fred Rafferty who had died only one year ago. "He worked right up to his late seventies. He was good, loved his work, did a great job. I tried to get him to come here when we lost our groundsman but he didn't drive and lived in Upper Stokesey just round the corner from the club. He had several assistants for cutting and raking who came and went." A sudden smile lit up her face. "I remember one of them: George. Gorgeous George I called him. He wore the shortest shorts and had a body to drool over."

Morrison's interest quickened.

"Do you know what happened to him?"

Norris sighed. "He didn't last long. Suddenly disappeared. Broke my heart. But I suspected he wasn't into females anyway."

She laughed infectiously so that Morrison saw the little girl she used to be.

"Do you remember when that was?"

"No. But it was a long time ago, when I still believed in love."

"Can you remember his surname?"

"I don't think I ever knew it. I didn't have anything to do with hiring the staff except in the golf-shop. But the club should have a record of all their employees; they had to pay insurance for them. The present groundsman is Dave Horton. He's been there a long time. He was Fred's assistant for a good fifteen years. I don't think he was there when Katy disappeared – but I can't honestly remember."

"I'll check him out – and Gorgeous George."

They both laughed and shook hands

"If you fancy trying golf I'd be happy to take you out sometime."

Julie Norris had made her feel much better. She had something positive to take to the Chief Constable when she had to face him with her report. Despite Jennings' scepticism she felt the idea that an electric buggy could have been used to move Katy and Jenny Challis was a promising one and now Julie Norris had given her another lead: a young, nubile groundsman who had the use of such buggies and wore very little other than shorts. It was not difficult to imagine how a meeting between such a person and Katy on Drovers' Hill could have developed into something more significant than a bit of flirting or chatting-up.

As soon as she left the Mountfield club she rang Ronald Baxter and asked him if they kept employment records. He told her their accountants did that. She found the accountants in Stokesey and explained to a man who looked as though he should have long been retired, the needle in a haystack she was seeking and gave him the date of Katy Lewis' disappearance. She was amazed and relieved when he went into a back room and came out with a thin ledger.

"This is our accounts ledger for Stokesey Golf Club for that year. What was the surname?"

Morrison admitted she didn't know. The man looked at her over his glasses rather as she remembered her father doing when she was naughty.

"He worked as a groundsman and his first name was George," she said.

The man stifled a sigh and turned the pages of the ledger.

"They were paid weekly then," he said. "Great nuisance that. I know the head groundsman was Fred Rafferty and then a chap called Horton joined him. He's still there." Morrison said it was before Horton joined the club.

"Well, it looks like someone called J. White was there in December…and January…"

"It would be in April," Morrison said.

"Ah. There's a G. Fuller – seems he was only there for three months."

"That's him. Would you have an address for him?" The man said the golf club might have that. "But I can give you his National Insurance Number," he added.

"Perfect." Morrison said and thanked him. Back at her office she called the Pensions Service. They soon traced the number she gave them.

"The file has not been active for many years," she was told. "The last record of his employment was over twenty years ago; somewhere called Stokesey Golf Club." She gave the last date of his employment and Morrison quickly noticed it was only two days after Katy Rose disappeared.

"Does that mean he hasn't worked since then?"

"It means he hasn't been legally employed in this country since then."

"Could he have died?"

"Not unless his death was not registered. HMRC would

automatically be informed from the General Registry if it had been. He could have moved abroad, of course."

Morrison had not thought it was an 'of course' possibility.

"Would any department have been informed of that?"

"Not our departments – the Passport Office might help."

"Do you have an address for him prior to the Stokesey Golf Club.?"

"Before that he was with the Bradford Office. He had an address in Otley, Yorkshire.

Morrison wrote the address then put a call through to West Yorkshire police. She explained she needed to find a George Fuller who once lived in Otley and gave them the address. It was two hours later when they called her back.

"That address you gave us is George Fuller's mother. She hasn't heard from him since he moved south many years ago. It seems they fell out when she remarried. She married her ex brother-in-law and he and George didn't get on."

"So she doesn't know where George is?"

"No. A bit sad really."

Very sad. She thanked the officer. She remained upright but her inside felt as though it was sliding downwards. A good lead, the only lead to Katy Rose, had disappeared – just like George had done, a few days after Katy herself. But it still meant George Fuller was more than a person of special interest and she now felt more confident of keeping the investigation alive when she faced the Chief Constable.

When she eventually knocked on his door she first explained the omission about the golf course being open to the woods and the find of a club near the spot where Katy's shoe had been found. Then she talked about the electric buggies.

"It would certainly explain how young Jenny could be taken down to the road," her chief agreed. "But it's not so easy to think that a club member could be involved."

Morrison ignored the sub-conscious snobbery of the remark and told him about the groundsman who had left the Club after Katy had disappeared. He considered the information and took some time to absorb it. She had watched his face closely, a face she had come to understand intimately over the two years of their association, and its light and shade had changed noticeably when she mentioned the buggies and George; she had timed their impact well.

"Have you tried to find this George chap?" he asked eventually.

She told him of the failure of that search.

"How could he disappear like that? Unless he won the lottery he must have been working somewhere. I know a lot of groundsmen are casual workers but he couldn't do that for twenty years without the tax people knowing about it?"

"The Pensions Service said he could have moved abroad. I'm requesting a search from the Passport Office."

"That is possible. He sounds a likely suspect – especially as he disappeared the day after Katy went missing; that's more than suspicious. Fleeing abroad would make sense. It would also explain why his mother hasn't heard from him too."

"Yes. But could he have just gone on the same day he left Stokesey? We're not talking about someone with a lot of money are we? Unless he caught a ferry across to France. And if he's in Europe we should be able to trace him. But if he went further afield he would have had to have got a visa if he didn't have the funds to be a tourist. So where was he staying before he left here?"

"Didn't the golf club know?"

"No. They didn't have an address for him."

"That is odd. Perhaps someone was hiding him. Did he

have any friends?"

"I've no idea. The golf pro – you know her, sir: Julie Norris – didn't know much about him except that he was very attractive and had a great body."

"Julie would notice that."

"The point being, sir, that it's not difficult to imagine what might have happened if Katy met someone like that on Drover's Hill."

"No. it's not."

"And a buggy would not only explain how Jenny could be taken down to the road, it would also explain how Katy's body could be moved elsewhere."

"Yes, I agree. So where are you going with this, Daphne?"

"Even with a golf-buggy there is no way off Drovers' Hill except along the path which was probably used to take Jenny down to the road, or through the golf course. The exits to Stokesey and Upper Stokesey are fenced off except for pedestrians."

"A golf buggy would be noticed on a road. So if Katy was removed from Drovers' Hill that way it would mean her body would have to be transferred to a vehicle."

"Exactly."

Her chief thought about it. "The only problem with that idea is that a casual groundsman is unlikely to have a vehicle. And transferring a body at the golf club would be difficult, there is always someone around at a busy club. During the day it would be impossible and in the evening it would be equally difficult, members use the bar and restaurant and they have social functions there. And after dark an electric buggy would be noticed buzzing around."

The explanation echoed that of Steve Jennings.

"That's why I think it more likely that a buggy was used to take Katy somewhere else where she could be buried."

"Such as?"

Morrison held her breath. "Such as the marshes."

Her chief's reaction was as she expected. Before the look of astonishment left his face she rushed on. "It's the only possibility. We've searched the woods. The rest of the hill area is sandstone with only a shallow topsoil. The marshes is the only alternative."

The Chief Constable leaned forward on his desk and tapped it annoyingly with a pen.

"That would be a hell of thing to search the marshes," he said.

"It need not be too complicated, sir. If the body is buried there it won't be too far from the Fender path. Hewlett told me the path is safe so if someone local buried Katy he would know not to stray far from that path. And the path is wide enough and solid enough to take a light vehicle. I think a small imaging team could do the job."

"I would have to consult Laxton and Chief Superintendent Faye. We couldn't do it quietly."

"Would you tell them about Penny Featherstone, sir?"

"I think not. The CID would make hay out of that; another crank as it were."

"They were wrong before."

"Yes. But we don't want to give them another bite do we?"

As he considered the problem Daphne Morrison wondered whether to ask him what he thought about the find of the golf-club but she decided against it, not only because she didn't want to divert him from authorising a search but also because of his disinclination to believe that a golf club member could be involved in anything so ghastly as a possible murder.

"All right, Daphne. I'll arrange a meeting."

Her release of tension might have been noticeable.

"Thank you, sir. Meantime, I'll put a request in to the Passport Office to see what address George gave if he applied for a passport."

The meeting was held a few days later. As well as Detective Superintendent Laxton Chief Superintendent Alec Faye also attended. Faye was the senior uniformed officer and Deputy Chief Constable.

The Chief Constable explained everything about Morrison's investigation without mentioning Penny Featherstone, only that someone had found the shoe on Drover's Hill which had been identified by Tom Lewis and his mother as being the same as that worn by Katy Rose on the day of her disappearance.

Laxton was naturally hostile to the idea that his original investigation was seriously flawed, even accusing Tom Lewis of creating the find of the shoe in order to get Katy's case reopened.

"Someone else found the shoe," the Chief Constable said evasively.

"Someone who knew about Katy's disappearance, no doubt?"

"A stranger who happened to be telling Tom Lewis about it over a drink at The Badgers," Morrison said. "And finding an earring also identified by Mrs. Lewis, which confirms that Katy Rose was on Drover's Hill on the day of her disappearance."

"We don't have to go into that at this stage," the Chief Constable said. "When Katy is found we can disclose the details."

"Surprise, surprise. No body found," Laxton said

"No. That's why we are having this meeting. The evidence that Katy Lewis and young Jenny Challis were accosted and abducted from Drovers' Hill is more than plausible and we have to proceed on that basis," the Chief Constable continued and stared at Laxton to dare him to interrupt.

"The problem remains of how that was done, by whom and where Katy is now."

"Miles from here very likely," Laxton said.

"Abductions of young women are never isolated cases," Morrison argued. "If someone is a sexual offender they will repeat the offence even after a gap of some years. I have looked up the county records. There have been no repeat offences since Katy Rose's disappearance and there were no such incidents before that."

"That is just in this county," Laxton said. "It therefore strengthens the conclusion of the original investigation that Katy was abducted by a motorist. There have been many cases of seemingly disconnected murders in various parts of the country which have later proved to be committed by someone who travels regularly."

"Wherever Katy was taken, her remains should have surfaced by now if she had been dumped or buried by someone passing through the area. Instinctive sexual offenders are not organised, they are opportunists and disposing of their victims is seldom pre-planned. They get rid of them as quickly as possible and not very effectively," Morrison responded.

"It would make sense that Katy decided to walk over Drover's Hill when she missed the bus," Faye said. "It's much shorter than going by road."

Laxton glared at Morrison.

"Have you re-enacted the scenario you're pushing, Inspector? Have you had a teenager try to carry a child and a pushchair up to Drover's Hill?"

"No. Crime re-enactments are your department," Morrison

177

responded. "Perhaps you should do that – if you can find a teenager as fit as a seventeen year-old Katy Lewis. Apparently she was the best athlete at her school."

"We are satisfied that Katy Lewis was on Drover's Hill," the Chief Constable repeated. "The point of this meeting is to decide what we should do next. If we accept that Katy and the child were abducted from Drover's Hill there is still a problem of how that was done, and how the child was left at that bus-stop. Morrison has discovered there was no barrier between Drover's Hill and the golf course adjoining it when Katy disappeared. The ground staff of the club and one or two Members used electric buggies. That could explain how Katy and the child were removed from the hill."

"We questioned all the members and staff who were at the club that day," Laxton said."

"Morrison has identified a young groundsman called George Fuller who worked at the club at the time and disappeared two days after Katy." The Chief Constable continued, ignoring Laxton's surprise and embarrassment . "But there is no record of him having worked in the UK since he left Stokesey Golf Club. That makes him a very likely suspect."

"Very likely," Faye agreed.

"It would seem very possible for Jenny Challis to have been taken down to the bus-stop using a golf-buggy," The Chief Constable continued. "Apparently, there is a path leading from Drovers' Hill to the road which is also hidden from the golf course. But what happened to Katy is more problematical."

He explained Morrison's two alternatives and why he supported the burial rather than a transfer to a car.

"You want to search the marshes, sir?" Laxton was

incredulous. "That would cost a million or so and could involve an aerial survey."

The CC explained Morrison's opinion that it would be a much simpler operation.

"So you're an expert are you, Inspector?" Laxton asked

"No. But I did talk to the tech officers during the hill search and I have consulted someone who knows the ground intimately."

"We know it had to be someone local," Chief Superintendent Alec Faye said.

He had been a uniformed sergeant based at Stokesey at the time of Katy Lewis' disappearance. The Chief Constable looked at him expectantly.

"There was the attempt on young Jenny's life after a psychologist told the media that one day Jenny could remember what happened to Katy through regressive hypnotherapy. So we knew then it had to be someone local," he explained.

"An attempt on Jenny's life?" Morrison gasped. "I didn't know that."

Faye looked at Laxton who shuffled as though his chair was suddenly uncomfortable.

"We tried to put a gag on it," he mumbled. "We kept it quiet. We didn't want the assailant to know he had failed. We thought he would be curious if there was no news about it and try again. We kept the Mill House under surveillance until the Challis's moved."

"But the locals knew about it," Faye reminded him. "Probably why they never attempted it again."

Laxton pressed his lips together but made no comment.

"Why would that exclude a passing motorist?" the Chief Constable asked. "Presumably, the Challis's involvement was known for the psychologist to make that statement?"

"Of course it was," Laxton agreed. "They were even interviewed by the press."

"Then why must it have been someone local?" the Chief Constable asked Faye.

Faye looked across at Laxton. Although their careers had run in tandem they had never been close, maintaining only a working relationship.

"I seem to remember that no one heard a car at the time of the attempt on Jenny's life, not even the Challis's. The Mill House and the cottages around the Badgers are quite isolated and when the culprit ran away it would have been expected that a car would have been heard at that time in the early hours."

The Chief Constable looked at Laxton.

Reluctantly, Laxton nodded agreement. "Yes, but that was only because the Challis' assumed that anyone going to the Mill House would park on the other side of the stream where they left their cars. It doesn't exclude the possibility that someone parked some distance away on the road so a car would not be heard by the cottages or the Mill house. The stream makes quite a babbling noise too." His increasing frustration showed. "Alec, you know what a state Mrs Challis was in even when you blokes got there some twenty minutes later. She was in no state to remember details like that."

Faye only nodded but made no answer.

"So it's possible that it could have been someone very local, even in the cottages around the Mill House?" the Chief Constable remarked.

"We questioned every one of them. Alec will tell you. We knocked them up in the middle of the night and found every one of them either in bed or in their bed clothes."

Morrison asked when the attempt on Jenny's life had been

180

made. Faye said it was nearly two weeks after Katy's disappearance.

"So if it was George Fuller, the groundsman, where was he staying until then? We know he left the golf club the day after Katy went missing."

"Perhaps he had an accomplice," Faye suggested.

Morrison thought of Julie Norris' remark that she suspected George wasn't into women. The doubts must have registered on her face for the Chief Constable to ask what she was thinking. But another doubt had quickly supplanted the first.

"If someone came back to kill Jenny, it would have to be someone local. Why would a passing motorist risk doing that with a major police investigation going on? If the killer believed this psychologist was right and a grown-up Jenny could recognise him, it had to be someone she would know. Not a stranger. Also the attempt on Jenny's life says something else about the suspect."

"Does it? Tell us what that is from your great experience," Laxton said.

"It's not about experience," Morrison replied. "It's about analysis. However Katy was killed and whatever the reason, it was not pre-planned. It might even have been an accident. But coming for young Jenny with the intent to kill her, to kill a child; that is something else. What sort of person would do that?"

There was a long silence as the three officers failed to answer and the frustration turned to anger on Laxton's face as he glowered at Morrison. Faye suggested it would be someone desperate and not very bright to believe what the psychologist said.

"Like a young groundsman," the Chief Constable added.

"But not a killer – or there would have been other murders

or sexual assaults." Morrison told them.

"So we are looking for someone local who knew how to find Jenny, and someone who believed Jenny would identify them when she was older," the Chief Constable said.

"But didn't you say, Daphne, that the groundsman had only worked at Stokesey for a few months?" Faye asked her.

Morrison agreed.

"Did you find if Katy had a regular boyfriend?"

"No. Her family said she didn't and her friends said she had a teen thing about a young builder but he wasn't interested in her. I don't think she could have been seeing someone regularly – and certainly not while she was looking after Jenny.

"Then why would this groundsman want to kill Jenny?"

"And just because a crank said she would recognise him years later. Bloody nonsense," Laxton said.

"What about this chap, Hewlett, Daphne? Didn't you say he lived in one of the cottages?"

"He wasn't living there at the time but his mother was."

"Who is Hewlett?" Laxton asked, astonished that it was someone he hadn't heard of. Morrison explained who he was.

"And why do you know about him?"

"I couldn't find a reference to him having been interviewed at the time."

"Why would we do that if he was living at Bredon?"

"Because he lived next to the Badgers for years and knew Katy from when she was a child."

Laxton failed to stop a degree of colour showing on his face. "I have no idea whether he was at the cottages that night, "he mumbled. "I'll have to check the files – or you will. You have them."

"I will," Morrison responded.

Not knowing about the attempt on Jenny Challis' life she had seen no reason to check where Hewlett was at that time.

"Is he on your radar, Daphne?" the Chief Constable asked.

"He fits. He had trail-bikes, he knows the ground, he was unmarried at the time, and he had seen Katy Rose grow from a child. But he says he has an alibi for the day she disappeared; he said he was in Stokesey delivering venison. He's been cooperative and even showed me where Katy could have been buried in the marshes. If he was staying at his mother's cottage when this attempt was made on Jenny then I would have to say he is a likely suspect – but since the information of a golf buggy being used and this George character disappearing, he wouldn't fit any of that criteria."

"I like that criteria," CS Faye said. "It is more than plausible."

"I thought it had been decided that the groundsman would have no cause to worry about what the crank woman said. And he disappeared soon afterwards. Why would he want to kill Jenny if he wasn't going to stay here?" Laxton argued.

"I think there might have been two people involved," Morrison said. She repeated Julie Norris's idea that George might not have been interested in women. "He could have been involved with one of the Stokesey Members. I didn't tell you, sir. A golf-club was found in the woods very near where Katy's shoe was found. I've sent it for possible DNA id. Perhaps Katy surprised George and a golf club member in the woods."

"You mean, homosexuals?" The Chief Constable asked.

"Yes, sir."

The men took a few moments to consider the idea. Faye nodded his approval.

"I've asked Jennings to look again at the interviews with the members of the golf club," Morrison added

183

encouragingly; she could see the doubt on her chief's face.

"It would certainly make more sense if two people were involved." Faye said. "One could have taken Jenny down to the road while the other hid Katy's body,"

"And later buried it somewhere or took it elsewhere," Morrison said.

There was further discussion about whether Katy would have been buried somewhere near Drovers' Hill or taken by car from the golf club. The Chief Constable reiterated his opinion that the first was more likely and he argued the difficulties of getting Katy away from a busy golf club. Morrison was asked to describe what she had learned about other possible sites for burial near Drovers' Hill and she repeated the most likely place would be the soft ground off the fender path across the marshes.

"Apart from the woods the rest of the area is shallow soil on sandstone. A local would know that,."

"So do we search the marshes?" the Chief Constable asked.

"It needn't be a big operation," Morrison said. "A small team could handle it."

"If there is any chance of finding Katy I don't think we can ignore it," Faye said. "The idea that two people could have been involved is a strong one, and it opens up the possibilities."

"All right. Let's do it. Alec, can you liaise with tech branch and arrange it?"

Laxton had been noticeably subdued in the last few minutes.

"What do you want from me, sir?" he asked reluctantly.

"If we find a body we'll want a murder investigation from you," the CC answered

"If you find a body. Good luck to that, sir."

184

The search of the marshes began a week after the abrasive meeting. A team of six, a police forensic anthropologist, a dog-handler and a GPR imaging team were collected and transported by Land Rover and trailer to Stokesey. Access to the Fender path and the marshes from the town was prevented to vehicles by a railed fence beside which a style allowed pedestrians to pass. The same restriction was repeated at Upper Stokesey for access onto the Ridgeway, a fact that Morrison had taken on-board when considering the restrictions for the physical transportation of a body from Drover's Hill. With the permission of the National Trust, part of the fence was removed to allow the police vehicles to access the area.

The demography of the search area was the narrow path which followed the River Fender towards the estuary and ran more or less parallel with Drover's Hill to the point where Morrison and Penny Featherstone had turned off it at a right angle onto the promontory which formed the western part of the crescent shape of the hill and was the boundary of the Bishop's estate. Before it reached that cross-point, the little river was no more than a running stream of eight foot width and beyond that it could not even be identified as it ran into the mud flats and trickled through them to the estuary.

A tent was set-up at the junction of the Fender path and the Ridgeway path and access to it from the Ridgeway path was taped and staked to keep walkers on the Ridgeway path. Inside the tent the various experts exchanged opinions as to how the search should be organised and listened to the Forensic Anthropologist's instructions of what they should and should not do if they thought they had found something needing further investigation. Daphne Morrison mapped out the search plan.

"There is no need to go to the other side of the Fender as, to cross it, they would have to go into Stokesey. So we need only test the ground immediately on this side of the path as no one would carry a body very far from the path."

The officers worked in twos, wearing harnesses and roped to each other. They carried steel probes to test the ground and wore waders. They worked in sections, twenty feet apart, and ventured in straight lines out from the path, testing the ground for firmness and where they found an area large enough for a grave to have been dug, the cadaver dog was brought in to investigate it and if it showed any prolonged interest the GPR device was used. GPR radar identification worked unpredictably on wet ground and at shallow penetration but it would respond to ground disturbance and trace any image such as a skeleton.

Dogs were even less predictable. They were trained to identify the gases of decomposition and, in one famous case had been successful even scenting such traces thirty years after the body had been removed.

The areas that were too wet were ignored as being too dangerous to bear the weight of someone carrying a body.

The teams worked slowly outwards and along the course of the path, marking each square that had been tested. It took them nearly two weeks to reach the junction of the path leading from the promontory of the downs and one or two of them were already sceptical as to the possibility of success.

"How far do you want us to go?" one of them asked Morrison.

"As far as we have to," she replied.

"We'll be in the bloody estuary if we go much further," the officer argued, addressing the remark more to his colleagues than to Morrison.

"There's at least another two months work before you reach that," Morrison told him. "Look, I know it's no fun, especially when it's pissing down as it has been sometimes. But just ask yourselves; how long would you do this if it was your daughter you were trying to find?"

They had been at it another two days when the dog showed interest at a point beyond the path that led from the Bishop's house and turned towards the estuary and the duck-shooting hides. It was a small hillock of tufted marsh-grass and was on a firm spur leading off the path. The dog ran around it and barked and its handler had to restrain its excitement. "Don't probe," the team leader instructed the men and the GPR equipment was brought to the scene.

"It's a firm reading," the operator announced, studying the monitor. The area was taped and the Forensic Anthropologist was called in.

The site where the object was found was tented and walk-boards were laid on the soggy ground. The forensic scientist examined the on-screen images from both the GPR camera and a thermal imaging machine.

"It certainly looks positive for a body," she said. "It's approximately two feet down. The sub-level will be very wet. There is a degree of sphagnum in it so there is a good chance the body will be in some state of preservation. We will have to recover it in-situ as much as we can," she told the collection of officers.

"How will you do that?" Morrison asked.

"We'll skim off the top soil for examination then stake-out the parameters, cut below the object, insert steel polls and lift the whole lot onto a trailer – or at least, that's what we'll try to do. It will take a lot of manpower and a four by four with a crane,I'm afraid."

Daphne Morrison could not help enjoying the

187

congratulations that were fed back to her from the Chief Constable and other officers – but not from Detective Superintendent Colin Laxton or his team. Her persistence had been vindicated.

The recovery of the body was difficult, as predicted by the forensic officer. It was essential, as a probable crime scene, to keep as much of it as possible intact. The trickiest part of the operation was to get a four wheel drive vehicle and craned trailer to the scene. The path was mostly packed well enough to hold the vehicle but had been made for horse-drawn carts and was barely wide enough for a modern wheel-base and a lot of usage was made of steel plates along the edges to prevent the path from collapsing.

The excavation of the body was less difficult than had been thought. The ground around the site was excavated and drained leaving the body entombed in a rectangle of peat, now raised like a pyre. The steel poles were easily inserted through the sub-soil and steel plates were then knocked under the whole using the poles as guide rails. Four poles were left under the plates and chains were threaded through them and attached to the swing crane. What then looked like a rectangle of peat, some one metre deep, was craned slowly upwards and swung onto the trailer. It was then sheeted over beneath a layer of ice-blocks to prevent it from drying out.

The most difficult part of the operation was for the vehicle to reverse its way back to the Ridgeway as there was no room for it to turn and, perhaps appropriate considering its cargo, that alone took one and a half hours of cursing and shouting.

Daphne Morrison inwardly waved it goodbye and gave permission for their recovery site to be de-camped and she and some of the other officers retired to the nearest pub, each of them feeling a sense of triumph, like marathon runners finishing the course.

Daphne Morrison's triumphalism did not last very long. Three days later the forensic scientist who had supervised the operation called her.

"It's not the body you wanted," she said. "It's male. But the good news is, it's in a remarkable state of preservation. A perfect bog body."

When she arrived at the forensic unit, Morrison found the body had created great interest in the local scientific world. There were many people in white coats standing around it, exchanging views, and it took some moments for the forensic officer to see her.

"Ah, Inspector," she said and the white coats parted and turned to regard her. She regarded them back, looking at each one in turn until one or two of them got the message and mumbled apologies and began to leave but Morrison stopped them before they reached the door.

"Just a minute," she said. "I don't want any of you talking about this outside of here. This is the victim of a crime and if any news of it gets out before we are ready to release it I will know where to come to chew your balls." The offenders filed out, hiding their embarrassment.

"Sorry," the pathologist said. "But you can't blame them; having our very own bog body is not an every day occurrence."

Morrison made no attempt to alleviate her censure. She looked at the body on the table. All residue of its entombment had been cleaned from it. It was dressed in recognisable corduroy trousers, a jacket and a pullover beneath it. It wore socks and leather shoes and the hands lying along its sides were a mixture of grey and red colour and looked like wax images. The face was of similar colour and effect, the skin looking like stretched, pale leather, the bones beneath it accentuated - a little like the pictures of starving prisoners she had seen in history books. But the face was noticeably of a young man and the hair above it was perfectly preserved even though it was now of the same reddish colour that predominated elsewhere. The clothes were all of recognisable origin but were loose as, she later discovered, the skeleton would have shrunk beneath them.

"Amazing," was her comment.

"Isn't it," the scientist agreed.

"How long do you think it's been there?"

"About sixty years."

The scientist enjoyed the look of surprise on Morrison's face.

"How can you tell?" Morrison asked.

In answer the scientist picked something from a table and handed it to her. It was a leather wallet and the gold embossed dedication was still clearly readable; *To Gerhardt. Xmas, 1945* she read. Again, her face registered her disbelief.

"Is it possible?" she asked.

"Oh, yes, Inspector. Bog bodies have been found in this state after two thousand years. The ground conditions were mostly fibric peat; the acidic and anaerobic conditions prevent the vegetation from decaying and the lack of oxygen in the wet conditions would prevent the soft-fibre decomposing. He had been put into the ground face-down which preserved his features even more than if he had been the other way round. My next problem is how to preserve him in this state long enough for an autopsy."

"To find out how he died?"

"I know that already."

She picked up a metal probe and held it above a dark patch on the man's chest. She then inserted the probe deep into the patch and twirled it round.

"A hole right through his body. I recovered lead shot and pieces of wood fibre from it."

"He was shot?"

"With a twelve-bore. I would say it was held against his chest and both barrels released. He must have been standing or lying against something made of wood."

"How awful. Someone didn't like him. Gerhardt sounds German and 1945 was just after the war. It could have been a hate-crime."

The scientist handed Morrison a metal disk on a chain.

"Hauptmann Gerhardt Muller, Luftwaffe. This is his ID tag. There were several prisoner of war camps in this area. My father remembers them. We've also got these."

She showed Morrison what looked like photographs but were unidentifiable as the images had faded.

"And this,"

She held a folded piece of paper in her callipers.

"Is there any chance of recovering them?" Morrison asked.

"I doubt it. We can do amazing things with science, but I don't think the paper will reveal much now. They were inside his wallet otherwise they would have completely disintegrated. We also found this packet of Lucky Strike in his pocket."

"What are Lucky Strikes?"

"Lucky Strikes were popular American cigarettes during the war."

"Well, it's not my case. CID will have to start an investigation," Morrison told her. "Have you taken any pictures of the body? I think that face is good enough to launch an information trawl."

"Yes. Your Photographic Unit could reproduce a perfect image. I can tell them what colour his eyes were and his skin and hair were fair. Should I contact you with the rest of the autopsy?"

"Until they decide who will handle it. Thanks."

Despite the interest and excitement in the forensic unit and the police sections regarding the find, Daphne Morrison could raise no enthusiasm for it. Her disappointment at not finding Katy Rose was palpable and it was not made any easier by the many sarcastic comments and jokes levelled at her from the CID section and Colin Laxton did not disguise his glee when he told her to keep on digging and she might find another Piltdown Man.

The Chief Constable was a little more sympathetic. "We've uncovered another crime at least. Not that we needed any more."

The CID appointed a detective constable, Christine West, to head-up what they considered to be a box-ticking exercise; no one had reported a crime, it was colder than the ice-age and who cared about a dead German prisoner of war?

The autopsy confirmed the cause of death was as it had been reported to Morrison by the pathologist. The victim's age was no more than twenty five years and the contents of his stomach were likely to have been processed egg and grain bread. He had a deep leg scar, probably a wound that had required surgery, and his liver showed signs of alcohol addiction. This information was telephoned to Morrison prior to a printed report.

"Have you sent the photographs to our photographic unit?" she asked and was told they would be included in the file. "But you may not need to use them," the forensic officer told her. "There are labels sown into the clothing with the name 'Geoffrey Foden' printed on them. The Fodens are still around aren't they?"

Like everyone else, the Chief Constable was intrigued by the find and the history surrounding it but when Foden's name was involved he was quick to see the dangers ahead. "I want you to work with Inspector Morrison on this," he told the CID. "She's already talked to Foden with regard to the Katy Rose Lewis case. He's a bit prickly and he told me he didn't mind Morrison."

He knew exactly how much Foden had minded Morrison but knowing the age and inexperience of the detective Laxton had detailed to investigate the German's death, he thought Morrison's diplomatic skills were needed.

Morrison suggested the dead image of Gerhardt Muller should be reproduced and brought to life by the visual imaging department so they would have a lifelike portrait for their enquiries.

"You don't think anyone is still around to identify him do you?" the detective asked her.

"I doubt if anyone who might have met him is still around; it was over sixty years ago. But someone might know of him," she replied. "There has to be a reason why he was wearing someone else's clothes."

She did not make the same mistake of going to the Foden's house without first making an appointment. Arabella took her call and said she would ask her husband to phone her. When he did, Charles Foden was less combative than on their previous meeting. He even sounded apprehensive, which Morrison was quick to recognise.

When she and the DC arrived at the house they were led into the kitchen by Arabella and offered tea or coffee which they both declined. Arabella left them to call her husband and Morrison studied the photographs on the wall. .

Foden surprised her by being atypically sociable, shaking hands with them both and offering them refreshment.

193

Morrison let Christine West take the lead.

"Do you recognise this man?" the DC asked, showing the reconstructed picture of Gerhardt to Foden. Foden's face expressed a release of tension.

"No. Should I?"

"We think his name is Gerhardt Muller," the detective told him.

It would be difficult to describe what happened to Foden; surprise, shock, interest, they all showed on his face like waves of light and when he spoke his voice was barely audible. "You have found him?" he said

"Do you know who he was?" the detective asked.

Foden recovered his strength. "He was a Luftwaffe pilot. He was at the POW camp at Stokesey."

"Is he on this photograph?" Morrison asked. She had been studying the pictures on the kitchen wall. Foden got up and pointed.

"That's him in the foreground."

"How do you know of him?"

He told them of Gerhardt's friendship with his father and his aunt.

"But I don't understand; why have you got his picture? Where did you find him?"

"Where did you think he was?" Morrison asked.

"He went back to Germany," he answered.

"How do you know that?"

He told them the story of his Father's plan to prevent Gerhardt returning because he would have been sent to a Soviet labour camp and how he had been handed to the police by his Grandfather.

"Why did he do that?" Morrison asked.

"I should have thought because it was the right thing to do. And probably to stop my father getting into trouble."

"But your family and your father must have been very fond of Gerhardt to take a risk like that to keep him here?"

"Yes, they were. My Aunt was in love with him. She spent the rest of her life hoping to find him. Where did you find him?" he asked again, puzzlement showing in his face.

"In the marshes," Morrison said and nodded her head towards the window. Foden's astonishment was dramatic.

"You found him here. You found Gerhardt here?" he said. "How could he be here?"

"With the help of two barrels of shot through his chest."

Foden almost fell onto a seat and stared at them.

"He was shot?" he asked weakly.

"Not handed to the police. We have no record of that happening," the detective said.

Foden stared at the table as though he expected the old wood to give him the answers to the many questions in his head. One of them suddenly made sense.

"How did you know to come here?" he asked.

Detective West told him of the clothes the German was wearing with the name Geoffrey Foden sown into them. Foden almost smiled.

"My Father went to boarding school. "We had to put our name on everything."

"It proves your story of what your father was trying to do. They must have exchanged clothes. Didn't your father ever tell you about it?"

Foden explained his father had died before he was born.

"So only your Grandfather really knew what happened to Gerhardt?"

Foden nodded emphatically. "Yes." Then a strange noise started deep in his throat that gradually became disjointed notes of sound, quavering between laughter and despair.

"All those years. All those years, Grandpa let me think we

could find him," he told them. "I promised Aunt Sheila, you see. I promised her I would find Gerhardt. Poor Aunt Sheila. She went mad worrying for Gerhardt. And he was here all the time. And Grandpa knew it."

His voice faltered. The officers let him continue his reverie in silence.

"I did find his family in Germany," he eventually concluded and seemed to be aware of them again.

"You know where they are?"

He told them how long it had taken for the German authorities to discover Gerhardt's mother and sister had moved to Frankfurt before the Russians had reached Cottbus. "Gerhardt's mother had a brother in Frankfurt. I went to the Frankfurt Trade Fair often and each time I went I searched the directories. Every year for three years. I spoke to dozens of Mullers and then I found his sister. She had married but had kept her own name, hoping Gerhardt would one day do what I did." He told them how young Germans were sent to Russian labour camps in Siberia. "That is what we all thought had happened to him," he said.

"Is his sister still alive?" the detective asked.

"I don't know. She would now be in her eighties if she is. We corresponded a bit. But she did have children," he said.

"Do you have an address for her?"

"I will find her last letter," he said.

He left them in the kitchen and returned some minutes later. He handed a letter to the DS, "This is twenty two years old," he told her.

"You kept the letter that long?" Morrison asked

"My aunt did. She read them often. She died recently."

"I'm sorry," the detective sympathised. She studied the letter. "She writes very good English."

The letter described how they had searched for her brother

and how their mother had died, not knowing what had happened to her husband or her son. It concluded, *"It is comforting to know my brother found some peace and happiness with your family, even if it was only for a short time."*

She handed the letter to Morrison. "Very sad," Morrison said as she handed the letter back to Christine West and asked her to note the address. "Let us hope we can still trace her or her family. At least they will be able to give Gerhardt a proper funeral."

"I will pay for his body to be sent over to them," Foden said.

"Why would you do that?" the detective asked.

"He had such an effect on my family," Foden answered. "I think we owe him a decent burial at least. And to return him to his family."

"That's good of you. Let us hope his sister or someone in the family is still alive to receive him."

The police officers prepared to leave.

"Can I see him?" Foden suddenly asked.

The DC looked to Morrison for guidance. "Why would you want to see a skeleton?" Morrison asked him. Foden looked surprised.

"But, you said he was found in the marshes," he said.

"So?"

"Wouldn't that preserve his body?" he asked.

"Yes, it did," Morrison answered thoughtfully.

"Isn't that how you got the photograph?" Foden asked.

"Of course, you know all about photography, don't you? Yes, Mr. Foden. that's how we got the photograph; his body is that well preserved. I don't see why you shouldn't see it if it's all right with Forensics. I'll arrange it."

"Thank you, Inspector."

They began to move towards the hall.

"Do you have any guns?" Morrison asked.

"No, Inspector. I gave up shooting in my teens. I prefer photography."

"But what about the photographs in your kitchen, your family seemed as if they did a lot of shooting?"

"Yes. Both my grandfathers enjoyed it. I sent their guns for auction when they died. Why do you ask? You couldn't match buckshot to a gun."

"No. But we might match the DNA off the body to a gun."

"Well, I'm sorry to disappoint you," Foden said. "It would be useless to find the guns now I suspect." He walked with them to the front door.

"We'll need you to write down everything you know about Gerhardt Muller and your family," the DC told him. Do you have a computer, sir?"

"Yes. I have several."

"You could email it to me and once I'm satisfied I've no more questions perhaps you would come to the station and sign it."

Foden said he would. They thanked him and stepped out onto the porch.

"What made you look in the marshes? Were you looking for him there?" he asked.

Morrison wondered why it had taken him so long to ask the question.

"No. We were looking for Katy Rose Lewis," she answered. "But whoever killed Katy knew not to put her body in the marshes."

As they walked to their car, Christine West looked at Morrison. "I'll bet there are a few more skeletons in that family cupboard," she said.

Morrison didn't answer. Her brain was still computing

many thoughts and as she got into the car she saw Foden still standing in the doorway, looking after them.

The Gerhardt Muller case assumed only administrative purpose as far as the police were concerned. Foden made his statement and was allowed to view the body. He stood for a long time staring through the glass at it but made no comment when he eventually turned away.

"There will be a coroner's inquest," the DC told him. "Then the body can be sent to Germany. We did find his sister."

Foden was genuinely pleased by the news. Afterwards West and Morrison ticked-off the bullet points on the To Do agenda. "Death by persons unknown," Morrison guessed at the coroner's verdict. "We can only go on what Foden has told us. Nobody else is going to be alive to tell us anything different," she said.

"Do you think the Grandfather killed him?" the detective asked.

"It looks like it. According to him he said he handed Gerhardt to the police, which he clearly didn't. So he must have shot him or got someone else to do it."

"Why? Why not just let him be sent home?"

"That's a damn good question," Morrison said.

"Perhaps it wasn't about stopping him seeing the daughter. Perhaps he did something else to her."

"Mmm. You could be right. Rape would be a strong motive for murder."

The case-file was closed after a coroner brought in the verdict Morrison had predicted. Foden kept his promise and paid for the body to be returned to the family where it was met by the mayor of Frankfurt and Gerhardt's tearful sister and children and grandchildren. The story received major media coverage and Foden spent many uncomfortable hours avoiding interviews and photographers. Two film companies approached him, offering to buy the story rights and his discomfort increased to the point where he threatened to sue a national newspaper who had carelessly suggested his grandfather had shot the German because he wanted to marry his daughter. The newspaper settled out of court and as Foden became increasingly litigious the clamour for his attention dropped away and after Gerhardt's reunion with his family and his burial the story was mostly forgotten.

But the case was not forgotten by Charles Foden. The discovery of Gerhardt's body had brought the past flooding painfully into his consciousness and the anger he showed towards the media was nothing compared to that which burned at his inside.

In the eye of the storm he had sent his wife and the dogs to stay with her sister but the cess pool still lapped around his office and factory buildings. He avoided personal contact with it by driving from the electronic doors of his garage to the office but when that became too annoying for his workers he decided to run his office from his photographic studio in his grandfather's old house which had not yet been discovered by the news-hounds.

He had done no photographic work for a long time and when he had used his studio he had walked there, but as he drove into the stable yard and reversed into the garage area and switched off the engine, his stomach registered his doubt that his desperate action might not have been the wisest decision. The past was everywhere around him. His grandfather's old Daimler/Jaguar was still there, shrouded under a cover like Miss Haversham's room, awaiting its reintroduction to the light, and the tethering rings on the walls reminded him of the stalls which had long been removed to make space for the mechanical horses of a new

200

age. He sat there for some time, staring up at the timbers of the ceiling, much as he remembered Aunt Sheila doing some years before. Her protests were still sharp in his memory and his anger was the deeper for the slow drip-feeding of the past, revealing the depths of deception and pain that had been inflicted on Aunt Sheila and on himself.

BACKSTORY 2.
THE FIRST CHRONICLE OF CHARLES HENDERSON FODEN

Charles Henderson Foden had celebrated his twenty first birthday in the Guildhall of the city as had his father, Geoffrey, two decades previously. The building had been renovated between the two events as if to demonstrate the financial progress made from one event to the other. The panels of Victorian murals had been cleaned to their original colours and their elaborate plastered frames had been re-gilded as had the plaster frieze of the ceiling. The four massive glass chandeliers which had been removed during the war were now in place and were reflected in the layered varnish of the oak flooring, and the fretwork of sticky safety tape was no longer protecting the stained-glass of the windows. The edible fare too had improved beyond the dreams of the rationed generation. Smoked salmon with quail eggs and asparagus was followed by medallions of Welsh lamb and fresh fruit with a chocolate parfait and Continental cheeses. Bottles of white and red Burgundy were generously positioned along the tables next to pyramids of roses, lilies-of-the-valley and gardenia. The music also reflected the changes of the times: on the balcony a pianist and cellist played Mozart and Strauss while the guests ate and talked and on the lower floor of the building the playing-style of Glen Miller and Geraldo had been replaced by a disco of disparate rhythms and frenzied interpretation.

Charles Foden was also more fortunate than his father in having many more contemporary guests. Having just received a First in Mechanical Engineering his university friends had joined many others from his boarding school to form a raucous and jolly core of youthful exuberance, unmitigated by wartime experiences. But those times and his father were not forgotten. Charles made a good speech. He held up a framed photograph of his uniformed father.

"This handsome young man was one of our many war heroes and, although you could not guess it from the genes assembled in my face, he was my father. He celebrated his twenty first in this very spot but soon afterwards met with an accident that took him from us."

He looked to where his mother sat with his grandparents on the top table but saw no reaction in her face.

"It has always been and will always be the greatest sadness of my life that I was not able to know him and he was not able to know me. But I hope that somewhere, somehow, he is able to see us now and know how grateful I am to him for giving me this day to share with all my friends and family and I would like us all to toast my gratitude. To Father."

He thanked his mother and both his grandparents for all they had done for him and then he he remembered his aunt and wished she had been there.

"Aunt Sheila, my father's sister, is another absentee who is not forgotten. She is unable to be with us but I would like to be able to tell her we remembered her and to wish for her, happiness and a full recovery." They toasted Aunt Sheila.

When the younger guests had departed to the lower floor and the noise of the disco, the older generations clustered together along the tables that bordered a space of clear floor where some of them shuffled to Gershwin now being played appreciatively by the pianist in the music gallery.

At the top table, Sir Toby and his wife and the Foden grandparents were visited by various friends and it was early into the evening that one of them, Reginald Simpson of Simpson, Jones and Simpson: solicitors, came and sat before grandpa Foden. He apologised that he had to depart early as he had to drive to London the following morning to prepare an important hearing at the High Court on the Monday following the weekend.

"I was hoping to have a word with Charles," he told grandpa Foden and took an envelope from his inside pocket. "I need to give him this."

Foden's shrewd eyes quickly assessed the envelope.

"A Birthday present?" he smiled, hoping it would contain a cheque.

"No, we sent that to the house," Simpson explained. "It's from his father."

Grandpa Foden's smile quickly disappeared.

"We were instructed to give it to Charles when he came of age," Simpson explained.

"I doubt if you'll have any success getting to him in that crush," Foden said, indicating the lower floor. "Why don't you let me give it to him tomorrow? I don't think he needs to be reminded of his father any more at this time."

"No. Quite," Simpson conceded. "Perhaps that is a better idea. If you don't mind?"

The envelope was handed over and grandpa Foden put it into his inside pocket.

Sir Toby and his wife were the first to break-up the party. Lady Henderson had noted her husband's fatigue had increased with the second glass of brandy he was sharing with grandpa Foden and she was concerned he would soon start being rude to people. Their daughter, Fiona said she would drive them back as she too had quietly decided that she had prolonged her duty beyond its need.

"We can leave the rest of the evening to the children," she said.

During the evening, Fiona had realised the event was as much of a milepost for her as it was for her son. She and his father had had no time to make a separate home together and she had continued to live with her parents in the old mansion after Geoffrey's death, so the physical aspect of her life had changed little from her childhood to the present and the desire for change had grown steadily since Charles had left for boarding school and it was now openly acknowledged by her as Charles' future seemed clearly defined, and an American lady, Jess Mavrolean, was foremost in her plans.

Fiona had developed her interest in horses to form a small stud which had become increasingly successful and sufficient to enable her to be financially independent from her parents, which was a great relief to Sir Toby as he found his army pension and his late father's investments as a Lloyds Name, insufficient to maintain the family home as the war had wrought a social revolution by destroying the selective benefits of cheap labour.

Although Sir Toby and his wife had been Charles' emotional and loving support as he grew up and his mother's time had been given mostly to her horses, Sir Toby had supported grandpa Foden in persuading Charles to take an engineering rather than an arts or language degree, which was his natural inclination, and he shrewdly realised that Foden's business might be the only chance there was to save the estate which had been in the family for four hundred years. He had only daughters and his hopes that Geoffrey Foden would answer his prayers had been cruelly dashed at his unexpected death. Now those hopes rested with his grandson.

Charles' grandparents had been the total influence in his life. His love for both families was deeply felt and although he recognised the emotional motives behind their arguments, he was not averse to the advantages of having an immediate income when he left university, and it had not been a chore for him to do an engineering degree as, from a little boy, he had been in awe of the huge machines grandpa Foden manufactured and some of his happiest memories were of riding on the tractors when they were tested after leaving the factory. So Charles Henderson Foden's future was, as his mother had reasoned, clearly defined.

It was almost midnight when grandpa Foden and his wife returned home. As Foden had paid for the celebrations he had naturally assumed the role of chief host and had remained at the party until the last of the parental guests had departed, leaving only the youngsters to continue the festivities. As his wife took herself to bed, Foden went into his study to pour himself his habitual bed-time whisky. Sheila appeared in the doorway.

"Hello, father. Do you know if there was any mail for me today?" she asked.

Her father sighed. "No, Sheila. You asked me that this morning and, no doubt, you will ask me that again several times tomorrow. Goodnight."

Sheila's face slumped with her shoulders as she turned and retraced her steps across the hall and climbed stiffly up the stairs.

Foden looked at the photographs of a young Sheila and Geoffrey upon his desk as he sipped the whisky, then he remembered the envelope Simpson had given him. He took it from his pocket and read, "To My Child" written on it in Geoffrey's hand. He unlocked a drawer in the desk and dropped the envelope into it, he then switched off the lights and went wearily to bed.

It was almost mid-day when Charles and his few house-guests assembled unsteadily in the Henderson's kitchen and it was mid-afternoon by the time the last of them had got themselves together and departed for the railway station and their separate lives.

Charles found his grandfather in the library smoking a cigarette and reading the previous days Times.

"Hello Grandfather. I hope you didn't mind my friend's disturbing your routine," Charles apologised. His grandfather put down the newspaper and smiled.

"Good Heavens! Not at all, dear boy. I enjoyed having them here."

He indicated for Charles to sit. "Did you enjoy your party?" he asked.

"Yes. Very much. I think everyone enjoyed it – thanks to you and Grandmother. You've been very kind to me. I do appreciate all you've done."

"Grandpa and Grandma Foden did their bit too."

"Yes. I'm very fortunate having you all as grandparents."

"Dear chap, you are the light of our lives. How could we be anything less than good to you." his grandfather smiled.

Charles nodded sadly. "I know. I wish...I wish Father could have been with us."

His grandfather felt the moment needed his wife's arms to enclose the young man who suddenly resembled again the little boy who used to sit on his knee and ask him endless questions. "So do I, Charles," was all he could give.

"What was he like?" Charles asked.

"Your father? He was a splendid chap," his grandfather said enthusiastically, pleased that the moment had passed.

"Then you did like him?"

"Good Heavens! Of course I liked him. I liked him very much."

"I'm glad you liked him. I think I might have liked him too."

"And he would have loved you, Charles. He loved having young people around – like me. I think it's something we soldiers learn: that friendship is important. Your father was very good at it. He was even friendly with the German POW's here. I admired that; making friends with the enemy."

"There were German prisoners here, in Stokesey?" Charles asked in surprise.

"Yes. There was a prison camp there. Italians and then German Luftwaffe. Your father became good friends with one of them: Gerhardt. He was a decent chap. He worked in our stables sometimes."

" Amazing. Were they allowed out like that?"

His grandfather explained how the prisoners worked on the farms and in his grandpa's factory once the war had finished. It was a world that Charles and his contemporaries were unaware of, even though the events were fresh in their parent's lives, and he listened attentively as his grandfather elaborated on his favourite subject: war and international relations. When the old man's brain became slower to answer Charles' many questions and Charles judged, correctly, that it was time for his grandfather's afternoon doze, he changed the subject to ease himself away.

"Grandfather. Do you know the Grangers? They farm over at Bredon?"

"Jock Granger? Of course I do. He was Colonel of my old regiment. Good chap. Caught a mortar shell at Tobruk. Big chunk of leg missing. Why d'you ask?"

"His granddaughter, Arabella was at my party. Pretty girl, wore a blue dress. Her parents are friends of Mother."

"Can't say I noticed her," his grandfather confessed. "So many pretty fillies there. But I know who you're talking about."

"I got on rather well with Arabella. I thought I might ask her over for dinner. Would that be all right?"

"Splendid idea. If she's Jock's granddaughter she'll be a decent gal. Well done, Charles. It's better to get those things over and done with early, so you can get on with life."

Charles was soon invited to his other grandparents for dinner and knew the main topic of discussion would be his future with Foden Agricultural Machinery. His twenty first Birthday celebration had been organised to coincide with his homecoming from university and after a short sabbatical he had taken to go with a group of friends to Norway, so there had been very little time to socialise with his other family before the celebrations and he looked forward to being alone with them even though he knew his grandpa would dominate the evening talking business as he normally had no opportunity at home to indulge his abiding interest. But Charles would not mind. His affection for his other grandparents and for Aunt Sheila was as deep as it was for Sir Toby and his grandmother.

Although he had lived with his mother's parents until he went to boarding school, he had been a regular visitor to his Foden family. Once he had learned to handle his own pony he was allowed to ride it across Drovers' Hill where he would regularly meet up with Aunt Sheila and together they would ride down to Stokesey and his father's home. He had always been fond of Aunt Sheila and had not noticed her oddities until he was older and visited during his school holidays.

When he had gone away to school, Sheila had then suddenly lost the urge to ride and her enthusiasm in helping Charles' mother at the stud had steadily declined until she stopped helping completely and showed no further interest in horses which had once been the main pleasure of her life. She had become more withdrawn and suffered increasingly with bouts of depression and Charles could not help feeling guilty that his absence had much to do with her condition, even though everyone had assured him that his company in growing up had only interrupted it. So his enthusiasm at seeing his Foden family again was tempered by his apprehension as to his aunt's condition.

He had been disappointed and concerned when he had been told by his grandpa that she was not well enough to attend his party but had not been given an explanation as to the reason so when he arrived at the house he was pleasantly surprised to see his Aunt looking healthy and he laughed as she hugged and kissed him until her father told her, "Enough, Sheila. You'll smother the boy," and Sheila ceased her demonstrations like a scolded dog.

During dinner, Sheila's interest in the conversation wavered between bouts of surprisingly incisive questions to almost comatose disinterest, which was not so surprising and not unlike his grandma's attitude as his grandpa launched enthusiastically into the business opportunities of the emerging international markets and the need to get a foothold for their products overseas.

"I think that is a role you could take on, Charles," he told him. "You're young and presentable. I'm too old to compete with the Germans and Japanese. We need someone to get over to the trade fairs and tell them that our machinery is the best there is. How do you feel about that?" Charles said he enjoyed travelling but also hoped to be able to contribute something on the design side of things.

Grandma Foden eventually steered the conversation to family matters when her husband ran out of prepared ideas and Charles took the opportunity of bringing Sheila into the conversation when his mother's stud farm was being discussed.

"You used to help Mummy with the horses, Aunt. Didn't

210

you enjoy it?" he asked.

Sheila seemed to take a few moments as if to understand what he had said then her face lightened.

"Yes. Fiona had a lovely horse called Hero," she offered.

Charles did not remember a horse called Hero and was about to ask his aunt about it when he caught his grandpa's eye and a slight shake of his head.

"She has quite a few horses," he said carefully. You exercised them for her," he tried again. "You used to ride over with me."

"Yes. That was fun," Sheila smiled vaguely but the smile immediately disappeared and she offered no further comment and Charles felt defeated. It was when the old Henderson mansion was mentioned that Sheila again showed interest. Grandpa Foden was elaborating on the need to modernise the house and the costs involved that were most certainly beyond Sir Toby's budget.

"I can't imagine what will happen to it when your grandfather dies," he was saying. "It will have to be sold and I don't think there will be many buyers for that sort of property."

"They could turn it into a home for people like me," Sheila said and her parents were silent and avoided the look of astonishment on Charles' face.

"What do you mean: people like you, Aunt?" he laughed.

"Bad people."

Charles felt the tension coming across the table from his grandparents and knew it would be better not to persist but he could not leave the statement hanging.

"You're not a bad person, Aunt Sheila. You're very kind," he said with some conviction and hoped his aunt would be satisfied, but she wasn't.

"No, I'm not," she answered defiantly. "I killed your father.

So I'm a bad person."

The words seemed to physically hit Charles so that he recoiled in his chair.

"Don't be ridiculous, Sheila," his grandpa barked at her. "Go and check the post. Have you done it today?" Sheila's face brightened again and she seemed unaware that it was Sunday and there would be no post.

"No, Father. I'll run and see," she said and hurried from the room. Charles looked from one to the other of his grandparents, his face still pale from Sheila's words.

"Take no notice, Charles," his grandpa said. "Sheila says silly things."

"My father's death was an accident wasn't it?" he asked.

"Of course it was," his grandma told him.

"But why would Aunt Sheila say such a thing?"

"She had a breakdown because of your father's death," his grandpa explained. "They were very close and she's never been the same since we lost him."

"Why does she keep asking about the post?"

"There was some business with one of the German prisoners, of war" his grandma added. "She was smitten by one of them and when he was sent back after the war she has been expecting to hear from him ever since."

"Poor Aunt Sheila. Grandfather was telling me about the prisoners. He said Father was friends with one of them."

"Yes. It was your father's friend Sheila liked" his grandma explained.

"Was that Gerhardt?" Charles asked just as Sheila re-entered the room.

Aunt Sheila's face brightened like a child's. "Gerhardt," she gasped. "Do you know him, Charles. Do you know where he is?" she asked and she ran to him.

"No, Aunt. But I could try to find him for you."

"Oh! Would you, Charles. Would you really?" She threw her arms around him and kissed his head repeatedly until Charles laughingly held her arms then stood and hugged her back.

The next morning Charles was in the kitchen of the Henderson house when his mother came in from the stables.

"Good morning, Charles," she greeted and kissed him on the cheek. "How was it at Grandpa's last night?"

"Very well. They were very pleased to see me."

"Did he offer you a job?" his mother joked as she poured herself some coffee.

"He wants me to go to trade fairs and sell his machines."

"Is that what you want to do?"

"I don't mind. I enjoy travelling – and it would be good experience to see what the opposition is like."

"It's probably better than sitting in an office at the factory."

"Much better – but I do want to do some designing. I have some good ideas."

"Like your Great Grandfather. He invented quite a few things. You must have his genes."

"I hope so. If it wasn't for him we would still be flour millers."

Charles had been studying the old photograph of Sir Toby's shooting party which had hung on the wall as long as he could remember. It was one of the few pictures available of his father and the family were accustomed to him standing in front of it as though trying to bring it to life. "Is Gerhardt in this picture?" he asked.

His mother looked at him quickly. "Why do you ask about Gerhardt?"

Charles explained the incident with Aunt Sheila. His mother pointed to the photograph.

"That's him, in the front with your father."

Charles peered closely at the two men laughing together, as he had often done.

"He's handsome," he said.

"Yes, he was," his mother admitted.

"Was Aunt really in love with him?"

"I think she might have been. Why are you asking?"

Charles told her how he had promised Sheila he would try to find out what happened to him.

"I think you've given yourself an impossible task. Your father did his best to find that out at the time," his mother said almost coldly.

"But if you'd seen Auntie's face when I said I would try... she was so happy. I can't not try. Would she have married him if he hadn't gone back?" he asked.

"I don't know," his mother said awkwardly. "She was certainly smitten by him."

" Were he and Father good friends?"

"Yes. They were. Your father tried to keep him here."

"How did he try to do that?"

They were now sitting on the bench seat at the kitchen table with their mugs of coffee. His mother related the story of how his father and Gerhardt had exchanged clothes and of the scheme to keep Gerhardt in England because of what would happen to him if he was sent back to Germany.

"That was jolly brave of Father," Charles interrupted.

"Yes. It was. Unfortunately your Grandpa heard about it from Sheila. He found Gerhardt hiding in the room above their garage. He arrested Gerhardt and took him to the police."

Charles imagined the scene and was confused as to where his sympathy should lie.

"Why did Grandpa do that?" he eventually asked.

"Because your father could have gone to prison if he had

214

been caught trying to hide him.."

"Not to stop Gerhardt marrying Aunt Sheila?"

"I don't think Grandpa knew about their relationship so I can't think that was the reason. He knew Sheila liked him but probably thought it was no more than an infatuation – as I did. I knew how much she thought she liked him. We talked about it and the four of us, Gerhardt and Sheila and your father and I used to go out together, but it wasn't obviously so serious that I didn't think Sheila would get over it once Gerhardt had gone away."

"But she never did."

His mother sipped her coffee before answering. "No. But I think that was more because it was her fault that Grandpa found Gerhardt hiding. She blames herself for what happened to him."

"I see," Charles said thoughtfully and he too sipped his coffee. "So poor Gerhardt might have been sent to Siberia. No wonder Aunt Sheila had a nervous breakdown about it."

They sat in silence for several minutes and then Charles looked earnestly at his mother.

"Mother. Father's death was an accident wasn't it?"

His mother looked quickly frightened. "Yes. Of course it was. Why on earth are you asking that?"

Charles explained what Aunt Sheila had said about killing him. His mother was genuinely concerned.

"Why on earth would she say such a thing? Are you sure she was talking about your father and not Gerhardt?"

"She said Father – but she was very odd so I suppose she could have meant Gerhardt. Grandma said she gets confused."

"Yes. I'm sure she did. She gets very muddled, as you know."

"How did it happen?" Charles asked.

"How did what happen?"

" To Father."

"It was just one of those terrible things that can happen when we do things so often that we don't think about them. I came off one of my horses once because I hadn't fastened the cinch properly, I could have been killed as we were taking a five-foot hedge at the time. Your father was cleaning his guns ready for the weekend shoot and there must have been a cartridge left in it. I think he was also a bit distracted. He'd just collected his first film from his new camera and when I asked him what was the matter he said he was cross with the shop because they hadn't made a good job of them. Then he said he would go and clean the guns. He was probably still cross and got careless."

"What happened to the film?" Charles asked after some moments.

"I've no idea. I think Grandpa had them. He did say they weren't very good, and many of them were out of focus. But I think it was probably because your father wasn't used to the camera rather than it being the fault of the shop."

"Who was it who found Father?"

"The housekeeper's husband. Jack."

"Were you living with Grandpa then?"

"Yes."

"Why didn't you have your own house?"

His mother laughed. "All these questions. You should have been a lawyer not a mechanic."

Charles returned the smile. "I'm a mechanical engineer, mother, not a mechanic."

"Whatever. We hadn't got round to thinking about buying a house. Your father didn't have any money, only his salary and he hadn't been working in Grandpa's factory very long."

"Were you happy?"

"Of course we were."

"But you didn't have a proper wedding. You were married in the Registry Office weren't you?"

"Yes. Your father didn't want a fuss. We got married rather quickly. He suddenly decided we should – and I said yes before he changed his mind."

"So he was happy – before the accident. He knew you were pregnant didn't he?"

His mother slid along the bench seat and put her arm around him and kissed his ear.

"Oh, Charles. Yes, we were happy and he was very happy I was going to have you. He was making plans for us to go to Germany as soon as you were born and look for Gerhardt. Your father would have loved you. But we have to accept what happened and get on with our lives."

Charles nodded and his mother kissed him again before getting up as though the situation had passed.

"Would you like more coffee?" she asked. Charles declined. His mother poured herself some and then sat next to him.

"Charles. Talking about getting on with our lives; I have been thinking about what I should do with mine." She ignored the way Charles looked at her in surprise. "Well, we know what you are going to do. You're going to work with Grandpa and make a lot of money. But I don't want to be alone here."

"You're not alone. You have Grandfather and Grandmother – and I'm not going anywhere yet. I may be away from time to time on business, but it would only be for a few nights."

"But I need my own life," his mother tried.

"Are you thinking of getting married?" he asked.

"No," she laughed. "But I do have plans."

"I wouldn't mind if you got married. You're still a bit of all

217

right. You know."

His mother attacked him, tickling his ribs.

"A bit of all right, am I? Where did you learn to talk about girls like that?"

"At that posh school probably," Charles said fending her off.

"I'll have to ask for our money back. No Charles. I was thinking of going to America."

"America?" Charles slid away from her as though she had made a smell. "What about your business? I thought it was doing well," he protested.

"It is. But it's a struggle financially and I haven't got the capital it needs to develop it."

"But why America? I don't understand."

"A friend, Jess Mavrolean, has a large stud in Maryland. She asked me if I would be interested in managing it. I wouldn't have the stress of worrying about the financial situation but I could still enjoy the breeding side of it."

She studied her son's face as he contemplated the idea and she wondered if he was as mature as he seemed.

"Who's this, Jess Mavrolean?" he eventually asked.

"I met her at Newmarket last year. She came here and seemed impressed by what I was doing. I met her in London a few weeks ago when she asked me if I would go over there."

"I see."

"Do you, Charles? Do you see that I have to make a life for myself?"

"Yes, Mother – of course. It's just that, well now I'm home I thought we could get to know each other."

"Oh, Charles. Don't we know each other?" She took hold of his hand.

"Not really. I've been away at school and university so we

haven't seen very much of each other, have we?"

His mother rested her head on his shoulder.

"We will, Charles. It's not going to happen yet and you're going to be busy working and you'll probably soon have a girl friend and I'll be forgotten. I don't want to be suddenly old and not have done something for myself."

Charles turned and put his arms around her and they hugged for some moments.

"What about Grandfather and Grandmother? They will be devastated if you go too."

Fiona's two sisters had left and married some years before.

"I know. That is a bit of a problem. But they're both in their eighties. And I don't have to go immediately. Jess' stud manager is nearing retirement but he's not looking to go until she's found someone to take over from him. So there's no great hurry. And you'll be staying here won't you?"

"Yes. I suppose so. There's no need for me to go anywhere else if I'm going to work for Grandpa."

"Are you happy about that, Charles? You mustn't do it unless you really want to."

"No. I don't mind. I can't think of what else I would do. I think I'll probably enjoy making money too." They both laughed and his mother took her arm from his.

"Then that's settled. Time will sort it all out."

"I think I will need another outlet though. I don't want to get like Grandpa and think only about business. I played golf a bit at school. I enjoyed it. But I need something artistic to keep me sane. I was thinking of taking up photography."

His mother suddenly jumped up. "Wait here," she told him. She returned after some minutes and put a camera on the table in front of him.

"What's that?" Charles laughed.

"It was your father's. Gerhardt gave it to him for his Twenty First. It was given to Gerhardt by his father who disappeared during the war and Gerhardt never knew what happened to him. Your father was very touched by such a generous gesture."

Charles picked up the Leica and examined it much as his father had done many years before. Then he held it to his chest and looked tearfully up at his mother.

"Thank you," he said.

His mother kissed his head.

"Think of it as your father's present for your Twenty First," she told him

****

Time began to sort things out when Sir Toby died suddenly while attending a regimental reunion dinner. He was buried in the family chapel of the little Norman church in Stokesey. His coffin was carried by troopers from his regiment and all of Stokesey and Upper Stokesey turned out to watch the horse-drawn hearse parade through the streets. There was later a memorial service at the cathedral in the city when all the dignitaries of the county and some high-ranked military officers attended. It was a memorial service for the Henderson family history more than for Sir Toby himself.

Grandmother Henderson attended, supported by her daughters and Charles, and then took herself to bed and died two days later.

As Sir Toby had promised when Charles' father had married his daughter and added the Henderson name to his, the first male progeny would inherit the Henderson estate, hoping they would keep the family home. The old mansion needed major investment even to repair the ravages of time and to bring it up to modern standards internally would require more than the Foden business could willingly endure. Grandpa Foden was not slow in discussing the subject with Charles.

"Even if the family agreed the estate should be sold, would I find someone willing to take it on?" Charles asked.

"It has land. Some good farming land and plenty of grazing and shooting land. Good land will always find a buyer," his grandpa answered.

"But what about the house?" Charles argued. "If we sold off the land we would never find a buyer for the house – and I couldn't let it be destroyed for development."

"I agree. The estate must be kept together. Besides, the house is Listed so it can't be altered. I'm sure there will be some romantic millionaire willing to spend money on it."

Charles was reluctant to sell, knowing how much the house meant to Sir Toby, but his mother concurred with his grandpa's opinion.

"I can't see what else we can do," she told him.

"What about my aunts?" Charles asked.

"They won't want to keep it. Neither of them is particularly well-off. I presume we are included in Daddy's will?"

"Yes. If in case of the estate being sold we all get an equal share."

"Then I'm sure they would agree."

"Would you still go to America?" Charles asked hopefully. "There should be some money to help with the stud if we sold the estate."

"The offer from Jess is still open. Even if we sell the estate there wouldn't be enough money for me to start up somewhere else would there?"

Charles reluctantly agreed. It took two years to sell the estate, then Charles and his mother moved in with the Foden family until his mother found buyers for her horses. She then departed for Maryland.

Charles was glad of the comfort of his other family and he immersed himself in work, surprisingly finding he enjoyed the experience. He saw Arabella Granger regularly and played golf at weekends and became increasingly interested in photography. He attended trade fairs in Europe and delighted his grandfather by finding new outlets for their machinery.

It was while attending a fair in Frankfurt that he remembered his promise to Aunt Sheila to try to find Gerhardt Muller. He had already made enquiries through the Red Cross and followed a chain of associations to discover that a Muller family had moved from Cottbus sometime during the war to relatives in Frankfurt. Without knowing if it would be Gerhardt's family, he began collecting telephone numbers and addresses for all Mullers in the Frankfurt area and on several visits there he would work his way through the telephone numbers and, in his limited German, explain that he was looking for a Gerhardt Muller. It took two years before he had some success; finding someone who had a cousin who had a brother called Gerhardt who had, indeed, come from Cottbus during the war.

The cousin, a woman some forty years older than himself, met him at his hotel. Charles had copied the photograph Gerhardt had given Aunt Sheila and he showed it to the woman. She held it for some moments and stared at it until her eyes watered and the tears began to run down her face.

"Yes. It's my brother," she told him and began to cry so much she excused herself and went to the toilets. When she returned she apologised and told him that her mother was

222

still alive but not very well. They had moved from Cottbus just before the Russians took the town. They made their way to Frankfurt where they had cousins on their father's side. It took them many weeks to reach Frankfurt and they arrived with only a little jewellery and small family items. There were many refugees fleeing the advancing Russian army, hoping to reach a part of Germany where the Allied forces would be in control.

"We never knew what had happened to Gerhardt – or my father," she told Charles in good English. My husband has tried to find out what happened to them but without success."

Charles told her about his father's plan to try to stop Gerhardt being returned to Germany and of his aunt's love for her brother. He met her mother, a frail woman made frailer by the rot of sadness from within. She held Charles' hand as though he was a direct link to her son and said how grateful she was that Gerhardt had found some kindness in England. Then she closed her eyes and when they thought she was asleep, he extracted his hand from hers and they crept out of the room.

Aunt Sheila got much comfort by exchanging letters with Gerhardt's sister and accepted an invitation to visit her but the next letter they received was to say Gerhardt's mother had died – without ever knowing what had happened to her husband or her son. Somehow, Aunt Sheila's visit never happened, though Charles was willing to take her to Germany, and the letters soon stopped coming.

Charles didn't marry Arabella Granger until he was thirty. His mother came over from America for the wedding, which was a swanky affair with many guests, and afterwards, Charles and Arabella accompanied her back to the States on the QE2 for their honeymoon.

Charles' influence on the Foden business was considerable and the overseas orders required them to extend their factory and his wedding present was a large bonus which he used as a deposit to buy a Georgian period house between the two Stokeseys and only a short walk from his grandparents.

Their life was a seamless one of privilege and pleasure; Charles enjoying his frequent business trips to the Continent and relieving any stress by working at his golf handicap and pursuing his photography while Arabella had two children and ran a charity for disabled and distressed ex military personnel.

The first blip in their lives was Grandma Fodens death. Charles then attempted to persuade his grandpa to live with them, arguing that his house was far too large and unnecessarily expensive to run for only him and Aunt Sheila – much as Grandpa Foden had reasoned about the Henderson home some years before – but his grandpa dismissed the suggestion aggressively; he was not a man to assume a secondary position, even in his eighties.

The first shock to their lives was the sudden death of Charles' mother from pneumonia after a skiing holiday in Aspen. Charles and Arabella had always been too busy with their lives to take up the constant pleas from Fiona for them to visit Maryland, always saying "Next year" and Fiona had only managed to return to England two or three times for the same reason. So Charles was suddenly aware that he had never got to know his mother beyond the physicality and practicality of their relationship and the realisation was strengthened when he went to Maryland for her funeral.

He was met at the airport by a distressed Jess Mavrolean and was rather surprised by the emotional display of her greeting, considering that he had met her only on two brief occasions in England and when he and Fiona had gone to the States for their honeymoon.

The surprise increased when he was taken to the estate. It was on a grand scale: the ranch-like property was set in over four hundred acres of prime grazing land with a dirt track in the centre, but it was in the sumptuous living accommodation that he was most surprised. In showing him round, Jess made no attempt to hide the fact that his mother and she shared the same bedroom and the same bed and it was obvious that she thought he was aware of her relationship with his mother.

After the funeral his host continued to display an outward affection for him that bordered on a desperate clinging-on to a tangible part of her lost love and she was demonstrably disappointed that he could not stay longer.

On the flight home, Charles felt an inner emptiness that was almost painful. How could forty years of shared genes disappear so quickly without ever feeling the sharing?

Grandpa Foden lived on until his ninetieth year. He was in good health and had chaired board meetings and still attended the office on most days and, on the evening previous to when he failed to wake the next morning, he had attended a dinner for a retiring alderman.

His death was deeply felt by Charles. Whereas his attachment to his Henderson family had been solely affectionate, his relationship with his grandpa had been beyond affection as he was the nearest Charles could ever get to his own father and his grandpa had been the major mentor in his life.

But Charles' emotion at his grandpa's death was nothing compared to Aunt Sheila's. The sudden loss broke the fragile shell of normality that barely contained the fractious state of her mind. She was inconsolable and required sedation and Charles was advised not to subject her to her father's funeral.

Her condition had never been treated nor even assessed and Charles' doctor immediately referred her for psychiatric analysis.

Charles' first inclination was to move her in with his family but the psychotherapy clinic of the local hospital thought it better to keep her in her normal surroundings, so Charles arranged for a nurse to live-in despite the housekeeper and her husband being there to look after her.

Advances in psychiatric medicine soon had a dramatic affect on his Aunt's condition and Charles constantly wondered why she had not been given the benefit of them many years sooner. Her condition improved so rapidly that he felt safe to dispose of her nursing care and she even began to show signs of assertiveness in the way she instructed the housekeeper as to what food she should provide and what jobs her husband needed to do around the gardens. But Charles realised she could not continue to live alone in the large house and the challenge of how he would manage to broach the subject arrived on a beautiful spring day when he and his daughter, Phillipa, were visiting his aunt and sitting in the garden.

"I can't believe how well you are looking, Aunt Sheila," Charles told her.

"Yes. I feel so much better, Charles – thanks to you. I feel alive again."

"Did you not feel alive before?"

"Not very much. I never wanted to go outside, did I? Now I'm so much enjoying being in the garden with you and Phillipa."

"Why didn't you want to before?" six-year old Phillipa asked.

Doubt returned to Sheila's face.

"Auntie was not very well," Charles explained."Don't you

just want to stay in bed when you're not well, like when you had Mumps?"

"Have you had Mumps, Auntie?" Phillipa queried.

"Not since I was about your age," Sheila replied and Charles was encouraged by the sensible answer.

"Aunt. Don't you think this house is too large for you now? Wouldn't you rather come and live with us?"

"Oh, yes please, Aunt. Please come and live with us. You can play with me a lot then," Phillipa said excitedly.

Sheila looked from Phillipa to Charles and her face changed each time from smiling to worried.

"It would be so much easier for you," Charles said persuasively.

"Would I be able to ride again?" she asked and Charles wondered if he had been misreading her signs of improvement.

"We don't have any horses, Aunt. We may get one for Phillipa and Edmund sometime. But I could teach you to drive," he added with sudden inspiration"

"Drive a car. Would you Charles? Aren't I too old to learn?"

"Of course you are not too old. It would be much easier and safer for you to learn to drive than to get on a horse again," he laughed.

"That would be fun," she said and then looked worried again. "But what about Margaret and Roger? she added, mentioning the housekeeper and her husband.

"They haven't been with you very long. Beryl and Jack only retired last year. I'm sure they would soon find another position and they could stay on here until they get fixed up. I'm not in any hurry to sell the place. What do you think, Aunt?"

"Well, it would be nice to be with you and the children.

227

Won't Arabella mind?"

"She'll love it. You could help her with the children. Settled then! You are coming to live with us."

Phillipa yelled her pleasure and pulled Sheila off the deckchair and danced her round until she fell back into it, panting for breath. They sat in silence, watching Phillipa throwing sticks for the dog.

"Would you like to hear a secret, Charles?" Aunt Sheila asked dreamily.

"Is it a nice secret?" Charles responded. Sheila's face changed.

"No," she said firmly. "But now I can tell it. Now Daddy is gone."

Phillipa had stopped playing and was standing, waiting to hear Sheila's secret.

"Phillipa, darling. Would you go and ask cook if we can have more scones."

Phillipa hesitated, scones were yummy but secrets were much better.

"Go on, darling," Charles insisted. Phillipa raced away, hoping she could please her father and still get back in time to hear Aunt Sheila's secret.

"Are you sure you want me to hear your secret, Aunt? Secrets are supposed to be secrets."

"Yes. I need to tell someone. It was not my fault," Sheila said.

"What wasn't your fault?"

"What happened to Gerhardt."

Charles had not heard his aunt speak of Gerhardt since she had last received a letter from his sister, which was then some two years before.

"We know that wasn't your fault. We know Grandpa sent Gerhardt away, not you,"

"But your father said it was my fault," Sheila insisted almost tearfully.

Charles saw Phillipa racing back to them, one hand holding the plate of scones and the other hand on top to prevent them bouncing off the plate.

"We'll talk about it some other time, Aunt," Charles told her. "Thank you, Phillipa. Just put them on the table."

"Have I missed Auntie's secret?" Phillipa asked breathlessly.

"It wasn't much of a secret," Charles told her. "It was only about Grandpa's wings."

Phillipa's eyes opened as wide as her mouth. "Grandpa had wings?" she asked.

"Yes. And when he died they took him straight up to Heaven. If you're good, you'll grow wings to."

"But I don't want to go to Heaven. Not yet," Phillipa protested and Sheila joined in Charles' laughter.

Aunt Sheila's mental and emotional condition continued to improve. She seemed to enjoy her visits to the clinic where they monitored her progress and balanced the Serotonin inhibitors that were a class of antidepressant. Her condition had been diagnosed as Obsessive Compulsive Disorder, even though it had manifested only as an obsession with finding Gerhardt, and her nephew was not convinced by what he understood OCD to be. But whatever it was the medication had changed her life – and that of the family. Finding Gerhardt's sister had probably helped and certainly had stopped Sheila's obsession with expecting Gerhardt to write to her, but she had continued to dip between anxiety and depression until her father's death had promoted the necessity of medical attention. Now she was a welcome member of the household.

Charles had kept his promise to teach her to drive and she looked forward to the weekends where she trundled his grandfather's old Jaguar-Daimler Sovereign automatic up and down the drive and around the expansive gravelled frontage and even learned to reverse it into the stable yard – but, curiously to Charles, she would always drive it straight out again and never attempted to reverse it as far as the garage where it was kept and she never followed Charles into the yard to get the car from the garage.

Her nephew had noticed her reluctance to go near the garage but had never commented on it as she was still a subject for observation rather than confrontation. He suspected it had something to do with his father's death and he had not forgotten her claim to have a secret about his father and Gerhardt, but he was loath to risk anything that might disturb the emotional equilibrium she now seemed to enjoy.

He had not yet begun the onerous task of clearing his grandfather's house, partly because his mind was concentrated on Arabella's recent announcement that she was pregnant with their third child and partly because of his reluctance to face the emotional challenges it would bring, both to his aunt and to himself. The house was more his family home than had been the Henderson estate for which he had felt no emotional attachment as he was away at boarding school and university for most of the time his mother lived there, and its clearance would be a psychological wrench for him and Aunt Sheila and might cause a relapse in her rehabilitation. As it was, visiting the house at weekends and using her family car had proved to be the perfect intermediary before a final severance, but he knew that would have to come.

It was at an event in the city to launch a business initiative to support a local care charity that he found an opportunity to raise the problem with a lady on his right who had informed him she was a psychiatrist. There was a buffet supper after the presentations so there were no place-cards to identify the sitters and he and the lady had used only first names to introduce themselves. He knew it was not good form to take advantage of anyone's profession in a social environment in order to indulge one's interests but the lady in question was keen to talk about her work for the recipient charity by providing free counselling for the mentally disturbed young people in its programme and after he had listened with interest to her for most of the supper he felt he had earned a question or two of self-interest.

"What is obsessive compulsive disorder?" he asked.

The question was not entirely out of context as she had mentioned OCD several times. The woman listed the many physical symptoms and the causal anxiety that triggered them and gave him many anecdotes to demonstrate her explanations, most of which were normal symptoms he recognised.

"Can one incident, cause a chronic compulsive reaction?" he asked when she had finished.

"Chronic?" She dwelt on the word. "That's very specific. Behaviour can become chronic by repetitive usage or a medical condition can be manifested in a physical manner…"

"There was no medical condition," he interrupted.

She realised he was talking about a particular case and was reluctant to go there.

"I can't be specific without a clinical diagnosis," she said carefully.

"Let me try to be," he said. "A man disappears and for the rest of her life his lover checks the post, every delivery, every day to see if there is a letter from him. Is that OCD?"

"Yes," she admitted. "I would say it is. It is a traumatic stress disorder. Checking the mail is compulsive, obsessive behaviour. It would be a way of reducing the associated anxiety of not knowing what happened to her lover."

As she spoke her eyes studied his face and her mind calculated his response beyond the answer she gave to his question.

"Of course," she continued as he contemplated her answer by frowning at the table, "It could be that the man's disappearance was not the catalyst for her behaviour. It was probably something more traumatic than his mere disappearance that caused it. Do you know why he disappeared?"

"Yes," he said. "He was sent back to Germany. He was a POW."

"Then I doubt that was the cause," she said. "She knew why he had left her. It would make her unhappy like thousands of other jilted lovers, but it would be unlikely to cause a trauma to that degree."

He explained the circumstances of Gerhardt's repatriation. "She thinks it was her fault he was sent back."

"She had no choice," the woman said. "She would have known his repatriation was inevitable. I can't believe it would have such a lasting effect as you describe. Guilt is certainly one of the causes of OCD but it would almost certainly be something much more traumatic than the reason you have given me."

"You think there is something I don't know?"

"Either that or you haven't told me everything," she answered.

She watched him carefully as his mind digested her answers and when he seemed unable or unwilling to offer more information she changed the subject and was soon relieved by the commencement of an auction.

At the end of the evening people were standing in groups talking together and Charles Foden was talking golf to the mayor and other councillors when his supper companion touched him on the arm.

"Goodnight, Mr Foden. I enjoyed our chat," she said and moved towards the door before the significance of her words registered with him; how did she know his name?

"Who was that?" one of his companions asked. "She's a handsome lady."

"Doctor Patricia Szernek," the mayor answered. "She runs the Psychiatric unit at the hospital."

A shock-wave of realisation hit Foden. He had been talking about Aunt Sheila to someone who was almost certainly aware of her case. "Something more traumatic than the reason you gave me." Her words echoed inside his brain for most of his journey home.

The next weekend, Aunt Sheila was looking forward to her weekly driving lesson and entered the kitchen kitted out in trousers and flat shoes. His grandparent's house was less than a half-mile away and he and Aunt Sheila usually walked there to collect the old Daimler-Jaguar. Charles was still drinking coffee as she entered the kitchen and asked cheerfully if he was ready.

"Not quite," he answered. "Why don't you go and pick-up the car and bring it here and collect me," he said.

His Aunt's reluctance was immediate. "No. I would rather not," she said.

"Why not, Aunt? You know how to open the garage doors. It will be good practise for you, make you feel independent."

He got up and took a set of keys from a hook. He threw

them along the table towards his aunt.

"No, really, Charles. It would mean driving on the road by myself," she argued.

"It's hardly a road, Aunt," he answered. "Between here and there are no more than four houses. You aren't likely to meet any traffic. You have to do this sort of thing if you're going to pass your test."

Aunt Sheila stared at the keys for a moment and then suddenly snatched them up. "All right," she said forcefully and walked out of the kitchen.

Arabella looked at her husband. "What's that all about?" she asked.

"I'm not sure," Foden told her. "But I'm going to find out."

"Don't upset her, Charles. The last thing I need at the moment is for Sheila to go doolally again."

Charles finished his coffee then put on his jacket. He waited on the outside steps and was wondering whether he had done the right thing as it was well over half an hour before the Daimler came into the drive and stopped below the steps. He opened the door, beaming his pleasure.

"There. Well done. You must feel very proud of yourself. Why don't you like garages, Aunt?" he asked. "It's only where cars sleep."

She stared through the windscreen. "Not only cars," she murmured, almost to herself, but Foden had understood – or thought he had.

"All right, Aunt. Put her into Drive and off you go," he said cheerfully. I think you are ready to try the lanes," he told her. Panic showed on his aunt's face.

"But we haven't got any learner plates on," she protested.

"Don't worry, Aunt. No one will know you're not an expert," he told her.

They did a circuit of two adjoining lanes and a small

stretch on the road between Upper Stokesey and Stokesey without a mishap and when Sheila drove back into the drive of the old house she was so elated by her success she drove into the stable yard and headed towards the garage.

"Well, done, Auntie," he said. "Now reverse her into the garage and we'll soon get you to take a driving test."

Her enthusiasm was child-like. "Do you really think I could, Charles, at my age?"

"Why not?" he laughed. "Age has nothing to do with it. You are starting a new life. Off with the past and on with the new."

She slumped a little into the seat and looked wistfully towards a misted horizon.

"If only I could," she said.

Charles reached across and took her hand. "You can, Aunt Sheila. What happened up there," he raised his eyes towards the ceiling of the garage, "is gone. It's over. It no longer matters."

His aunt snatched her hand away and turned and looked at him with a sudden authority. "You know? You know what happened, Charles?"

He smiled indulgently. "I think I do, Aunt. You were in love. That's nothing to be afraid of, nothing to be ashamed of either."

Understanding mixed with horror on his aunt's face. "No," her voice quivered. "Not me. Not me." She opened the door and stepped quickly out of the car. "I'm going back to the house," she said, again with a vocal authority he had never heard before. His eyes watched her walk into the rain, striding determinedly across the yard until she disappeared like an apparition into the haze.

They did not meet again until dinner. Charles had taken his wife into the city to her natal clinic and they had lunched there and shopped afterwards and when they returned Sheila was in her room and then the children came back with their nanny and they all had tea together but Aunt Sheila did not join them. Charles thought nothing of it as she often preferred to spend time by herself to read and to rest as her medication tended to make her sleepier than what would be considered normal for a woman in her sixties. When she appeared for drinks before dinner, her sudden confidence was noticeable and Arabella remarked upon it.

"Goodness, Aunt. You're in a chipper mood."

"Am I? I do feel so much better. I believe it's all down to Charles and his driving lessons. I feel that I can do things again."

"Jolly good. You'll be able to run the children around if you pass your driving test. I'm going to be out of action soon and nanny doesn't drive," Arabella told her.

"Oh, that would be fun. Do you really think I could pass the test, Charles?"

"I don't see why you shouldn't, Aunt. A few more turns around the lanes and then we can go into Stokesey and frighten the horses."

"There aren't many of those any more – mores' the pity."

"You should have gone with Mummy to America," her nephew remarked.

"Yes. I should have liked that." Her confidence disappeared and anxiety showed on her face as it had done for almost all the years Charles could remember. He hastily tried to amend the situation.

"Grandpa and Grandma needed you here. They didn't want to lose you too."

"That's right, Aunt. They loved you too much," Arabella supported her husband, fearing Aunt Sheila was about to slip back to her old moods.

But she need not have worried. Aunt Sheila soon rallied with the same vehemence that Charles had witnessed that morning in the garage.

"Daddy just wanted to keep me here so I couldn't talk about what I knew. He had no right to make me promise. It wasn't my fault. Your father had no right to blame me. It was not my fault." she said and emphasised her point by putting the sherry glass down so that it slopped a few drops onto the mahogany.

Arabella stole a look towards her husband.

"What wasn't your fault, Aunt?" she asked but without conviction.

"Let's go into dinner," her husband said quickly and helped his wife off the settee.

Later that evening, when he was alone with a whisky after his wife had taken herself to bed with a book, Charles considered Aunt Sheila's behaviour, both in the garage and during their pre-dinner drinks. Her assertiveness he welcomed as the continuing improvement of her medical condition, but the considerable anger that seemed to drive it was less understandable.

"Something more traumatic than the reason you gave me." He recalled the words of Doctor Patricia Szernek.

All his adult life he had been led to believe that his aunt's psychological condition was caused by the disappearance of her German lover but Sheila's recent words, and the anger behind them, weakened that probability. When they were spoken his mind had immediately rejected them, like a safety curtain closing them out, but now, in the silence of his isolation he repeated them aloud; " Not me." and "Daddy just wanted to keep me here so I couldn't talk about what I knew."

What did Sheila know? His mind was again reluctant to

dwell on the question, even though his nature was to be decisive rather than conjectural, but he could not ignore it. He was acutely aware that Sheila was still attending the psychiatric clinic that Patricia Szernek headed-up and that Doctor Szernek mixed with his many peers in the city. He decided that in the morning he would ask his aunt for an explanation. He emptied his glass in a swift movement and went purposefully to lock-up the house before going to bed.

Sunday morning came slowly. Charles had slept fitfully only until four am. He could not blame his wife as she was having a good night. He spent some time in his office but was pleased to be interrupted by his two children and Nanny. They were excited because Sunday meant they could take the dogs onto the Ridgeway and kick a ball about. He looked in on his wife and took the newspaper and a cup of coffee up to her. She declined the offer of breakfast but was happy to stay in bed and read the paper.

"Right. I think I'll take Auntie a cup of tea," he said.

"Why? You never take her a cup of tea," his wife answered.

"I want to see if she's all right. She was a bit strange last evening and she's not usually this late coming down."

He went back to the kitchen and made the tea and some toast. He put them onto a tray with a pot of honey which his aunt enjoyed. He knocked on her door and when there was no answer he called her name. Again there was no reply. He thought quickly of the medication she administered herself. He opened the door and stepped into the room. Sheila seemed to be sleeping. He put the tray down and opened the blinds. She didn't stir. He called her name quietly. There was no response. Her arm was outside of the duvet and he bent and touched it – and quickly snatched his hand away. It was cold. Fearfully, he reached down and put his hand onto her neck. That too was bloodless. Aunt Sheila was dead.

****

The family watched as the covered body was carried to the ambulance. The children were frightened and clung onto Nanny's skirt. Even the dogs seemed to understand the occasion and sat dolefully watching. When the ambulance was ready to leave, the doctor extended his hand to Charles.

"I'm so sorry, Mr. Foden."

He was not their regular GP.

"It wasn't her medication," Foden told him. "I counted her tablets."

"Most likely her heart," the doctor answered. "It's comforting when it happens like that."

But Charles was not comforted. Sheila was the last of his own family and the depth of his grief surprised him. It pressed against his body and made him open his mouth and suck in the air to relieve the pressure.

"Go for a walk," his wife suggested incisively.

He nodded and walked quickly away as though he thought to run after the ambulance.

He walked in a straight line, much as his unborn son, Noel would do at a future date, heading down towards the river. Tears came and went as grief was replaced by fits of anger. The anger was mostly for the injustice that Auntie's life had been snatched away just as it had begun after being stifled for so many years and such thoughts made him scream at the hedgerows and put sparrows and tits to flight. But as his legs slowed so too did his brain and numbness descended and wrapped him in an emollient blanket.

****

On the Monday morning after Aunt Sheila's sudden death, Charles Foden wakened having slept surprisingly well.

"I'll take the week off," he told his wife.

"I should damned well think you would," his wife responded, even though the funeral would not be for another week.

He had a good works manager and had no fears for the business because of his absence, but he had his grandpa's work ethic and did not take time away from the business without good reason.

"I thought I would make a start on clearing the other house," he said.

His wife looked at him as though he were mad.

"What do you mean? That's a mammoth task. Aren't you just going to get a firm in to clear it all? There's nothing there that we want."

He winced inwardly at the harshness of her appraisal.

"I will need to go through Grandpa's study; sort out his papers, that sort of thing."

As he turned into the drive the old house loomed before him like a sad monument to an ancient past and its gloom seemed to reach out and envelope him as he climbed the steps and opened the front-door. He forced himself forward, past the iron umbrella stand with Grandpa's walking sticks still being held ready to accompany the dogs on their exercise. He opened the door to the sitting-room and lingered in the doorway, remembering the evenings around the large fireplace, listening to the radio as his grandparents liked to do. Grandpa's pipe was next to his seat, the cushion indented still from his weight and Grandma's sewing-table was beside the settee where once she sat, working her intricate tapestries.

He jumped visibly as the mantle clock suddenly chimed the hour. He smiled to himself that Aunt Sheila or the housekeeper had kept it primed.

He crossed the hall to Grandpa's study. He had kept it locked since his Grandfather's death, meaning constantly to go in and sort out the papers. He unlocked the door and swung it open. The odour of tobacco smoke and leather escaped into the cooler air. The curtains were drawn across. He opened them and the window and then surveyed the room. He looked wistfully at the photographs of his young father and aunt and the sudden realisation that photographs were all that were left of them brought tears quickly to his eyes. He took a deep breath and forced himself on with his task.

He had not been in there very often, only occasionally to report on a business trip that required a private hearing. One side of the room was covered by glass-fronted mahogany bookcases. His grandfather had not been a regular reader, preferring to use his hands rather than other people's brains, and as he studied the leather-bound volumes Charles wondered from where they had come. Was his great grandfather a reader? He would never know; there was now no one to answer the questions.

On a side-table a Tantalus of brandy and whisky was locked. Although it was only morning he thought he would enjoy a whisky before settling into his task. He went to the desk and searched several drawers for the key. A bottom drawer was locked. He studied the ring of house keys for a likely solution and eventually found one to unlock the drawer. A small, silver key inside it caught his eye and successfully unlocked the Tantalus. He poured a whisky into Grandpa's glass and took it to the desk. He settled into the leather swivel chair and sniffed the whisky before taking a sip and washing the liquor around his mouth to prolong the flavour.

The drawer that had been locked was still pulled open. He decided that any papers of importance would be in there. He removed a ledger that contained financial details written in his grandfather's small and precise lettering. Although his grandfather had been dead for over two months Charles had done nothing about his estate other than to have it made over solely to him as in the terms of the will. He put the ledger on the desk as one to take away and study. He delved in the drawer again and found a large envelope containing share certificates which surprised him as he thought they had been kept on deposit in the bank. He placed them with the ledger.

He rifled through another file and a small envelope and several photographs fell from it. He quickly saw the photographs were the same size as his Leica prints and was not surprised to see they were black and white. But as he looked at them his feeling of loss increased as he suddenly remembered a conversation with his mother many years before when she had told him his father had been to collect his first film on the morning of his death. He recognised a young Sheila and his grandparents taken in their garden and several shots of his mother even though they were slightly out of focus and justified his grandpa's opinion of them – and then there was another picture, perfectly composed, of several naked or almost naked men, holding bottles and glasses and wearing bits of what were clearly German airforce uniform. One of the men was blatantly wearing only flying boots and a tie and was facing the camera, raising a bottle towards it.

He threw the photographs onto the desk and picked up the other envelope that had fallen from the folder with the photographs. He turned it over and read the words; "To my child" handwritten across it. He sat back in the chair as if to warm his spine which had suddenly gone cold.

He took a longer sip of whisky then reached for a paperknife. He slit open the envelope and withdrew a single sheet of paper written on two sides. He read the date, January 16th. 1947. He knew the date well; it was the date on which his father had died. With trepidation he continued reading.

My dear, dearest child.
Forgive me that I cannot think how else to address
you as I know, if my instructions have been followed,
that you will be at least twenty one years old when
you are reading this.   Of all the pain I feel, not
knowing you, not even knowing if you are my son or
my daughter, is the greatest pain of all.
 Why then, you will no doubt think, would I do what
 I am about to do? Ah! If only I could take you into
my arms now and tell you how I could love you.
How I would cherish you into my dotage if you
could forgive me for being who I am, what I am.

Love is the greatest thing, my child. It is the only
 thing that makes sense of our existence when it
is felt, and when it is reciprocated it is the ultimate
 gift of life. This gift I wish for you, however it comes,
wherever you may find it and whomsoever you share it
with. But it is not universal. It is rare and it struggles
to exist in a world of hate and fear. 'Love thine enemy'
the Bible tells us. I did. Out of the horrors of war I

*found this jewel of love in mine enemy. But those
who have not found such love, those who still harbour
feelings of hate, of violence, of jealousy, of greed and
revenge, those people cannot understand what love is
and strive to destroy it in others. They have destroyed
mine the moment they knew of it. I cannot face their
world. I have seen it at its worst. Once lost, Paradise
cannot be regained.*

*You may feel, like those around me, that I am selfish.
But I am not. I am destroyed and would become a
father of pity, hating the world as it is, should I not
do what I am about to do. Without me you will have
the chance to be who you are and not what I would
make you: ashamed.*

*God Bless you my child,
Your father, Geoffrey.*

He read the letter several times and his feelings were similar to those on his walk the day before; grief and anger. But there was another emotion in the mix, one he resisted to recognise. If it had a name it hovered somewhere between contempt and shame.

He folded the letter, now damp from several tears that had dripped from his face, and replaced it in the envelope and put the envelope into his inside pocket. He looked again at the photographs of the naked German airmen.

"Which one are you, Gerhardt?" he asked himself. "Which one of you stole my father's life?"

He flicked the photographs back into the drawer and slammed it shut.

He sat there for a long time, until he became aware of a

chill on his back from the open window. He got up and closed it then left and locked the room and walked out into the late afternoon.

He started towards the gate then suddenly turned to his right and walked into the stable yard. He went to the side of the garage and tried the door and found it locked. He inspected the house-keys and tried several in the lock without success. He cursed and with a sudden burst of energy went into the garage and took a crow-bar from a shelf. He returned to the side door and inserted the bar into the jamb and put his weight on it until the door split around the lock and eased open. He pushed it wide and the first thing he saw was that two rungs of the laddered stairs were splintered and stained. He carefully wet a handkerchief and rubbed at the staining then examined the result. It was not conclusive but was sufficient for him to think that it was the spot where his father had ended his life. He scraped at the splintered wood with the crow bar and soon exposed what he recognised as buckshot. He fell back against the wall and the tears came again. Then anger returned. He climbed the ladder, carefully avoiding the damaged steps, and climbed up to the floor above. There was a paraffin heater against a wall and a mattress on the floor. The windows had not been cleaned for decades. The paper tape had been removed but cobwebs covered most of them and spiders were scurrying everywhere to escape his intrusion.

He stood for some moments then kicked at the mattress violently before descending the stairs.

When he arrived home his wife was anxious. "I've been phoning you," she protested.

"Sorry," he muttered.

"What kept you so long? I thought you were just going to look at the papers?"

Her husband sighed.

"I found other things to do. I'm going to have a shower."

"Don't you want to eat something?"

"Later."

He was already climbing the stairs.

It was two days before he told his wife about the letter. Her reaction was one of relief; he had been morose and bad-tempered and she had worried that Sheila's death was affecting him more than it should.

"Your father committed suicide?" she exclaimed. Put into words the act was graphically recalled and provoked again the anger he felt.

"Yes. The selfish, selfish," he did not finish the sentence, he had always avoided profanities. His wife got up and put her arms around him. The tears began again. There was nothing his wife could say that would not seem inadequate or unnecessary. She gave him a tissue and he dried his eyes.

"Grandpa knew how he died. Mummy knew. Everyone knew except me. And that letter should have been given to me when I was twenty-one but Grandpa kept it from me." His anger was raw.

"Why didn't they tell you?" his wife asked. He looked at her stupidly then realised he had not told her why. He took his father's letter from his pocket and gave it to her. He watched as she read it, waiting anxiously as he suddenly remembered he had done when his mother had got his school reports. She must have read it again as it took her a long time before she handed it back without a word.

"Well?" he asked.

"I'm so sorry," she said.

The inadequacy of her response made him laugh. "Sorry? Sorry? So am I sorry."

His wife struggled to put the various pieces together. She

was frightened by her husband's fragile emotions but she had to ask the question that was absent from the letter.

"Who was his great love?" she eventually asked. Her husband looked at her again as if he didn't understand the question, and then he did.

"Gerhardt," he almost shouted. "Gerhardt of course. The German prisoner. He wasn't Aunt Sheila's lover; he was my father's."

A sort of laugh squeezed from his throat.

"But..." Arabella hesitated, unsure of how much she dared ask. "But why was Aunt Sheila so anxious to find Gerhardt?"

The question drove the anger from her husband's face and was replaced by a blank expression. "I don't know. She knew about them. She tried to tell me, in the garage. I don't know why. I don't know."

"But Aunt Sheila said they blamed her. What did she mean?"

"I don't know. I don't know."

"Then we shall never know. Don't torture yourself, Charles."

But he was torturing himself, it showed on his face and in his shoulders which were projected upwards as though he were trying to bury his head beneath them. He moved his lips as if to speak but no sound came from them.

"Poor Sheila," his wife said, hoping the words might soothe his anger but they seemed to have the opposite effect.

"Poor Sheila. Poor Sheila indeed. They tortured her. All those years they tortured her. She said she had promised Grandpa not to tell. He had to die before she could live again. Just for a few weeks. Her life was just a few weeks..."

He smashed his fist down onto a table then cuddled the pain with his other hand. His wife hurried to his side and drew his head down and kissed it and then the tense situation was relieved by the sound of Nanny bringing the children in from school.

The next day his wife found him calmer but still brooding. She knew he had been up several hours before her and felt the tension radiating from him

"Why don't you go and play golf," she suggested. "The weather forecast is good for the week. Haven't you got some sort of tournament this month?"

"The Harlequin Trophy," he mumbled.

"If Sheila's funeral is next week you won't have much time to play then," she said.

"Perhaps I should. I could do with some air ."

THE PRESENT
4

The Gay Hussar was not busy on a Monday. The Doggers Crew: Warren and Elvis and their cousins, were together in a booth, an array of bottles covering the table between them. They were bantering across to other cronies in an adjacent booth when a dark-skinned youth hovered near them. He had his hair greased back and caught in a pony-tail and wore sunglasses and a patterned cotton poncho despite the warmth. The youth stood next to the table and looked at the twins.

"We don't do wogs," Warren said and they all laughed. The youth sat down on the edge of one of the bench seats.

"I said…" Warren began and his arm came out to push the youth off the seat but stopped as the boy took his hands from under the Poncho and fanned several fifty-pound notes as though they were playing-cards.

"I have a business proposition," he said in a squeaky, lisping voice with a slight accent. The arm flopped and Warren sat back in the seat. They were all looking at the money. Boys didn't pay them. Boys didn't want to do business with them.

****

Noel Foden's esteem had climbed considerably since his strong performance at the Union debate. He had received several telephone calls from local organisations enquiring about his availability for speaking engagements but the one that pleased him most was from the Chair of the district Conservative Association asking if he had considered putting his name down as a prospective candidate. He was already a member of the University Conservative Association but had come quite low in their pecking-order. Now he had suddenly leapt ahead. It was in such a mood of self-congratulation that he received another call from a Mr. Pickles who introduced himself as the Secretary of the local branch of the Motor Trades Association. Mr. Pickles explained they were in something of a fix because Jeremy Clarkson had had to cancel a speaking engagement and they wondered if Noel could step in and speak on taxation and small business.

"When?" Noel wanted to know, feeling rather pleased that he was second-best only to Jeremy Clarkson.

"Tomorrow," was the reply.

Noel made a thing of having to consult his engagement diary but soon admitted that he was free.

"Wonderful," Mr. Pickles said. "We're holding the meeting at the Town Rowing Club." Noel knew it. "Would seven-thirty be too early, we wanted to chat before the members got there?" Noel agreed seven-thirty would be fine. "Do you want us to pick you up or do you have transport?" Noel told the man he had a car.

When he drove into the car park behind the Rowing Club it was a dark evening, threatening a thunderstorm but only the lights in the upper meeting room were on. There were two cars, both Jaguars, in the car park and Noel wondered what time the meeting was scheduled to start and his enthusiasm dissipated at the possibility of speaking to only a handful of people. The lower part of the building was the boat-house where the rowing skiffs were stacked. It had no windows but as Noel got out of his car he could see the rear pedestrian door was open and it was dimly lit from the inside and the silhouette of a man was standing in the doorway. As Noel approached the man stepped forward to meet him.

"Mr. Foden? Pickles. Arthur Pickles. So nice of you to step in at such short notice."

They shook hands as Pickles stepped backwards into the boat-house and he was still holding Noel's hand when someone from behind grabbed Noel's jacket and pulled it down to his elbows, pinning his arms to his sides and even before he could react a plastic waste-bin liner was put over his head and the draw-string pulled tight. His arms were seized and his jacket pulled off him and his wrists were taped behind his back. The bin-liner was large but Noel quickly realised he needed to conserve oxygen and closed his mouth and breathed only through his nose. He heard the door close behind him and then he was aware of light showing through the plastic. The liner was pulled from his head. He looked around. Mr. Pickles had disappeared and several men in black leathers were standing about him, all of them wearing masks.

"What do you want?" he asked, aware his voice sounded rather high and off-key.

"Your body," one of the men said in a rough, accented voice. Noel struggled but he was held firmly by the men and frog-marched to where a skiff was set upside-down on one-foot-high blocks.

"Better switch off the upstairs lights," one of the men said.

Noel's shirt was stripped off him, tearing in the process. He screamed a protest and the bin-liner was immediately replaced over his head. He was thrown onto the upturned skiff and he felt ropes being tied to his wrists. The tape was then cut and his arms were separated and pulled forwards and he was forced face-down onto the boat. His arms were pulled down and the ropes from each wrist were crossed under the boat and brought up and tied to his ankles. He was now straddled and hog-tied across the skiff. His trousers were pulled off and then his underpants. There were crude comments and jokes from the men and much laughter. The draw-string on the bin-liner was loosened but the sack remained over his head so his cries of protest were muffled.

"Pass me the fat, Mick," someone said and Noel felt the grease slapped into his anus and then he was penetrated. The sodomy lasted an hour, each man taking his turn. Noel's protests had turned to cries of pain and then to whimpers and at some stage the bin-liner was taken off and photographs were taken on mobiles, one in particular from the front, showing clearly his face and the bare torso of someone's body straddling him from behind.

Eventually he was led out into the car park, still naked, his eyes covered by his shirt which had been tied around his head. The rest of his clothing was thrown at his feet. The lights had been put-out in the boat-house and the door was closed and the men calmly walked to the two cars in the gloom, laughing and chatting as though they had just had a meal together. They waved to Noel as they drove away.

THE PRESENT
5

Daphne Morrison was reluctant to return to her office. The amusement at the failure and circumstances of the search of the marshes had not abated on the lower floors of the CID section but it was not Laxton's mockery she wished to avoid, it was facing the Chief Constable knowing his reaction would almost certainly be that the Katy Rose investigation had nowhere else to go unless new evidence, not just speculation, was produced. Her fears were realised when her chief suggested she should take two weeks leave.

"You need a break. You've been pushing it too hard. You need to step back and take a fresh look at things. We all do."

The platitudes did nothing to alleviate her feelings, which were a mixture of guilt, disappointment and anger. When she thought about it she decided there was no cause to feel any guilt; the failure had not diminished her view that Katy Rose was taken from Drovers' Hill in a golf-buggy; there could be no other explanation. She reminded herself that if one body could be buried in the marshes another body could also be buried there – but the thought of suggesting a further search was quickly abandoned. There was also the other alternative, one that she had not pressed when it was agreed to search the marshes: that Katy was taken, like Jenny, either down to the road or the golf club and transferred to another vehicle. If that were true the possibility of finding her was remote. But if it were true, it probably meant that George Fuller, if he was the guilty party, did not act alone.

The Chief Constable's argument that a young casual worker was unlikely to have a car was a strong one and Morrison could see that any behaviour outside his normal work schedule would immediately be noticed by the

Members or his boss which made it unlikely that he could remove Katy without either being noticed in doing so or without the aid of someone else.

She was thinking such thoughts as she drove from the police station towards her cottage. She was wondering whether to drive on to The Badgers to assure Tom Lewis and his mother that she was not about to stop her investigation even if she had to do it out of police hours, when she passed a small building that announced the offices of the local newspaper. She stopped the car, turned around and drove into the car park.

She had had no time to think about the extraordinary circumstances of Gerhardt and the other prisoners of war and her curiosity was tinged with a copper's instinct of not ignoring any information, no matter how insignificant it might seem to be.

The editor was younger than herself and knew nothing about prisoners of war, but he was friendly and led her to a small, windowless room and introduced her to a microfiche. He apologised.

"We are hoping to computerise our archives but, as you can imagine, it's a long job and the owners won't commit the funds as yet. Do you know what dates you're looking for?" She did and he said that would save a lot of time. She had all day, and as long as a fortnight, she told herself.

She took the year 1945 and whirled through the pages. There were several stories about the camps in the area and about the repatriations, first, of the many Italian prisoners and then, much later, the Germans. She learned how the prisoners were interrogated and labelled white, grey or black depending on their propensities for retaining Nazi affinities. The black cases were sent to Scotland where they had less chance of escaping or of mixing with the local population.

Officers were camped separately and were not made to work but by 1946 thousands of German prisoners were working on road and building repair and on the farms. They were important and vital labour and the government was not quick to repatriate many of them, some of them not going home until as late as 1950. It was cheap labour, they were paid only pocket money for cigarettes and personal needs, but they were fed and housed and most of them would not have been either if they had returned home. Many were sent home and some came back again, staying and marrying in Britain and those that stayed in Germany retained friendships they had made whilst working as prisoners of war. But officers did not have to work if they chose not to and they were the first to be repatriated, their usefulness being of a lesser order than other ranks.

There were anecdotal personal memories, of locals marrying ex-prisoners and of their experiences from capture to repatriation, but Morrison could find no particular reference to the Stokesey camp or to its inmates.

Having taken a few notes and exhausted the subject she was about to leave, being reminded by her stomach that she had had no lunch and it was then late afternoon, when the present clicked in. She sat down again and searched the index for Katy Rose Lewis.

There was a lot of material which she speed-read, knowing it would take her beyond their closing hours to read it all. From the day of her disappearance the story was newsworthy for several months and there was a lot of coverage.

It was a revelatory exercise for Morrison to get an outsider's perspective of the case and she wondered why she had not thought to do it sooner. Probably, she admitted, because of the natural inclination for police officers to disregard media reports as uninformed speculation doing more harm than good. But what she got was the public's perception of how they thought the investigation was conducted as well as many conjectural opinions of what had happened to Katy Rose. Then she came across the picture of the Challis family: young Jenny, her mother and her father. It had probably been taken in the early days of the investigation when Jenny was left alone at the bus stop.

  She studied the picture closely and when she was ready to leave she requested a copy. She took it home and studied it again under a strong reading light. She thought about the Challis family and of the fears that had driven them away. There was no reference in the newspaper to the attempt on Jenny's life – at least, covering that up was one thing Laxton had got right – but she felt and understood the fear and turmoil that it had wrought on their lives. She had read what the psychologist had said and understood it to be meant as no more than a provocative hypothesis to attract interest to herself and her practice but the consequences had been profound. Especially on the person who had attempted to take Jenny's life. A person who thought that Jenny might recognise them. Not a stranger. Not a passing motorist. Someone with long connections to the local community.

  As she ate and sipped a glass of wine she thought of Penny Featherstone and her extraordinary experience on Drover's Hill that had reopened the investigation into Katy Rose's disappearance. Wasn't that just as unbelievable as Ivana Katowice's idea?

  After dinner, she rang Penny and asked if they could meet. Penny had not entirely forgotten the Katy Rose enquiry or her part in it. It had remained in her subconscious and had only jumped to the front of her brain in unguarded moments between sleep and more pressing interests. She might have admitted to herself that her experience of the case fascinated her as much as it did the few other people who knew about it but there was still an element of fear that further involvement might reveal more about herself than she wanted to know.

Daphne Morrison would not say why she wanted to see her except that she wanted Penny to confirm something that might help them both. She said she would stay overnight and booked a small private hotel with a four-star restaurant and chose a midweek rendezvous when it was unlikely to be busy and a table in an alcove where they were unlikely to be overheard.

They were each pleasantly surprised at the warmth of their greeting and that their brief friendship was still alive. They found conversation easy. They talked about careers and relationships just as two friends might do. Daphne Morrison was not going to mention the Gerhardt Muller case as she did not want it to dominate the evening and divert her from the purpose of the meeting, but Penny opened the subject. Being a student who typically got any world news via their laptops or television, she had only seen the story flagged-up as a Google headline but had then noticed where it had happened. She asked Daphne if she had had anything to do with it and Daphne had to relate how it had occurred.

Penny was fascinated and more so because a Foden was involved, and as Daphne had speculated, it did take up most of the conversation. But it also gave her an opportunity of saying what the failure had meant to the Lewis's who's hopes of the search had been crushed, leaving them depressed that the investigation might now be abandoned. That had the effect on Penny that played into Morrison's purpose.

"Do you think that will happen," Penny asked with

concern. "That would be terrible."

"Unless there is a new development. I'm on two weeks gardening leave."

" That is so unfair. After all you've done."

"I haven't done much. You did it all."

She didn't mean it to sound like a criticism but by the look on Penny's face she realised she had taken it personally and she rushed to reassure her that she believed in her and hoped she would be able to keep the investigation alive.

"How?"

In answer, Morrison asked about her parents. Although puzzled by the response Penny told her where they lived, what they did and about her younger brother.

"What are their names?"

"Mother is Virginia, Dad is Ian and urchin is officially Cedric. Why do you want to know about them?"

Without comment, Daphne pushed the newspaper photograph of the Challis family across the table. Penny looked at it and then squealed with surprise.

"That's us. Me and my parents," she said and then the realisation of the fact registered and her face clouded quickly. She looked across the table at Morrison for an explanation.

"That's the Challis family," Morrison told her.

"No. It's me and my parents."

Morrison explained who the Challis' were and of their involvement in the Katy Rose Lewis disappearance.

"You are not psychic," she said. "You had a recall of memory when you saw Katy in Drovers' Hill woods."

"That is ridiculous," Penny protested, not far short of anger but also close to fear.

"Have you told your parents about your experience

"No. They would be frightened for me."

"Phone them," Morrison said. "Ask them who you are."

Penny realised the inspector was serious and was not going to back down.

"All right," she said. Morrison handed her a mobile phone. "Use this."

Penny called her parents and Morrison sat back and sipped her wine and watched her. The student's facial expressions, her voice and her emotions went through many changes in a conversation that lasted almost an hour. There were moments of anger and loud protests and even some tears before she handed the phone to Morrison.

"My father wants to talk to you."

Ian Challis was not happy and wanted Morrison to leave his daughter alone and reminded her of what they had done to try to keep her safe.

"We changed our names We moved away and had to make new careers and now you are threatening to make it happen all over again," he told her.

Morrison tried to soothe his emotions. She explained that what had happened to Penny was out of their control.

"It was an amazing coincidence that your daughter just happened to visit Upper Stokesey. You could say it was fate."

She reminded him that Katy Rose had never been found, that her mother and brother were still hoping every day for news of her.

"I would like her mother to find her before she dies."

She assured him that his daughter was in no danger, that only Katy's family and two other officers knew of the reason why they had reopened the case.

"And only I know who Penny really is and I won't let anyone else know that until we have found Katy."

Challis was pacified but still concerned. He spoke to his

daughter again and made her promise she would not do anything she was not comfortable with. When Penny handed the phone back the two women looked at each other in silence and only when Morrison was sure that Penny was calm did she speak.

"You're so like your mother," she explained. "It's not quite as bad as suddenly discovering you were adopted," she added and got a smile.

"Jenny Challis," Penny said.

"I suppose your parents chose Penny because it sounds like Jenny to a twenty month old child. But why Featherstone?"

"Apparently it was my grandmother's maiden name,"

"Your parents are positive people," Morrison said and Penny told her how they had remade their lives in the Midlands, even moving one of her grandparents there.

"How do you feel about it now?" Morrison asked.

"Angry," Penny said. "Confused but definitely angry," and she remembered how she had felt when she had confronted Charles Foden and his wife.

"Angry with whom?"

"With whoever did this to the Lewis family and to mine," she said. "They tried to kill me. Did you know that?"

"Yes. I found out during the Gerhardt Muller search."

"Who would do that: kill a baby?"

"Someone desperate."

"Someone evil."

"Do you want to help?" Morrison asked hopefully.

"How can I? I'm not psychic, remember?"

"The psychologist who said you could one day remember what happened is called Ivana Katowice. I read what she said to the local press which was silly of her but I think she might be right. She said the mental processes start to work as soon as other senses and that visual image especially is retained even in babies. That is how they recognise their parents and objects long before they understand speech. She believes that visual images are retained even from the age of one year and if they are particularly dramatic they will be locked away in the brain forever."

"And you think that is what happened to me on Drovers' Hill?"

"Yes. I'm sure of it. What else could you remember with some help?"

"What sort of help?"

"Ivana Katowice specialises in hypnotherapy."

"And you want me to try it?"

"Ivana is still practising. We could just speak to her; ask her to explain her techniques. She claims to have regressed people's memories to their birth."

"Do you believe that?" Penny asked sceptically.

"Not really. But Darwin never did explain how the evolution of experience works. Perhaps memory is passed on through the genes too."

"I don't want to be an experiment."

"Nor do I want you to be. But it wouldn't do any harm to talk to Ivana would it?"

"I couldn't cross the bridge to the mill house," Penny told her and explained how she had visited it. "I just had a feeling about it. I didn't want to cross and I didn't know why. Do you think I could have remembered that too?"

"Ivana Katowice would think so."

"Can I stay with you? I'll feel safer."

"I would love you to"

THE PRESENT
6

Mrs. Foden expected, and was usually obeyed, that her children would ring her once a week. Phillipa, the eldest, worked in London and Grant, the youngest, was at boarding school. Edmund, the eldest boy who was in the army, was on a quick visit from his barracks as he had been told his unit was being posted overseas. His mother was complaining to him that she had not heard from Noel for more than a week.

"I've rung him several times and left messages," she was saying as her husband came home and joined them for lunch in order to see Edmund. He stopped as he entered the hall and stared at Edmund.

"Hello, Father. What is wrong?"

Foden recovered then shook hands and embraced his son.

"Sorry Edmund. You looked the image of my father, standing there in your uniform."

"Doesn't he look nice," his wife smiled.

"Yes. He does. Very handsome. How long are you home for?"

They went into the living-room where Foden poured sherry as Edmund explained his unit was being sent to Cyprus.

"I thought that was all RAF."

"The helicopter squadron is doing joint manoeuvres with them. Everyone's getting a bit worked up about what is happening in Turkey. They think Cyprus might need a bit more attention if it gets out of hand."

They sat around, catching up on various topics until Noel's name came into the conversation.

"I was just telling Edmund that I haven't heard from him for ten days. Arabella told her husband

"Is it that long? Perhaps he's too busy with his new

political career," Foden laughed.

Noel had reported his success at the Union debate.

"It doesn't take two minutes to say hello and tell us he is all right. It's quite unlike him and I've left three messages on his answer phone."

Only she and her husband knew of the Caroline incident, as they liked to refer to it, and it was an unspoken anxiety with them that Noel could still react badly to it. But the Union debate had lessened the anxiety as Noel had obviously been elated by his success.

"He could be unwell," Edmund suggested. It was the wrong thing to say.

His mother immediately reacted.

"Yes. I think I should phone the Dean."

"Don't panic, darling. If we don't hear from him tonight I'll go up there in the morning," her husband said.

Betsy announced that lunch was ready. As they went through to the dining-room, Foden sifted through the mail on the hall table.

"There's one there for you, from America," his wife told him. "Who do you know in America?"

"Jess Mavrolean," her husband said. "But I expect she died some years ago."

He slit open the letter and was reading it as they sat at the dining-table. Although it was only two sheets of small paper he took a long time over it and frowned noticeably.

"Who's it from?" his wife asked.

"A friend of George," he replied

"Who is George?"

"The chap who helped me do-up Grandpa's house and garden."

"I remember George," Edmund smiled. "Phillipa and I helped him in the garden."

"Yes, you did," his father smiled back. "He enjoyed having you and Phillipa help him."

"What happened to him?"

"He went to America."

"And became a model," his wife reminded him

"Did he really?" Edmund asked. "I seem to remember him being very nice. Did you know him, Mother?"

"I think you met him once, but you never came over to the other house," Foden said as she hesitated to answer.

"Certainly not. I hated it. What about George?"

"He died."

"Good heavens! He couldn't have been very old," Edmund said. "He was younger than you, wasn't he, Father."

"Yes. He was only forty-two."

"I won't have a starter, Betsy," Arabella said as the housekeeper attended them.

Edmund and his mother did most of the talking over the meal with Foden joining in only when necessary. His silence was noticed by Edmund who commented on it by asking if he was all right.

"Yes, Fine. I've just got one or two problems at work."

As Betsy began to clear away the table and Edmund said he would take a walk and stretch his legs, Foden surprised them

"I think I might drive up to the university and see how Noel is."

"Are you worried about him?" his wife asked with concern.

"No. But the new hybrid could do with a good work-out and that would give me the excuse to call and say hello."

"But you won't get back for hours,"

"I'm not tired and it will give me a chance to think about a small problem in the factory. Don't wait up."

But he didn't think about the factory on the drive; he thought about the letter in his pocket and his thoughts brought tears to his eyes.

By university standards Noel's flat was large. It was off-campus in an old Victorian house. It was seven thirty when Charles Foden found it and parked. He had been to the university only once, when Noel had first arrived and he had helped move him in. He had then roomed on the campus but had had to find other accommodation in his second year The university was not to Charles' conservative tastes - old and beautiful, cold and uncomfortable - nor was it a modern purpose-built university of architectural merit. The main building was akin to a Whitehall ministerial block, which was no surprise as it had originally been built for a similar purpose, and other buildings had been commandeered around the city as the university expanded but the establishment was very much part of the hub of the city and despite its comparatively recent history it had gained a good reputation in several faculties.

He rang the bell of Noel's flat. He rang several times and could hear it ringing inside the house but it was sometime before someone came to the door.

"I'm looking for Noel Foden," he told a young man who looked as though he hadn't changed his clothes for several weeks.

"I don't know if he's in," the man said. "I haven't seen him for a while. You can go up and knock if you like."

Charles Foden followed his directions up the uncarpeted stairs. He knocked on the chosen door and waited. He knocked again and thought he heard a noise but still the door was not opened.

"Noel? It's your father," he called, beginning to fear

Edmund had been right.

There was another noise, a long pause and then shuffling. The lock on the inside of the door was turned. The door opened slightly and an unshaven Noel peered past it.

"What are you doing? Are you all right?" his father asked. Noel reluctantly opened the door and moved away. His father pushed it further and followed him inside.

"God. This room is awful," Foden said and immediately opened a window. He turned and his son was cowering in an armchair, looking at him with pained eyes.

"Are you all right?" Foden asked again and Noel began to cry.

Once begun, the tears flowed profusely. His father took a handkerchief from his pocket and gave it to him then waited. He pulled up a desk-chair in front of him.

"I'm sorry, father," Noel mumbled eventually.

His father stood up. "Have you got any tea," he asked.

He walked through to the small kitchen and curled his nose at the sight of the unwashed dishes on the draining board. He filled a kettle and looked in the fridge, it was almost empty but he found some long-life milk. He made the tea and brought two mugs back to the other room and gave one to Noel and resumed his seat opposite. They both sipped their tea and Foden waited.

"Have you been ill?" his father asked, giving up the waiting-game. Noel shook his head. "Then tell me what the problem is and I'll try to help you."

Noel almost started to cry again and spluttered into the mug.

"I was raped," he mumbled.

If his father had dwelt on the problem for weeks it was not an answer he would have imagined but he immediately began to make connections.

"By whom?" he asked grimly. Noel shook his head.

"I don't know," he said and was crying again. "There were several of them."

Gang rape was only a phrase Charles Foden had heard from television programmes. He stood up and walked to the window and stared out at the skyline of the city.

"I had to do engineering. I learned mechanics and welding and how to use lathes. I could have gone to Oxford or Cambridge, I was bright enough, but Grandpa wanted me to do what he did."

He turned back into the room and saw that Noel was now listening to him. He resumed his seat.

"I was determined that I would let you all do what you wanted to do. Edmund wanted to go into the army. Phillipa wanted to publish books and you wanted to be a politician."

He let the silence make his point before continuing. "Politicians do not give way to crisis; they oppose it and find a way to defeat it."

"I have resigned," Noel mumbled.

"Resigned? You have resigned your degree with less than one year to go? Noel, I know how you must feel about this and the other incident, but running away is not the answer. You will be coming down soon for the summer. Give it until then and see how you feel in the autumn

"I wrote to the Dean," Noel said.

"God!" His father got off the chair again and paced about the room.

"Have you told the police?" he asked.

Noel shook his head.

"Why not?"

"If I did that they would soon find out about Caroline wouldn't they?"

By his silence, his father concurred

"They took pictures," Noel whimpered. "They're probably all over Facebook by now."

"She did this," his father said. "That girl, Caroline."

"How?" Noel responded. "How would she know men like those?" and he looked as though he would cry again at the memory.

"Tell me about them," his father said and Noel reluctantly, painfully, tried to describe them and some of his ordeal. He told his father about the phone-call and Mr. Pickles and of the boat-house.

"How do I get there?" Foden asked.

"It's no good, they won't know anything. They hire out the upstairs room for meetings," Noel told him. "It was Wednesday. They don't meet on Wednesdays. The men must have got the keys from somewhere."

"Where does this Caroline live?"

"Dad, please. I want to forget that."

"You will never forget it," his father said, bending low and thrusting his face at him. "You will never forget this. She arranged it, don't you understand? She will know who they were. She arranged it to get even for what you did. Where does she live?" Noel told him. "Right. I want you to have a shower and a shave and I want you to put on some clean clothes and wait here. At some stage you'll have to go to the hospital – but I think you'd better do that at home."

"Hospital? I'm all right."

"How do you know? You will have to have an HIV test."

Noel's face crumpled again.

"Don't snivel, son. Do as I say. I will be back in half-an-hour."

Charles Foden left and drove to the address Noel had given him which was near. It was a terrace of small houses. He rang the bell and when someone opened the door he said he was looking for Caroline. The man turned back into the room and called upstairs.

"Pen, someone wants Caroline. Is she in?"

Penny Featherstone appeared from a door at the top of the stairs.

"Who is it?" she called down but then saw who it was as Foden stepped inside and began to climb the stairs towards her.

"Mr Foden," Penny exclaimed. "What do you want?"

Foden was now at the top of the stairs.

"I wanted to talk to Caroline. Noel didn't tell me you lived here too," he said. He seemed nervous by the discovery/

"Why do you want to see Caroline? She's not in."

Foden's manner softened as he realised he had a problem.

"I wanted to talk about what happened," he said conspiratorially and looking down as though he were afraid the lower tenants were listening.

"You'd better come in," Penny said.

As soon as he was inside the room his manner changed.

"Where is she?" he asked aggressively.

"I don't know where Caroline is," Penny answered. "And I don't like your tone, Mr. Foden. We haven't yet decided whether Caroline will bring charges against Noel so I would advise you to leave."

Foden stepped forward and gripped Penny's arm forcefully.

"Charges? You've done worse than charges. My son has been gang-raped and he has resigned from the university. Where is she?"

"You are hurting me," Penny cried.

The adjoining door opened and Caroline stepped into the room. She brandished a canister, held in front of her like a gun and pointed it at Foden.

"Leave her alone," she said. Foden did so and turned menacingly towards Caroline.

"Get out," she said and pushed the canister towards Foden's face.

"Who were they?" Foden asked

"Who were who?"

"The men who raped my son."

"Did someone rape your son? How awful. I know how he must feel."

"You did this. I know you did this. Who were they?"

"I think you'd better leave," Caroline told him

"I'll phone the police," Penny said and opened her mobile. Foden backed away towards the door.

"This isn't over," he said. "This isn't over."

"Yes it is," Penny told him. "If you or Noel come near either of us again we will go to the police. We have four witnesses and I have photographs of what Noel did to Caroline."

Foden hesitated only for a moment before looking at both of them menacingly then walking out and slamming the door loudly behind him. Both girls sighed audibly.

"What's that?" Penny asked.

"Pepper spray."

"Noel raped?" Penny said.

Caroline shrugged her shoulders. "What goes around comes around."

When Foden got back, Noel was dressing. He had showered and shaved.

"What happened?" he asked anxiously.

"They pretended not to know anything about it. Is there a special meeting place for homosexuals?" .

"Dad...I don't want..." his son protested.

"Is there?" His father asked again

"The Gay Hussar," Noel told him.

"Would you recognise these men?"

"They wore masks, but I would know them."

"Think. What do you remember about them?"

"They were dressed in leather jackets and jeans mostly, and they all had shaven heads and wore earrings. They drove two Jaguar cars and they stank of a mixture of cologne and oil."

"What sort of oil?"

"Car oil."

"Are you ready?"

"Where are we going?"

"First, we are going to this Gay Hussar and then we'll get you something to eat."

When they found the pub, Foden told his son to wait in the car then went inside.

Although it was then after nine the bar was not busy as it was early in the week. There were a few people drinking around the bars but the cubicles were mostly empty. There was no sign of anyone answering Noel's description of his attackers. Foden was about to leave but a young man smiled at him and asked if he was looking for someone.

"Yes. Two men damaged my car. They said they would meet me here and get it repaired,"

"Do you know their names?" the young man asked.

"I've forgotten it. I was in a rush. They were a bit rough-looking, shaved heads, wore leather jackets and drove a Jaguar."

The man's face hardened. "The Batleys. They don't come in till late," he said.

"Blast! I should have taken their details. I don't suppose I'll see them again. But I did take down their car registration."

"They own a garage on Hall Street. They will probably be all right about doing your car but don't let them do anything else."

"What do you mean?"

The man just grimaced and turned back towards the bar. Foden thanked him and returned to his car.

"Do you know Hall Street?" he asked Noel.

Noel guided him to a road on the edge of the city. The buildings stopped almost immediately and a sign announced it was a through-route to a motorway. They quickly came to a small garage with no other building near-by. It had two petrol pumps on a forecourt and a small shop. The petrol station was closed but there were lights showing in the accommodation above which was extensive and ranged over the full extent of the lower buildings.

Foden went slowly past and pulled in to the side. He looked at Noel who seemed to be asleep, his head resting sideways on the window. Foden got out and walked back to the garage. He inspected the premises from the other side of the road, looking for any security cameras, but saw none. He crossed over to the garage and read a sign that declared it was the premises of JJ Batley and sons. There was a passageway leading to a rear yard with an MOT facility and steel doors to the main workshop. Two Jaguars were parked there. Foden examined the yard and the rear of the building and then returned to the front. As he emerged onto the forecourt he was confronted by four leather-clad men with shaven heads. They all stared at each other until Foden found his voice.

"Hello. I'm sorry. I was wondering if anyone was about," he said.

"We're well closed," one of the men told him.

"Yes, I realise that. Is there another garage near. I think I've run out of petrol."

He nodded towards the road and the men turned and looked towards his car.

"Tough," one of the men told him. "The nearest garage open is the supermarket in the centre of town."

Foden made an annoying sound.

"I suppose I'll have to walk back there. I could phone the AA but they could take hours and I'm in a hurry. I don't suppose I could persuade you to sell me a can of fuel? I'll pay cash and you can charge me what you like. I'm rather desperate to get somewhere quickly."

"You should 'ave thought of that before you ran out of petrol," another man told him.

"I know. But it's a new car and I don't think the gauge is working. It says I still have some in the tank – but it's been saying that for some time."

"It will cost you," the first man said.

"Anything."

"Fifty quid and you can keep the can."

"Thank you. Thank you. I'm very grateful," Foden said and took out his wallet.

The man spoke to the others and they walked past Foden towards the rear of the premises where the cars were parked. The first man walked back to the forecourt, rattling a set of keys. Foden followed. The man opened the shop and switched on the lights. Foden noticed the shop was well stocked with various goods including foodstuffs and a shelf of motor oils. He also noticed that a door behind the counter seemed to be the only access to the living accommodation above and that the door of the shop had a letter-box,

The man selected a five-litre plastic container from a shelf. He switched on the pumps and Foden followed him to where he proceeded to fill the container. Foden studied the man's face and found it difficult to understand how a normal, quiet and sombre appearance could hide a loathsome, sadistic nature.

"I'm sorry for holding you up," Foden said.

The man shrugged his shoulders. "No problem. Only going to the pub."

He screwed the lid on the container and handed it to Foden who took out his wallet and gave the man two twenty and one ten-pound note. He inwardly smiled at the look of satisfaction on the man's face as he quickly folded the notes into his back pocket.

"Thanks guv," the man said and he looked at Foden as he might at a child.

"No. Thank you," Foden responded and he looked into the man's eyes so intently that the look of satisfaction and amusement on the man's face became one of puzzlement.

As he walked away, Foden wondered at what precise moment the man, the man who raped his son, would realise the significance of that look and understand that what he thought was getting one up on a stranger with more money than sense was instead, a contract with the devil, and the inner smile escaped onto Foden's face at the thought of the perfect beauty of the agony the man would then feel.

He waited until he saw in his rear-view mirror a Jaguar drive from the yard and head towards the city. He then turned the car around and slowly followed in the same direction.

He found a small restaurant that was suitably ordinary for them not to attract particular attention. Noel found it difficult to eat but his father insisted that he should finish what he'd ordered.

"Where is your car?" Foden asked when Noel eventually pushed a dirty plate away.

"At the back of the house. There is off-road parking there."

"Are you up to driving home?"

"I think so…I'm not too sure."

"Better not. I doubt if you've slept in days. I can arrange for the car to be collected – that is, if you are adamant that you can't return to university?"

"How can I?" and the tears came again into his eyes.

"All right. We can give it time. You can always start another course elsewhere."

When they were in the car Noel asked where they were going

"We're going back to your flat. I want you to take a book and wait for me in the bar of the Pickwick Hotel." Foden knew the hotel because he and his wife had stayed there when they had brought Noel to the university.

"Why. What are you going to do?"

"I'm going to tidy up your room and collect some of your things to take home. I may be some time. Just have a drink and wait for me."

"Why can't I help you?"

"Because you'll just get in the way."

At the flat Foden was pleased to find the other occupants of the house were not there; 'Probably won't be back until the pubs close' he thought.

He packed Noel's books in a holdall and carried it down to the car then waved Noel on his way to the Pickwick Hotel, telling him the walk would do him good. He then returned upstairs and quickly set-about clearing the mess in the kitchen and throwing Noel's clothes into another suitcase. By the time he was finished it was almost eleven pm. He locked the flat and left a note for the downstairs tenants to tell them Noel would be away for some time and someone would return to take away his car.

He drove to the garage on Hill Street and waited beyond it in a lay-by with his lights off. It was not long before he saw the Jaguar return to the garage. He waited another fifteen minutes and then got out of the car and carried the container of fuel and a rag to the forecourt.

In the flat above, one of the Batley twins was breaking eggs into a frying pan while bacon sizzled in another. His twin was having a shower and their cousins were eating crisps and talking above the loud music. Below them, the cartons of biscuits and motoring books had caught fire and then several cans of oil had expanded and split and the fire had soon spread along the floor and was leaping up the door in tongues of orange flame to the wood joists of the ceiling.

From the doorway of the bar of the Pickwick Hotel, Foden attracted Noel's attention where he was sitting in a leather armchair staring into space, an unfinished glass of beer on a table next to him. He got up and waved to the barman and followed his father to the car. They exchanged only a few words before Noel was soon asleep, snoring loudly for most of the journey home.

****

Noel's mother had been told only that Noel was depressed and didn't want to finish his degree. She immediately blamed 'That awful girl,' but received no support from either Noel or her husband and seethed quietly.

The following day, Noel was taken by his father to A&E at the hospital where he was treated for post-exposure prophylaxis and kept telling the doctor and nurses that he wasn't gay. At home he became more withdrawn and stood in his bedroom staring out of the window for much of the day. It was in such a position two mornings after his return home that he was sub-consciously listening to the local radio station that had been his habit when in his rooms at university, when the music was interrupted for a news bulletin.

"Breaking news on the story we reported about the arson attack on a garage in Hill Street. It has now been confirmed that a fourth person has died from injuries sustained in the fire two nights ago."

Noel turned into the room and stared at the instrument, now giving details of the police enquiries regarding the case.

"It is believed it was a deliberate homophobic attack as the victims were known to be practising homosexuals. Detective Superintendent Simon Townsend told this station that enquiries were progressing within the gay community but he has stressed they will leave no stone unturned in their quest for the person or persons responsible. 'No one deserves to be burned alive,' he told our reporter Sally Gray."

Noel switched off the radio. He walked down the stairs and out through the front-door without closing it behind him. He continued down the drive and through the main gate, walking as though being fetched by a silent lure. He continued down the lane walking in a straight line across the Stokesey road and two others. The lane was the old route from the city to Stokesey long before the roads were built but was now no more than a track, the surface grown over and worn only by farm vehicles.

He had walked some four miles, oblivious of the distance or any physical features, when he was suddenly confronted by the river. It was the main river, a flowing tidal expanse under the five-arched bridge that crossed it to the outskirts of the city on the other side. The tide was flowing in and conflicting with the current making eddies and whirlpools against the buttresses of the bridge. He stood on the bank, staring down at the whirling mass of water as though unable to understand the impediment to his progress. He felt suddenly exhausted and his knees began to tremble and his brain seemed incapable of directing his body as to what it should do.

"Can I help you?"

The question was repeated again before the voice penetrated Noel's brain.

He turned and saw a young woman, probably no older than himself. She was wearing a long, knitted cardigan over a striped smock-dress with black stockings and her hair was pulled back from a clear, pretty face and tied in a knot behind. Noel looked at her as though she were an alien species.

"No. Thank you," he managed to mumble.

"Are you visiting?" she asked

"Visiting?" he repeated

She nodded her head in a direction behind her. He turned and saw a low building set back with pretty gardens between it and a low wall which bordered the tow-path on which he was stood.

"What is it?" he asked

"The Hospice," she said.

"Hospice?" he queried.

"A home for terminally ill patients."

He wondered why she thought he would not know what a hospice was.

"You look rather tired," she said. "Why don't you come inside and I'll make you some tea?"

"No. I couldn't. I shouldn't," he said and began to panic. "I'll just sit here for a moment."

He retreated to the wall and sat on it.

"Why not?" she laughed and her laugh was light and full of expression. She sat next to him and Noel turned his face away and pushed it towards the ground as though trying to escape her closeness. She put out her hand and touched his arm and he almost jumped away from her.

"Come in, please?" she said. "I'll make you some tea."

He turned and looked at her. She smiled at him and her hand opened as though she expected a bird to land on it. "Come." Noel lifted his arm and her hand slipped into his. "Come," she said again and Noel allowed himself to be guided from the wall and followed her through the garden towards the house.

"I'm Tracy," she said as they walked.

"Noel," he told her. "Do you work here?"

"Yes. I'm a nurse. "Do you like reading, Noel?"

Again he looked at her as though struggling to understand the question.

"Yes, of course. I am, was, reading English."

"Would you read to a patient for me?" she asked. "She loves books but her eyesight is not good and she would take so much pleasure if someone read to her. We don't always have the time."

"Yes. All right."

Tracy smiled all the way into the hospice.

It was a pleasant, modern building and he was led through a reception area into a kitchen where two other staff looked from Tracy to Noel but made no comment as Tracy made the tea in a mug from a simmering hot-water machine.

"Come and meet Claris."

They walked along a corridor and entered a room. It was furnished with a bed and two armchairs and had French Windows opening onto a pleasant patio-garden. An old lady was seated in one of the chairs and turned as they entered.

She smiled at Tracy.

"Hello, my dear. Who is this handsome young man?"

"His name is Noel, Claris. He's going to read to you if you would like him to."

The lady offered her hand, it was almost skeletal on an almost skeletal arm and the fingers were crooked but they managed to grip Noel's proffered hand quite strongly.

"How d'you do Noel?. That's awfully kind of you. You see, my eyesight is not quite what it used to be and I do so love reading."

"I understand," Noel said. "What sort of things do you like to read?"

"I like adventure or biography or even history, but I'm happy to read anything if it's interesting. What do you like?"

Noel dropped into the other armchair.

"I like good stories, with interesting characters."

"Like Dickens?"

"Yes. I think he qualifies rather well," he smiled and Claris laughed.

"I think he does," she said.

They discussed books and writers while Noel sipped his tea. Tracy had indicated that she would be nearby as she crept out of the room.

"Do they have many books here?" Noel asked.

"Oh, yes. They have rather a good library, quite eclectic. People keep bringing books in when they've read them."

"Where is it?" he asked.

"I'll show you," she said and attempted to rise from the chair but Noel was quickly on his feet and had almost to lift her from it. She clung onto his arm and used a stick with her other hand and they made very slow progress into the corridor and then across it to a lounge which was lined on all sides by bookshelves.

"There," Claris said. "I'll just sit here while you browse."

Noel lowered her onto a chair and began to promenade along the shelves. Someone had tried to organise them into sections by subject but it was rather haphazard. Noel called out author's names as he inspected the titles and Claris would make comments.

"H.E. Bates," he said.

"Oh, yes. I like him. I haven't read him for years. He was one of us, you know."

"One of you?"

"An airman, during the war."

Noel had taken one of the books off the shelf but he now turned quizzically towards the old lady.

"You were an airman?"

"The Air Transport Auxiliary. We delivered all the aircraft from the factories to the squadrons."

"How amazing. I would like to hear about that?" Noel said.

"Later perhaps. It's all rather boring. What have you selected?"

Noel looked at the book

"The Purple Plain," he said.

"Splendid. I remember that. It's about a pilot who crashes in Burma and walks back to his base because he is in love with a local girl and if he is going to die he wants to die in her arms. Very uplifting."

"Do you want me to read to you here?" he asked

"No. It's rather dull in here. Let's go back to my room and we can sit on the patio."

Noel helped her to make the slow journey back and out through the French Windows where chairs were already placed on the patio. The sun was warm and roses and azaleas were wafting their scent in a slight breeze. He read for over an hour until he realised Claris was asleep. He heard the door of the room open and he had just got quietly to his feet when Tracy looked out at them. He put his finger to his lips and crept up to her. He followed her into the room.

"Thank you," she said. "She would have enjoyed that so much."

"I quite enjoyed it too," he answered. "I hadn't realised I could read quite well."

"Who was it said something like, 'Reading is almost as great an art as writing?'

"I think it was David Cecil. What's wrong with Claris. Just old-age?"

"Cancer, I'm afraid. She won't have very long."

"Has she got any family?"

"No. She was never married."

"That's sad," Noel sympathised.

"I don't think so. She has had a remarkable life. You must come back and talk to her."

"Yes, I would like that."

"Should I take you home now?"

"It's quite a long way."

"I have a car."

"Don't you have to work?"

"No. I've finished."

They had continued into the corridor and were now at the reception area.

"Isn't that a rather short shift?"

They walked outside and she took his arm.

"I was on the way home when I saw you standing by the river."

He stopped and looked at her.

"You thought…"

"Let's not talk about it now."

Noel found himself going to the hospice every day. His visits did not always coincide with Tracy's shift pattern so he cycled, something he hadn't done since getting his driving licence. He found the journey along the lanes almost magical, the only noises were birdsong and the clicking of a loose cotter pin. He not only read for Claris but each morning he read all of The Times for a Mr. Bramble who was very political and Noel was surprised that he was able to listen to prejudiced opinions without feeling the need to correct them. Tracy's colleagues soon got used to his visits and seemed to look forward to them as much as the patients did. He made himself useful, moving furniture and beds for cleaning, running errands to the city and even helping some of the patients to eat.

Claris was continually entertaining and surprising. She told him about the war: the rationing, the bombing in London, the wild parties with airmen of all nationalities and of knowing Amy Johnson and of reprising her solo flight from England to Australia.

Tracy had taken to kissing him goodbye, no more than a lingering press of her lips to his cheek, and one evening, after she had driven him home, he apologised for never asking her inside.

"I don't think you would like my parents," he explained.

"Why not?"

"Because I don't."

"Then you will have to share mine," she told him and after a morning shift had finished she took him home for tea. Her parents had a small house not far from his own. They had two dogs and a large garden including a vegetable plot which her father guarded with ferocious zeal from rabbits and foxes and all kinds of insects. They both smiled a lot and he knew why Tracy did the same. He was immediately at home in their company apart from the terrors that were now buried deep inside.

He had nicknamed Tracy 'Angela'. "That's who you are," he had told her. "And to me, that's what you will always be."

She had kissed him then, her lips soft and warm and moist on his. All her personality seemed to travel through them into him. He wanted to hold her, to press her body to him but instead he took her hands and looked at her face which was asking questions.

"I can't marry you," he said. "I can't marry anyone, ever."

His voice seemed, to himself, to belong to someone else.

The absurdity of his statement seemed not to register with either of them. Tracy smiled as she usually did and held his hands and led him back inside the house.

It was a warm, sunny afternoon when Claris died. Noel was reading Kipling, insects were humming about the flowers and the Rhododendrons were beginning to burst into bouquets of cerise and lilac. He thought she would like Kipling as she had said she loved India. Her thin arm had crept towards his and her hand rested on his fingers.

"Thank you, Noel," she whispered and then she was silent. Her eyes had been closed against the sunlight and Noel thought she was asleep but then her arm had dropped and he had panicked. He shook her gently and then ran inside and called for Tracy who came quickly and went to Claris and examined her. "She's passed," she told Noel who could not then prevent his eyes from watering. He had never seen anyone die.

"What do people think about, in that moment, the last moment before the dying of the light?" he asked later.

"We won't know until it's our turn," Tracy answered. "But I think it will be about love."

"I hope so," Noel said.

He went to her funeral and placed a rose on her coffin. There were very few people there apart from the staff of the hospice.

"She once told me that the worst part of getting old is losing one's friends," Tracy had said. But there were many letters from all around the world and her obituary surprised Noel by being in the Telegraph. "She was an MBE," he said, reading it to Mr. Bramble.

A few weeks later, Tracy had felt confident enough to ask Noel why he had dropped-out from university.

"One day, I hope I can tell you," he answered.

"What will you do? Won't you ever go back?"

"Perhaps. I was thinking about reading medicine."

"I think you would be very good at that," Tracy said.

"I have no idea if I am strong enough."

"Why don't you come to India with me?" she then asked.

An explosive charge going off inside his body could not have moved Noel more. They were sitting on the wall opposite the river, eating their lunchtime sandwiches which Tracy's mother had made. Noel leapt upwards and stared down at her, his mouth open and threatening to drop Tuna mayonnaise onto her lap.

"India?" he eventually repeated.

"The Mission wants me to go to Mumbai. They have two orphanages there. I would like to go. It would be a wonderful experience."

Noel swallowed and regained his voice.

"When?"

"In three weeks time."

Noel turned towards the river as though hoping that when he turned back again she would be different, but when he did so her face was still watching him carefully. He walked

285

about, shaking his hands then he came back to her and sat on the wall.

"A passage to India," he said thoughtfully. "What would I do?" he asked.

"Read to the children. Make them love books as you do."

Daphne Morrison found Ivana Katowice living in a semi-detached house in a suburban street of the city. It was not the style of establishment she expected for a qualified psychologist. She had checked her qualifications carefully before contacting her. She had a doctorate from Bristol University and had practised in one of the London clinics for some years before starting on her own.

A small plaque next to the front-door announced her profession. It was another surprise; practising from one's own home seemed, to a police officer at least, unwise as psychologists tended to have unstable patients.

She had made an appointment in her name without telling the woman either that she was a police officer or the reason for her visit.

She announced herself through an intercom and was told to enter. As she stepped inside she was surprised to find herself in a narrow passage that led only to the rear of the house, the hall having been converted. At the end of the passage, framed in the doorway, was the silhouette of a large woman.

"Come through, please," the woman called in a pleasant voice.

Morrison followed the figure through the doorway into a room that had been built onto the rear garden. Now in the light she could see Ivana Katowice was a woman of early middle-age. She wore a flowered, flowing smock-dress which clashed with her red-died hair and large earrings and Morrison had the uncomfortable thought that she resembled a gypsy fortune teller she remembered from her childhood.

The woman smiled broadly and gestured for Morrison to go before her into the room. The room was carpeted and decorated in a restful shade of green. There was an armchair with a small table beside it and opposite to it a very modern, leather reclining chair with a matching foot-stool. A small sofa was against one wall with a coffee table and the single window had a view of a pleasant garden and was framed by dark-coloured vertical blinds.

"Do have a seat," Ivana Katowice said and gestured to the sofa. "Would you like some tea or coffee?"

"Coffee would be very welcome. Black, no sugar. Thank you."

Katowice disappeared through a door at the opposite end of the room from the entrance. Morrison hadn't noticed the door as it was painted black and the rest of the end wall seemed to be covered by dark glass. She sat on the sofa and wondered how long she would be welcome when Katowice learned of the purpose of her visit. The psychologist returned and set a tray down on the coffee table then sat on the sofa next to the inspector.

When she had poured the coffee she smiled that large smile.

"So, my dear. You said you only wanted to talk prior to a possible consultation. My fee for a preliminary consultation is sixty pounds. Is that all right for you?"

Morrison agreed that it was. "Doctor," she began but was stopped by a raised hand.

"Please call me Ivana. Titles are the worst thing for patients to have to face. The chances are they have been surrounded by them prior to seeing me."

"Fine. Ivana. Firstly, I have to confess that I am not here for myself. I am a police officer, an inspector."

Ivana Katowice lost her smile but showed no sign of commenting. She stared at Morrison coldly, patiently.

"Do you remember Katy Rose Lewis?"

The name had a noticeable effect. Katowice put down her coffee-cup as though she didn't trust her fingers to hold it any longer. "Yes," she answered softly.

"I know that you suffered a great deal of condemnation for what you said at the time of Katy's disappearance," Morrison continued.

"It was stupid of me to say what I said without thinking of the possible consequences."

"The consequences?"

The attempt on Jenny's life."

"I thought that had been kept quiet."

"I think the police managed to keep it from the press but I knew about it when the officer in charge blamed me for it."

Morrison had another insight into Laxton's culpability.

"That's why the Challis' moved away. They even changed their name, Jenny is now called Penny."

"It was stupid of me to say those things. I was much younger then. We all need experience to teach us lessons."

"Yes, we do. And I am not here to criticise you. I need your help. Would you be willing to help me, Ivana?"

"If I can."

"Thank you. But first we must agree that anything I say to you now will not go out of this room. If you find that difficult please tell me now."

"I have never broken a patient's trust – even when I have been put under considerable pressure to do so."

"But you work a lot with children don't you. Isn't that difficult, dealing with their parents and Social Services?"

"Very difficult. Parents mostly cannot understand their child has the right to be an individual outside of their influence. That is why a child, more than an adult, must trust me if they confide in me."

"You once said that Jenny Challis might one day remember

something about Katy's disappearance."

"I did. And I still think that is possible.".

"It is. You were right. It did happen."

Ivana Katowice fell back into the sofa. Her breath escaped noisily and she seemed visibly deflated because of it.

Daphne Morrison told her of Penny Featherstone's vision on Drovers' Hill, of how the family had changed their identity, but did not disclose their new names, and of the coincidence that had brought Penny back to the area. But she did not mention the police search operation or the shoe and earring that Tom Lewis and his mother had identified as belonging to Katy Rose. When she had finished Ivana sat forward eagerly.

"That's fascinating. So interesting," she said. "Such recall of deep-seated experiences usually happens over time, piece by piece. But for Jenny to have such a strong reaction to a location is absolutely fascinating."

"You haven't heard of it happening before?" Morrison asked

"Yes, I have. Location influence is very common. Our visionary sense is more developed than any other. Sound too. We all know how certain tunes or sounds can evoke the same responses we experienced when we first heard them. But Jenny's experience is as good a case that I have heard of. If she had had that vision after seeing Katy's photograph in The Badgers I would have suspected it. But the interesting thing is that she did not recognise Katy's picture, she had no memory of what Katy looked like – or rather, that it was Katy's face that was locked in her mind. Fascinating. Absolutely fascinating."

"Obviously, we are hoping that other memories of that incident are locked away in Jenny's head. Perhaps who Katy's abductor was," Morrison said.

Katowice looked doubtful.

"That is very unlikely, I'm afraid. You see, Daphne, often the most dramatic details of a trauma can't be recalled. It's rather like an attack by our immune system on a virus; sometimes the immune system damages the cells more than the virus – but prevents the virus killing us. It's the trivial details of a trauma that we remember."

"Sometimes trivial details are enough." Morrison answered. "Tell me about hypnotherapy. How does it work?"

"Often it doesn't. People think hypnosis is a magical weapon that can make us do anything or become something we are not. All hypnosis can do is to isolate our conscious mind and release our sub-conscious mind in a controlled way. Think of it as dreaming but being able to control those dreams. It works very well when a patient wants to remember something but it often fails to unlock memories of emotion that a patient does not want to remember."

"Like sex-abuse?"

Ivana opened her hands in a gesture of annoyance. "That is the one subject that divides our profession most aggressively. You see, it is possible to lead a patient by suggestion and I'm afraid some hypnotherapists are guilty of that. So there is a danger in hypnosis of getting a false reading."

"How do you avoid that?"

"By being very careful. There is no technology as sensitive as the human brain."

Daphne Morrison had heard what she wanted to hear. She knew she could trust Ivana Katowice with Penny Featherstone's security.

"How would you approach the Katy Lewis case with Jenny?" she asked.

291

"As any other patient. First I would have a chat, rather as we have done, and then, for a first session I would use a light level of hypnosis, rather like being in a relaxed state after a good nights sleep; listless, half awake and almost asleep. I would ask her to concentrate on the spot where she saw Katy in the woods and then I would see if her mind would take me somewhere else. In another session I would use a deeper method of hypnosis when she would be completely unaware of any extraneous objects or sounds. It might be that Jenny can't remember anything voluntarily – but I would know that after the first session."

"She's only just willing to do this," Morrison said. "Her parents are very apprehensive about it. I don't know if Jenny would try it more than once."

"Then what I would suggest is that you and Jenny first walk the route through Drovers' Hill, the way you did before and then bring her straight here for her session while the woods are still in her mind."

"That sounds like a good idea."

"But tell me, Inspector; have you thought of bringing her parents to see me?"

Morrison looked puzzled.

"Why I ask is that they saw the man who tried to abduct, in fact murder, young Jenny. Surely they are the best people to remember something about him?"

"Mrs. Challis could only give a description of the man's height and build. It was night."

"Then we shall just have to hope Jenny can remember something more," Katowice said.

Penny Featherstone agreed to make herself available the following weekend and Daphne Morrison said she would meet her at the railway station in the city on the Friday afternoon. Morrison had not told the Chief Constable or any other officer about the visit or of the consultation with Ivana Katowice. As it happened, Penny's visit did not go undetected.

Morrison was delayed in traffic getting to the station and Penny waited outside as agreed. She watched a car draw into the drop-off area farther along from where she was standing. A young woman got out and went into the station. The car drove off but stopped next to her and the driver opened the nearside window. "Hello," he called.

Penny was about to ignore the call but then she recognised Charles Foden. "Hello," she answered and stepped nearer to the open window.

"Would you like a lift somewhere?" he asked.

Penny explained that she was waiting for a friend to pick her up.

"I didn't realise you knew people down here. I thought your visit to us with your friends was the first time?"

"It was, but I do know someone here. How is Noel?" she asked, wanting to change the subject although not wanting to know about Noel.

Foden pulled a face. "Gone off to India to work with some charity or other."

Penny was visibly pleased. "That's good."

"Is it?" Foden said and by his tone he did not think it was. "Well, goodbye. It was nice meeting you again."

Penny smiled and nodded. The Car swung round to leave as Daphne Morrison's drove in behind it.

In his rear-view mirror Foden recognised the inspector as he waited to filter onto the road.

When she had settled into the car Penny told Morrison who she had been talking to.

"That's unfortunate. Is he likely to tell his son? I don't want your friends to know who you are?"

Penny was still excited by the thought of Noel's decision to go to India and spoke before her brain caught up. "No. He's gone to India to work for a charity. Isn't that great?"

"Is it? Why?"

Penny realised her mistake and her voice dropped to sombre.

"It is so unlike him," she said.

"Has he graduated? I thought he was in the same year as you?"

Penny squirmed inside, she was incapable of lying.

"He dropped out."

Morrison didn't pursue the subject but Penny's changes of mood told her there was more to learn of it. It also told her why Penny was likely to make a good subject for Ivana Katowice.

That evening they ate in. Morrison had prepared a seafood salad with saffron rice and sweet peppers. They drank a bottle of Sauvignon with it and finished with profiteroles and fresh fruit. Penny ate like any university student would. During the meal Daphne Morrison explained her visit to Ivana Katowice and what she had suggested about walking the Drovers' Hill route again.

"Do you mind?" she asked. "Or would it bother you?"

Penny said she was okay with it – and had brought her boots knowing how Daphne liked walking. After the meal they settled on two small sofas and spoke generally about work and people. A CD had been playing quietly beneath their conversation and when it ended Daphne Morrison got up to change it.

"What sort of music do you like?" she asked.

"All sorts," Penny answered. "A lot of group bands. I like Soul too and Blues." Then she laughed. "But I'm a bit ancient too. I love Blur – and their later albums as Gorillaz.

My friends laugh at me."

Morrison stopped what she was doing and turned to her young companion.

"What?" Penny asked.

"Katy Rose Lewis loved Blur too. "

Penny screwed up her face in the. silence. "Oh God. That's so weird. How do you know?"

"I read it in the case files. Apparently there was a Blur gig somewhere and we sent a police unit there looking for Katy."

Penny closed her eyes and sank back into the sofa. Daphne Morrison sat beside her and put her hand onto hers.

"Don't worry, Penny. What it means is that you may lead us to her after all."

The walk through Drovers' Hill woods needed some careful planning and Daphne Morrison had to get the help of Tom Lewis to do it. She wanted Penny to reprise the route from The Badgers that she and Katy Rose would have taken so many years before. But she then needed a car at the other end to take them into the city for the appointment with Ivana Katowice. Tom agreed to collect them from Upper Stokesey and take them to the pub for the start of their walk. He made a great fuss of Penny and Daphne Morrison needed to tell him that he should not be too optimistic for a result. She did not tell him they were seeing Ivana Katowice.

Before they started, Morrison suggested they go into the pub for Penny to have a good look at Katy's picture so her face was firmly in her mind prior to their walk.

It was a fine afternoon. They climbed the slope up to the Ridgeway with much puffing and pausing. "I don't know how Kat would have carried me and a pushchair up here," Penny complained.

"What did you call her?" Morrison asked.

"Kat. Isn't that what Tom calls her?"

Morrison nodded. "I believe Katy was a strong girl with lots of energy."

They reached the path and started through the trees. "We won't talk now," Daphne Morrison said. "Ivana wants you just to walk slowly and feel. Don't look for anything or think of anything. Just enjoy the walk."

She let Penny set the pace which gradually slowed to what Morrison hoped would be the pace of Katy wheeling a pushchair. They emerged from the trees and began the descent on the path to Upper Stokesey without Penny making any comment or registering any expression or reaction at any point in their journey through the woods. Daphne Morrison suddenly turned to their right. "Let's go this way," she said as they reached the end of the golf course and she led the way to the path skirting the course and dropping down to the road. As they reached the path Penny hesitated before following her. The path was just wide enough for two people to walk abreast but brambles and other plants had intruded onto it through lack of use so Morrison mostly led the way. It was stony and rough and they were both pleased to reach the road. The only pavement was on the other side of the road where there were a few houses set-back. Where they were standing and to their right there was a grass verge bordering the fenced-off golf course which led to the clubhouse and the car park. Morrison pointed. "That's where you were left. At that bus-stop."

Penny stared across the road. "You think someone pushed me down that path and left me over there?"

"I'm pretty sure that's what happened."

"But what about Katy. Where was she?" Penny asked, concern in her voice.

"That's what we don't know."

They crossed the road and followed it almost into Upper Stokesey where Morrison had left her car. They changed from their boots then drove to the city, only speaking when Penny wanted to, which was mostly to ask questions about Katy's disappearance and Morrison was careful not to give her too much to think about before they got to Ivana Katowice's house.

Ivana greeted Penny warmly, taking both her hands and leading her into the consulting room. The blinds were drawn across but not quite closed so the room was dimly lit but not dark. They were asked if they wanted anything to drink. Penny chose a glass of water and Daphne said coffee would be good.

"Come, I'll show you where you can make yourself some."

She led the way to the black door at the end of the room. They went into a narrow space. Along the back wall were three kitchen units on which there were the facilities for making tea or coffee. The other wall, which from the room side had appeared to be a dark glass window, was only a fret worked decorative board covered with a film of dark blue transparent material.

"That is my cheap version viewing window," Katowice smiled. "You can see and hear what is happening during the consultation. Sometimes it is necessary when dealing with children."

Daphne agreed to stay in the kitchen space and settled on a stool. She watched as Ivana took the water through to Penny.

"You are very pretty," she told her. "You were a pretty child from the photographs that were published in the papers."

Penny was surprised. "I've only seen the one picture."

"There were several."

Penny told her how her parents had never spoken about the

case. How she only knew of it when her grandma told her.

"That's good," the psychologist said. "The more information you have the harder it is to separate the things you really remember. Sit here, my dear. Make yourself very comfortable. The back of the seat will adjust."

Penny allowed herself to be ushered into the reclining seat.

"Put your feet up on the stool. That's it. I don't want you to go to sleep, just get very comfortable and relaxed."

She adjusted the back of the seat so that Penny's head was back and able to look easily at the ceiling and straight ahead at Ivana Katowice who had taken a seat in the armchair opposite. Ivana then talked to her in a soft, slow voice. She explained the practice of hypnosis as she had done with Daphne Morrison. Penny became aware that a globe on the ceiling, which she had assumed was a light shade, was slowly revolving. It was made up of small pieces of glass set at angles much like a huge diamond and the dim light from the half-opened blinds caught it and refracted from the prisms in coloured spots.

As Ivana talked, Penny's eyes went from her constantly to the ceiling until her eyes were closing increasingly.

"I want you to think about the walk you have just done on Drovers' Hill," Ivana said, her voice getting softer. "See the trees and the sunlight through them. Can you see that?"

Jenny said she could. Her voice was quiet and she was smiling as though being warmed by the sun.

"You are in a pushchair. Is it comfortable?"

"No, it's very bumpy," Penny smiled. "Bump, bump, bumpety bump," she said musically.

"Can you see anything besides the trees?"

"No. I can hear someone singing," and then she began to hum a tune in the high part of her palette. She suddenly stopped and her expression changed. A frown, then her head went from side to side as though she were at a tennis match. "What can you see?" Ivana asked almost in a whisper.

"Nothing. There's a lot of noise. Shouting."

"Who's shouting. A man or a woman?"

"Both. I can hear different voices." Then she laughed. "There's someone naked. Hopping. A man. He's fallen over. He's gone into the trees."

Her expression changed abruptly and she opened her eyes and sat forward and Ivana knew the spell was broken. She clicked a plastic snapper that was used for getting the attention of dogs and then Penny was completely awake.

"What was it?" Ivana asked.

"I'm sorry," Penny apologised. "Suddenly all I could see was Mister Foden."

"Who's Mister Foden?"

"He's the father of someone from university. I saw him yesterday and he's been on my mind ever since."

"Why is that?"

Penny shrugged and took a sip of water. She didn't know Daphne could hear what was being said.

"It's a horrible story."

She sat back again but took her feet off the stool.

"We were staying at his house, a group of us with his son, Noel. He was at uni with us. We came for a concert but there was an incident with Noel forcing himself on Caroline, my flat-mate. It was pretty nasty. Another friend hit Noel with a chair to get him off Caroline. He had to be treated in hospital. Foden tried to bribe us to keep quiet. Then, apparently, Noel was gang-raped and Foden blamed Caroline. He forced his way into our flat and threatened Caroline and when I saw him yesterday at the station it brought back the whole business again."

Daphne Morrison walked in from the back room. Penny

looked at her as though she had forgotten she was there.

"I heard," Daphne told her.

Ivana Katowice hastily explained that sometimes someone had to witness consultations. "I didn't think it mattered that Daphne was listening.

"No. Of course not," Penny agreed.

"That's pretty serious stuff," Daphne said.

"I sort of wanted to tell you about it but I didn't want it to get any worse than it was."

"Tell me about it later – if you want to," Morrison told her

"Right," Ivana said. "I don't think we can take the session any further now. But what about this naked man?" she asked Penny.

"I don't know," Penny laughed. "It was funny. I think he was trying to put on some shorts or trousers as he was sort of hopping or trying to get away."

"Did you see him? Was he young, old?"

"I didn't see a face. Just his back. I think he was young."

Daphne Morrison remembered Julie Norris' description of George: with a body to drool over and wearing the shortest of shorts.

"That was a very good first session." Ivana was saying. "Don't you agree Daphne?" Daphne agreed.

"See how you feel tomorrow," Ivana continued. "If you feel like coming for another session I will be here."

In the car Daphne smiled sideways at her young companion.

"Are you all right? Did you know you were humming a Damon Albarn song? I think probably Katy would have been singing as she pushed you."

"That is scary."

"How do you feel about another session?"

"I don't know if it would do much good. I don't seem to

know any more than what we already know."

"We didn't know about the naked man. Perhaps, if you told me all about this business with Foden and his son it will clear it from your mind and you may be able to recall more about Katy."

"I don't know how much I should tell you. We asked Caroline if she wanted to take it further. At first she wasn't sure but now she just wants to forget about it. She changes the subject if I mention it."

"I can understand that. But rape is serious and gang-rape is something else."

"I know" Penny agreed and Daphne could see it troubled her.

"Tell me about it over dinner."

They went home and changed then walked to a local pub where they sat in a corner and had fish and chips. Slowly, skilfully Daphne got the whole story of Noel's assault on Caroline and of Foden's visit to their flat.

"Caroline should have reported it," the policewoman in Daphne said. "That's almost as bad as it gets."

"She was worried about ruining Noel's career."

"That I can understand, but Noel could do the same thing again. How will Caroline feel if that happens?"

Penny didn't know. "But if Noel has given up on politics and gone out to India to help with a charity, he must have changed," she argued.

"I think being gang-raped probably had more to do with that." Morrison said.

"He was contrite afterwards, when he got back to uni. He sent flowers and wrote letters of apology. Caroline was okay with that until we all saw him speaking at a uni debate. He was really aggressive and horrible so we thought the apologies were not heart-felt. Then Caroline got all depressed again and I told her she had to talk to someone."

"Did she?"

"Yes, her course tutor. She's a clinical psychologist. She told Caroline to think of it as bad sex and not to let it destroy her."

Morrison decided not to comment on the advice.

"What about the gang-rape. What do you know about that?" she asked.

Penny said they didn't know about it until Foden accused Caroline of having something to do with it.

"Do you think she might have had something to do with it?" .

"No. No. How could she? Neither of us talked about it. Then we heard from someone that a picture of Noel being raped had been put on Facebook. It was taken down but not before a lot of people had seen it."

Daphne Morrison realised she was being made aware of several criminal offences.

"I thought you would have known about it," Penny continued. "Soon afterwards, there was the arson attack on a local garage and four men were killed and everyone seems to think they were the men responsible for the gang-rape. They were known locally as the Doggers Crew and all the gay community hated them."

Morrison sat back and stared at Penny. Penny realised how casual it had sounded.

"I know. I know. It's all horrible isn't it? We've tried to ignore it. Caroline hasn't mentioned it so I haven't talked about it either. She seems much better now. Probably because she doesn't have to see Noel any more."

Daphne Morrison had a lot of questions but she did not want to play the heavy policewoman and she knew a serious investigation of the arson attack would be under way.

Instead she concentrated on what did concern her.

"Tell me about Foden threatening you. How did that happen?" she asked.

Penny told her of Foden's visit and how they threatened to report Noel to get rid of him but how he also told Caroline she hadn't heard the last of it.

"And have you or Caroline heard any more from him?"

"No. I think he's scared that Caroline might still report Noel."

"No wonder Foden was on your mind. Heavens! You really have given me a lot to think about."

By the time they got home it was after eleven pm. They listened to the television news and then decided to go to bed.

"Don't worry about anything, Penny." Daphne told her and kissed her goodnight.

It was in the early hours that Daphne wakened to a noise. The walls of the old cottage were timber-framed with wattle and daub fillings. She thought she had heard Penny call out and as she listened she heard what sounded like her moaning and then, quite clearly crying. She got out of bed and went in to Penny's room. She saw the girl turning and moving her arms wildly. She sat on the bed and touched her shoulder. Penny jumped awake.

"You were having a nightmare."

Penny groaned. "It was horrible. I was in something, being tossed around and then falling, faster and faster. I was trying to get out but I couldn't move. It was like being in one of those Big Dipper cars that had gone off its rails."

"I told you not to worry about anything," Daphne laughed.

"I know. Oh, God. I'm a mess. But I haven't had that nightmare for years."

"You've had it before?"

"Yes. When I was a child. Then I seemed to grow out of it

– until now Why now? I suppose it's all this Foden business.."

"Come on. Move over. I'll stay with you."

Penny moved across the bed and Daphne got in beside her.

"You're so kind," Penny said over her shoulder. "You should have been a nurse, not a policewoman."

Daphne put her arm around her waist and Penny covered her hand with her own. "Go to sleep," Daphne told her.

She felt Penny's breathing getting slower until she knew she was asleep. Suddenly she thought that she would quite like to have a baby and fell asleep thinking how it wouldn't happen.

They slept until late in the morning. Daphne got up and made some tea and Penny was still asleep when she took it back to the bedroom but she woke as Daphne set the mug on the table beside her.

"Hello," Daphne said. Penny smiled and sat up. "I don't think we'll go back to Ivana," Daphne told her. "I think you've had enough for now. You need to go back and get on with your work and forget Katy and Foden and everybody for a while. I'll drive you back today."

"But that will take you two hours," Penny protested.

"I know. But I only have to drive, the car does the work – and there won't be any traffic on a Sunday,"

"Are you worried about me?"

"Only that I don't think you get enough rest. You're like me, you won't let go of things. If I run you back at least I will know you'll get there safely and not fall asleep on the train."

It was lunch-time when they eventually got themselves together and set-off for the university. When they arrived outside the little house which Caroline and Penny shared with two boys, there was a moment of awkwardness as

Penny didn't know how they should part.

"I would like to ask you to stay rather than make that drive back but we don't have a spare bed – or even a settee," she said.

"I don't mind the drive. Don't worry about me. But a cup of tea would be nice. Could you manage that?"

"Of course," Penny laughed. Then she looked concerned. "I don't think Caroline should know that I've told you about the Noel business. You don't have to mention it do you?"

Daphne Morrison had suggested tea only because she was hoping to be able to talk to Caroline.

"Don't worry about the tea. I'll have a meal before I drive back. You're welcome to join me if you would like to."

Penny said she had to prepare a paper for the morning.

"Then go and do that and don't work all night on it. Thanks for coming Penny. You are giving us all hope that we'll find Katy."

They hugged. As Penny opened the car door, Morrison leaned towards her.

"Penny, I can't ignore what you told me. What happened to Noel can't be isolated from what happened to those men in the garage."

Penny sat back in the seat again and looked miserable.

"But don't worry about it. It's possible you and Caroline might be questioned about Noel. But unless Caroline wants to, she needn't tell the police anything about what Noel did to her. They will only be investigating what happened to those men and whether Noel had anything to do with it."

"Do you think Noel could have had something to do with the fire?"

"I don't know. I don't know him. Do you think he could?"

"I don't think so. But what happened to him must have been a frightening experience. I just don't know how he would react to it. I know how it's affected Caroline."

"The local police will be investigating every possibility."

"Do you think that is why he's gone to India?"

"Possibly. One way or another it seems like a good thing for him to have done considering what he did to Caroline and what someone did to him."

Daphne Morrison checked in to a hotel.

****

The university town was the county police headquarters and the next morning she was admitted to the underground car park. As she entered the police station the first thing she saw was a notice about the arson attack. There were photographs of four men who were identified as Elvis and Warren Batley and Morris and John Tate. The notice was obviously the flyer the police had circulated for information about the murders. She identified herself to the desk sergeant and asked to speak to the officer in charge of the arson investigation. She was shown into the office of Detective Superintendent Simon Townsend who wanted to know why she was interested in the Batley case. Daphne explained that an incident had come to her notice in her investigation of the Katy Rose Lewis disappearance.

"I remember that case," Townsend told her. "I was a uniformed inspector, like you, at the time. The county were asked to do CCTV searches on the motorway links. Have you got new evidence then?"

Daphne Morrison only said that a possible connection had turned up and they were rechecking the files. "But it's nothing substantial," she added. "That's why they gave the job to me instead of the CID. Has the name Noel Foden come up in your investigation?"

Townsend repeated the name until his memory worked. "Yes. Foden. Wasn't that the name in the bog-body case down your way?"

Daphne agreed it was. "Same family, but that wasn't Noel. Noel was a student here until a few weeks ago. He was gang-raped and everybody seems to think it was by the Doggers Crew."

Townsend lost his polite, friendly manner. His eyes narrowed defensively.

"How do you know this, Inspector?"

"I've been in touch with one of the students here. It was when a few of his University students were visiting Stokesey for the music festival at Easter that one of them found something that has been identified as belonging to Katy Lewis. I dropped the student back here yesterday after a recreation of the find and learned about the gang-rape and the arson attack. It's all around the university. Apparently, a picture of Noel Foden being raped was put on Facebook."

She watched the Detective Superintendent carefully but his eyes only briefly showed surprise.

"My team would know about it," he said. "They're processing a heap of information. We've interviewed about fifty people in the gay community and elsewhere."

"Then I'm sure they will know about the Foden incident. But it seems the arson attack occurred around the time that Noel Foden left the university and went home. I just wanted to be sure you'd made the connection, sir."

Townsend softened a little. "The problem is, Inspector; the Batleys and the Tates were about as popular with the gays as a dose of HIV. Everyone is happy at what happened to them and no one wants to put anyone else in the frame for it."

"That must be difficult for you. I hope my information might help in some way."

"I'm sure it will. And if your student contacts can give us any more information then we'd be grateful. Did they by any chance mention a foreign youth?"

"Another student?"

"No. We think not. He was seen talking to the Batley crew in the Gay Hussar – the local gay pub. He was described as thin with his hair in a pony-tail and wearing a poncho."

"Mexican?" Morrison asked with a smile on her lips.

"Probably from Tonipandi. But he was seen flashing some notes at the Batleys. He hadn't been in the pub before."

"Sounds positive for a suspect," Morrison agreed. "I'll ask my contacts about him for you."

"Thank you. That would be helpful. Also, there was an older man asking questions about the Batleys. Have you heard anything about that?" Morrison said she hadn't.

"I assume you'll want to speak to Noel Foden," she said. She put a sheet of paper on his desk. "That's the Foden's home address. "I believe Noel has gone to India. I hope that won't be a problem for you, sir."

****

Detective Superintendent Townsend's guarded response to the information Daphne Morrison provided was forgotten when he addressed his team later that morning.

"Why do I have to learn from an outside force about a student from the university who was gang-raped by the Doggers Crew," he wanted to know. No one could answer the question. They all stared uncomfortably awaiting a further onslaught.

"Noel Foden," Townsend continued. "A PEP and English student who happened to leave here about the same time as the arson attack. Do we believe in coincidence? No."

Again he awaited a response without success.

"For Christ's sake. I thought we had covered all possibilities. Get out there and ask about this Foden. There was a posting on Facebook of the rape. Find it. It was downloaded and circulated around the university. It should not be beyond your capabilities of getting a copy. Johnson, talk to the college and find out when this Foden resigned, and where he roomed. Talk to his flatmates and get the exact date and time that he left. Jeremy: Noel Foden has apparently scarpered to India. I have a home number for the Fodens. Talk to his parents. We want to speak to their son even if it means going to bloody India to do it. And I want answers soonest; the University goes down for the summer in two weeks. "

When Detective Constable Jeremy Bolton phoned the Foden house he spoke to Arabella Foden. Charles Foden had decided it was better for his wife not to know of the real reason for their son's decision to leave the university and had only said that he was too unsettled after the unpleasant incident with the Caroline person to continue. So when Bolton spoke to her, her body and mind tensed with fear.

Despite her husband's assurances that they would not hear from the Caroline person again the possibility was never far away and when the officer asked if he could speak with Noel it seemed only too real.

"Why do you want to speak to my son?" she was brave enough to ask. The officer ignored the question and persisted.

"Is he with you? We understand he has left university?"

"He's not here. I think you will have to speak with my husband if you require any further information," she concluded and put down the receiver.

When Foden got home early after his wife had phoned him at his office, she was in quite a state.

"Calm yourself, Arabella," he told her.

"I can't bloody well calm myself. Noel is going to be charged with rape and you think I should stay calm?"

Foden flopped into a chair.

"He's not going to be charged with rape. He was raped. I didn't want to tell you about it because Noel was in no state to talk about it. He did not want you or the family to hear about it."

He told his wife how he had found Noel in his flat. How he had tried to persuade him to stay on at university. "But he was in no state to listen," he continued. "This girl, Tracy, seems to be what he needs. Going away with someone he likes is the best thing for him right now."

His wife's panic was over and had been replaced by a deep feeling of concern for her son and an equally deep feeling of loss and helplessness.

"But if he hasn't made a complaint why do the police want to speak to him?" her brain eventually found the energy to ask.

Foden then told her about the arson attack and fear took over her body.

"And they think Noel had something to do with it?"

Her voice rose with her astonishment.

"I expect they are interviewing everyone who had anything to do with those people."

"What people?"

Foden told her about the Doggers Crew and watched the effect an unknown, unsuspected, and incomprehensible world had on a woman from a wealthy county family with a military tradition whose tenet was family, love, charitable giving and loyalty to a Christian faith.

They did not speak again for over an hour. Charles Foden had a shower and changed from his suit and his wife busied herself in the kitchen until it was time for drinks. "What are you going to do about the police?" she then felt calm enough to ask.

"I suppose I'll have to speak to them," he answered.

"Will you tell them how to get in touch with Noel?"

"No. As far as they know I have no way of getting in touch with him."

"What if they arrest you?"

"My solicitor will get me out immediately. They have no proof that I know where Noel is."

"Is that wise, Charles? Won't it make them suspicious that we have something to hide?"

"What we have to hide is the damage this would do to Noel. I hope he is feeling better but there is no way of knowing that. It could be that he isn't. Can you imagine what a police interview would do to him – especially if they want to go all the way to India to do it?"

They drank in silence for a while and then his wife asked,

"How did you know about this – Doggers Crew?"

"Noel told me about them."

"Then if he knew who they were why on earth didn't he report them?"

Her husband was showing some irritation.

"He was in no state to do anything when I found him. I don't think he had moved from a chair for several days. He thought someone had posted photographs of his ordeal on Facebook. He was terrified of going out."

"Poor Noel. How could anyone do such a terrible thing?" the mother in her asked.

The irony in her her remark was ignored by Foden. He was pleased for her mind to take another direction, until she then said; "That girl Caroline. She's responsible for this." He knew she was right but felt helpless to do anything about it.

The next morning Foden rang DC Jeremy Bolton.

"Thanks for calling back, sir. We want to speak with your son, Noel. Could you tell us how we can get hold of him?"

Foden said he couldn't, that he had gone abroad and they had no contact number for him.

"Really? Has he disowned you?"

Foden was vocally irritated. "He doesn't own us so he cannot disown us."

"I'm sorry, sir. I didn't know how else to phrase the question. What I mean is that it sounds as though he doesn't want any contact with you if he hasn't left a forwarding address or a phone number. Do you know where he has gone?"

"To India. He is having an emotional crisis and just needed to take himself off for a while."

"I'm sorry to hear that. We understand he has dropped out of university?" Foden confirmed that was so. "Would that be because of what happened to him?"

"That depends to what you are referring."

"We understand he was gang-raped."

There was silence as Foden wondered why or how they would know of it.

"Yes," he eventually admitted.

"I'm very sorry, sir. That would be a traumatic experience."

"It was."

"Did he or you report the incident?"

"No. Noel was too traumatised to want to talk about it. That's why he took himself away."

"I understand. But we need to talk to him because he may have information regarding the people who did that to him."

"He is not going to bring any charges so there is no need to subject him to anything else that can only worsen his condition."

"We have officers who are specially trained to deal with rape cases, sir. We do need to talk to him."

"I'm sorry, I cannot help you. When and if Noel does contact us I will let him know you wish to speak with him."

Foden put down the telephone.

When DC Bolton reported the conversation to DS Townsend he knew immediately what to do. "Right. We'll do it the hard way. We'll question this arrogant bastard under caution."

Townsend's request was put to his Divisional Commander who then spoke to Morrison's Chief Constable. He explained why they needed to interview Noel Foden because he might have information regarding the arson crime.

"Apparently this Foden chap is not being very co-operative. He says he has no way of contacting his son. One of your officers, Inspector Morrison, brought the matter to our attention. Perhaps she could sit in on the interview as she seems to know about Foden and his son."

The Chief Constable had an uncomfortable feeling that giving Daphne Morrison what was thought to be a preliminary task in investigating the Katy Rose Lewis case was building into the greatest work-load that had landed on his desk. His discomfort was more acute that it was now somehow involving Charles Foden. He was well aware of the influence Foden had in the city and the surrounding area. But the other direction the phone request took was that Daphne Morrison had not informed him of this latest development and had chosen to tell another force about it instead. Was his PA getting above herself? He thought she understood that she was on leave, pending her standing-down from the Katy Rose Lewis case.

He had no alternative but to agree that Townsend's officers could interview Foden but emphasised to the senior officer at the other end of the telephone the need to handle Foden with the utmost respect or both of them could be scraping shit off their office walls.

Before he could ask his secretary to get Morrison into his office, she knocked on his door.

"Good morning, sir. Have you got a moment? I want to bring you up to date on what's been happening in the Katy Lewis investigation."

"I thought I was up to date with the investigation – or at least I was up to the point where I told you to take time off."

Morrison knew her chief well enough to sense when an admonition was brewing.

"Yes sir. But it was hard for me to switch off, so I thought I would research newspaper files about the prisoners-of war-camps in the area."

The Chief Constable wondered what prisoners of war had to do with Foden or Katy Rose Lewis. He gestured Morrison to sit and she continued while she had the opportunity.

"While I was there, I read the reports about the Katy Rose Lewis case. I found a photograph of the Challis family, including the young Jenny Challis. I recognised the likeness of the child and the mother to Penny Featherstone."

Her chief's face now lost all expression except astonishment. "Good God!" was all he could say.

"Yes, sir. Penny's parents confirmed she is Jenny Challis."

She let him compute the information in silence.

"So she isn't psychic. She's something else," he eventually commented.

"Yes sir. It makes her information even more important, wouldn't you agree?"

The Chief Constable did agree.

Morrison pressed home her advantage.

"We can't drop the case yet, can we? Penny, or Jenny, has more to give us."

"How?" her chief asked.

Morrison told him about Ivana Katowice and what she had predicted could happen which had led to the attempt on Jenny's life.

"Her parents are still worried for her safety and I promised them no one else would know Penny's real identity. But I had to tell you, of course."

He nodded agreement and gestured for her to continue. She told him of the visit to Katowice, quickly adding she would pay her fee as she saw the censure on his face. He interrupted her when she recalled the reference to a naked man.

"A naked man. Are we being serious? A child less than two years old could remember a naked man?"

Morrison's reaction surprised him.

"We are being very serious, sir. Penny is a serious girl and she and her family have been through a terrible ordeal. The girl is frightened by what is happening to her. We can't let her down by ignoring it."

Her chief muttered an apology.

"But what difference does it make? It doesn't take us any further in the investigation does it?"

"Unless we put a naked man, a lost golf-club and George Fuller together. If a member of the club was involved with George Fuller it would make it easier for two men to get Katy off the hill and down to a car wouldn't it?"

While the other officer pondered the possibility she told him about Penny Featherstone's nightmare.

"She said it was like being in one of those big-dipper cars that had come off the rails. I think being taken down to the road in the back of a golf-buggy on that rough track would be rather similar, wouldn't you agree, sir?"

The senior officer was aware that agreeing would emphasise the wrong choice he had made to search the marshes.

"It sounds very plausible, Daphne. But where does it all get us? How can we prove that is what happened? Unless we find George Fuller we're not going to be able to question him and I don't see how we can make a link between him and a member of the golf club. Unless we find Katy's body and get some DNA from it – which is very unlikely after twenty years – I don't see how any of this, fascinating as it is, is going to get us any further. And if you are right and Katy was taken away by car how are we going to find her?"

Morrison had asked herself the same questions and the answers she had found were more in hope than expectation.

"I'm still waiting for a response from the Passport Office to find what address Fuller had given them and I've sent the golf-club for DNA analysis; both of which are taking a bloody long time. The address could lead to a link to someone local and the golf-club could put someone from the golf club in the frame."

"Good. Good. If either option proves successful then we can progress the investigation. If not..." He didn't need to explain the alternative. "Meanwhile; I've had a call regarding a DS Townsend and an investigation into an arson killing."

"Ah! Yes, sir. I was coming on to that."

Her chief leaned back on his chair and waited. She told him about Foden's accidental meeting with Penny and how it had interrupted the hypnotherapy session and how she had then unburdened herself about what had happened to Caroline and what Noel Foden had done to her.

"I took Penny back to university and I thought I should alert DS Townsend about the connection with Noel while I was there. I don't think they knew about the gang-rape."

The Chief Constable leant forward onto his desk and tapped it with a pen; a frequent, annoying habit.

"My God, Daphne. You attract crime like a magnet. What else are you going to uncover?"

She smiled apologetically.

"You say Foden's son, Noel, attempted to rape someone and then he was gang-raped?"

Morrison confirmed the information.

"Then it sounds suspiciously like revenge for what he did to the girl, doesn't it ?

"It does. But Penny couldn't see how Caroline could have anything to do with it."

"Well, its not our case. Someone else will have to sort it out."

He told her of the request to interview Foden.

"They want you to sit-in on the interview. You know how brittle Foden is. If we let other officers loose on him they may well end up arresting him and that will give me an awful headache. I don't want Townsend and his crew crawling all over him. You can tell him we only want to speak to Noel in order to find out who did that awful thing to him."

"I don't like Foden, sir. But he is no one's fool. He will know they want to put Noel in the frame for the arson attack in revenge for his rape."

The implication had not occurred to the Chief Constable.

"Really? Do they think that?"

"It's an obvious possibility."

"Is the boy capable of that sort of thing?"

"I don't know him. But Penny said he could be arrogant

and aggressive. If he's anything like his father I would say there is a distinct possibility that he would want to get even with his assailants," she answered.

Her chief was thoughtful.

"Foden is very competitive," he admitted. "He certainly doesn't like to lose a pound or two at golf."

The request for an official interview was put to Foden's wife over the telephone and she was told that Foden could be interviewed at home, in his office or at a police station and that he should ring them back to arrange a suitable date.

Foden telephoned DC Bolton and agreed to be interviewed at his offices in the city on condition they did not wear uniform, used an unmarked car and did not disclose their identity to his staff.

****

DC Bolton was duly impressed that a senior officer looked so attractive in a skirt and short jacket with a pink blouse under it and standing quite tall in high-heeled shoes. Foden too was affected by Daphne Morrison's appearance – but for other reasons.

"Why are you here?" he asked rudely.

DC Bolton explained that it was customary for a member of the local force to observe an interview from an outside constabulary.

Bolton had been well briefed, mostly by Daphne Morrison. First he cautioned Foden that the interview would be recorded and may be used for future reference. He took out a notebook and asked for the date when Noel had left the university and returned home. Foden said he could not remember the exact date.

"Noel's flatmates seem to think it was Friday, the 9th. Do

you think that would be right?" Foden conceded it was a Friday but had nothing in his diary to confirm the date. Bolton then asked how he got home.

"He has a car," Foden replied.

"Did he go from the university to home by his car?" the officer persisted knowing that enquiries at Noel's flat had established that his car had been collected after Noel had left.

"No. I collected him," Foden admitted.

"But you had forgotten that, sir?"

"No. I had not forgotten that. I wanted to know how well you were doing your job. If you know what happened to Noel I assume you know where he lived and would have spoken to other people that lived in the same house. So why are you wasting my time by asking questions to which you already have the answers?"

It was an assault that baulked the young detective and Foden pressed on with the advantage.

"We hadn't heard from our son for over a week. My wife was worried because he did not answer his telephone so I drove over there to find out what was going on. I found him severely traumatised. He had not eaten for days. He was afraid to go outside. He would not answer the telephone. It took me some time to get him to tell me what had happened to him. I cleaned him up, took him for something to eat and then we drove home."

The detective was also taking notes and used it to slow Foden's stream. He finished his notes and then asked. "What time did you arrive at your son's place?" Foden thought it was about seven pm. "About what time did you leave the city to go home?"

"I can't remember exactly. By the time we'd had a meal and I had collected most of Noel's things from his flat it took quite a long time. So it was quite late"

"How late approximately?"

"Gone eleven I should think."

"That is late. What were you doing in the four hours between arriving at your son's flat and leaving for home sometime after eleven?

"It took time to get Noel together. He was in a very poor state. By the time I had persuaded him to have a shower and tidy himself up and we had had a meal that took up most of the evening."

"Was Noel with you all of the time?"

"Not exactly. He waited for me at the Pickwick Hotel while I got his things together and tidied up his flat."

"Why was that, sir?"

"Why was what?"

"That he waited for you at a hotel?"

"He was of no use. He was just sitting around and getting in the way, so I told him to take a book and wait in the hotel for me until I'd cleaned up his room.""

"Can you give me the times he was at the hotel?"

"I can't be sure. I was not looking at my watch, my mind was on other things, like Noel's state of mind and the fact that he had resigned his degree course."

"Did he return to his flat before you came back here?"

"No. I collected him from the hotel."

"You must have some idea how long he was waiting there."

"Possibly about an hour – but I couldn't be sure."

"Did he drive to the hotel?"

"No. He walked. It is not far from his flat."

"Did you call on anybody else before you went home?"

Foden's brain quickly recognised the connection Morrison had with Penny Featherstone and why she was probably sitting-in on the interview.

"I went to see another student, a friend of my son's from university."

The DC wanted to know the student's name and address. Foden could only tell him her name was Caroline and could not remember her address.

"Twenty four Church Avenue," Morrison answered.

Bolton looked quickly at her but Foden's eyes lingered longer on hers.

"Of course, you would know Inspector; being a personal friend of one of the girls."

"My relationship with Penny Featherstone, Caroline's flatmate, is purely professional."

"Is it? Even though she stays with you?"

Morrison could not help her surprise showing and Foden enjoying it. Her brain worked quickly; how did he know Penny had stayed with her; had she told Noel? She doubted that very much. Then she remembered their near meeting at the railway station; did Foden follow them? Why would he do that? She had no time to consider the reasons beyond the obvious one that a personal relationship with a witness could jeopardise a prosecution. Was that the reason for Foden's smirk and steady look?

"You must be taking a personal interest in Penny Featherstone to know that. Why would you do that, Mr Foden?"

Foden lost his surreptitious smile. "Because, according to you, she told you she had left a camera in The Badgers when my son said she had only one camera with her, which I know she had with her when she returned to university. So either she lied or you did and I am curious to know why. If she lied about that she could lie about anything."

Morrison was secretly astonished at the way the interview

had changed and was grateful for Bolton's interruption.

"All of that has nothing to do with this interview. Could you please just answer my questions, sir. Why did you go to see this Caroline?"

"Because I believe she was responsible for what happened to my son when she stayed at our house."

"Why would you think that?"

Foden didn't know how or why Morrison was connected with Penny Featherstone but he had to assume she had told the inspector about Noel's assault on Caroline.

"She accused my son of attempted rape. She was with a group of students enjoying Noel's hospitality at our house. They went to a pop concert, had too much to drink and were waltzing around the house the next morning in a state of undress when Noel was foolish enough to think that this girl Caroline's state of undress was an inducement to a sexual advance."

He watched the blood flow quickly to Morrison's face and stared at her challengingly.

"I see," Bolton said. "And you think she might have had something to do with what happened to Noel ?"

"Yes."

"Because your son raped her?"

"My son did not rape her. I have explained what the situation was."

"Then why would you think she was to blame for what happened to Noel if he did not attempt to rape her?" Morrison interjected.

"I thought you were only here to observe."

"Unless my personal knowledge can help DC Bolton's investigation."

Foden realised his accusation was putting Noel's relationship with Caroline onto the police agenda.

"Look. I went to see the girl because I was very angry for what happened to Noel. I did accuse her of having something to do with it because she was equally angry with my son for what happened when she stayed with him. If she hasn't made a complaint I don't want to talk about it. I have no way of knowing if she could have had anything to do with what happened to Noel so there is no point in pursuing the matter."

"We'll decide that after we have spoken to Caroline," Bolton told him. "How long were you at the girl's flat?"

"Less than five minutes. They asked me to leave and I did."

"And where did you go then?"

"That was before I took Noel for a meal, so I went back to his flat."

"Well, sir, this is a preliminary investigation. It's very possible we will need to speak with you again. It would seem we have to confirm certain facts and timings you have given us so it is important that we speak to your son so he can corroborate or change anything you have said. Are you still saying that you do not have any information as to his whereabouts or that you have no means of contacting him?"

"Yes. I am saying that."

"Do you have any questions, Inspector?" Bolton asked.

"Have you ever been into a pub called The Gay Hussar?"

"I have been in many pub's who's name I have had no cause to remember or even to know, so I cannot say I have or I have not been in one called that. Is that all, detective?"

"Yes, thank you for your time, sir." Bolton said.

"Not at all. If Noel does get in touch with us I will let him know you wish to speak with him."

"That's okay, sir. We'll be issuing an international arrest warrant for him. We will need you to provide a photograph of Noel. You could either fax it to us or let Inspector Morrison have it."

The effect on Foden was immediate. "Is that necessary? He's done nothing wrong?"

"Apart from being accused of rape and failing to report a crime," Bolton responded. "Goodbye, sir."

Outside Morrison smiled. "Well done, Jeremy. You handled that well."

"We both did. Is that true about his son and Caroline?"

"Yes. But she doesn't want to bring charges, so I don't want her questioned too heavily about it."

"We'll have to check her out, just to confirm what Foden told us."

"Then be careful; she's very brittle."

"What was all that about you and a Penny Featherstone?"

Morrison explained that Penny was helping with their investigation of the Katy Rose Lewis case.

"Is Foden involved in the case?"

"Not that I know of."

"Then what was that all about?"

"I don't know. I'll have to think about it."

"It sounds a serious business with Noel and the girl, Caroline."

"It was," Morrison agreed.

"It's all a good reason for Noel to go to India. Can you believe Foden doesn't know where his son is?"

"No. I can't, and it will be interesting to hear Noel's version of who did what on the night of the arson attack."

"How d'you mean?"

"We know both of them were there when the arson attack happened and Foden has just told us they were separated for some time. So, either of them, or even both of them would have had time to set the fire."

324

"We'll check the Pickwick Hotel and see how long Noel spent there. The timings are important; we know fairly accurately when the fire was set; a nearby farmer reported seeing the blaze at 11.30 and we estimate it was started no more than ten minutes before then."

"There are quite a few things you will need to check."

"We're doing a CCTV search around the town. Now we know Foden was there we'll check to see if his car was caught anywhere. And when we find Noel we'll see if his version agrees with his father's."

From his office window, Foden saw the exchange. He stood there for some time even after they had driven away. Then he phoned the shipping company.

THE PRESENT
8

When Morrison called in at the police station to report on her interview with Foden, she met the Chief Constable in the corridor before she reached his office.

"Hello Daphne. How did it go?" he asked cheerfully. She told him how it went.

"Mm! So he wasn't very co-operative?"

"Not at all. They're issuing an arrest warrant for Noel."

"God! That's going to raise a stink. How did Foden take that?"

"Not very well. I think it might persuade him to suddenly discover he knows how to get in touch with Noel."

"I hope so. Why would he pretend he didn't know?"

"To protect Noel, I suppose."

"One can't blame him; what would we do if it was our son?"

"I have no idea, sir. I hope we would act according to our conscience and within the law."

"Yes. But it would be a hard decision to have to make. It's not our case anyway, thank God. Well done, Daphne. Thanks for doing that."

He was about to move on to his office.

"There's one other thing, sir. I want you to know that when Penny Featherstone has come down here on our behalf, she has stayed with me."

The Chief Constable looked puzzled.

"She wouldn't have helped if she was put into a hotel alone," Morrison explained.

"I can understand that. Did you want to claim for her accommodation. Or is it something else?"

"Of course not. I just wanted you to know about it because Foden seemed to think it was important."

"Really? How did he know?"

"I don't know, sir."

"Odd. But he is a bit odd sometimes. All right, Daphne. Go and enjoy the rest of your leave."

She watched him disappear into his office.

'So he didn't tell him' she told herself. She went into her office and checked her mail. She found a response from the Passport Office in her In-tray.

It showed that George Fuller had applied for his passport a year after leaving the golf club and gave his address as Upland House, Uplands Drive, Upper Stokesey.

The news excited her but before she set-off to check the address she had to warn Penny that she and Caroline would probably be interviewed. Penny was apprehensive for Caroline's sake.

"Don't worry. They will only want to check the timing of Foden's visit. Caroline need not talk about her ordeal unless she wants to bring charges against Noel."

She then asked Penny if she or Caroline had heard anything about an older man asking about the Doggers lot in the Gay Hussar or anything about a Mexican-looking boy wearing a poncho giving them money. Penny said she hadn't but she would ask Caroline.

"I thought your friend, Camp Freddie might have mentioned them. I'm sure the police there will get in touch with him too - if they haven't done so already. Have you had any more nightmares?"

Penny laughed. "No. I've been sleeping really well lately."

"Good." Morrison said but was disappointed.

She set off to find Upland House, feeling now that the information as to where George had been staying was not going to be helpful. If it was a lodging house it was very unlikely anyone would still be there to remember him.

She found the house situated between Stokesey and Upper Stokesey. It was a large Victorian corner building in a high position with gardens all around and a circular drive. There was a rental board outside for one of the flats. She parked in the road and walked up the drive and saw an expansive garaging area to her left in what must have once been the stabling area. There were only two cars in it. She continued to the front door and counted six name plates. She pressed three of them before getting a response. A woman's voice asked what she wanted. Morrison hadn't prepared for the house to be let into flats; she needed to find out who owned it and decided it was better not to be a police officer for that.

"I'm supposed to have met the estate agent here about the flat that's vacant. He said he would meet me outside but I've waited quite a long time. I wondered if he was inside?"

"I haven't seen anyone. I can check the hall for you," the voice responded.

"Thank you."

After some minutes the front-door was opened and a pleasant looking woman in her seventies smiled at Morrison.

"I'm afraid there's no one around. Perhaps she's forgotten. I don't think they're very good. They are the managing agents, not estate agents, and one does have to remind them when things need doing."

"Yes, I got that impression too. I'll have to phone them. But I'm not happy. I've made a special journey and I don't know when I can get back."

"Oh, dear. The vacant flat is above mine. It's quite similar but not as big. Would you like to see mine? It would give you an idea of whether you will like it or not."

" That's very kind of you. It would help."

328

The woman introduced herself as Mrs Courtney as she led the way up a beautiful staircase to the first floor and into a hallway. She pointed to the kitchen and two bedrooms off it then led the way into a spacious living-room with large windows overlooking the rear garden.

"How lovely. And what a beautiful garden," Morrison enthused.

"Isn't it? I spend a lot of time down there."

Morrison asked how long she had lived there and was told eighteen years. "We were the first tenants – apart from George."

Morrison held her breath to stop the air escaping in a rush.

"My husband was alive then. He loved it here. He liked to do things and helped George and Mr. Foden's builders quite a lot, especially when they were landscaping the garden. You see the pond?"

Morrison recovered her breath and said it was a lovely pond.

"I call it Adam's Pond. He loved ponds and planted all those wonderful wetland flowers and grasses and the lilies; aren't they splendid? They're at their best right now. Monet would have loved them."

Morrison enthused again, her mind being on other things. But Mrs Courtney's was still in memory lane. "Of course, Adam didn't actually build the pond, George had just done that with one of those digger machines before we moved in. He landscaped all of the garden."

"George sounds like a useful chap. Who was he?" she asked as casually as she could.

The woman smiled.

"Dear George. He was such a lovely boy – well he wasn't really a boy, very much a man. But he looked so young and was so full of energy. I always think of him as a teenager," and her eyes took her somewhere in the past. "He was Mr. Foden's right-hand man and supervised the builders and managed the house and was the gardener too."

"What happened to him?"

"We don't really know. He suddenly left. Mr. Foden was very upset. Especially after he'd done so much for him."

"In what way?"

"He was very attractive and Mr. Foden took photographs of him and got him modelling work. He got quite well-known. Do you remember the ads for Love Frost deodorant? They were all over the television at one time. Anyway, that was George,"

"How long did he live here?"

"About two to three years I think. He said it had taken a year to convert the house and they were still doing the gardens and converting the stables after we moved in. And it must have been nearly another year before everything was finished and all the flats were occupied. It was sometime after that when he left. I think he probably felt it was too quiet for him here when he had got that big modelling job."

"You mentioned a Mr Foden. I presume he is the owner? Does he have anything to do with the house, or does he just collect the rent."

"I don't think he has to bother about that sort of thing. He owns Foden's Agricultural Machinery in the city. He does come quite often, but not so much as he used to. He's a keen photographer and has a studio in the basement. But he lets the agents deal with everything. They're not so bad really, just a bit slow sometimes. I think you would be very happy here," she added hopefully and Morrison had to back-track and say she was looking for somewhere for her mother.

"Well there isn't a lift and the vacant flat is above this one. But the stairs are wide and easy to climb, but it would depend how agile your mother is."

"Not very, I'm afraid. That would be a problem. It's such a shame because they are lovely flats and in such a beautiful position."

She thanked the woman and said she would let herself out. She opened the front door, called up to say goodbye and closed it loudly. When she heard the flat door close she looked around the hall and found what she hoped would be the entrance to the basement. The door was locked and she saw it had a mortise as well as a security lock. She let herself out of the house quietly.

She returned to her car, almost dizzy from a rush of adrenalin. She sat, waiting for her body to stop tingling so that she could think calmly about the link between the mysterious George Fuller and Charles Foden. She had expected her visit to Upton House to be another dead-end, instead it had opened up a vista of new possibilities.

That Charles Foden had suddenly emerged as a significant figure in her own investigation did not surprise her as much as it would have done prior to his interview by DC Bolton a short time before. Then, as bizarre as it seemed, she pointed out to DC Bolton that if they suspected Noel Foden of murdering four people they had to suspect his father too. It had been a cool appraisal of the situation but she had not seriously considered that Foden could be responsible. It would have had to have been the work of an emotionally disturbed person and that was not an image one could easily apply to Charles Foden. But if his description of the emotional state in which he had found his son were true, then it would be even less believable that Noel would have been able to set the blaze that destroyed his violators. But that was someone else's problem and it was only important to her as a window to her own investigation.

There could be innocent explanations as to why Foden had employed George Fuller after he left Stokesey Golf Club but at the moment she could find only puzzles and no solutions. Why would he give him work? It was possible that Foden knew George the groundsman as he was a member of the club. It was possible that he offered George a job because he had found him to be a good worker. But why would he have chosen to do it so near to Katy Rose Lewis' disappearance? That day must have been chaotic with police enquiries everywhere and anyone behaving outside their norm would have attracted attention. But George Fuller had somehow escaped those enquiries; DS Laxton had no knowledge of him when his name came up at their meeting. Even allowing for a misguided or slack investigation, surely everyone at the golf club, only a few hundred yards from where young Jenny had been left, would have been questioned? Why would a significant member of the club employ George in those circumstances? Was George living at Upland House while he worked at the club? Is that how Foden knew him? Was Upland House then a lodging house and Foden decided to turn it into flats with George's help? Was that why George left the club? Were either of them questioned in the police enquiry? Laxton was so sure it was a motorist who abducted Katy that a lot of people probably escaped questioning. But Laxton had said that members and staff of the golf club had been questioned.

She rang Steve Jennings. They had not spoken since their last frosty meeting and she had felt disinclined to call in for tea and cake as she often did. They greeted each other politely.

"Steve, how are you getting on with examining those statements from the traffic reports and the club members?

He said he and one of his team were trawling through them

when they had the time to spare. It did not reflect any belief in the task.

"I would like you to concentrate on two people. One is someone called George Fuller who worked as a groundsman at the golf club and a Member called Charles Foden."

"Should I know of any special reason for targeting them?"

"Only that I want you to do it and I want you to do it urgently."

"Right then. I'll get on with it."

"Thank you."

She had no time to waste wondering about Jennings' continued grumpy mood, apart from a vague feeling that somehow she had upset him when they argued about the golf-buggies. She had more important things to think about.

She rang the forensic laboratory and asked for the chief pathologist with whom she had worked on the bog-body case. She explained she had taken a golf-club in for DNA analysis and wondered if it had been done.

"So sorry, Inspector. We've been a bit off our heads here. I have two technicians off sick and your bog-body case did set us behind schedule a bit. I'll try to get on to it soonest. Is it urgent?"

"Nor urgent. But it is important."

"When it's done I'll phone you with the result. I promise."

Morrison was still sitting in her car outside Upland House. After twenty minutes of stimulating, mental activity her brain had suddenly stopped, not sure what it should do next. She looked up at the rental sign and noted the name of the agents. Would there be any useful information to be had by visiting them? She could only think that they could tell her how long Foden had owned the house and whether it was a lodging house before being converted. But she could see no purpose in that information and it was more than likely that her visit would get back to Foden and instinctively she knew that it was never a good idea to reveal to someone they were being investigated until you were ready to question them – and it was too early to question Foden; there was a lot more information she needed before she could do that Then the unhappy thought occurred to her that when that time arrived, if that time did arrive, it would not be her place to do so, it would then have to be a CID investigation.

But there were things she could do. If she couldn't question Foden yet she could still try to find George. Mrs Courtney had said he had modelled. She could try to trace the agency that had handled the Love Frost deodorant contract.

She went to the central library and searched their commercial directories for modelling agencies. She found only two in their part of the country and then only concentrated on the many London-based ones. She made a list and took it home. She spent two hours on the phone. Many of the agencies had gone out of business or had been merged with bigger ones and she picked up bits of information from each call which led to other bits of information like a paper-chase. She eventually reached a London agency called Sally Redfern. They told her they would search their archive but were not very happy when she gave the dates they should look at. She expected them to call her back in days, if at all, so she was surprised when an Edna Fielder caught her soon afterwards with her mouth full of pasta salad. She explained she was the Projects Director of Magnox.

"But I once ran the Sally Redfern agency and I remember George Fuller very well."

Morrison spat her mouthful of pasta into the sink and explained as calmly as she could who she was and that George had come up in an investigation.

"I don't know that I can be of much use to you. He did some work for us but we also acted as London agents for Magnox. They had seen pictures of George and put him in touch with us and when the Love Frost assignment came up they remembered George and contacted me. He got the contract. It was a big break for him. I went to work for Magnox when they opened their own branch in London. Unfortunately, Love Frost was bought by an American company and we lost that account."

"What happened to George?"

"The American agency handling Love Frost liked George and offered him work.

"Did he go to the States?"

"He did. Then he informed me he had signed with a New York agency. I was not happy; I had big plans for him. He was special."

"Did he stay in America?"

"I assume he did. We never heard from him again."

"Do you know which agency he was with in New York?"

"The Josh Brown agency. They are one of the big boys."

Morrison thanked her. She went online and found Josh Brown. She checked her watch and estimated it was mid-morning in New York. She rang the agency and spoke to three different people and each time had to explain who she was and what she wanted. They were all very polite but unhelpful until she lost patience and said it was a police enquiry and was very important. She eventually spoke to an executive vice-president.

He wanted to know what her business with George Fuller was. She bit back her anger and explained again who she was and that George was identified as someone of interest in a crime investigation.

"Then I'm afraid he won't be able to help you. George died

a few weeks ago."

All the waiting, all the hope deflated inside Morrison like a pricked balloon and spilled her frustration into the room.

"Did he work for you?" she forced herself to ask, knowing somewhere in her mind that such useless questions would be asked by someone else.

"He was still on our books but he hadn't done much work for some time. I don't really think he had to."

"Was he financially secure?"

There was a trace of a smile in the voice.

"You could say that, or rather, his partner was."

"He was married?"

"I don't know if he was married but he had been living with Wayne for several years. Wayne is a very successful property developer here."

She asked if he could provide a number for Wayne, which he eventually did.

She thanked him and flopped onto a sofa. So Gorgeous George was gay. She remembered Penny's vision of a naked man. The idea of Katy Rose having a confrontation with two gays had then crossed her mind but she had forced it to concentrate on the facts one at a time. But even the Chief Constable had acknowledged there could be two men involved with getting Katy and Jenny off Drovers Hill. But he would never, she decided, never accept one of them could be Charles Foden.

Charles Foden gay? It was an intriguing if not convincing possibility. She knew enough to know that being married and having a family did not inhibit the possibility, but she would not have guessed it from her several confrontations with Foden. Then she thought of the arson attack on the Doggers Crew. Perhaps that wasn't just a case of revenge – or at least, not revenge for what happened to Noel.

336

A new dimension was emerging of Charles Foden. Was he the monster in a suit and tie? Is that why he sheltered George after he suddenly left the golf club? It was making a lot of sense. According to Mrs Courtney, he was responsible for George's modelling success. Then George went to America and lived with someone else. Did that leave a deep scar; a scar that was responsible for the murder of four gays? Then she remembered someone had tried to kill Jenny Challis. That also did not fit with her estimation of Foden. Killing rapists was one thing, trying to kill a child was on another planet. Or was that down to George? And if it was, would Foden have known about it? The police had kept a lid on the attempt. Was that why George escaped to New York?

Her head ached with all the speculation and she surprised herself by a sudden feeling of wanting to throw the case out of a window. She knew the signs of brain block. The Chief Constable was right; she needed a break. She could visit her mother, but that wouldn't stop her thinking. She could get stoned. Alone? She trawled through her phone book.

"Julie? It's Daphne: that nosy copper who doesn't play golf. I need someone to get pissed with. Are you up for it?"

Julie Norris told her to come over.

THE PRESENT
9

The container ship *Ramallah Maru* had only two cabins for passengers. Both had a shower and toilet but neither cabin was large. One had two cot-beds bolted to the steel floor and the smaller cabin had two bunk-beds. Tracy and Sister Agnes Malone shared the larger cabin and Noel had the other to himself.

The journey from the port of Bristol had not started well for any of the passengers. Heading into the Atlantic the natural forward pitch of the wide vessel was regular enough to be tolerable for the non-sailors but when they cleared Land's End and the Channel Approaches a persistent south easterly contested the seasonal flow of the ocean and for two days and nights through Biscay the ship pitched and rolled and the passengers never left their cabins, refusing food and only drinking bottled water and it wasn't until they rounded Cape Finisterre that the winds eased off the coast and the ship settled to a regular rhythm and the passengers felt their unsteady legs could take them farther than the bulkhead doors.

Sister Agnes was the first of the passengers to venture out onto a balcony surrounding the third level of the accommodation block. She was met with bright, temporarily blinding, sunshine and a decent breeze which she sucked in, hoping it would cleanse the stale taste of vomit from her tubes. She was then joined by Noel Foden whose great bulk sagged from the waist and made his shoulders hunch forward like a chimpanzee's. He was dressed only in a pair of shorts and slip-ons and as he shuffled forward to take hold of the rails the professional nurse in Sister Agnes could not help thinking what a difficult patient he would make when he was old and infirm.

They exchanged morning greetings as if to speak was a painful experience. Noel asked after Tracy and was told she was sleeping.

"I think that's what I'll do," he said and shuffled back to his cabin.

The crew of the ship were headed-up by only four permanent officers: the captain, his first and second officers and the chief engineer. The rest of the crew, including the other two engineers, were engaged on a voyage-only contract and were moved about by the shipping company between vessels.

Each day the passengers had been attended by one of the Indian crew. The attention being only to enquire whether they wanted anything to eat or drink and was usually a knock on the door and a shouted greeting every few hours and all three passengers had separately decided the regular greetings were to see whether or not they were still alive.

Later that afternoon the response from all three had been more positive and they agreed to take tea together in the officer's mess. They assembled and greeted each other with smiles and more energy and were able to withstand the jolly natures of the captain and chief engineer who were already sat around the steel dining table and seemed to find their passenger's existence more a source of amusement than relief.

"Just eat a little cake and have some sweet tea," the captain advised them. "Then you will feel better. Tonight I will have the cook prepare some steamed fish and vegetables and when you have eaten that, tomorrow you will feel like tigers."

Captain Dillip Dhoni was a man somewhere in his fifties. He spoke almost flawless English and had a quiet confidence commensurate with the responsibility of handling a fifteen million dollar vessel with cargoes of several millions in value per voyage. He told them that as a young cadet he had attended the Merchant Training College in Dulwich, South London and exercised his knowledge of London and the surrounding areas where many of his relations lived. From experience he knew that listening was, for passengers recovering from seasickness, easier than talking and kept their minds away from concentrating on the possibility of further attacks.

But for the passengers even listening became a burden and Tracy was the first to declare that she thought she would go and lie down until dinner and Noel and Sister Agnes soon followed her to their cabins.

When they were called for dinner they all felt a lot better. Noel had shaved and was dressed in slacks and a shirt and wore sandals instead of his annoying flip-flops. The women too looked as though they had made efforts to hide any trace of their afflictions that still paled their skin and they all walked with firmer legs.

Tracy greeted Noel with a gentle kiss on his cheek and held his hand as though he might suddenly run away and hide. They ate the fish and drank more tea and even managed a little of the same cake they had before declined but they all felt that a sponge and syrup pudding which the Captain and Chief Engineer ate as though it were their favourite, would be too much for their stomachs to appreciate.

Afterwards, they accepted the captain's invitation to see the Control Room. The captain and Agnes took a small lift but Noel and Tracy followed a crewman who had been detailed to take them to the bridge. They climbed another six levels and arrived knowing their legs were not yet recovered from their ordeal. They entered the control room where the captain was already introducing Sister Agnes to another officer.

The huge room, the whole forty three metre width of the ship, was immediately comforting. The only light was from the many instrument panels, blue screens, green waves and red dots, and from the night sky outside and it reminded Noel of when he and his father had been taken into the cockpit of a Boing airliner by a pilot friend on a trip to Canada – but without the noise.

The captain took them round the consoles like a proud father, explaining what the various instruments were and Noel was again, annoyingly, reminded of his father when he was showing a customer one of his agricultural machines.

"And this is what you steer it with?" Tracy asked pointing to a traditional wheel. "But no one is steering," she said, suddenly alarmed.

The captain laughed at her. "Everything is automatic, like the automatic pilot in an aircraft. That wheel is only used when we have to manoeuvre her ourselves, going into a birth or a tight mooring. This is what we use if we want to interrupt the auto pilot for some reason," and he pointed to a joy-stick no larger than the gear-change of a car.

Then they were all staring out of the forward windows, thirty feet above the top containers that stretched out in regimented rows below them over two hundred and thirty metres to the bow.

"There are so many," Tracy said and her excitement pleased Noel; she had recovered.

"Seven thousand," the captain smiled. "But they are not all full. We usually carry a full cargo into Europe but not on the return."

Noel was tempted to make a correlation with the bureaucratic trading rules of Europe but resisted.

"We are what is termed a Post Panamax Plus Container."

He explained that ships were categorised by their ability to get through the Panama Canal.

"We are by no means the biggest. They are making them now in South Korea almost twice this size, but not for this route. They are too big for the Suez Canal," he explained to an enthusiastic Tracy.

"We are going through the Suez Canal?" she asked and almost forgot as she jumped up and down that she was less than a few hours from feeling that she was going to die

"Yes. Tomorrow we will be in the Mediterranean. If you are up early enough you will be able to see Gibraltar," the captain told her.

Tracy grabbed Noel's hand. "Isn't it exciting Noel?" she said and Noel agreed that it was.

"Then I think I had better retire if I am to get up early," Sister Agnes told them and the Captain said he would escort her down.

Noel and Tracy descended to a lower deck and held each other as they stared out across a moonlit ocean.

"I thought the ship was huge," Noel said. "But it isn't even a speck on that," and he waved a hand westwards towards the Azores.

"Are you glad you came with me?"

"Yes." Noel agreed. "I'm very glad."

The next morning they were all up to see the ship enter the Mediterranean and they were able to look back and get a clear view of the extraordinary rock before they went down for breakfast. The weather was now settled and seasonally hot and all three took a tour of the decks with one of the crewmen. The Chief Engineer met them and asked if they would like to see the engine room. Noel and Tracy said they would but Sister Agnes chose to sit on deck and read a book.

The young passengers followed the engineer down the several steel stairs through various levels and labyrinths of piping and cables to the depths of the great hull where the two diesel motors were housed. The Chief explained the various functions and had an appreciative audience in Noel and Tracy. Noel looked upwards and around him at the network of steel and said how his father would love all of it.

"Is he an engineer?" the Chief asked.

Noel explained what he did – and quickly changed the subject to obliterate the memories of all he'd left behind.

"What do you all do to pass the time on these voyages when you're not working?" he asked the engineer

"In the old days a lot of officers drank too much," the man told them. "If you weren't a Conrad or a reader it was hard being away from the family but now all the crew have laptops and they can access the social media."

Noel quickly ignored the thought that the engineer had heard of Conrad. "You have website access?" he asked, shifting his surprise.

The Chief laughed. "Yes. On a ship like this we have satellite access all the time. We can talk to other ships anywhere in the world."

The answer gave Noel an uncomfortable feeling that there was nowhere in the world to hide any more.

Their progress along the Mediterranean was mostly uneventful and pleasant. They looked through binoculars at the coast of Africa but at Cap Bon, Tunisia was so close the glasses were not needed. They went between Sicily and Malta and Tracy felt the disappointment they could not go ashore. "Next time we'll take a cruise ship," Noel joked and Tracy inwardly glowed that he thought there would be a next time.

Between meals, when the weather was not so fine, they sat

in the women's cabin around a small writing table attached to the wall and played simple card games. Agnes was a Bridge player but neither Tracy nor Noel had the desire to be taught. "Perhaps when we're in India," Noel said.

"You won't have the time then m'boy," Agnes told him and took the opportunity to talk about the three orphanages where they would be working. Two were in Mumbai and the other eighty miles inland at Poona. Agnes had been going there for twenty years. The staff worked a two-year stint and the charity relied on volunteers who got a little spending money and their food and fares provided.

"I think you'll love Mumbai," she told them. "It's everything our world isn't. It's noisy and dirty and takes an eternity to get permission to do anything. But it's constantly fascinating and the people are lovely – especially the children. They will love you, Noel. Do you play cricket?" Noel said he did a little but rugby was his game. "Then you can teach them rugby. You will find them very rewarding."

That evening, after dinner, Tracy and Noel were together on one of the decks, endlessly looking at the sea and the trail the great ship was making through it.

"Agnes likes you," Tracy told him. "I don't think she would mind if we shared a cabin," she said hesitantly and felt Noel tense. When he made no reply she untangled herself from his arm and looked up at his face. "Don't you like me, Noel?" she asked. The pain and frustration showed quickly.

"Of course I like you," he said. "I like you very much Trace…" He left the sentence unfinished and there was an awkward silence but when Tracy realised he was not going to find the words she said, "I know you're not married."

Noel made a sound between a laugh and a snort.

"I'm only twenty. How could I be married?"

"What then," she asked. "Are you gay? – I won't mind if you are," she quickly added.

Then Noel did laugh; it was a sound deep in his throat and Tracy did not know what it meant.

"Are you?" she asked again.

"No. I am definitely not gay," he told her and there was now a seriousness to his voice. "I am... I am just, right now, asexual," he said.

Tracy struggled to understand and a thought alarmed her. "Are you ill, do you have a condition?" she asked and her worried face made Noel spontaneously take hold of her and hug her close to him.

"No." he said into her neck. "I'm not ill. Soon I'll be able to explain, Trace. It's getting better. Just keep being my friend and you'll soon make me whole again."

They never spoke again of the problem and the next day they approached the coast of Egypt and Captain Dhoni was there to point.

"You see that haze; that's Alexandria," he told them.

They all saw the pink haze on the horizon and watched for an hour as it got nearer until it was a white line between the blue of the sky and the deeper blue of the sea and soon the white line emerged as buildings reflecting the sun like a mirage. Noel remembered his history and thought of the great general after whom the city was named. He thought of Caesar, Marc Anthony and Cleopatra and he stood for another hour as the city slowly merged back into the haze.

They passed the mouth of the Nile and suddenly there seemed to be ships everywhere. Captain Dhoni explained there were two passages through the canal, north and south and ships went through in convoy as the canal was too narrow for the ships to pass except in certain places.

"Our convoy south starts at midnight," he said. "But I

don't know how long we will have to wait. You can count the ships in line as we get nearer. But the good news is, you will be able to take the tender and go ashore and shop in Port Said. Two of my crew will take you."

Even Sister Agnes was excited. She had always flown out and back on previous visits, this being the first time she had supervised and accompanied the three containers of supplies. It was late afternoon when they anchored and were told they would be in the second scheduled convoy but that meant they would have almost a full day ashore.

Port Said was a busy city. They had not expected to find so many new modern buildings but the one's from the previous two centuries were handsome with their many balconies and reflected the French culture of the men who had built them when the Canal was being constructed.

Two crewmen accompanied them on the Captain's orders and one of them spoke Arabic and both Noel and Agnes had enough French when it was preferred by the traders and café owners. They walked and shopped and ate and drank until one of the crew told them it was time to get back and make ready for the voyage through the Canal. They were so exhausted and relaxed that even the journey to the ship in the small tender was enjoyable – but being winched aboard was less so.

They had bought wine in the city and they sat on deck and watched the incredible fall of the sun, sipping the wine in iced glasses and each of them knew that it had been a day they would always remember.

After dinner they all three were allowed onto the bridge to witness the manoeuvre to get into line with other ships and wait for the convoy to snake gently forward out of the Mediterranean to the other side of the world.

They were almost the last in line and did not enter the

Canal until the early hours, by which time they were all ready to sleep.

"It will take about twelve hours to get out of the canal at Suez," Dhoni told them. "When you wake we may be in the Gulf of Suez and then the Red Sea."

They all went to sleep with the sounds and sights of a new world slopping in their heads and thoughts of more adventures to come. All three slept and woke and slept again until a knock on the door got Noel to his feet and a crewman told him he was wanted on the Bridge by the Captain. He splashed water on his face and put on a T-shirt over his shorts and stepped out into blinding sunshine and immediately felt the heat of it. He saw buildings very near on the Port side and looked at his watch; it was nearly noon and as he got into the lift he wondered why he was needed on the bridge. The Captain greeted him and handed him a telephone receiver. "You have a phone-call," he told him and retreated discreetly to the other side of the bridge.

"Noel, it's your father," a voice said and Noel felt his body go cold.

"How are you?" his father enquired and Noel began to hope it was only a reconciliatory social call.

His hopes increased as he was asked about the voyage and even how Tracy was and he described the bad start but the wonderful cruise through the Mediterranean and then the trip ashore at Port Said.

"So you are enjoying it?" his father asked and Noel said he was enjoying it very much.

"That's good. Your mother and I think it was perhaps the right thing to do," and Noel was lifted before the fall.

"Noel. I've had a visit from the police. They are making enquiries about that arson incident."

Noel's body almost froze and he knew it was not just the

air-conditioning on the Bridge. He did not trust his voice and his father continued.

"Unfortunately, they learned about your awful experience by those monsters. They want to speak with you."

"When. How?" Noel stuttered.

"I think they may send someone to interview you when you stop at Aden. I don't know. I just gave them the shipping company's number but they told me you were only stopping at Aden to unload some cargo. Otherwise they will have to wait until you get to India."

"Can't they speak to me on the telephone like you are?" Noel pleaded.

His father told him they would need a statement.

"Noel, all you have to say is that I picked you up from the university. That we went for a meal and then I left you in the Pickwick Hotel while I tidied your flat and collected your things, then I collected you and took you home. Nothing more. Do you understand?"

When Noel failed to answer, the question was again put to him and it had the connotations of legal advocacy. He put down the receiver and mumbled his thanks to the Captain and stumbled out into the oven-like heat.

He was disturbed in his cabin by Tracy asking if he was awake and did he want to go down to lunch. He said he would join them there and was pleased the Captain and another officer were with them as they were already explaining to the others where they were and where their route would take them.

"The convoy will open out now we are out of the canal and we will soon be able to get up to our normal speed," the Captain was saying. "By tonight we will be in the Red Sea."

"How long will it take to get to Aden?" Noel asked.

"Three days depending on the traffic."

Tracy laughed. "It sounds like the M25," she said.

The Captain carefully explained they were restricted to a narrow channel along the Saudi Peninsula patrolled by military shipping. "There have been one or two incidents of piracy." He added that it was now very safe with American warships patrolling the area.

"And we stop at Aden?" Noel said.

"We shall be there for a day or two," the captain explained.

"How did you know we would stop in Aden " Tracy asked and gave Noel a playful dig in his side but Noel only gave her a weak smile in answer.

They had been warned of the heat they would now experience and the Captain told them to be sensible and stay in their air-conditioned cabins.

"Just come on deck for short periods until your bodies adjust to the conditions," he added and Sister Agnes supported the idea.

"You will need to adjust slowly so you are ready for the humidity and heat in Mumbai," she said. "We don't want anyone getting heat-stroke before then."

After the first day, when the many ships ahead of them and the lines of shipping awaiting access to the Canal at Suez gradually disappeared from their view, there was nothing of interest for them to see and they spent most of the time in their cabins. Sister Agnes was content to read unless they played cards but Noel had a laptop with him and when they learned the ship had access to the internet he and Tracy spent much of the time accessing social media sites. Tracy sensed Noel's detachment but did not comment on it as her previous efforts had told her she had to be patient.

In the evenings they went on deck and drank a little and talked a lot and watched the amazing panoply of stars, Tracy surprising them by her knowledge.

"Daddy's a big star-gazer," she said.

It was an evening when they were out of the Gulf and into the Red Sea that one of the crew told them about the dolphins. They were taken to the bow and in the phosphorescence of the wash they saw the pod, diving and leaping and keeping up with them effortlessly. They watched them for over an hour until they suddenly disappeared as though on a signal but the next afternoon they were there again and Noel seemed mesmerised as he looked down and watched them but inside he was thinking only of Aden getting nearer.

After dinner he said he would have a shower and read for a while. He kissed Tracy goodnight and shook Agnes' hand. He waited until he heard their cabin-door close and then he went on deck and down the stairs to the gunwale deck. He told a crewman he was going for a walk, the only long route for exercise was a circuit of the ship on the bottom deck, but he stopped at the bow and looked down and saw the dolphins were there and wondered how far they swam at such speed. He continued to stare downwards and remembered doing the same at the river back home when Tracy had appeared behind him and taken him into the hospice.

He walked back a few paces where the high bow gave way to the rails. He climbed onto the top of the rail, balanced perfectly for a moment and then stepped out into the night.

Daphne had no idea that golf pros got up so early. It was six am when Julie Norris kissed her and said there was a coffee on the bedside table. When Daphne managed to open her eyes she saw that Julie was fully dressed including her outside jacket.

"Will I see you tonight or was it a one-nighter?" Julie asked in typical, laconic to-the-point character. Daphne stretched out her arms in invitation and they were filled by Julie's torso. Their lips pressed with gratitude.

After Julie left, Daphne sat up and smiled to herself. She sipped the coffee and looked around the room that had been only an alcoholic haze the night before.

It was casually tidy: a nightdress thrown on a chair, a pair of socks on the floor and an odd shoe outside the wardrobe. But the dressing table was neatly arranged, the flowered curtains fully draped and a bowl of daisies and pansies on an occasional table. The tough little sportswoman was still a tough little girl.

The alcohol had been dissipated by the best sleep Morrison had had for a long time. Her body was floppy and her inside was just as relaxed. She still smiled as she stepped into a shower; the smile that new lovers have in the spring of pleasure. It was only later, when she closed and locked Julie's front door, that the old world intruded, but even then it seemed not so bad.

Her leave time had finished and it was back to an office. She vaguely wondered as she drove whether she would fail a breathe test but even that thought failed to suppress the smile. Gradually her mind reverted to business. It was still a waiting game for her: Jennings to find the interviews with

Foden and George, if there were any, and for the laboratory to give her something solid to work on. She wondered what she should tell her boss. Was it time to declare her interest in Foden and ask to bring him in for questioning? She thought not; everything was still speculative and she knew what Foden would do with that.

She had no time to take her coat off when her mobile rang. She was apprehensive when she saw the call was from Penny Featherstone and more so when she heard her voice.

"Daphne, I need to talk to someone. Not someone; I need to talk to you."

"I could drive up."

"No. No. I can't let you do that."

"Can you tell me over the phone?"

"I'll try. I'm sorry, I'm being silly. But I don't know what to do."

"Just try to tell me."

"I was cleaning the flat - the landlord lets our room in the summer to tourists. It means we don't have to pay rent in the holiday. I was washing the bedroom floor and under Caroline's bed, right in the corner against the wall, I found a plastic bag."

There was a pause.

"What was in it?" Daphne asked helpfully.

"A Mexican poncho."

The silence was much longer.

"Are you there?"

"Yes," Daphne answered.

"I don't know what to do." Penny's voice was near to tearful.

"Did you ask Caroline about it?"

"No. I'm afraid."

"What are you afraid of?"

"Of what she might say, what she might do."

"What do you think she might do?"

"I don't know. She's still a bit flaky. You said a boy in a poncho gave those Doggers money."

"Quite a lot of money according to a witness."

"Caroline had money from Foden."

"Yes, you told me."

So what should I do, Daphne?"

Her voice was pleading, desperate.

"I'll have to think about it, Penny. I'll call you back."

"When?"

"In a few minutes."

She closed her phone and thought. She was able to shut out everything when she had to concentrate. After several minutes she rang Penny back.

"What Noel did to Caroline was a terrible thing," she said. "He deserved to be punished for it – but not like this. What Caroline seems to have done to him is just as bad, even if she didn't do it physically herself. If she had reported Noel for what he did to her he would probably have gone to prison. It certainly would have ruined his career. But as it is, what has happened to him has now done that – and probably affected his life. If I report what you've just told me it will ruin Caroline's career and will probably ruin her life. She would almost certainly get a prison sentence."

There was an audible sob from Penny.

"What Noel did started a chain of destruction; four people dead and two people damaged for life. I think its time for the destruction to stop."

The sound from Penny was an outpouring of breath and a yelp.

"Daphne, I love you. You are the best friend I'll ever have. Thank you. Thank you."

"Don't tell Caroline what you found. But keep that poncho somewhere. Take it home with you. Let her wonder what happened to it. She deserves to suffer that much."

"What if she asks me about it?"

"Then pretend you don't know. Let her sweat – unless you want to stay friends."

"No. I couldn't. I think I'll share with Graham next term."

"Do you like him that much?"

"I think so. I want to see how we get on."

"Then it's best to find out now rather than later. Good. I won't have to worry about you so much if I know someone is looking after you."

"Thank you, Daphne. I love you."

"And I love you."

She closed the phone and lingered on the thought of what she had just done. If ever the facts emerged it would be the end of her career. She had chosen to be a human-being instead of a police officer. It had not been an easy choice and she vaguely wondered how much the previous night had affected her choice. She felt more human.

She drove her mind back to her day job. What to tell her chief? She wished now she was still on leave, just to keep out of his way until she had more ammunition with which to face him. Bugger! Why is everything taking so long? She was so near to getting answers. So near to finding the truth about Katy Rose and Gorgeous George – and Charles Foden.

Her mobile rang again. She expected it to be Penny – she had a strong conscience too – and she didn't look at the number. She was surprised. Perhaps a god had been listening. It was the forensic pathologist.

"That golf club you brought in."

Morrison held her breath. "That was quick," she said.

"It didn't take long."

Morrison already felt the disappointment.

"Two lots of DNA on it. One matched the DNA and finger-print on the map you gave us and the other we found in our own backyard."

Morrison said she didn't understand.

"The bog-body."

"The German?" Morrison exclaimed in disbelief.

"Not the German. The other one. Foden."

A chemical rush passed through Morrison's body and sent acid into her throat.

"It's not an exact match with the jumper on the bog-body but definitely the same family," the pathologist was saying.

Morrison recovered enough to speak.

"What's the division between family members?" she asked.

"Minute. This is son-father or brother-brother. I promised to give you a heads-up. Sorry about the delay. Should I send the report to you?"

Morrison was still struggling with her excitement.

"Yes please."

"Do you want us to bag the club as evidence?"

"Definitely."

"It's a goer then?"

"A goer? It's a bloody miracle. Thank you. Thank you."

She closed the phone and had to stand to relieve the need to scream. She punched the air instead.

"So, Mr smart-ass Foden. We're coming to get you," she told the empty room.

It was tempting to speculate with the evidence but it was not the time for speculation, it was time to get Foden in for questioning. But then her enthusiasm waned; that would mean handing the case to the CID. She saw Foden answering the questions put to him by DC Bolton; arrogant, confident aggressive. DC Bolton had already confirmed the barman in the Pickwick Hotel had given Noel an alibi for the time the arson attack took place which would put Foden in the frame for the attack. But he showed no fear of them finding evidence of his involvement. They would need indisputable evidence before they questioned him about Katy Rose Lewis. Indisputable evidence – like a body. A groundsman might not be able to remove a body from Drovers' Hill without attracting attention and take it elsewhere, but a golf club member?

She thought about Upland House and George landscaping the gardens. Could they get a search warrant? Did they have enough evidence for that? A golf-club left in the woods with his DNA on it, employing someone illegally – the Pensions Service had said George had not worked legally after he left the golf club – and so far, no evidence of where he was on the day Katy disappeared. Was that enough evidence? It was enough to question Foden but not enough to get a warrant to search Upland House. But it made Foden her number one suspect.

She remembered Foden had never supplied the pictures of Katy she had requested. That could be another reason for a search; Penny had said photographers would never destroy their work. He might have destroyed prints of Katy but would he destroy the negatives?

Bugger! They needed to get into Upland House and turn it over.

She opened her phone again and rang Steve Jennings. She was in no mood to waste any more time.

"Steve. Have you got any results with those interviews with the golf club members yet?"

"We couldn't find anyone called George Fuller."

"What about Foden?"

"We haven't got to the traffic stops yet. He wasn't interviewed at the golf club."

"Doesn't urgent mean urgent? I would have read every damn report by now. What the hell is the matter with you, Steve; are you getting too old for the job?"

She immediately regretted the barb

"Maybe I'm just not rushing to make mistakes," Jennings replied coldly. "We don't want to find any more bog-bodies do we, Inspector?"

Morrison took a deep breath. She wondered how their relationship had deteriorated to swapping insults.

"That golf-club that was found in the same place as Katy Rose's shoe had Charles Foden's DNA on it. So I need to know exactly where the hell he was on the day Katy disappeared. If you can't find a sighting of him on that day I need to know before we haul him in for questioning and ask him to explain exactly what he was doing that day. If you can't do that, tell me now and I'll get the Chief Constable's authorisation to have the CID go through those files to save you the trouble."

There was a long pause.

"No need. I'll do it," Jennings replied softly.

Morrison closed the phone, still shaking with anger. The phone rang; she saw it was Penny. She took a deep breath before answering.

"Hello Penny."

"Daphne. Sorry. I forgot to tell you something else. You know, every time I've seen Charles Foden he's always been wearing a suit and tie. But when I dreamt about him after seeing Ivana he was wearing..."

"A golf shirt."

"How did you know? Daphne, you're amazing."

"So are you. Thank you Penny. Go home and forget all of this."

She closed her phone and the temper she poured over Steve Jennings was still closeted somewhere inside and clamped her jaw and tightened her face. Her door opened and the Chief Constable walked in.

"Daphne. Welcome back. Someone thought they'd seen you. I hope you had a good break."

Because of her emotional state she was slow to respond and he quickly rushed on. He was in a peculiar mood too.

"Are you busy? I wondered if I could ask a favour."

"I'm not doing anything special. What do you need sir?"

"Noel Foden's gone missing."

Her shock replaced everything else.

"In India?"

"Off the ship. In the Red Sea."

"Oh!"

"Exactly. DS Townsend has just phoned me. The shipping company called him, knowing they were planning on questioning Noel."

"Does his father know?"

"No. They wanted us to break the news. I wondered if..."

"Not me, sir. Honestly, I know Foden hates me."

"No. You're right. I should do it. It's just that I'm really tied up to-day. I'll call him."

"I'm really sorry. But I know it would not be well received coming from me. We have a few issues after the arson thing and I've got a lot of questions hanging over him. I would just bungle it and upset him even more."

"Really? Well, I'll manage. He's only just down the road. I could take a few minutes."

"I'm really sorry, sir. But it's very sad news, isn't it?"

"It is. I just hope he's not going to blame us."

"Why would he blame us?"

"We did force him to contact Noel. That must have sent Noel over the edge – literally."

"You think he deliberately jumped ship?"

"What else? It's difficult to fall off a container ship."

"Why would he do that?"

"He was going to be questioned about the arson attack. You know that."

"He isn't guilty of that. His father gave him an alibi and DC Bolton has confirmed it with the hotel bar he was in when the arson happened.."

"Then why..."

"He was protecting his father ."

"Daphne, you can't think Foden had something to do with that."

"I need to talk to you, sir."

"I've got a hell of a day; three scheduled meetings."

"Yes, sorry. All right, sir. I'll give Foden the news, if it will help."

"Really? It would help very much. Thank you, Daphne. We'll talk tomorrow."

"Yes, sir."

Morrison stared at the door after he had closed it. Her mind almost numbed by the confusion of electrons that bombarded it but the anger still smouldering inside.

She walked to Foden's offices, hoping to clear her mind. She was shown into his office and found him scowling at her from behind his desk;

"I hope this isn't going to take long, Inspector."

"No, sir. It should only take a moment. Have you had any news of Noel?"

His scowl increased and his voice was threatening.

"I've already told you people..."

"He's gone missing off the ship."

His face cleared. It almost became featureless.

"When?"

"Last evening. He didn't turn up for breakfast. They searched the ship but didn't find him."

There was a long silence.

"I'm sorry, Mr Foden."

The colour had returned to his face, heightening the contortions it performed. His lips curled as he looked at her.

"Sorry? You are sorry? You should be more than sorry. If your lot had listened to me... I told you Noel was in no state to be interviewed..."

"A serious crime had been committed. We could not ignore the possibility that Noel had something to do with it."

"Of course he had nothing to do with it."

His temper exploded and sent him jumping out of his chair

Morrison's voice softened to counteract the gesture.

"We think we know that now. But he knew who might have had something to do with it, didn't he, sir?"

Foden stood, glaring at her.

"Get out, Morrison. Get out."

She walked to the door and turned with her hand on the knob. Her temper had risen with his.

"We are sorry for your loss. We are sorry about Noel – and we're sorry about George."

"George. What George?"

"Your old gardener. I believe you've lost him recently too."

She opened the door and closed it behind her.

"Fuck" she told herself.

Behind the door Foden stared and then fell back into his chair.

Foden went straight home and told his wife. Her response was traumatic. She spat questions at him as she gulped for

360

air and wiped the tears that kept filling her eyes. She moved about the room as though she wanted to physically amend the situation and she pushed him away when he tried to calm her by holding her still.

"That girl. She started all this."

"Yes. I think she is responsible," Foden agreed but then his wife screamed at him.

"And why did you give in to the police? You said you would not tell them where Noel was. If you hadn't he would now be in India, on dry land and would still be alive. You said you knew what you were doing."

"I'll phone Phillipa and ask her to come home," Foden said and as his wife finally sat down and sobbed. He telephoned their daughter.

Betsy took his wife up to her bedroom and persuaded her to take a Diazepam tablet. Foden hung around outside the bedroom like an expectant father until Betsy told him there was nothing he could do, that his wife would soon be asleep.

"I'll go and wait at the station for Phillipa," he decided.

"But she won't be here for two hours or more."

"I know. I'll get something to eat so I won't bother you. Phone me if you need me."

He left the house quickly, as though desperate to escape. Outside, he sucked in draughts of air, it felt as though he had been holding his breath since leaving his office. He stretched his back and looked towards the sky, hoping to find an answer there. But the sky was sullen and unresponsive. He got into his car and drove, not consciously aware of a destination until he found himself at the railway station. He pulled into the car park and found a space at the farthest end where trees overhung, making the day even darker.

He walked back to the cafe attached to the station. He bought a sandwich and a coffee in a paper cup and took them back to his car. He sipped the coffee and stared into the grey surroundings. It was too early for the car park to be busy with returning commuters and the greyness and silence matched his mood. It began to drizzle and soon the windscreen blotted out the dreariness of his view. Depression closed in on him like the weather

His head still echoed silently to so many questions but one found a voice and cried helplessly; 'Why? Why? There was no need. You only had to answer their questions.'

A vision of Noel, happy and animated, flashed into his head but was gone just as quickly. Noel, his son, his blood, his genes; of the same image, of the same temperament and perhaps of the same fateful flaws. He thought of when he was born, and the moment, so clearly remembered, brought other memories rushing in: his grandparents, his mother, his father, Gerhardt, Aunt Sheila and... George.

He sat up quickly and gulped down a mouthful of coffee, almost enjoying the pain of its heat as it seared his throat. He heard Morrison's last words, saw the look that accompanied them before she closed the door. She had found George. Somewhere, somehow she had found George had worked for him. What else had she found? And why? He knew Morrison was working the Katy Rose Lewis case, but how had she made the link to George? Then he remembered Noel telling him it was something about Penny seeing Katy on Drovers' Hill.

His throat tightened as though to prevent him scouring it again. But now the whole of his body was reacting. He noticed how his hand trembled holding the paper cup and how his back had gone cold. He put the cup in a holder and switched on the engine to heat the car. Outside the drizzle had strengthened to a constant rain. He switched on the light then fumbled in his jacket pocket and withdrew the letter he had fatefully received the day he had collected Noel from university.

He read again the lines he had read several times, as though they might change.

"...*George sometimes spoke of you. He was very grateful for all you did for him. He once said that, but for you, he might still be cutting grass and sleeping in sheds. I shall miss him dreadfully and I'm sure that you too will be saddened by his sudden death. When I asked about you he gave me that teasing smile and said you were his secret. But he would never tell me what he meant. Whatever it was, it will now be his forever.*

If you should ever come to New York I would love to meet you, I'm sure George would like that too."

It was signed, *Wayne (Duke) Gilbert*

The words no longer generated the shock and anger he had felt when he had read and reread them several times before, when feelings and events had rushed out of an envelope after so many years of forgetting. That wave had receded, leaving only the detritus of its wake; the detritus of his life.

BACKSTORY 3
THE SECOND CHRONICLE OF CHARLES HENDERSON FODEN

By the fifth hole he had decided his wife's suggestion that he should play golf to take his mind off his father's letter and Aunt Sheila's death had not been a good idea. He had played badly; slicing shots, over-hitting, and generally spending more time in the rough than on the fairways and by the time he reached the top half of the course only the thought of Nigel Farringdon winning the Harlequin Trophy and being made Club Captain kept him playing.

The course was plateaued as it rose up to border Drovers' Hill but the top fairways still presented hanging lies and made shot-making more difficult and the fifteenth, sixteenth and seventeenth holes, which formed the boundary between the woods and the course, were the trickiest of all.

As Foden stood on the first of those holes he already felt exhausted, mentally and physically, even though he was using an electric golf cart to get around the course.

His brain was still analysing the contents of his father's letter and the implications of Aunt Sheila's accusations and his anger kept bursting out of his body as visions of his father's relationship with Gerhardt slipped past his mental defences. His grandpa's compliance in keeping the truth from him, and what that had done to Aunt Sheila's life tore at his inside and threatened to consume his brain entirely.

He sat for several minutes on the fifteenth tee and surveyed the golf course below him, trying to calm his body and shut away everything except the next shot he had to play.

He had started the round at seven am and only now, two hours later, were people beginning to tee-off by the clubhouse and only four other cars were in the car park.

It was a beautiful morning and normally such days on a golf course soothed his body and soul like nothing else. His artistic eye took-in the swathes of different greens, the little ponds where wildfowl darted to and fro between the water and the banks and the small clumps of strategically placed trees bursting with new leaf against the backdrop of a perfectly blue sky. Golf courses were the palettes of Man's love affair with nature, but that morning, although his eyes sent the message to his brain, he did not feel it.

He got to his feet and took a two-iron from the golf-bag and looked ahead, willing himself to concentrate on the shot that would start the toughest holes on the course.

The woods were on his left and the ground fell away from them requiring just enough draw on the shot to keep the ball from running down the slope and off the fairway but not so much to curl the ball into the woods. An oak tree intruded a little into the course two hundred yards away and good players, as he was, would fly a draw-shot around the tree to set up a mid-iron shot to the green.

He placed the ball on a low-tee and took his stance taking a stronger left-hand grip. He lined-up the shot a little to the right of the tree expecting the ball to curl around it and hold-up on the sloping fairway. He took in a gulp of air and held it in his chest, flexed his knees, loosened his wrists, pushed his chin towards the ball and took the club away with a good left arm, his right elbow hinging the back-swing. He brought the club down against a firm left side and watched the ball arc away straight as an arrow as he held the follow-through, but as the ball began to fall the strong left-hand grip worked the spin and it began to curve too soon. It clipped one of the branches of the tree and shot off into the woods.

Foden cursed and smashed his iron into the ground. He got into the buggy and drove to the tree. He took a nine-iron from the bag and stepped over the shallow ditch into the trees hoping he might have a clear shot back to the fairway if he found his ball.

The side of the woods between the course and the Ridgeway path was not heavily foliaged. There were several large beech trees well-spaced with only light saplings in between them and wayward golfers were often able to find their ball and have a line-of-sight back onto the course.

Foden had kept an experienced eye on the divergent flight of the ball and as he stepped carefully towards where he judged it to have settled he saw what appeared to be a trainer-type shoe at the end of a bare ankle protruding from behind the trunk of one of the large beech trees. He edged forward and the bare ankle became a bare calf and the bare calf became a bare thigh.

"Hello," the man said, smiling up and sideways at Foden as he stepped beyond the tree and looked down at him.

Foden stared, open-mouthed. The man was young, in his early twenties, and completely naked. He was lying in a pool of sunlight with his back against the tree and his legs stretched out in front of him. Some light clothes were on the ground next to him. He had blond, curly hair that fell about his ears and over his brow, and large brown eyes that surveyed Foden's astonishment with unflinching interest. His body might have been modelled by Michelangelo, there were no angular parts, every muscle was defined by smooth curves and Foden noticed that the beech leaves dappled his chest in spots of purple shadow and his genitalia resting on his pectineus muscles were a large impediment to the smooth contours of the rest of his body.

"Aven't you seen a naked man before?"

The voice had a strong north country accent and was spoken from thick, sensuous lips that curled in an amused expression as they shaped the words.

"C, can I take your picture?" Foden managed to gasp.

"It'll cost you," the man said and his lips curled even more in a smile.

"Yes. Yes, of course," Foden said. "Please, don't move. I'll get my camera."

He leant the golf club against a tree then rushed back to the golf buggy to get his Leica. When he returned, the man hadn't moved but he held out his arm and worked his thumb across his fingers as Foden positioned himself to take a picture.

"Yes. Of course," Foden said.

He took a ten-pound note from his back pocket and handed it to the man.

"Thanks," the man said and held his head on one side and smiled up at Foden. Foden took several pictures and then the man got to his feet and walked towards the camera, lips pouting playfully. He was taller than Foden had realised as, on the ground, he had looked like an overgrown teenager. and as he got nearer, his hips swaying to his measured steps, he only had to tilt his head upwards a little to look into the camera. Foden lowered the camera and looked at the man who was then only an arms length away from him.

"Would you like to touch?" the man said in a teasing voice. "For another tenner?"

Foden was transfixed. He could feel the heat from the man's body as he took one of Foden's hands from the camera and began to pull it down to his groin.

****

Katy Rose Lewis was glad she had chosen not to wear knickers as she reached the top of the climb up to

Drovers' Hill. She was sweating all over her body and the thin cotton dress was already sticking around her waist. She sat Jenny on the grass as she reassembled the pushchair then strapped the girl back into it.

"That was a bit of a puff wasn't it m'darlin?" she said and got a smile in answer. "Right, now we can enjoy the walk,"

She started to sing as she wheeled the pushchair along the Ridgeway path.

> 'I ain't happy, I'm feelin glad,
> I got sunshine in a bag,
> I'm useless but not for long
> The future is comin on.'

In the shade of the woods her body soon cooled and they got up a good walking pace to make up the time lost by the climb but before they got to the end of the woods Katy's bladder told her she would have to relieve it before they reached Upper Stokesey.

"Won't be a mo m'love," she told Jenny and stepped off the path and behind a large clump of gorse alive with yellow flowers. She waved to Jenny before dipping below the gorse. As she squatted she thought she heard voices. She hurriedly finished her toilet and peeped over the gorse. She saw no one so she stepped back onto the path. Then she heard a voice again, coming from the other side of the path. She cautiously edged towards the noise and peered through a screen of saplings. She saw two men, one of them completely naked, holding the other man's hand. She gasped air into her lungs and fell backwards and sideways and out of the screen of saplings. The man with his back to her turned at the noise and she recognised Charles Foden and her shock increased so that she had difficulty breathing. The naked man said, "Oh shit," and swept up his shirt and shorts and staggered past her onto the Ridgeway path, trying to put his shorts on over his trainers as he went.

Charles Foden was now looking at Katy Rose and recognising the implications of her astonishment.

"It's not what you think," he said. "I was looking for my golf ball."

Katy Rose found her voice. "That's why you didn't want to touch me. That's why you wouldn't take those pictures of me," she said, the remembered anger of rejection reasserting itself.

"No. No," Foden said and stepped towards her. "It wasn't, I'm not..."

But Katy Rose interrupted him.

"Yes you are. You're a dirty queer, just like your old man."

The words stopped Foden like a smack on the face.

"Our Jack told Dad all about your father and that German. What they got up to in that room above the garage. You're a queer, just like him," she snarled and all the hate of what she thought she had discovered shone from her face.

Foden swung his fully stretched arm to hit her but it was the lens of the Leica, still in his hand, that made contact with her temple just in front of her ear. Katy Rose Lewis fell back, uninterrupted by anything other than air, and crashed heavily to the ground.

Foden looked down at the stricken figure, her legs and arms stretched out from her body, her head tilted back, her open mouth showing the pink of her tongue, her eyes wide and her lovely hair spread around her head like a whirlpool of golden chocolate.

He looked at the camera in his hand then he stepped forward with a foot carefully placed on either side of Katy Rose's body and focussed the camera. He took two pictures before the blood trickled from her nose and then he saw that it also ran from an ear.

He sprang back as though out of a dream, making a noise somewhere in his chest. He dropped the camera and knelt down and lifted Katy Rose's lifeless face in his hands. A swelling was getting visibly bigger on the side of her temple and the round indentation of the lens housing of the Leica was clearly marked in the centre of it. The noise in his chest became a whine somewhere near the back of his throat – then he heard Jenny cry.

He let go of Katy Rose and got to his feet. He looked out onto the Ridgeway path and saw the little girl in the pushchair. She stopped crying and looked back at him and for a moment they stared at each other before she started to cry again. Foden looked from the girl back to where Katy Rose lay and then back again as Jenny's cries became louder and constant. "Shush," he said in a soothing voice and bent close to the girl. She stopped crying as she looked at him, but only for a moment. Foden's brain struggled to know what to do before he lifted Jenny up in the pushchair and carried them both away from the path. He set the pushchair down beyond where Katy lay and he saw Jenny looking at Katy lying on the ground. She had stopped crying and her trembling lips mouthed "Kat" and she reached out a hand towards the body.

"Katy's all right," Foden told her. You wait here and she'll be all right in a moment."

He turned the pushchair so Jenny could no longer see the body then took hold of Katy under her arms and dragged her towards the Ridgeway path. He looked along the path before dragging her across it and past the gorse where Katy had performed her last physical function. He dragged her farther into the woods to where a copse of saplings and other plants mixed with bracken and brambles, into the heart of the jungle of growth, then covered her body with the bracken which he tore up with frantic hands. He studied the result then heard Jenny crying again.

He hurried back to the child and wheeled her to the edge of the trees where he had left the golf cart. He looked down the course. Another foursome was teeing off on the first hole and the two before were still on the bottom of the course at the fourth hole. He moved his golf-bag out of the receptacle at the rear of the cart to the front seat then he lifted Jenny and the pushchair and manoeuvred them into the receptacle vacated by the golf-bag.

Jenny had now stopped crying, her brain trying to work-out what was happening to her. Foden jumped into the cart and drove it as quickly as it would go to the top edge of the course and onto the footpath leading down to the road and prayed they would not meet anyone from the few houses on that part of the road using the footpath to take their dog up to Drover's Hill. They reached the road and, using the last of the footpath to remain out of sight of the houses on the other side, Foden lifted Jenny and the pushchair from the golf-cart. With his golf-towel, he cleaned all the parts of the pushchair he had handled. He surveyed the road for traffic then, with his gloved hand, pushed Jenny to the other side and into the bus shelter. He hurried back and with difficulty reversed the cart back to the top of the course then drove it down to the clubhouse.

He changed his shoes and got into his car, then on impulse, he got out again. He stood and surveyed the area as though looking for someone and then his eyes lingered on Drovers' Hill. He locked the car then walked past the clubhouse and started the upward journey bordering the eighteenth hole to climb to the lowest point of the hill.

Without knowing exactly why, besides a feeling that he did not want to pass young Jenny on the way home and the instincts of a dog that returned constantly to a place where it had buried a bone, he had decided to walk home via the Ridgeway. It was not a long walk. When he reached the Ridgeway he stood and looked back along the path towards the woods; there was no one about and he hoped it would continue that way. Fortunately it was too early in the season for tourists.

His wife asked how he'd got on and he told her he had played badly.

"I'll go back later when the course isn't busy and get a bit more practise," he said.

His wife was relieved that he was making the effort to put Sheila's death and his father's letter behind him but during lunch she sensed his preoccupation and made a great effort to maintain a conversation about the children and schooling and members of her family but by the time they had taken their coffee into the sitting-room she had admitted defeat realising, wrongly, that his father and Sheila still occupied his thoughts. So she was understandably astonished when he suddenly announced that they might keep his grandfather's house.

"What on earth for. What will we do with it?" she asked.

He told her they could have it converted into flats. "There is a growing market for that sort of thing," he added. "It will be an investment for the children and if any of them should need a home sometime they could use it. It has a good basement too. I could make a proper photographic studio down there."

His wife declined to argue that it would be an unnecessary bother, grateful that his mind was on other things. She answered the telephone in the hall. He heard her ask if they wanted her husband. She reappeared in the doorway.

"It's Stokesey police station." She continued quickly, not

noticing the blood drain from his face. "Something terrible has happened; "You know the Lewis girl from The Badgers, Katy Rose?" her husband said he did. "She's gone missing. There is a police search and they need a photograph of her. The Lewis' thought you might have taken some of her at the fair."

"Yes, I did."

"Do you want to speak to them?"

"No. Tell them I'll sort one out." He looked at his watch. "Tell them to give me an hour or so and we'll ring them to collect it."

His stomach churned as he waited. His wife returned and gave him a message page.

"That's the number. They have some school photos but they're not very good. Isn't it awful?"

"When did this happen?"

"This morning. She went into Upper Stokesey to collect the meat for her father but didn't come back."

"How strange. What do they think has happened to her?"

"They didn't say. But they are taking it seriously."

He noticed the depth of concern in his wife's voice and on her face. He thought they couldn't have told her about the child or she would have been in a worse state.

"I'd better go and see what pictures I have of her. It sounds serious."

As he left for the old house, he thought how fortunate the call was to give him the excuse to go there. He used one of the rooms of the old kitchen for his printing and developing.

The basement had been the 'below stairs' kitchen and scullery but had been used mostly for storage after his grandmother had had a modern kitchen built onto the rear of the house but he remembered that his grandparents had continued to use a large chest-freezer down there. He found it was still there and had been defrosted and cleaned by the cook sometime after his grandpa's death when there was only his aunt to look after. He plugged it in and switched it to quick freeze.

It was almost two hours later when he returned home with two eight by ten prints of Katy Rose.

"What a marvellous picture," his wife enthused. "Such a lovely girl. I hope nothing terrible has happened to her."

"Yes. Will you ring the police station and tell them they're ready."

"Where are you going?"

"I promised Brady I would do a few holes with him."

"Then do take a sandwich with you. You hardly ate a thing for lunch. I know you, you'll be gone ages."

"I'll get something there."

It was late afternoon when he returned to the Club, walking back along the Ridgeway. He was carrying the waterproof travel cover in which he transported his clubs whenever he took them abroad. Before he started the descent to the clubhouse he hid the cover behind a clump of gorse at the top of the path leading to the road.

He had tea in the committee room and chatted to other members and was even polite to Nigel Farringdon and enjoyed the forced concern on his face as he told him he was playing badly and thought he would have a few holes before dinner.

It was an hour before dusk when he drove up to the top half of the course. He practised around the fifteenth green as a foursome played ahead to the seventeenth but when they had teed-off at the eighteenth and started on the long trek towards the clubhouse, he walked into Drover's Hill Woods.

He carefully traversed in both directions beside the Ridgeway Path, making certain that no late walkers were

374

using it, then returned to where he had laid Katy Rose's body. He dragged the body out of the copse then lifted it onto his shoulders. He shivered as Katy's head lolled into the small of his back and his arms held her stiffening legs to his chest.

It was already gloomy in the trees as he carried the body across the Ridgeway and past the spot where he had fatefully encountered the naked sunbather. He set it down just inside the trees then took the golf-cover from the golf cart. He unzipped it and laid it beside Katy's body and as he got hold of her ankles he realised she was wearing only one shoe. He knew it was then too dark on the ground for him to find it easily and he could not risk leaving her on the edge of the trees while he looked for it. He pushed her legs into the cover then turned her and pulled it up past her head. He pulled one side beneath her then rolled the rest of her body into the cover. He zipped it closed then lifted her again and carried her to the golf-buggy and dropped her into the rear section where he had previously carried Jenny and the pushchair. He put his golf-clubs on top of the body then he returned to the trees.

He walked the parts of the wood where he had dragged the body but failed to find the missing shoe, but it was just light enough for him to be certain that it was not on the Ridgeway path where it could be easily spotted. He returned to the golf-cart and drove down to the car park.

A departing member called to him from his car saying he must be damned keen to win the Harlequin Trophy playing in the dark. Foden responded that he needed the practise or he didn't stand a chance of winning it.

There were only three other cars in the car park; it was too early for social members arriving for drinks or dinner and too late for players.

He opened the boot of his car. He put his clubs on the rear seat then, using the long, strong handle of the cover, he lifted Katy Lewis' body and put it into the boot and closed the lid. He leant against it until his body had stopped shaking. He put the golf-buggy away then sat for some time in his car before he felt able to drive.

Before he got into Upper Stokesey several police cars passed him in both directions and as he got into the village he was stopped by a police cordon.

"Good evening, sir," a young constable said. "Can you tell me where you have come from and where you are going to please?" Foden told him. "And how long have you been at the golf club?" the policeman asked. Foden explained his movements of that day.

The police constable had been looking inside the car as he asked the questions. "That's a lot of clubs," he smiled. Foden said the way he was playing he needed them all. "They won't do your leather seats much good," the policeman continued.

Foden anticipated his next thoughts. "I know, but I've got my golf-cart in the boot. Do you play?"

"I try," the constable smiled. "I just go up to the golf-range in the City sometimes with one of my pals. Can't afford a set of clubs yet."

Foden looked concerned. "That's a shame. I've got my grandfather's old set at home. You could have those if you'd like them. He died recently and I'm clearing his house."

The constable's face registered his surprise and pleasure.

"That would be fantastic, sir. Are you sure?"

"Certainly. Give me your name and contact address and I'll get them over to you."

"Jennings. Steve Jennings," the constable said and gave his address in Stokesey.

"I know the cottages," Foden replied. "I'll pop them over there tomorrow. Still no sign of poor Katy?"

"You've heard about her then?"

Foden explained that he had provided a picture for the police earlier.

Jennings looked at his notebook. "Ah, yes. Mr Foden. I spoke to your wife. It was a great photograph."

"Let's hope it gets a result," Foden said

"We hope so. Thank you Mr Foden – and thank you for the clubs; really generous of you.

"Not at all, constable. It's a pleasure."

Jennings wrote Foden's name and address and the car registration number into a notebook and then waved Foden off.

"What a nice bloke," he said to one of his colleagues.

Foden drove to his grandfather's house. He carried Katy Lewis' body down to the basement and dropped it into the chest-freezer then padlocked the lid. He went upstairs and into his grandpa's library and poured himself a whisky and sat at the desk. He stared at the photographs: his grandma, Aunt Sheila and his father.

"We, none of us, know who we really are, do we?" he asked them in a quiet voice.

He looked intently at the handsome, smiling face of his father almost willing him to speak – then he remembered his nine-iron.

He jumped up from the desk as though he could immediately do something about it, and sat down again. He could take a torchlight and go back for it, but someone might see the light from the clubhouse. There was no hurry; tomorrow would do.

By the time he had taken his wife to the anti-natal clinic the next morning and got to the course it was well into the afternoon and the nine-iron had gone.

It was a further two days before he forced himself to return to the course after his wife enquired several times why he was not playing. He arrived earlier than usual not having slept very much and as he drove into the car park he had a view of the rear of the clubhouse and the yard where the green-keeping machines were kept and the greenkeeper's workshop was situated.

He could see Fred Rafferty, the groundsman, gesticulating to someone hidden by the fence. He was obviously animated and angry.

Although the Members didn't have much to do with the ground staff because of their work schedules, Fred Rafferty was known for his good humour and calm demeanour so it was with some curiosity that Foden wondered as he got out of the car as to who had upset him.

He saw Rafferty move his arm in a cutting motion as he walked away and disappeared farther into the yard and as Foden took his clubs from the boot of the car and closed the lid he saw a young man wearing shorts walk from the yard into the car park.

Foden's body stiffened and his breath choked somewhere in his chest. He tried to walk around the car so that it shielded him from the man who was now walking past the car towards the exit of the car park.

"Hello," a voice said with a northern accent.

Foden turned and saw the man had half circled the car and was looking at him. "Good morning," Foden responded.

The man smiled and his teeth shone youth-bright from his tanned face.

"I thought it was you," he said. "We didn't finish our photo session did we?"

He laughed and cocked his head sideways and pursed his

lips as if to give the question hidden meaning.

"No," Foden agreed. He smiled briefly but felt embarrassment and fear inside.

The young man was still looking at him, still smiling. He flicked his head to remove the thick, sun-bleached curls away from his ears. "

"Was it you who was just upsetting Fred?" Foden asked, his voice still struggling to sound normal. "I haven't seen him get excited before."

The man's face changed, it seemed endlessly expressive. He curled his nose towards his eyes.

"Yeah, 'fraid so. He found out I was sleeping in the tool shed,"

Foden relaxed a little as his mind found something else to occupy it rather than what he thought the young man was thinking.

"Why were you sleeping there?" he asked.

"I've nowhere else to sleep."

"Can't you find a room in the village?"

"I suppose I could but I can't afford it yet. Specially not now; Fred's just sacked me."

Part of his brain told Foden that further questions would increase his involvement with the man and that that was not a good idea. But somewhere his instincts were working in a different direction; he didn't know what the man had seen on Drover's Hill or what he had heard. So far he had shown no sign that he knew more than when he had made a hasty and awkward exit at Katy Lewis' appearance. He had an infectiously relaxing personality and seemed not to be threatening.

"That doesn't sound like Fred," Foden said. "It seems a bit unfair to sack you for that. You weren't doing any harm."

"I don't think he likes me," he smiled. "I'm not his type."

Foden thought of little, weather-gnarled Fred and his bowed legs with the young man standing in front of him looking like a beach life guard, and he too smiled.

"What are you going to do?" Foden asked.

"Dunno. Find some work if I can."

"I mean, about somewhere to sleep?"

The man shrugged and smiled; he was very easy to like.

"Have you got any money?" Foden asked and was told that Fred had just paid him for the week.

"Look, I may be able to help you. Can you meet me in about two hours, I must get some practise in first."

"Sure. Do you want me to come back here?"

"Better not. I'll meet you in the village – by the market cross. Say about ten?"

The man held out his hand. "Thanks. The name's George."

Foden took the hand. "Charles," he said.

Foden persevered on the lower half of the course, playing it twice rather than the nine holes which would take him up to Drovers' Hill, but his mind was in many other places and he knew he would be in no state to win the Harlequin Trophy the following week. Something that once mattered a great deal to him now seemed trivial and irrelevant and he knew he was going through the painful motions only to pacify Arabella's fears for his emotional stability. If only she knew, he thought and shivered at the idea.

George was waiting at the cross, talking to a young woman who seemed to be enjoying his company. He crossed the road in three athletic strides when Foden peeped the horn.

"Who was that?" Foden asked.

"Dunno. Some girl called Irene. She came on to me as I was sitting on the wall waiting for you."

"I should imagine that happens to you quite a lot," Foden smiled sideways at him.

George laughed. "Yeah. If I was interested I would have been in a lot of shit by now. Did you know about all the police activity in the village?"

Foden looked at him but there was no sign of anything other than the question on his face.

"Yes. It's about that girl we saw: Katy Rose Lewis. She's disappeared," Foden kept looking at his face but it showed no emotion.

"The one in the woods? She's disappeared? And the kid?" George responded.

"The child was left at a bus stop."

They drove in silence for some moments, Foden waiting expectantly for George's next comment.

"Did you know her; the girl?"

"I knew of her. Her father owns a country pub called The Badgers."

Another pause

"Did she recognise you?"

"Yes."

"Is that why she seemed so upset?"

"I think that might have had more to do with you being naked."

George laughed.

"I think she got the wrong impression about what we were doing."

He continued to laugh

"We'd better not tell anyone we saw her up there had we?" he said. "We don't want anyone else getting the wrong impression."

"I agree. I think it could get awkward for both of us."

"Has she really disappeared; just like that?"

"Apparently. She was walking to Upper Stokesey. She must have met someone there who probably offered her a lift back to The Badgers. The police seem to think it was something like that."

"Then it could be serious?"

"I think so."

"Whew! You're right. We don't want to get involved, do we?"

They exchanged looks and an understanding went between them as firm as a handshake.

"Did the police speak to you in the village?"

"They asked a few questions. They were stopping people, showing them a photograph of the girl and asking if they had seen her."

"What did you say?"

"I told them I hadn't. I didn't know it was the girl we saw."

"Did they ask anything else?"

"They asked me if I had a car. They seemed to lose interest when I said I couldn't even afford a bike."

When they drove into the drive of his Grandfather's house, Foden was explaining how it was now empty as his aunt had recently died. They got out of the car and George stood and looked up at the house and the surrounding grounds.

"It's not very elegant is it?" Foden said.

"It's incredible," George answered. "It's like something out of Gothic Horror. I love it."

Foden led the way into the marbled hall and George was still looking around him. He ran his hands over the mahogany doors and the heavily carved staircase. and Foden watched him with amused interest.

"I'm thinking of converting it into flats," Foden said.

George looked at him with sudden enthusiasm. "I could do that for you, Charles," he said.

He explained that his father had been a builder. "I worked with him from when I was a kid until he died. I know everything about converting a house like this. We did dozens of them around Bradford." His great brown eyes pleaded.

"Why didn't you continue doing that?" Foden's shrewd brain asked.

The enthusiasm disappeared and George just as quickly looked disconsolate.

"Mum married Dad's brother. They shared the business." he explained.

"And you didn't like that?"

George told him how he suspected his mother and uncle had been having an affair while his father was still alive.

"I found a note in Dad's work bench in our garage. It was in Mum's writing. It said, 'Desmond' – that's Dad's name – 'would be visiting his sister on Thursday.' It was a few years old. Dad must have intercepted it somehow. It was addressed to my uncle."

"Do you think your father knew they were having an affair?"

"Of course he did." His voice reflected his anger.

"And he didn't say anything to your mother?"

"I don't think so. Dad wouldn't, because of me. But just before he died, when he was in hospital with cancer, he said; 'Don't be hard on your Mum, son. She loves you too.' He died a few days later."

"So he knew you would find out?" Foden said.

George snorted. "I didn't have to find out. They wasted no time getting married once Dad had gone."

Foden took his arm. "Come on. I'll show you the rest of the house."

As they toured the rooms George recovered his enthusiasm. He praised all the fine woodwork and craftsmanship and the big Victorian windows.

"Charles, you won't destroy it too much will you?"

"Well, it's not exactly modern taste is it?" Foden answered.

"No. But it could be converted into really nice flats without changing too much. Quality always sells," and Foden saw another side of the casual, flippant, surprising George.

"This was my aunt's room."

George looked around the spacious room. It still exuded a feminine touch: from the flowered, patchwork bedspread and matching headrest to the pink silk, cloche-shaped lampshades and the tasselled curtains.

George smiled. "I can still smell her perfume. Has she been gone long?"

"Only a few days. We still haven't had the funeral. But she lived with us for a little while before she died."

"I'm sorry, Charles. When you said 'recently' I didn't think..."

"That's all right, George. We were very fond of her. I shall miss her."

There was a moment of silence as a trace of emotion showed on his face.

"Come and see where you can sleep," he said gruffly.

They went into the bedroom that had once been his father's.

"This was our room, when we were first married," he explained.

"You lived with your Grandparents? What about your mother and father?"

"I didn't know my father, he died before I was born. And my mother chose to go and live in America when her father died."

He explained a brief history of his grandparents and as he did so he wondered why he was able to talk so easily about his life to someone he had just met.

"So there we are," he concluded. "This room was only used occasionally as a guest room so it is probably the best one for you to use."

"Charles, are you sure it's all right. Won't your wife mind?" Foden laughed.

"Good lord, no. Arabella hated this house, she couldn't wait for us to get our own place. She would come over sometimes when Aunt Sheila was here but she didn't enjoy it. I'm not sure why."

"Didn't she get on with your grandparents?"

"Yes, perfectly. I think it was a female thing. This house is a bit intimidating isn't it?"

"I love it. Charles, let me help you. I could make some drawings. Most of the bedrooms have bathrooms already. It will be so easy to convert the place. I'll do some drawings with several options. It will just give you some ideas to help you decide what to do."

Foden smiled at his enthusiasm. "All right. Why not? I have to do something with the place. I'll have to have an architect at some stage – but you could site-manage couldn't you?"

"Yeah, definitely. And I could work on the gardens while the house is being done."

"That would be very helpful. I've only had someone come in once a week to cut the grass so there is plenty that needs doing there. I'll pay you of course. Do you drive? There's an old Daimler in the garage."

George laughed infectiously. "Of course I can drive. I can't believe this; one minute I'm homeless and workless and suddenly I'm living in a mansion, driving a Daimler and doing what I love. Thank you, Charles. Thank you."

He stepped quickly towards the older man and hugged him before Foden could react.

"Good. That's settled then," Foden said awkwardly. "Let's go downstairs and look at that."

He led the way down and George followed, smiling to himself, amused that he had embarrassed Foden by his show of warmth. They toured the lower floor and briefly discussed ideas as to how it could be converted, then Foden opened the door to his grandfather's study. He watched as George admired the bookcases.

"I suppose we can send things like that to auction," Foden said. "I can't see much use for them in a modern setting."

George made no reply. He looked at the photographs on the desk, picking one up and studying it closely.

"That's my father."

"He's right handsome."

"Yes. I didn't inherit his genes, unfortunately. I think I'm more like grandpa,"

George looked at him. "You're not pretty, Charles. You're different. Imposing. You have presence. That's how my mum would describe you. You're like this house. You've got quality."

Foden was visibly embarrassed, no one had ever praised his looks.

"The other one is my aunt," he said quickly.

"She's beautiful too. Wasn't she married?"

"No. I'll tell you about it sometime. Let's go and look at the basement. I want to make it into a studio. If you want any paper you will find plenty in that desk."

They went down into the basement with Foden explaining it was the old below-stairs kitchen. He opened a door off it.

"This is my dark-room and laboratory," he explained.

"You're really keen on photography then?"

"Yes. I would like to take some pictures of you if I may?"

"Of course you can. As many as you like."

"I haven't done much portraiture. I really need a studio. I thought the main kitchen area could be converted."

George looked over the large central space. "No problem. I could do that myself. We'll just have to insulate and line the walls, do the electrics for the lighting and off you go."

"I would like that very much."

George had wandered around the room, admiring the old cooking-range which was still installed, then he looked through into a larder-space and Foden went cold.

"That old freezer's still on."

Foden felt the blood flowing into his cheeks. He forced a laugh.

"Yes. You'll think this very silly of me. One of our dogs died. The children were very fond of it and wanted to bury it in the garden. I told them, as it used to belong to Auntie, it should be buried in this garden and we could do it in the holidays. So I put it in the freezer. I hope they will forget all about it when the holidays are here."

"What was it called?"

"Sandy."

"Poor Sandy. I'll make a nice coffin for him and the children can help me bury him."

"They would like that. Phillipa, my youngest, loves a bit of drama. She'll probably want flowers and the vicar to say a few words."

They both laughed and went back to the ground-floor.

"I'd better be getting home. Will you be all right? The village store is open until seven if you need to buy anything. I haven't had anything turned off so you will have water and electric and, if you know how to work it, the Aga in the kitchen is good for heating and cooking."

"I know all about Agas. Thank you, Charles."

Remembering how Foden had reacted to his enthusiastic

thanks before, he held out his hand. Foden shook it and nodded his head as a way of returning George's gratitude.

"I'll call round in the morning before I go into the office. I'm supposed to be playing golf this week but I think I'll call that off. I'm playing so badly."

"And I'll start putting some ideas to paper to give you something to work on."

George stood on the porch and waved as Foden got into his car and drove away. He closed the door and stood in the hallway for a moment and then he bent forward and clenched his fists and exploded with a yelp of joy.

****

Foden slept that night only in draughts of exhaustion between nightmares and waking shocks. He relinquished the battle soon after light permeated beyond the curtains. He looked at his wife, uncomfortably on her back, snoring gently.

He got up and quietly went downstairs into the kitchen. He made coffee and sipped it thirstily. He looked around the large room where his family had their noisy, chatty breakfasts and his eyes rested on the photograph of the shooting party. He took the picture off its hook and held it in front of him. He saw clearly both of his grandparents, his mother, his aunt, his father and...Gerhardt. The past that was ever present. Then he saw Katy Rose Lewis, so beautifully dead, like a butterfly caught in a frost.

He put the picture angrily back on its hook and gulped the now cooled coffee. His anger just as quickly was replaced by a feeling of helplessness, of weakness and despair. 'Why, why am I subjected to this, to other people's problems?' he asked himself and felt so deeply the injustice of it all that several tears wet his cheeks and the anger returned as he wiped them away. Then he thought of George and his body calmed as his brain started to work again. What to do with George?

He had worked by instinct and intuition when doing what he had done with the charming, alarming young man who's beauty had snatched up his life in a moment of admiration. So far, George had responded predictably to his manipulation, but Foden knew that under the facade of the ne'er-do-well there lurked a smart brain.

His grandpa's genes asserted themselves and the shrewd, practical Foden now considered the situation clinically. He did not know what George had seen or heard on Drovers' Hill. He did not know if his innocent reaction on learning that the girl who had disturbed their brief encounter and was now being sought by the police was innocence or convenience. For now, it was a quid pro quo situation: George now had somewhere to live and a means of making a living and Foden had found someone to solve the problem of what to do with his grandpa's house – and what to do with Katy Rose. But for how long could the situation last?

Would George be able to ignore the publicity that Katy's disappearance would inevitably generate without asking question of himself or of Foden? And when he does, how long will it take for him to arrive at the most likely, the probable, cause of her disappearance?

What to do with George?

What he had done seemed, so far, to be a satisfactory solution. George was more than happy about it. But for now was not forever. What if George got to know people in the village? Would he tell them where he was living, what he was doing? Would he boast of his friendship with Foden when he knew how well he was regarded far and near? That would not do. Not for a long time at least, long enough for people to stop thinking about Katy.

When he called round to Upland House he found George in the modern kitchen built onto the rear of the property. He could hear loud music coming from a radio that Aunt Sheila had kept in there. George was frying eggs on the Aga. He wore jeans and a vest and he didn't hear Foden arrive as he was also singing to himself. When Foden went behind him and touched his arm, he jumped then laughed like a child and made Foden smile too.

"Would you like some breakfast?" he asked

"No, thanks. But you go ahead. I can see you know how to cook."

"Eggs and fried bread; no problem. Sausage and mash, Cottage pie, Corn-beef hash, spag-boll...I won't starve."

"Or keep your figure," Foden laughed.

"I don't eat during the day when I'm working, so no problem – as long as I'm working."

Foden realised it was a question.

"But you are working, at least you will be soon. There are plenty of tools in the woodshed if you want to start on the garden, and a good mower."

He saw, slight as it was, the relief on George's face. George flipped the two eggs and fried bread onto a plate and sat opposite Foden at the table.

"I've done some drawings," he said and slid several sheets of paper across the table. Foden picked one up and studied it, turning it several ways. He did the same with all the sheets and then looked at the young man.

"These are very good, George. I'm very impressed. How did you learn to do plans like that?"

"I like drawing. I wanted to go to art-college but somehow it didn't get to happen."

"I'll give these to our architect. We use a firm in the city, we have developments from time to time."

"They're only ideas. They'll probably want to do something else."

"No, I think they are a good starting-point. I'll get Robert to work with you on them."

George beamed his appreciation.

"There's one thing we'll have to be careful about," Foden continued. "I don't want your wages going onto our books. I want to keep them private, just between the two of us."

"Sure, Charles. Whatever you think best."

"Employment law is a mess and it's easier if I pay you cash. Is that all right for you?"

"Fine with me."

"But it means we'll have to keep the arrangement quiet or I will get into trouble. If anyone should ask, and I don't anticipate that happening, you can say you are just looking after the house for me. You can say you are a distant relative if you like."

"A second cousin from Aus."

"Not with your accent. Better say from Yorkshire. In fact, George, it's best not to tell anyone that you're living here; they're a nosy lot and it will soon be all over the county."

"No problem, Charles. I'm good at minding my own business, and I expect other people to do the same. But I've used the village shops quite a bit, they know me there. They know I work at the golf club – or did. I'll just let them think I still do."

"Good. Good."

"You look as though you haven't slept much."

"No. I had a terrible night. My wife is pregnant and is a bit fidgety and restless."

"Is it your first baby?"

"No, we have two other children: Edmund and Phillipa. Remember? We have to bury the dog for them?

"Of course. I'd forgotten that."

Foden looked quickly into his eyes but saw nothing to be afraid of.

"But Arabella has always had a bad time until she gets well into the pregnancy."

"You're a busy man, Charles: office, pregnant wife, two children. No wonder you don't get much sleep. I don't suppose I'm going to see much of you."

"I'll get the phone reconnected and then you'll be able to reach me if you have to."

"Great. Meantime, breakfast over. I'll find the mower."

"I do have a gardener come in once a week to keep it tidy,"

"Would you rather I did something else? I could crack on with starting to convert the basement for your studio."

"Do you think you can do that by yourself?"

"Sure. It's not a big deal. It just needs the walls and floor insulated and finished and then wiring for lighting and heating."

"And you could do that?"

George laughed. "Course I can. How would you like the floor finished; timber or tiled?"

"Timber would be warmer, don't you think?"

"Easier too, I'm used to handling timber."

Foden took out a pen and wrote on one of the sheets of paper George had been using for his drawings.

"I'll give you details of our account with the builders merchants. Order what you need. I'll phone them when I get home and tell them you are working for me." he handed the paper to George and smiled. "I can't believe I'm going to get a proper photographic studio."

George returned the smile. "And I can't believe I met you.

I'm going to love doing this."

"Good, George. Good." Foden held out his hand across the table and the young man took it firmly.

After he left, Foden found himself still smiling. There had been black, frightening moments in the midst of the night when he thought of what he might have to do to solve the problem of George, to protect himself, to protect his family.

The serious consideration of killing someone is a rare phenomenon, despite the attempt of fiction writers to make it seem like a popular occurrence, and when the realisation that that was what he was sub-consciously doing jerked him awake from his nightmares and his sweating body cooled with his mind, he saw the possibility clearly. But that is what it remained; a possibility. His mind did not go beyond that, to the How, the Where or the When. He had been waiting, testing, watching George with the instincts of a wild animal stalking an enemy, but he had found nothing threatening in the young man. If George had thought he knew of what might have happened to Katy Rose, he showed no sign of it and Foden was now sure he wasn't going to let it interfere with his sudden good fortune.

But as he neared home, his smile disappeared and depression descended again and pressed inside his head. He now had two lives separated by a short walk. How long could he keep them apart, he wondered.

"Are you going to play?" his wife asked.

"I suppose I should," he told her.

His lack of enthusiasm was evident.

"For goodness sake, Charles. If you don't feel like it, don't push yourself. It won't be the end of the world if Farringdon gets the trophy."

Part of Foden thought it would be, but now it was a very small part. Farringdon had dropped well down his stress-list.

"You are right. Let's get the funeral over with, then I hope I'll feel better."

The funeral took place six days later and did nothing to alleviate Foden's deep depression. The week leading up to it had been an inexorable journey of sleepless nights and stressful encounters. The news of Katy Rose's disappearance had made the national press and television and the local evening news featured the search for her persistently. Then the announcement of door-to-door enquiries sparked a sense of panic in Foden. The telephone company had restored the line to Upland House within two days as it had only been disconnected at the exchange and Foden rang George as soon as the house enquiry was announced.

"Don't answer the door to anyone, George," he told him. I'll get into trouble if I'm suspected of employing you illegally."

"Can't you make it legal, Charles. I don't mind paying tax and insurance?"

"Not for now. Perhaps later."

"I've ordered stuff from the builders. I can't very well hide can I"

"It's only for this one police door-to-door enquiry. Have you seen any sign of them?"

"No."

"Then just check from the window before answering the door. I just think it's not a good idea for anyone to know about you working for me yet. It might not look good if the golf club knew I'd taken you on after Fred sacked you. They're a nosy lot and they might get the wrong idea."

"I see what you mean, Charles. That's no problem. I'll keep a low-profile and keep out of the way."

The police in the form of constable Steve Jennings, knocked at Foden's door the next day. He beamed as Foden opened the door to him.

"Allo, sir. This is where you live. Thank you for dropping the clubs off to my wife. I was going to contact you at the club to thank you."

"Now there's no need," Foden managed to smile at him.

"No, s'pose not. It was very kind of you. I hope I can do them justice."

They chatted pleasantly before Jennings got around to the reason for his visit. He wanted to know who else lived there and when he was given the names he smiled again.

"All women 'an kids then. No need to worry 'bout them, then."

"And one of them is pregnant."

"Not likely to have been drivin' about much, I reckon."

"No. I'm usually her taxi," Foden laughed. "Are you still thinking it was a motorist responsible for Katy's disappearance?"

"That's what CID think. I don't get to have an opinion."

"Don't you agree with them?"

"It looks the most likely thing to 'ave 'appened," he said.

"Yes, I suppose it does. Steve, have you been to Upland House yet?"

Jennings was impressed that Foden had remembered his first name.

"Upland House?

"At the top of Upland Rise. My aunt lived there. She's just died. The house is empty/"

"I know where you mean. I'm sorry to hear about your aunt, Mr Foden."

"Thank you. I'm just about to have the house converted. There might soon be one or two builders looking at it."

"Thank you for telling me. I can give that one a miss then. Thanks, Mr Foden. 'an thanks again for the clubs."

Foden closed the door and felt his body exhale slowly; perhaps his good fortune was not permanently shredded.

He went back to the office as soon as Aunt Sheila had been buried beside her parents and brother in the local churchyard. Visiting the graves again had regurgitated the deep feelings of love, deceit, anger and abandonment that had only recently been suppressed by the pressing weight of guilt and fear from the events on Drovers' Hill. His anger was also with himself that he was unable to ease the sadness and loss that his wife and children were also suffering after Aunt Sheila's death, but going back to work was one step further away from an emotional meltdown.

The following weekend, Nigel Farringdon easily won the Harlequin Trophy and Foden's abasement was complete.

The local media still concentrated on the search for Katy Rose and every evening the television news bulletin featured interviews with local people including Katy's school friends and family and constant updates and appeals by the police, and the pressure Foden felt was remorselessly increased by his wife and and nanny wanting to talk about it.

"Who would want to hurt a lovely girl like that?" the nanny wondered.

"There are plenty of depraved people about," the housekeeper added.

"I just cannot think how her parents can live with it. Imagine not knowing what might have happened to your child."

Mrs Foden put her hand to her stomach as though to protect it.

Her husband stood up quickly.

"Are you all right, darling" his wife asked him.

She had been observing him carefully since Aunt Sheila's death and had hoped his obvious stress would have diminished after the funeral.

"Yes. I felt a little chilled. I'll go and put a cardigan on."

"I hope you're not getting a cold, Mr Foden," Nanny told him. "We don't want the children catching anything."

"No. I think I'm just tired. I might lie down for a bit."

He lay on the bed, face down, and wanted to cry but no tears came. After a while he beat the duvet with his fists and then got off the bed and went to the window as though he would find an answer to his problems in the garden. But the garden reminded him of George.

He had spoken on the telephone twice in the two weeks since he had last seen George. The conversation had mostly been about ordering building supplies as George said he would start on the studio. But as he stared at the garden he remembered George saying he would bury Sandy for him and a sweat quickly smeared his back. If George was doing things in the old kitchen would he need to move the freezer? Panic, which had never been far away, now seized him. He went downstairs, taking a coat from the rack and shouted to his wife he needed to go for a walk.

He walked to Upland House, giving himself time to calm his mind. As he entered the house the sound of an electric drill came from the basement. He descended the steps and stopped on the bottom. The level of the kitchen floor had been raised and wood planking shone newly bright almost level with the bottom step. He trod carefully and called as he moved from the small corridor into the old kitchen. The drill stopped and as he entered the kitchen he too stopped just as abruptly. The walls were covered in plaster board and new skirting and architrave had been added to finish it off. But his astonishment was emphasised by the new flooring which spread into the kitchen and was almost complete. George was standing there, smiling at him.

"Allo Charles. What d'you think?" he asked.

"I'm astonished," Charles replied truthfully. "You have done all this in two weeks?"

He ran his hands along the smooth plaster-board, noting the many electric points cut into it.

"I don't believe it. You have even wired it too?"

"Not connected yet. I'll have to get a certified electrician to check it and connect it to the meter," George said, almost apologetically. "I've also run cable up to the ceiling; thought you would want some sort of overhead wall lighting."

"Amazing. Absolutely amazing. Haven't you been sleeping?"

George laughed and immediately Charles felt better.

"Slept like a log every night. I've never slept in a bed like that before. No, there's not much to it when you know what you're about. The walls have got three inch insulating set between posts every eighteen inches. And I've done the same with the floors. So it all looks a bit smaller and the floor's higher but I think it's okay for what you need. I think you will have to use electric heating as I couldn't see any central heating down here."

"No. They didn't think about the servants when this was built," Foden laughed. "George, you are amazing. I had no idea you could do all this."

"I told you, Charles."

"Yes, you did."

"So is it okay if I carry on?"

Foden laughed again. "Okay? It is very much okay, George. Thank you."

"What do you want me to do with the other rooms?" He swept his arm towards the ancillary rooms off the kitchen. "I can raise the floors up to this level if you want them insulated. Depends what they'll be used for."

"I suppose we could make a dressing-room out of one of them. It would be nice to have some insulating for heating in there. And I could use the old scullery for my processing and developing room. I don't need anything special in there, it's better to keep it cool.

"So I'll leave that one as it is. What about Sandy?"

"Sandy?" It took Foden two seconds to remember. "Oh, yes. Sandy."

"I'll have to move the freezer," George explained.

Foden was unable to answer, his brain had frozen.

"If you don't want the freezer, why don't I just bury the whole thing in the garden when I do that? I was planning on doing a bit of landscaping."

Foden's brain thawed.

"What a good idea. I never thought of that. I think the children have forgotten about the dog now so that would be a good solution. I certainly don't need the freezer. When you start on the garden I can send one of our small diggers over. They're easy enough to learn."

"No need. I've used one a few times."

"There you are then. George, you are amazing. I cannot thank you enough."

"No need, Charles. You are thanking me. And thanks for the cash, by the way."

"Not at all. I'm going to open a building account for you. You'll have to come over to my bank so they can identify you and get your signature, then you can withdrew anytime. We could have lunch together."

"That would be great."

"Good. I'll arrange it and phone you."

"Charles, if you don't mind me saying so; you still look terrible."

"Do I? I haven't been sleeping. We had Auntie's funeral

last week and I have so many things to think about."

"You need to offload. Don't worry about this place, it will all come together soon enough. Your architect came over a few days ago. We got on fine. He liked my ideas and said they were preparing the drawings. So you don't have to worry about that."

"Yes, he did phone me. He said he liked you and could work with you."

"Then what else is worrying you?"

For a moment Foden's defences almost slipped. Confession was something his inner self longed for but his brain kept denying. There had been a moment, up on Drovers' Hill, when he had wanted to turn to someone and say how sorry he was, that he only wanted to slap Katy for being so rude. But there was no one there to listen, except Jenny, and it was her cries and the thought of what to do with her that had awakened his brain and sealed his fate. But repentance was a strong magnet that constantly dissembled his thoughts.

"Have you been watching television?"

"No. I didn't even know if they would work," George laughed. "I'm fine with the radio, I like music. I haven't been finishing work until late and by the time I've had something to eat and a shower I just collapse in bed. Have I been missing something?"

"The local news is all about Katy Rose."

"Haven't they found her?"

"No. They still think a motorist took her. She was supposed to be catching a bus from where she lived to Upper Stokesey."

"What was she doing up there, in the woods?"

"I think she must have missed the bus and decided to walk; it's much nearer than going by road."

"Don't the police know that?"

"I don't think they've thought that's what she might have done."

"Could she get up there? She had a kid with her didn't she?"

"It would be quite a climb up to Drovers' Hill from The Badgers where she lived. But she was a determined girl."

"Did you know her well?"

"I took some photographs of her once – and I know her father. I think I should tell them that we saw her on Drovers' Hill. What do you think?"

George took some moments to consider the question. Foden waited for his answer, mentally on edge. He could see the indecision in George's face and he hoped it was a good sign that his gamble had worked.

"I dunno, Charles. It's a bit awkward isn't it. I mean, the police will ask us a lot of questions. Like you said."

"They'll want to know what we were doing there."

"That's what I mean – not that we were doing anything bad."

"No. But if we tell them you were sunbathing and I was just looking for my golf-ball, will they believe us – especially now you're living here?"

"I don't think they will. It would be awkward for us."

"I know. That's what I thought. But I want to help them find Katy."

"What do you think happened to her?"

"I don't know."

"The police were all over the village. They must think she went there."

"I know. That's why I think I should tell them we saw her up on Drover's Hill."

"That might be a bit awkward for us."

"So you don't think I should tell them we saw her?"

401

"I don't see how it will help find her."

"No, I think you're right."

"And it will certainly mess up your life."

"And yours; we'd definitely not be able to see each other or the police really would get suspicious as to why we were on Drovers' Hill."

"I don't think it's a good idea, Charles."

"Nor do I. But it's a terrible burden for me. Now you see why I haven't been sleeping?"

"Charles. If you go to the police they'll suspect you had something to do with it. They'll make your life hell – and mine. Your wife's expecting a baby, what will it do to her? And it won't help find the girl. You can't get involved. Let the police get on with it."

"You're probably right, George."

"I know I am."

"Thank you for listening. I feel better already."

"Good. Why don't we go upstairs and have a beer?"

"You've got yourself organised then?" Foden smiled.

"A trip to the shop once a week. Haven't had much time for anything else."

"Don't overdo it, George. There's no great hurry. We're not on a schedule."

"I know. I'm enjoying myself. I love working. What about that beer? You can tell me what else you need in the studio."

George took two beers from the refrigerator and handed one to Foden. Foden was pleased that the beers were real ale but he hesitated about what to do with it until George put the bottle to his lips. He noticed Foden's hesitation.

"Sorry, Charles. You want a glass."

"No, no. fine," Foden told him and drank determinedly from the bottle.

They sat opposite each other at the table and Foden felt the presence of their companionship and, with a touch of excitement, realised he had not enjoyed the feeling since leaving school. He had friends at university but there had been no one he could sit with without feeling the need to talk. Strangely, George had that affect.

"I don't know anything about photographic studios, Charles so you'll have to tell me what you want me to do when I've finished the floor."

"I don't know much about them either," Foden laughed. "I know that windows are not a good idea because they interfere with the lighting."

"There aren't any so no problem. How did they manage cooking down there without ventilation?" "The ancillary rooms have windows and no doors – apart from the old larder. I suppose they made do with those. Also, as there would be no heating except from the cooking range and the basement is half below ground, it wouldn't ever get too warm."

"So I should leave it as it is? It would be expensive and damn noisy to put an air-conditioner in."

"I think we'll manage. I'm going to use the scullery, where the freezer is, for my developing room and the old larder can be a dressing room. The other two small storage rooms can be left open. Perhaps you could fit a fan into those windows?"

" No problem."

"It would also be nice to be able to have some sort of system so I could change the background for photo-shoots."

"I could put runners along the walls, top and bottom, then you could use panels that slide along."

"That is a good idea. I could then either project pictures onto them or use graphics on them. You are clever, George."

"Just practical, like my Dad."

403

"No, you have imagination too, a useful combination. You would have made a good engineer, then you could have come and worked for me."

"I am working for you."

They both laughed. They talked for another hour. George told him how he had come to be working at the golf club.

"On the train down I was talking to some bloke. I was going to change and go to London but he lived down here on the coast and he was telling me how great it was in the summer. I love sea-swimming but not up our way; the sea is freezing even in the summer. Anyway, I thought it would be nice to spend the summer near the coast. So I stayed on the train until the ticket-inspector found me and said I should have changed trains and would have to get off at the next stop. So I ended up in the city, went to the Job Centre and they sent me here to the golf club."

They talked easily together, swapping anecdotes and laughing quite a lot, which Foden hadn't done for a long time. Without either of them being aware of it, they were laying the foundations of a friendship that defied their cultural and background differences.

Foden went to work the next morning, having slept better than he had for over two weeks. He didn't go to the house again for another two weeks. Work, and his wife's condition kept him busy and he managed to avoid the television news by returning later than usual from the office, arriving in time for dinner, and afterwards chose to read a newspaper while his wife felt free to watch what she normally knew he wouldn't enjoy. But he could not avoid the news all of the time and an appeal by Katy Lewis' father and mother was particularly distressing and revived his anxieties and stress to a physical degree so that when he arrived at Upland House as arranged to inspect George's work on the studio, his enthusiasm was noticeably subdued.

George had consulted him several times by telephone and the result was an open space with hidden strip lighting around the three walls and panels of six foot tall, heavy plywood that could be moved around within runners. It had been decided to keep the old cooking-range as Foden thought it would make a useful feature for portraiture and George had installed a two-way ventilation and extractor fan and a stainless steel lining in the chimney above it. With the wood flooring and white-painted panelling and the fitted lighting it was an impressive result and Foden did his best to show his appreciation but it was just muted enough for George to sense the lack of energy behind the compliments.

"Are you in a hurry, Charles? Have you got time for a beer?"

Foden was beyond hurry; the Katy Lewis appeal he had watched before arriving had not only revived his anxieties, it had condensed them to a deep depression.

"That would be good, George." His voice reflected his inner turmoil even though he smiled.

They went up to the kitchen, but instead of handing him the beer, George carried them into the sitting-room and Foden followed him demurely. He sank into his grandfather's old armchair and smiled down at the worn upholstery of the arms, and the worn damask reflected the melancholy of his thoughts. George handed him the beer.

"Cheers," he said.

"Cheers. I think it should be Champagne to celebrate all the incredible work you've done," Foden told him.

"We'll keep that until it's all finished. I hear you've arranged for a lot of stuff to go to auction next week."

"Yes. As you are getting on so quickly I thought we'd better make a start. Robert has submitted plans for the conversions so there's no reason why it can't be started."

"Yeah. I spoke to Robert. I can get on with the garden while that's all happening."

The lack of response from Foden was noticeable, almost embarrassing.

"Charles, what's worrying you. Can I help?"

Foden tried to respond, but suddenly the words wouldn't come. Instead, several tears defied the squeezing of his eyelids and ran down his face. George put down his beer and was suddenly at Foden's side, kneeling by his chair. He put his hand on Foden's knee.

"Hey, Charles," was all he could think to say but the way he said it and his gesture was enough for Foden to feel the intensity of his concern.

"I'm sorry, George," he mumbled.

George rose and knew where to find a box of grandma's tissues. He extracted several and pushed them into Foden's hand. He pulled up a footstool next to Foden's chair and perched on it and waited.

Eventually Foden recovered his voice as he dabbed his eyes. He took a sip of the beer and smiled wanly at his friend.

"I know I should tell someone," he said.

"About the girl being in the woods? I thought we'd decided that wasn't a good idea."

"About me killing her."

He saw the surprise, almost disbelief in George's eyes and his own response was similar. "I thought you knew," he said.

"No. I believed what you told me."

Foden felt the guilt of his duplicity which added to his misery. "I'm sorry. I'm sorry, sorry, sorry." The tears started again.

George put his hand on Foden's arm.

"Whatever happened, Charles, I know you didn't mean it."

Foden dabbed his eyes and looked at him.

"She was rude, aggressive. She called me a queer. I just meant to slap her."

"I know."

Foden then quickly related the actions of the events on Drovers' Hill. He spoke as though he couldn't control the way the words tumbled out like unbottled insects. He described how he hid Katy's body and took the child down to the road and then he threw himself backwards into the chair as though the process had completely exhausted him.

"So, Sandy is..."

Foden opened his eyes and nodded. "It's Katy."

"Fuck!"

George rose and stood, taking a large mouthful of beer.

"I'll go to the police." Foden's voice was now quiet, normal. George put down his beer and resumed his seat on the stool.

"Charles, you can't do that." His voice and his eyes were pleading, serious.

"I don't really have any choice."

"Yes, you do. Think of your family. Your wife. Your new baby. Think of spending twenty years in prison while they try to manage without you. What happened wasn't your fault. The girl was a bitch. She had no right, no need to say those things to you – just because she thought you were different. Another pretty slag that can't believe the world doesn't love her."

"It's unfair to you. I've involved you."

"By trying to help me. Don't you see, Charles; if you go to the police you'll ruin a lot of lives, not just your own."

Foden looked into the large, pleading eyes.

"I don't know if I can live with it, George."

"Yes, you can. You can live with it better than you can live with being in a prison. It was an accident. Accidents happen. But a jury might not see it that way. What you did, you did for your family. You can't ruin all that now. And going to prison isn't going to change what happened – and it isn't going to bring the girl back."

Foden looked at him for some moments and it was the old Foden who eventually answered. He realised that what George had been saying was exactly what he had told himself in fractions of time when he did what he did on Drovers' Hill.

"You are right, George. I know you are. No matter how bad I feel about what happened I can't take it back, can I?"

"No, Charles. You can only live with it, knowing it wasn't your fault. I will help you."

"You are proving to be a good friend."

"We'll do it together, Charles."

"What about...."

"We'll pretend it's Sandy. Do what we were going to do."

"Can you live with that?"

"I can if you can."

"Together?"

"Together."

Foden raised his beer and George brought his to the stool and they smiled as they clinked the bottles and drank

For several days after that, they only spoke on the telephone. George was attentive, caring, wanting to know how Foden was. Foden assured him he was now all right, that he was sleeping better. But a week later, when the news of Katy's disappearance seemed to be dying down, the interview with Ivana Katowice got maximum coverage. It was broadcast on a Saturday afternoon as a Breaking News item when Foden, his wife, the nanny, Betsy and the children were having tea in the nursery. A young Katowice was asked about a comment she was supposed to have made to a local newspaper reporter.

"It is very possible that the child will be able to recall what happened to Katy at some future date, depending on how traumatic the occasion was. It could be locked away in her brain for years, then suddenly another event, even a particular sound or image, could cause her to recall what happened. But it would be more likely to happen in stages; she might have nightmares which could increase as she gets older. They would probably be repetitive, without detail but the detail could be extracted with proper analysis and treatment."

"You mean, with hypnotherapy?" the interviewer asked.

"Yes."

"When could that happen?"

"Almost at any time if something triggers a strong reaction. But it is more likely to be when Jenny is older, when her brain has developed."

"And events could be hidden away for that long?"

"Yes. The brain retains images forever. It would just be a matter of getting the brain to recall them. Regressive hypnotherapy can be very successful."

The little group in the nursery were attentive, even the children. Ivana Katowice had an addictive personality.

"What's hyp..." Edmund was the first to react.

"Hypnotherapy," the nanny explained. "It's a way of putting someone almost to sleep so they can concentrate better. We must try it with you when we're doing sums."

The women and and the children laughed but Foden was still staring at the television.

"She sounds a bit of a nutcase," Mrs Foden commented.

"What's a nutcase?" Edmund wanted to know.

"Someone who talks like a squirrel," his mother told him and tickled his ribs, making him squirm beside her on the sofa.

"Can squirrels talk?" Phillipa wanted to know."

"Course not, silly," Edmund teased her.

"Do you believe someone can be hypnotised to remember something from childhood?" Arabella asked her husband.

"I don't know anything about hypnotism."

"Can a child of eighteen months remember things like that anyway?" his wife persisted.

"A child's cognitive awareness is quite active at that age," the nanny added. "But children do differ. Some are much brighter and develop quicker than others."

Charles Foden saw quite clearly the little, tearful face of Jenny Challis watching him tending Katy Rose's body and he shivered inwardly.

"Well, I think that woman is talking nonsense," Arabella Foden decided.

"So do I," her husband agreed, but the image of Jenny Challis looking up at him didn't go away.

At Upland House, George too watched the interview. Having got a television working he now, with good reason, regularly watched the news.

He had no one with whom he could swap opinions and Ivana Katowice's personality and performance remained with him into the evening.

He wondered if Charles Foden had seen the interview and, if he had, of the effect it might have on him. He knew his friend was still very emotional despite the efforts he had made to alleviate his fears. He also knew that one thing could push him over the edge and damage all their lives – one thing like the Ivana Katowice interview.

410

As he worked, such thoughts swirled around his brain until he made a mistake in measuring a window-frame he was fitting. He decided to give up before his lack of concentration did more damage.

He had a shower and put on a clean shirt and jeans. For several weeks he had only worn shorts and a vest and as he admired the effect of his new self in the mirror he realised a change of scene and some relaxation would do no harm. But, where could that be? He remembered Charles' caution about talking to anyone in the village. Then he hadn't realised the significance of the warning, but now he did. It would not be a good idea for either of them if local people knew of their relationship.

He stood in front of the mirror for some moments, feeling like a bride dressed for a wedding that had just been called-off. Then he remembered the Daimler. He had had no need to use the car, but it was there; a means of escape. He could take it to the city, have a meal or a drink in a nice bar, but even driving the car anywhere would be a pleasant way to relax.

He put a sweater around his shoulders and found the car keys.

He sat in the leather seats and admired the walnut fascias and smiled as he remembered the only vehicles he had driven were vans and mowers. He spent a few minutes familiarising himself with the controls and then he started the quiet engine and put it in Drive and smiled again as the car slid almost silently out of the yard. He drove down Upland Rise but at the bottom, instead of turning left to go through the village and onto the city, he turned right. He passed the golf club where he had worked and there was a second when he nearly turned into its car park – he would have loved to have seen Fred's face when he got out of a

Daimler– but he drove on. His brain soon acknowledged where he was heading; subconsciously it was taking him in the direction of The Badgers.

The pub had been mentioned enough in the news bulletins of the Katy Rose Lewis affair to be known as her home, from where she had started her last, fateful journey with young Jenny Challis.

Only two days before there had been a police reconstruction of a young woman wheeling a child in a pushchair away from the pub and onto the road and standing at the bus-stop. But he was not conscious of why he was making the journey apart from the need of somewhere to go and a vague feeling of curiosity and attachment.

He parked in the rear car park of the pub and noted there were only two other cars there. He checked his watch and saw it was nine pm, not exactly late or too early for a country pub to be attended on a fine, Saturday evening. He got out of the car and looked around. Behind a blend of trees he could see the tops of a few cottages and a larger building that he assumed was an old mill as he could also hear the babbling of a stream.

He entered the pub. There was a man and a woman sitting at the bar and three men and two women at the tables. There was a back-room that was laid out for eating and he realised he was hungry, but there were no lights on in the section. The barmaid seemed to be the only person behind the bar; she was very young and her eyes lit up and her face beamed with country health as she asked him what he would like. He selected a local brew.

"Do you do food?" he asked.

"We do normally, but we don't have a chef at the moment," the barmaid told him hesitantly. "We've got pies," she added hopefully. "They're home-made. Mrs Lewis does 'em herself. 'an we could do a few micro chips wiv 'em."

"Okay. That'll do," he told her.

"I'll bring 'em over if you want to sit at a table."

He chose a table near the empty fireplace. He noticed that the customers who were sitting at other tables, whom he assumed were locals, looked at him individually and sometimes in harmony. He smiled and nodded to them and they got the message that they were being nosy. He assumed the couple sitting at the bar, who were better dressed, owned one of the other cars in the car park.

He sipped his beer, wondering what he was doing there, and was pleased when he saw a woman emerge from a door and put his pie and chips onto the bar. The girl was about to pick it up and take it to his table when a scruffy old man entered the pub. He seemed to appraise the scene in a second.

"Oi'll do that'n, Chris," he told the barmaid. She looked disappointed and nodded in the direction of George. The man took the plate and a knife and fork over to George's table and placed it carefully in front of him.

"Want any sauce or anything?" he asked him.

"No, thanks," George told him

"Want anuvver ale, then?"

"You could top me up."

The man took George's glass to the bar. The barmaid gave him a sour look as she poured the beer. He carried it to George.

"Thanks. Have one yourself."

"Well kind of ee. Thanks. Oi'll 'ave an 'alf wiv ee."

The barmaid gave him an even sharper look as she served his half.

He carried it to George's table.

"Your good health and thank ee," he said.

413

"Cheers. And thank ee too," George responded.

"You a tourist then?"

"No. I'm just on the way somewhere," George answered.

"Ain't we all? But some un don't know where they're agoin. I know where I'll be agoin soon."

"Home or the lavatory?"

The old man cackled when he got the joke.

"Is it always this quiet here?" George asked.

The old man frowned, then sat down opposite to George. He leaned forward conspiratorially.

"You don't know wot 'appened then?"

"No. What happened?"

The old man related in a whisper what had happened. George looked suitably shocked and concerned.

"That's terrible. Is that what they were talking about on the television? I saw something at the hotel I was staying in last night. Something about a girl being hypnotised to be able to remember what happened."

"That's um. Poor Jen. Don't 'elp sayin' things like thaat, though, do it?"

"I thought it sounded a bit far-fetched. "Does the girl live here, too?"

"No. No. Over at yon mill," and he pointed in the direction of the car park."

"Are you family?"

The man cackled again. "No. I'm old Jack, the potman an' cleaner. Better go an' work I s'pose. Thank ee for the drink."

"You're welcome, Jack."

He watched the man go to one of the tables and collect empty glasses. Then he sat down again and started talking to the locals

George paid the girl at the bar and waved to Jack as he left.

In the car park he stood again and looked towards the mill.

He got into the car and at the main road he turned left and quietly slid along the lane that went behind the pub towards the mill house and cottages. There were lights on in the mill house and the windows were open. He saw a woman in an upstairs room. bending out of sight and then straightening and drawing over the curtains. The light went out in that room and he saw the same woman appear downstairs.

He turned around and drove back to the road. It was then dark. He wanted to continue driving, enjoying the car, and he turned left at the road and drove in the direction of Bredon. There was almost no other traffic and it was a new experience for him to wind a luxury saloon along a twisting country road at night.

At Bredon he parked and walked around the small town and sat by the river where young people were still gathered, smoking and laughing together. Two girls spoke to him and he enjoyed teasing them until he realised some of their male friends were getting less friendly. He wished them goodnight and walked back into the town.

It was gone midnight when he started his drive back. He was doing seventy miles an hour but as he recognised the fall in the road towards The Badgers hamlet, he slowed down and was doing less than twenty as he reached the pub. He looked down the lane towards the mill house as he passed. He saw no lights. He continued to drive at a slow speed until he reached the bus stop after The Badgers. He pulled into the cutting and stopped the engine. He sat for several minutes and then he got out of the car, switching off the lights before he did so. He walked back towards the Badgers and the mill house.

****

415

Charles Foden had rung Upland House twice without getting a reply. He assumed George was making a lot of noise and hadn't heard the phone but when he rang again late one evening from a phone-box while taking the dog for a walk and still got no answer, his nerves began to tense.

The following morning, before driving to the office, he called at Upland House. As he entered he heard no sound of activity. He called towards the basement but received no response. He checked the living-room: it was empty. He climbed the stairs and, for no known reason, he didn't call. The door to George's bedroom was ajar. He pushed it further. George was lying face down on the bed, wearing only a pair of thin, cotton shorts which Foden assumed was what he slept in. He called his name in a hesitant voice but George didn't move. Foden put his hand on his back. George turned and sat upright with a startled cry.

"I'm sorry," Foden smiled. "You were fast asleep."

George responded only with a pained expression.

"Are you ill?" Foden asked. "I tried phoning you several times."

"Sorry Charles."

"Are you all right, is there something wrong?"

George nodded and then put his hand to his face. "Oh God!" he murmured.

Foden sat next to him on the bed. "George, what on earth is the matter?"

He was aware it was a role reversal from his last visit and an ache started in his stomach. George took his hand away from his face and wiped it on his shorts, but his eyes remained tearful as he looked at Foden.

"I killed someone."

Foden recoiled physically and it took a few moments for

him to ask the question.

"Who. Who did you kill?"

"The child. Jenny Challis."

Foden's shock was mixed with puzzlement and a degree of anger.

"How?"

"I drowned her."

Foden got off the bed and walked to the window and back again.

"Why?"

"That woman, the psychologist on television, she said Jenny would remember what happened. She could identify you."

Foden sat on the bed. "Oh, God! George."

He put his arm around the young man's shoulders. George turned into him and cried into his chest. After some moments Foden spoke into his hair.

"There was no need. The woman was talking nonsense. How could an eighteen month old child remember what happened? She might have dreams, or nightmares, but to remember any detail... It was all nonsense."

George freed himself and looked tearfully at Foden but said nothing, his eyes spoke for him.

"How did you drown her?"

George recalled what he did on the Saturday evening, how he felt being in The Badgers, seeing the mill house and the lights going out. How, when he went back, the window to the child's room was still open, how easy it was to stand on a water-butt and reach the open window.

"It was so easy. The girl was asleep, she didn't even wake when I lifted her off the bed wrapped in a duvet. I carried her downstairs, opened the door and then a women screamed, and then a man was shouting. I started to run across a bridge but realised they would catch me. I threw the girl in the water... "

"I don't know what I was going to do with her. I had some stupid idea I would just frighten her parents; leave her somewhere."

There was a long silence before Foden spoke.

"You weren't involved, George. Why did you do it?"

"I believed what that woman said," he protested in a whining voice.

Foden surprised himself. He put his arms around George and hugged him. Then he let go as a thought occurred to him.

"This was on Saturday night? Why hasn't there been any news of it?"

They looked at each other.

"It's now Wednesday. I've seen the local news several times. There has been no mention of it. I'm sure it would have been a big story."

Neither of them had an answer, but there was a glimmer of hope in George's eyes.

"I'll find out about it," Foden told him. "I can't believe they could keep the murder of a little girl quiet. I have an idea. It's something I should have done a week ago. I'll need to go down to the darkroom. Don't worry, George. I think you might be wrong."

"But I threw her in the river."

"There has to be an answer. I must find out. I'm going to the darkroom for a while."

He went downstairs and into his darkroom. He emerged over an hour later, holding a large print. George was tidying up in the studio, unable to concentrate on anything more serious. Foden showed him the two foot by three foot print of a photograph of Katy Rose.

"What do you think?" Foden asked.

"Is that her? She's beautiful. It's a wonderful photograph. What are you going to do with it?"

"Give it to her parents. But first, I'll get it framed. George, Don't worry. I'll speak to you tomorrow."

Foden took the picture into a framers on the way to the office. He collected it before they closed and then bought a large bouquet of flowers. He rang his wife to say he would be late and then drove to The Badgers. The same girl was behind the bar and there were no customers. He asked to see Mr or Mrs Lewis. The girl was hesitant but decided he was not a reporter or a policeman.

Mr Lewis emerged, showing the strain of his ordeal. He recognised Foden although he could not have seen him for several years.

"Charles, isn't it?"

"It is. Hello Mr Lewis."

"I don't think I've seen you since the cricket club closed."

"No, probably not. I don't get to come this way."

There was an awkward pause before Foden produced the flowers and laid them on the bar. "I thought Mrs Lewis might like these."

"Thank you. Very kind of you."

And then Foden lifted up the framed photograph of Katy Rose and held it up in front of her father. He stared at it for some moments. His lips trembled.

"It is the photograph I gave the police – with a lot of touching-up. I thought you should have it."

Mr Lewis took the picture in both hands and held it in front of him. He struggled to keep back the tears. A door opened behind him and Mrs Lewis appeared. She took in the flowers on the bar and then saw the picture. She stood by her husband's side and made no attempt to stop the tears flowing down her face. Her husband put his arm around her and lowered the picture to his side.

"Thank you, Charles. Thank you," he said.

"I would have brought it sooner, but I didn't think you wanted any more fuss."

"No. It has been a bit hectic."

"No more news?"

The Lewis' both shook their heads.

"How is Jenny, is she all right?"

"Oh, yes. Jenny's fine. Her parents are talking of moving. I know how they feel. I can't blame them."

"No, of course. It's understandable. Well, I just wanted you to have the photograph. I hope there will soon be some good news." Neither of them replied. "Goodbye."

The Lewis' seemed to come out of a trance.

"Goodbye, Charles. And thank you. Thank you," Mr Lewis said.

Outside, on the way to his car, Foden almost bumped into Jack coming from the cottages. Jack recognised him.

"Allo young Charles. Wot brings you up 'ere?"

Foden, who had never liked Jack, without any reason for the feeling, took a minute to remember he and his wife had retired to a cottage behind the pub. He also remembered, with a spurt of blood to his cheeks, Katy Rose's remark about Jack telling them of his father's liaison with Gerhardt. He forced a smile and a polite greeting He was about to walk on when Jack stopped him.

"Terrible business 'bout young Jenny, ain't it?"

"What was that?"

"Thought you might 'ave 'eard. Someone tried to drown 'er."

"Good Heavens! When?"

"Saturday night. Fortunately, 'er dad got 'er out afore she

drowned. But it were a near thing."

"How terrible. Is she all right?"

"I think so, but the Challis' are movin' cos of it."

"I don't blame them. Do they know who did it?"

"No, but I 'ave me suspicions. There was an 'andsome young feller 'ere. Said ee was passin through. Aven't seen 'im afore."

"Do the police know?"

"I told em 'bout 'im."

"Did he have a car?"

"S'pose so. But I never saw it. He seemed a nice enough feller though."

"Probably an innocent traveller. I can't imagine whoever was responsible for Katy's disappearance would have the nerve to drink in the pub."

"That's wot I was athinkin. But there are some queer folk around nowadays."

Foden squirmed at the adjective. He made a suitable reply and excused himself.

He went straight to Upland House and told George that Jenny was all right. "Her father pulled her out of the river. They said she was fine."

George was physically affected, his body went slack and Foden thought he might faint. They were standing in the kitchen and George put his hand on the table to steady himself. Foden caught him before he collapsed and eased him onto the bench seat. Foden sat side-on close to him, afraid he might still faint.

"But it wasn't a good idea to go into The Badgers. The police have a description of you. You'll have to lie low for a while. I'll shop for anything you need."

George was wearing only his usual shorts. His hair was wet and his body was warm and moist as though he had just had a shower and Foden felt the heat of his body through his jacket as he sat next to him.

George turned his tearful eyes so they were no more than nine inches from Foden's. He nodded then leaned his head against Foden's and muttered a thank you into his neck before lifting his face and looking into Foden's eyes. He made a movement towards Foden's lips and as their bodies twisted towards each other Foden slid off the bench onto the floor and George fell on top of him. They both laughed but George didn't move, lying across Foden's body.

"I should go," Foden gasped. "I'm already so late going home."

George smiled and got up, holding out his arms. Foden took his hands and George easily lifted him from the floor. George kissed him on the cheek.

"Thank you, Charles."

"I'll call tomorrow," Foden said breathlessly

"Please. I love you, Charles."

Foden didn't know what to say or what to do. He nodded again and hurried from the kitchen and didn't slow down until he reached his car.

At home he found his wife was about to go to bed and read, having had a bad day. Betsy had kept dinner for Foden and he ate it alone, for which he was grateful because his mind was full of many thoughts. They assembled in his head in a kaleidoscope of dissociated faces and words.

When he went upstairs his wife was asleep. He looked at her, serenely radiating the potency of her pregnancy, her face composed with the suggestion of a smile on her lips. He wanted to make love to her as she slept. Instead, he kissed her forehead. She opened one eye and moaned a greeting

"I won't disturb you. I'll sleep in the other bed. It's so hot."

She smiled an acknowledgement. He took his pyjamas and

went into a spare bedroom. He stripped off and looked at himself in the mirror. He was, as he remembered George had said, physically imposing, and, in the nude, not overweight as he seemed to be when dressed. His body was naturally heavy and his face only reflected the overall pattern of his genes. He showered then decided it was too hot to wear anything. He climbed into bed and lay on his stomach and the warmth and smell of shampoo brought the feel and touch of George into his mind and body and he pressed his erection into the mattress and tried to shut the confusion of feelings out of his head.

He kept away from Upland house for several days but he was conscious he had said he would shop for George and on the Friday he left the office early and went to the supermarket in the city and bought a stock of food and beers that would last George for over a week.

He heard the noise of a strimmer coming from the garden at the rear of the house as he got out of the car. He took the groceries into the kitchen and stocked up the fridge and the freezer then went into the garden with two cold beers.

George was wearing his usual shorts and cutting around the edge of the lawns. He didn't hear Foden call but as he turned and saw him. He smiled enthusiastically.

"It's beginning to look a bit tidier," Foden said and handed George a beer. He had decided that would be a safe introduction to their meeting and even conceded they could drink out of the bottles. They chatted easily and Foden was grateful for the normality.

"Charles, what do you think about a pond over in that corner?"

"I think it would be a good idea. That part of the garden is a bit bland."

"I thought it would make a nice feature, with lilies and

water-iris and wild grasses around it – like the one on the golf course."

Foden laughed. "Then you could paint it and I could photograph it – the Monets of Upper Stokesey. But it may have to wait. I spoke to Richard yesterday. He has permission for the building changes and thinks they could make a start next week. So you might be busy with other things."

"Great. What about the auctioneers?"

"They're picking up the first lot next Wednesday. They've marked all the items they want to take. We'll just have to send what they don't take somewhere else."

Once the builders arrived and started work, Foden only visited occasionally to give an opinion that had been sought either by the architect or by George. They saw each other for lunch on two occasions and it was over one such lunch in the city in an old restaurant where Foden was very unlikely to meet anyone he knew, when George asked him when he was going to start using the studio.

Foden shrugged apologetically.

"I've had so much to think about that taking pictures hasn't entered my mind."

"All the more reason why you should make yourself do it."

"Perhaps you're right. But the house is a building site right now."

"The studio is finished. You can lock yourself away down there without being disturbed by anybody."

"I've got nothing to photograph."

"You've got me. You said you wanted to photograph me."

They looked at each other. It was a question and Foden wasn't sure how to answer it. He laughed instead.

"You're so busy, George. You're working into the evenings.

I wish you would take a break."

"I love work, you know that. But I'll always make time for you, Charles."

"I know. Let's get that first flat finished and then I'll celebrate with an album of the work you've done. How is that?"

"It's a good idea to have a record."

"Arabella will be giving birth at the end of the year. Then we'll be into the winter and by next spring we might be ready to let one of the flats."

George felt it was a timetable of excuses.

"It's awkward for you being with me isn't it?"

Foden wasn't sure how to interpret the question. He had wondered how other people would see their relationship. George was half his age and could be his son, but instinctively Foden didn't think most onlookers would see it that way. Was it because George was too handsome to be related? Or was it for another reason? George was not in any way effeminate in his manner yet Foden was careful not to give anyone any reason to suggest their relationship might be anything but normal.

"What makes you ask that?" Foden laughed.

"I sense it."

He looked around the small, quiet restaurant.

"Do you come here often?" George asked. He raised his eyebrows to make the question a tease.

"No, I don't." Foden admitted. "But at the moment, you need to be anonymous. The police might have a description of you. You are not ordinary."

Anxiety clouded George's face.

"Do you think I should still lay low?"

"I think it's all right coming to somewhere like this but I don't think it would be a good idea for you to be seen too often locally, like in the village. Someone like nosy Jack or one of the locals at the pub on that night might recognise you. Also in parts of the city where people visit, like the railway or bus station."

"Should I change a bit, disguise myself? I could cut my hair short or even colour it."

Foden smiled at his seriousness.

"Not before I take some pictures of you."

The answer made George smile too and the hint of tension to disappear.

A waiter brought their meal and smiled at George and brushed his arm as he put the plate in front of him. George saw that Foden noticed.

"Charles, I could go, you know."

"Go where?"

"Anywhere."

"You mean, leave here?"

"Yes."

"Why would you do that?"

Foden sounded genuinely puzzled and a touch of panic flashed into his eyes.

"You don't have to worry about me, Charles. I mean, we both have secrets now don't we? You needn't be afraid of me any more."

"You don't think that's why...surely?"

"Perhaps it would be safer, for both of us?"

Neither of them spoke for some moments. Foden took a sip of water and George watched him, fork poised above his plate. Then Foden looked at him.

"I don't want you to go, George."

George smiled broadly and his foot found Foden's ankle under the table and rubbed it gently.

"I don't want to go either," he said. They both began to eat and exchanged looks between forks of fish pie.

Foden took to visiting during the week when the builders were present. He enjoyed watching the progress from tearing things down and filling of skips to the conversion stage. He saw how easily George blended in with the other builders. There was an easy camaraderie between them and George's position of being the site foreman didn't seem to bother anyone despite his different accent and youthful looks.

It was a scene of bustling, jocular activity with several radios competing in the various parts of the house and Foden felt the absence of such companionship from his own youth. Some of the men worked on Saturdays too and Foden took his Leica with him and enjoyed taking photographs.

On one occasion he took Edmund and Phillipa to the house. George took their hands and guided them safely around and Foden smiled at how easily they seemed to accept his company. Then George took them into the garden and played with them while the builders got on with their work.

Back home, the children told their mother and Nanny about their experience and mentioned George several times.

"Who is this George?" Arabella asked her husband.

"Where did he come from?"

"He worked at the club for Fred, the groundsman. Fred didn't like him and sacked him. He was without a job and had nowhere to live so I thought I would make use of him."

"Can you trust him?"

"In what way?"

"What if he runs off with something?"

Foden laughed

"You said there was nothing there that we wanted."

"Yes. But that's not so say that anyone should have it."

"Darling, Almost everything has gone to auction. I'd be delighted if someone took what's left. But why would George do that; I'm paying him for working and he has somewhere to live?"

"Does he know what he's doing?"

"Yes, his father was a builder. He's very good."

"He's a nice man, Mummy," Edmund suddenly interrupted and Phillipa nodded in agreement. Both Foden and his wife laughed.

"There you are: an endorsement from the children."

"Am I going to meet him?"

"When you're in a condition to pick your way around a building site;"

"By the sound of it, the house will have been finished by then."

Arabella always had difficulty in the first months of pregnancy and had twice had miscarriages. As her condition intensified, Foden took her regularly on Saturday mornings to the private natal clinic and his visits to Upland House were restricted to calling there in the week for a brief conference with George and Richard, the architect, and the builder and other conversations with George were done over the telephone.

The publicity over the Katy Rose Lewis affair had died down. Foden had found that the Challis' had left the area and there was no noticeable police activity either on the roads or in the village and Katy's presence seemed to diminish in Foden's mind too. Only occasionally, when he visited the studio, did her presence there loom in his consciousness.

George seemed to accept his absence as their working relationship took the feel of a partnership. Foden had continued to shop for him for several weeks but it was

George who said he thought he should go into the village occasionally so that his absence and then his reappearance would not be noticed.

Foden thought it was still a risk but he saw the danger of trying to keep George closeted too much, although he knew that he had taken the car into the city on one occasion. He decided on a bold solution.

Foden was well known in the local shops as they seldom changed hands and he had been visiting them since he and Arabella had lived with his grandparents. He chose a Saturday morning, when his wife did not attend the clinic, to take the children and the dog to Upland House, telling his wife they could go onto the Ridgeway and give the dog a run. The children enjoyed exploring the house as it was then cleared of debris and was in the conversion process.

"Let's all go into the village and take some ice creams onto the Ridgeway," Foden announced, much to the enthusiasm of the children and raised eyebrows by George.

The two men took the children's hands and they walked into the village They went into several shops where Foden was known and bought small items and chatted. Foden briefly introduced George and said he was looking after Upland House. Some of the shops George had already visited and their owners nodded and smiled their recognition and seemed pleased to be able to identify George's new role as someone associated with Mr Foden and his family. It was as they came out of the ice-cream shop that they almost bumped into Constable Steve Jennings.

"Allo Mr Foden," Jennings said.

Foden hoped his nervousness didn't show.

"Steve, Good morning."

Jennings smiled at the children and patted the dog. He looked briefly at George.

"My nephew, Constable Jennings," Foden said.

The two men smiled and nodded to each other.

"Got a nice morning for ice-cream," Jennings said to the children.

"It is. We're just going onto the Ridgeway to give the dog a run," Foden explained. "How are things, Steve? Any news about Katy?"

"Not much I'm afraid. The investigation's still ongoing. How is Mrs Foden getting on?"

"She's doing quite well, thanks. I think she's out of the discomfort stage."

"I wish her well. I know what it's like."

"Thank you Steve. How is the golf coming along?"

Jennings laughed.

"Well, Oive learned to 'it em but not in the right direction."

They all laughed.

"Keep trying. It takes time," Foden assured him.

The men nodded to each other as they parted. Jennings had not given George any noticeable attention but both George and Foden heard their respective sighs of relief as they walked away.

On the Ridgeway the children threw a ball for the dog and rolled down a grassy slope while Foden and George sat together on the grass.

"I think that went quite well," Foden said.

"Bit scary meeting the copper like that, though."

Foden explained how they had met.

"You had Katy in the boot?"

George was incredulous.

"I know. I thought it was all over when they stopped me." .

George made a whistling sound. "You're amazing, Charles. Most people would have gone to pieces in that situation."

"It was lucky he was interested in golf. Anyone else would

have wanted to look in the boot. I managed to divert him by offering him Grandpa's clubs."

"Still, you were pretty cool about it."

They sat in silence for a while, watching the children rolling around and the dog trying to join in. Then George asked, "Do you believe in fate?"

Foden thought hard about the question but nothing specific came into his mind.

"I'm not sure I know what that is," he decided.

"The way some things happen outside our control and take over our lives."

"Like death?"

George laughed at the joke but continued to look serious.

"Like the way we met. I was sunbathing, you were playing golf, Katy was walking somewhere, then 'Bang'; all our lives changed."

Foden didn't answer. He looked backwards and upwards, towards Drovers' Hill woods and then continued to look into the distance.

"Accidents happen," he said eventually.

"Is that what you think it was: an accident?"

"There was nothing planned or deliberate about it so it had to be accidental."

"So is life just a series of accidents?"

"Possibly."

"But some people, most people, don't have accidents. Their lives just tick along without anything unusual happening to them. Like yours was – and mine."

Foden turned and smiled at him.

"You're being very philosophical, George."

"Yeah, I suppose I am.. But it's not every day two normal people become killers. I don't know how it happened. I'm bloody scared now what I might do next."

"I know. Suddenly realising that you're not the person you thought you were."

"That's it. That's suddenly how I feel. I thought I knew myself."

"I don't think any of us ever does. We only know who we are where we are. Perhaps we can all be killers in the wrong place, at the wrong time."

"That's scary.

"Yes. It's like falling out of the sky. Not being able to hold on to anything. Wondering how it's going to end."

"Is that how you feel?"

"Yes. I think it is."

They both stared across the estuary.

"Are you having nightmares, Charles?".

"I wake up before they get going."

"Me too."

Foden looked at him.

"We'll get over it, George. We can't change what's happened."

"I know."

George looked across the alien landscape to an alien horizon, but Foden knew it well. The grass on which he sat he had walked since childhood; across the estuary he had shot with both his grandparents; his grandpa had walked the dogs every evening where the children now played; Aunt Sheila and his mother had ridden up the Ridgeway and over Drovers' Hill, and down there, somewhere down there, his father had met Gerhardt.

The sun was warm, the air was fresh and but for the insects seeking the clumps of heather and the children's cries and the barking of the dog, the elements were tranquil, peaceful, eternal. But what moved unseen? Was there a malevolent spirit about Drovers' Hill that infected people like a poisonous mist? That fed on love and consumed them from within? Or was that what George called fate?

"Will you ever get married, George?"

George showed his surprise.

"I've never thought about it." Then he laughed. "I don't think so."

"Don't you like women?"

He struggled for an answer, wondering whether to joke about it or to seriously consider the question.

"Some are all right I suppose. But they don't do anything for me. You know?"

"You mean sexually?"

"Yeah."

"But you find men attractive."

"Yes, but...Sort of...What I mean...Not any man. Some of them are horrible. But It's not just a physical thing is it? I mean, I've got to like someone before I find them attractive. Is that silly?"

"Not silly. Interesting."

"Why?"

"It's usually a female perception. They seldom admit they want a man for his body. It's either his sense of humour or kindness..."

"Or his money."

They both laughed. Then George frowned

"Are looks the most important thing to you?"

"Beauty is important to me. Sometimes it just overwhelms me. It makes me afraid that it might be damaged or disappear. That's why I have to capture it so it will always be there. But I know it can flatter to deceive. A spider's web is exquisite, but it has a deadly purpose. Nature is clever at making things appear to be what they're not."

"Does that apply to people?"

"Yes. We've gone full circle haven't we? We don't know who we are or who someone else is. It takes a lifetime to know ourselves so how can we ever know someone else?"

"Don't you trust anyone?"

"If they trust themselves."

"How do you know that?"

"You don't, until you do. You just hope a Katy or a Gerhardt doesn't come along to test you."

"Who's Gerhardt?"

"He was my father's lover."

He knew what the effect would be on George's face but it took some moments for him to turn and look at him to confirm it.

Edmund threw the ball which landed near them, with the dog in pursuit, The dog paused to lick Foden's face before retrieving it.

"Come on, children. We'd better get home," Foden suddenly called and got to his feet.

George sat on.

"George?"

"I don't have a home," he answered quietly.

Foden bent and put his hand on his shoulder

"You do. You are building it."

George looked up at him and smiled weakly.

"Come back for lunch, you can meet Arabella."

George's smile got stronger.

"Are you sure?"

"Yes. Why not?"

He scrambled to his feet and was just in time to catch a racing Phillipa and twirl her round.

Arabella was in the garden when they arrived, dead-heading roses. The children and the dog ran up to her and made a fuss, telling her what a super time they'd had.

George shook hands and said it was nice to meet her. Arabella quickly took in the jeans, the trainers, the tousled hair and the vested body and blinked as she realised George's eyes had been doing the same.

It was decided to have lunch in the garden and Agnes and Nanny brought out trays of olive-bread, cheeses, salad and jugs of lemonade. They sat in a circle and Arabella asked George about Upland House.

"It's going well. Charles' studio is finished and we've started on the first flat. It should all be done by the spring" he told them.

The women showed no sign of noticing his accent beyond the blankness of their eyes.

"Trust Charles to have the studio done first." Arabella smiled at her husband.

"We had to start somewhere and it's easier to build up rather than down," he said.

"I think they'll make lovely flats," Agnes said. "The house was too big for a modern family."

"Well, it will be nice to have it finished so that we don't have to worry about the place," Arabella agreed. "But if Charles has got a studio I'm not sure we'll see much of him here from now on."

"You'll all have a new baby to keep you busy," Foden laughed.

George asked polite questions about the baby and started a conversation about names which the women and the children entered into with some enthusiasm. Foden smiled sideways at him as though to acknowledge it was a smart move to enable them to talk between themselves about the next steps in the conversion process. He noticed George had been looking beyond them to the house.

"How old is it?" George asked.

"Most of it is late eighteenth century, but the portico was added much later. Do you think it spoils it?"

"It's a bit grand."

"I know. But it's jolly useful when it rains. Would you like to see the house?"

"I'd like that."

Foden told his wife where they were going.

"I shall be going to have a lie-down in a minute," his wife told him as though to warn him not to be too long.

Foden watched George take in the rooms without comment but his enthusiasm showed in his eyes and he wore a constant smile. When they reached the main bedroom-suite at the rear of the house, George admired the garden from the window.

"I can't promise I can do the same with Upland House but I'll have a go," he said.

"That garden has been a work in progress for two hundred years," Foden laughed.

"I can't promise I can stay that long either."

"How long will you stay?" Foden asked quietly, almost hesitantly.

"As long as you want me to."

They looked at each other for a moment, questions lay like a chemical cloud between them.

"Hello. Where are you?" Arabella's voice called up to them.

Foden led the way out of the bedroom.

Arabella was making slow progress up the stairs.

"There you are," she said. "How do you like the house, George?"

"Very much."

"It's a bit better than Upland House isn't it?"

"At the moment, Mrs Foden. But wait until we've finished

it and then you might be surprised."

Arabella laughed breathlessly as she reached them.

"You're an optimist, George. I'm sure you're very good but I think you'd be better knocking it down and starting again."

"You wait, Mrs Foden. We're going to make some lovely flats"

"I wish you luck. I hope they'll pay for all the expense of building them."

"Many times over."

Arabella laughed again and held out her hand.

"Nice to have met you."

"You too, Mrs Foden."

As they reached the bottom of the stairs Foden apologised.

"Arabella never liked the house. She thinks it's a waste of money."

George stopped and touched Foden's arm.

"You don't think that do you? When the flats are finished and I've done the garden that house will be worth more than this one."

Foden raised his eyebrows sceptically.

"Honestly. No one wants houses this size any more. Those flats will keep increasing in value."

"So you think I should let them rather than sell them?"

"Definitely. On short leases. Or, sell the one on the first floor with a fifty year lease, that will pay for all the work, then let the others. The house will be a fantastic legacy for your children. Don't sell it."

Foden found it puzzling to equate the casual worker sleeping in Fred's tool shed with the man standing in front of him, giving him financial advice. He smiled.

"I wouldn't do that. I would lose my studio."

"It's no damn good having a studio if you don't use it."

"I haven't really been in the mood, George."

"Sorry, Charles. Course not."

The old tensions showed on both their faces.

"But I've ordered some lighting for it," Foden said.

"Great," George enthused.

The nanny and Agnes came in with the children.

"Did you decide on a name?" Foden asked them.

"How could we do that, Mr Foden if you don't know if it's going to be a boy or a girl?"

"Good point," he conceded.

George said goodbye to the children and Foden walked him down the drive.

"Is that right; you don't know what you're going to have?" George asked.

"We know it's human That's a start."

"You've got a lovely family, Charles. Thank you for letting me meet them."

The significance of his words was understood by both of them. Foden tried to lighten the atmosphere.

"If you were having a baby, what would you call it?"

"Apart from Miracle? When is it due?"

"Sometime in December."

"Then if it's a girl it's got to be, Chrissy."

"And if it's a boy?"

"Noel."

"Noel. I like that."

They had reached the gate and Foden held it open. Their shirts touched as George stepped past. He looked up towards the house and Foden looked round. He smiled and put his hand on George's shoulder.

"I'll see you tomorrow," he said quietly.

Arabella, having forgotten her book, was on the landing to call down to someone to fetch it for her. when she looked through the window and saw her husband and George laughing together and Foden's hand on Georges shoulder.

The first time they made love was a week later. Foden had called at Upland House and received no reply when he called George's name. He heard no work noise and decided George must be in his room. He climbed the stairs and saw the door to the room was open wide as though it had been pushed back by the wind from an open window. He heard the noise of a shower as he reached the landing and approached the room. From the doorway he could see into a full-length mirror on the bedroom wall. It was opposite the en suite and reflected the view of it and the shower from which George stepped as Foden reached the doorway to the bedroom. Foden stopped, mesmerized by the beauty of the youth as he reached for a towel and dabbed his wet body and hair. With each movement, muscles moved subtly together like a warm breeze over sand. He stretched a leg and bent easily to the ankle, unwinding his back as he pulled the towel up to his groin. He straightened to dry his pelvis and saw Foden in the mirror.

They stared at each other, neither of them moved – and then George smiled. He made no attempt to hide any of himself; he held the towel at the end of a hanging arm and his other hand rested along the thigh that was a step ahead as though it was poised to run.

Foden had a clear memory of the statue of Hermes on his visit to Greece and had the same urge that must have driven Praxiteles to preserve such beauty forever. He stepped towards the mirror.

"I have to photograph you," he said.

Another step and the image disappeared and he was looking at himself.

He turned his head and George was at his shoulder. He put

his arms around Foden and moved his hand down and inside his trousers and leaned against the other man so that Foden was unable to turn. With one hand firmly holding Foden's genitals, George unfastened Foden's trousers with his other hand. The trousers slid down Foden's legs and his underpants followed. Then George had both hands on Foden's penis. When it reacted, he released the pressure of his body so that Foden was able to turn. They came together, their genitalia touching, their lips meeting. George almost ripped off Foden's shirt and they fell onto the bed, kissing and fondling and gripping each other in various holds, rejoicing in the physical conjunction of their naked bodies until they climaxed then lay exhausted, their legs intertwined, the sweat running over them like summer rain.

After a while, George untangled himself.

"I'll fetch us some lemonade," he said.

Foden watched him walk leisurely across the room, the sweat glistening on his back and running between his tight buttocks, his hair matted in curls around his neck and he thought again of the Greek statues at which he had marvelled. Here now, he had his own Greek god.

Foden settled against the pillows. He looked down at his own body and felt the freedom of his nakedness. He realised he had never before displayed it so openly. He thought of making love to his wife and that it had always been in the confines of a bed and almost always in the dark. That they had never savoured each other's body with eyes wide open.

George returned. He handed Foden a frosted glass and climbed onto the bed, smiling as though to a friend he had met on the street. The naturalness made Foden smile too. They touched glasses.

"Cheers," they said

Their arms were touching, their heads close together.

George was several inches shorter than Foden and his lips pressed against the soft muscle of Foden's shoulder intermittently between sips of lemonade. Foden responded by leaning his head against George's and then George put his free hand on Foden's stomach and played with the hair around his pubis until his penis reacted. He put down his glass and his wet lips caressed the nipple of Foden's breast then slid down his body until they took in his penis. Foden fondled George's hair and then George pulled away and smiled up at Foden then turned on his stomach and took Foden's hand and inserted his fingers into his anus. Foden straddled him and clumsily penetrated his anus until all the tensions of the past few weeks and his wife's condition flowed out of him until he was limp and fell onto George's neck, kissing it gratefully.

"Tell me about your father," George said later. They had pulled a sheet over their bodies. The late afternoon had clouded and the light inside the room hazed the shapes and colours and left indistinguishable patches of dark in the corners and across the floor, and even the details of their faces were softened by the gloom.

The question mimicked Foden's thoughts. His mind had settled as much as his body and even in the moments of extreme ecstasy he had thought of his father and the love he could not live without.

He told George about Gerhardt and his father's desperate scheme to keep him from being sent back to a certain death. He told him about his aunt and about his grandparents and why he was led to believe Sheila's illness was for the love of Gerhardt. And he told him of how he had found his father's letter which had been denied him for twenty years and of his father's love for Gerhardt.

In the soft light his tears were hidden until he turned

towards the window and looked at George.

"Now it's easier to understand," he said.

George took his head in his hands and pressed his lips to it.

"What happened to your father?" he asked.

"He killed himself."

George reacted sharply, going back and staring at Foden and then he put his arms around him and hugged him close.

"I'll never let that happen to you," he mumbled into his neck.

They talked until it was dark. Foden told him about his father's letter and Aunt Sheila's obsession and fears and how he had only just discovered it all when Aunt Sheila died.

"And that was when you played golf and we met in the woods?"

Foden nodded.

"That's fate if anything is," George responded. "No wonder you hit that girl. I would have wanted to kill her."

"Do you think it's wrong, what we're doing, what Father did?"

"What can be wrong about it? It's what we feel. Love doesn't have a formula, Charles."

"Is it love?"

"I think it is. Even if it's only sex, what's wrong with that? Sex is great. Sex is how we're made. Who has the right to say how it should be. If it feels right it's right. Right?"

They both laughed.

"Did it feel right?" George asked.

"Yes."

"And does it still feel right?"

"Yes, George. It does."

Their lives progressed uneventfully for several months. The house development took up almost all of

George's time. There were bricklayers, plasterers, plumbers, electricians and even scaffolding for fitting new windows and replacing damaged roof tiles to look after and if he wasn't needed there he worked in the garden, tearing out old shrubs, digging borders and pruning trees. His energy and enthusiasm were incorrigible.

Foden called in whenever he could. Sometimes it was only on his way to the office, to give his opinion or consent whenever it was needed, or in the evening when he would walk the dog before bedtime. Then he would share a beer with George and if the mood was right, they would make love. It was not a wholly satisfactory situation for either of them but it was the dog who was the least satisfied.

When he thought about it, Foden realised it was the same situation that most illicit lovers faced but he did not feel in any sense unfaithful to his wife. He recognised the contradiction of such a view but only questioned it so far as to wonder how he would feel when his wife was ready to resume normal, marital relations.

When the studio lighting arrived he had more reason to be able to visit during the weekend, telling his wife enthusiastically about the exciting possibilities of having a studio. His wife accepted his excitement with patient good-humour and was mostly pleased and relieved that his mind seemed to be recovering from the stress of losing Aunt Sheila and of the awful business of his father's letter.

George helped him set-up the lighting and was his first model for his test pictures. For those Foden chose to use monochrome film which was more effective for experimenting with various exposures. George was usually dragged away from his work for these experimental sessions and Foden would develop the film, study the results and then call on George again until he got the effect he wanted.

Sometimes the children went with him and they then became his models but showed less patience than George and soon wanted to be taken into the village or onto the Ridgeway which helped to soften his absence from home as it relieved his wife and Nanny to do other things.

Foden would take his prints home and offer them to the household for comments and study them over a whisky and make notes as to how they might be improved. It was his wife who, studying a picture of George sitting on a stool, holding a hammer, commented that George was beautiful enough to be a model then handed the print back to her husband with the question still on her face.

"You think he's beautiful?" Foden was surprised by the adjective.

"Yes. Don't you?"

"He's handsome I suppose. But, that's not what I was trying to capture. I hoped his personality would show," and he sounded disappointed as though the remark was a criticism.

"Well, even though he's holding a hammer I think he looks more like a model than a workman," his wife laughed. "What do you think, Nanny?"

She handed the print to be studied.

"Definitely beautiful," Nanny agreed.

Foden took the print away and made no attempt to hide his petulance at their frivolous remarks.

"Don't worry, darling. I'm sure you'll make a workman of him eventually. Can't you just mess him up a little? But I think those pictures of the children and Lucky are marvellous."

Foden stopped taking the prints home, especially as those of George became less workman and more artistic.

But taking-up portraiture was a diversion his mind and

body needed and he pursued it with the obsessive concentration that was part of his nature.

He used his big Nikon, hawking it around Upland House to capture the many workmen concentrating on their tasks, often unaware they were being recorded, and he printed them as a series, which he entitled 'Art On Craft', which was selected for an exhibition featuring local businesses in the Guildhall of the city.

After a visit to the natal clinic, he took Arabella into the exhibition and let her discover with surprise the portfolio of pictures. After her delight and pride had registered she then asked in genuine puzzlement, "But where is George? There's not one picture of him."

The omission had not registered with Foden as being odd and for a moment the question threw him.

"I couldn't make a workman out of him. You were right, he is too beautiful."

His wife looked at him, unsure of whether he was making fun of her or was serious.

The summer went by rapidly. As she got heavier ('Are we sure it's not twins?' Foden asked), Arabella became voluntarily confined to the house and the garden and was less demanding of Foden's time for driving her to various locations and he was able to spend more time at Upland House and in dog-walk time, with George. He took many photographs of his favourite model and became totally immersed in his new craft.

The development of Upland House also proceeded at a rapid pace. It was divided mostly front and back, with two flats on each floor varying in size, being smaller on the ground-floor because of the staircase and hallway. The first-floor was considered, following George's advice, to be the prime development and utilized all of one side of that floor with only a studio flat on the other side of the stairwell. It was to be the first to be fitted-out and was scheduled to be put on the market before the others. It was during a discussion about the scheduling of this with the builder and George that Christmas was first mentioned.

"I hope we can sign off the building work by then," the builder told them. Foden said his wife was expecting their baby two weeks before so that would be a good target.

"Then you can start the fitting-out after Christmas and think about marketing them in the spring," the builder continued. "But you'll soon have to decide what you want us to do with the top floor if we are to get it all finished by then."

After he'd left, George reopened the subject

"The top floor is only three rooms and a bathroom. You could either let them as two bed-sits with a shared kitchen and bathroom or as one flat,"

"They were the staff rooms," Foden explained. "Even though the rooms are a decent size they are in the roof so there's restricted head-room. I don't suppose we would get a lot renting them out separately and I wonder what sort of people would want them."

"Students."

"That could be a problem if the rest of the flats are up-market."

"What do you want to do with them?"

Foden suddenly realised what was behind George's urgency.

"Where are you going to live?" he asked.

They looked at each other. It was the first time their relationship had required a future.

"When the flats are ready and I've finished the garden I'll probably head down to the coast and find some work."

446

"You won't have a problem after the reference I'll give you. Is that what you want to do?"

George shrugged. "I dunno. What else? I like building work, I like gardening."

"Is that what you want to do for the rest of your life?"

"I don't know, Charles. I've never really wanted to do anything. If my father had lived I would have worked with him. I always thought that's what I'd do ."

Foden let his emotions subside

"You could do other things."

"Like what?"

"You underestimate yourself. You are capable of learning anything. You could do a design course."

"I love being outside. I love being free and using my hands."

"You could be a model."

George laughed.

"A model? What sort of job is that?"

"A profitable one. Arabella thinks you're beautiful and would make a good model. So do I. I could make a portfolio for you."

"You're serious?"

"Yes."

"Would you want me to do that?"

"I want you to be happy."

"Charles, I'm very happy now."

"But for how long?"

"I dunno Charles. Why have we got to think ahead like that?"

"So that things don't just happen. Like Katy Rose."

"We couldn't stop that happening. How could we? We had no control over what happened."

"I did. She wanted me to take nude pictures of her. She

wanted to be a Page Three model. I refused. That's why she was so mad with me and called me a queer."

"So you knew her that well?"

"Not really. She asked me when I was taking pictures of her at a local fair."

"Why wouldn't you take the pictures she wanted?"

"I thought she was demeaning herself. She was a beautiful girl. I told her she could be a genuine model but that she would have to learn the trade. She wanted instant fame and thought her breasts would give it to her."

"Poor kid."

"Yes. If I'd agreed she wouldn't have been mad at me and she might now be a Page Three model. On the other hand, if she'd taken my advice and let me make a portfolio for her she might now be getting some work and would still be alive. So, you see; it's all about the decisions we make. It's not fate

"I don't think I could plan ahead like that."

"Why not?"

"Because you don't know how you'll feel about something in a year, or two years, or three years. Can you know that?"

Foden agreed that he couldn't

"There you are then. You can only make decisions on how you feel and what you know now."

"How do you feel now?"

"I said. I am happy. Are you?"

"Happy? I thought I was, until I found my father's letter."

"Because he loved a man?"

"Because he loved someone more than me."

"But if he'd known you he would have loved you too."

"Yes. But he didn't try."

"Oh, Charles. Come here. Give me a hug"

Foden smiled weakly and held up his hand.

"It's all right, George. I'm dealing with it. I'm still angry that he did what he did. But you've helped me understand how he felt."

"Is that how you feel?"

"Sometimes. You must know that. I suppose if I was only twenty-one as my father was when he met Gerhardt I would have felt the same. But I'm not twenty one."

"I'm not much more. But I don't think I could do what your father did."

"Be that much in love?

"I know I can be that much in love. But you said it happened in wartime. We can't know how people felt then."

"Desperate?"

"He must have felt something like that."

"He thought Gerhardt was being sent to a certain death. How would we feel if one of us was being sent to a certain death?"

"Or even to prison for life."

"Even that," Foden agreed.

"Desperate."

"Suicidal."

They hugged each other.

"It must have been terrible for your father not knowing what happened to Gerhardt."

Foden suddenly felt the impact of George's intuition.

"That's how the Lewis' must feel," he said.

"Hey, Charles. Come on. Don't go there. There's nothing we can do. We've been over it. I know how they will feel but what can we do? Even if we both fell on our knees and told them what happened it might make them feel better but it would ruin so many other lives. You know that."

"I know. But they would have Katy."

George saw his misery and reacted with a touch of anger.

"If Gerhardt had died. If your father had him in a grave, would he have felt any better?"

"Probably not."

"'Of course not. He would have still done what he did."

"Are all Yorkshire men like you?"

"Worse. I'm the soft sort."

"What would the hard sort tell me to do?"

"Stop whingein. Owt good cryin' over spilt milk."

Foden smiled weakly.

"Okay, Charles. Let's do what you want to do."

"What do I want to do?"

"Go to the police and tell them what happened. Come on, let's do it. I'll come with you. You can plead manslaughter."

"But that would make you an accessory."

"It would make me a bloody child murderer. But if you can't live with what we did then let's get it over with. I'll be your age when I get out of prison but you'll be an old man."

"Why are you doing this, George?"

"To make you wake up. Accept what you did. Accept who you are and what you are. I'm not proud of what I tried to do, but who I was then, is not who I am now. We live and learn. You can't live your life in a box."

"So you think I should tell Arabella about us?"

"That's different."

"Is it? Isn't that accepting who I am? Isn't that living outside of a box?"

"Okay. Yes. It is."

"So you think I should tell Arabella who I am, what I am?"

"You're twisting what I meant. I was talking about the other business."

"The murder business."

"Yes. It's not the same."

"Isn't it? Don't you think that telling Arabella about our

relationship would be the same as me going to prison? Do you think I would still have a family? Do you think I would be able to see my children? Do you think I could still see clients and run a business with everyone knowing I was a queer? What would you have us do then? Would we live together in one of these flats and only mix with other queers?"

"Sorry, Charles. You're upset."

"Of course I'm upset. That's why my father killed himself."

The tears came. George held him as the accumulation of stress seeped from his body until it was still.

"Let's just do what we're doing, Charles. Let's just be friends and not think too far ahead."

He felt Foden nod into his shoulder and held him away. They smiled at each other.

"In answer to your question, George. I think you should do the top floor flat to your liking. That can be yours,"

****

Two weeks before Christmas there was no sign of the baby's arrival. Arabella was examined and was assured there was nothing to worry about, that everything was normal and that the baby was just taking its time.

"It's too bad," she told everyone. "Very inconvenient. At this rate it will arrive with the turkey and my sister and her family."

Her sister and her two children had been scheduled to spend Christmas with them so that she could be on hand should Arabella need assistance and to see their parents who lived at Bredon nearby. Her husband had to stay on in London right up to Christmas Day because of work, for which Foden was grateful as he did not gel too well with the pompous civil-servant. But when the baby was five days overdue and the clinic thought Arabella should consider an induced birth or a C-section it threw her into a panic; not being organised was about the worst thing that could happen.

"Don't worry. We'll manage," her husband assured her.

"And who is going to help Agnes with all the cooking?" his wife wanted to know.

"Your sister is quite capable of managing. She's a very good cook."

"She was supposed to enjoy herself, and give me support. Not do the cooking."

"All right. I'll hire someone. In fact, I'll order all the Christmas food from our Club caterers so no one has to do much cooking."

"Really? You could do that?"

"Why not. Even if they can't do it I'm sure they can find someone who can."

Despite Foden's assurance he did not feel confident that the golf club caterers would be able to provide assistance as the club had several dinners scheduled before and through the holidays up to New Year's Eve. But, as he had hoped, they did find someone who could help.

"Justine will help out. She does the breakfasts but we won't be doing any over Christmas. She's a damn good cook generally – and she could do with extra money."

Justine agreed and Arabella was pleased. Foden thought it a good time to suggest that George should join them.

"Your builder chap? Why? Hasn't he got family to go to?"

"His mother remarried and George left home because of it. He would be useful to have around to help. He's quite good at looking after himself."

"Well, if we must. I suppose one more won't make much difference."

"Good. I'll ask him. And I'll order everything from that farm shop who were boasting they could provide all we need for Christmas."

"Let's get this birth over with. I can't think too much about anything else."

Foden phoned George and told him he had been invited to spend Christmas day with them.

"How can you bother with all that if Arabella's going to give birth a few days before?" he asked.

Foden told him about ordering everything in and getting Justine to help?"

"Justine from the golf club?"

"Yes. Oh, God! Do you know her?"

"Yeah. She cooked our breakfasts. I think she fancied me."

"I'm sure she did. Damn!"

"Sorry, Charles. You'll have to do without me. It would be too much of a risk if she knew I was still here."

"And I'm sorry, George. I should have thought of that. What will you do? Can't you go home? I'm sure your mother would love to see you."

"No. Don't worry. I thought I would help out at the homeless charity in the city. I stayed there last Christmas when I arrived and had nowhere to go. It was good fun. I enjoyed it and I feel I owe them."

Foden smiled to himself. Trust George to find a positive solution.

"All right, George. That's a good thing to do. You won't be alone so I won't worry about you."

"I'll worry about you – and Arabella. Will she be okay?"

"I'm sure she will. There's nothing wrong. Just a lazy baby. I'll phone you as soon as we have a result."

A room was provisionally booked at the private clinic and the next day Foden took Arabella for a pre-admission consultation.

They were met at reception by the shift manager. She spent time going through Arabella's file and asking many questions of her medical history. They were then shown to a residential floor and a further reception area where a medical officer explained prostaglandin, oxytocin and artificial rupture procedures as though he were lecturing a class of midwifery students. He looked up and saw the effect on their faces.

"Don't worry. I know it all sounds a bit alarming but there is not much to worry about. If there are any risks they are very small and only concern patients with particular problems. But yours only seems to be macrosomal. A large baby," he added as their expressions worsened.

"What sort of unit would you like?"

"Unit?"

"We have single rooms, double rooms – if your husband wants to stay with you - and birthing suites.

"Birthing suites?"

"They are equipped with a birthing pool for water births."

"I don't think we'll need that," Arabella laughed.

"I know it sounds odd but It does make the birth easier, especially if you are to be induced."

"Does it. Why is that?"

"Inducement can be less tolerable and warm water is soothing. Why don't I take you up to the intake floor and hand you over to one of our midwives. She can show you everything and explain the procedures in detail."

The midwife was a large lady of Caribbean descent called Sophie. She had ultra-white teeth and a huge smile to match her body. She greeted Arabella warmly.

"Let's show you where everything is my dear."

She took Arabella's arm and led her gently along a corridor. They looked into rooms and the birthing suite, which was exactly the same as the other rooms but larger to accommodate what looked little different from a normal bath with space on either side.

Sophie had talked the whole way, asking the occasional question and studying Arabella surreptitiously as she explained what the various procedures mentioned by the doctor entailed. She had a musical, soothing voice and Foden, following reluctantly behind, saw that Arabella didn't mind the protective hand on her arm and seemed quite relaxed with the woman.

They returned to a room where Sophie offered them coffee or tea. She sat next to Arabella on a small sofa. Foden asked for directions to a toilet and when he was gone the two women were noticeably relieved.

"I don't think my husband wants to know too much about it," Arabella laughed.

"No. Some don't, especially the older ones. Some of the youngsters want to know it all. They would have the baby if they could. Is this your first?"

Arabella explained she had two other children.

"But they were no problem. I think this one is going to be like my husband and do it his way."

"You know its a boy then?"

"No. But I hope its not a girl at this size."

The words were out before Arabella's brain could stop them. Sophie smiled at her embarrassment. She patted Arabella's thigh.

"Don't you worry 'bout that. If it is a girl she will find a lovely big man to keep her warm. I never had a problem."

They both laughed and Sophie's was as bright as her smile.

"So you know all about it then," she said.

"I thought I did but all this talk of suppositories in the vagina and intravenous hormone stimulation is a bit off-putting."

Sophie leaned close and almost whispered.

"How long is it since you and your husband had sexual relations?"

Arabella's embarrassment showed.

"Well, it's not easy in this condition."

"How long?" Her voice was even quieter.

"Some time. Months."

Sophie patted her hand and sat back.

"It does help. Semen contains prostaglandin. And nipple stimulation releases oxytocin. They are both needed to dilate the cervix."

Arabella was physically uncomfortable with the conversation.

"How...what is the best way?"

"There are more ways to break an egg, my love. Your tummy needn't be a problem. Think of doggies. It's much easier."

Arabella flinched as if wanting to hide.

"Have you had a membrane sweep?"

"I don't think so. What's that?"

"If your cervix is slightly dilated it may be possible to ease it a little from the uterus. It doesn't take a moment. I can have a look now."

"All right," Arabella agreed.

Sophie helped her from the sofa. They were met at the door by Foden.

"Just make yourself comfy, dearie. We won't be long."

She led Arabella into an examination room and propped her on a bed then donned surgical gloves.

"The cervix is not tight. I don't think you need a lot of help. I've eased it a bit. A little more stimulation will probably do the trick."

She looked at Arabella and winked, then her big laugh made Arabella smile.

"Just a minute," she told Arabella. She went to a cupboard and brought out a little glass bottle. "Put this in your handbag."

"What is it?"

"Aromatherapy. It's a nice soothing oil with lavender and eucalyptus.

"What do I do with it?"

"Not what you do, my love. It's what your husband can do with it. Tell him you have to massage your lower parts, especially your vagina and you can't do it yourself."

Then the wink and the laugh again.

"And tell him otherwise it could mean a C-section – and a large scar. I won't book a room for you. We needn't worry for a day or so. I hope you'll tell us your contractions have started before then."

They were both laughing as they went back into the other room to an anxious Foden.

In the car, Foden enquired about the consultation.

"Sophie thinks inducement might not be necessary."

"Good. So we just have to wait do we?"

"Hopefully, not for long. I may need your help."

Foden turned and looked at her.

"It's not something I can do alone. I have to massage with an oil they gave me."

Foden nodded and assumed a serious expression as though he knew and approved of the procedure.

"Would you mind?"

"Why would I mind?"

"Massaging me?"

"No. Of course not," but his voice did not match the confidence of his words. Arabella reached across and put a hand on his which was idling on the centre consul.

"Thank you, darling. It will be wonderful if I can do this naturally rather than going through all that nonsense."

Foden smiled his agreement. Arabella felt more confident,

"Sophie said normal relationships can't do any harm. In fact, she thinks they might help."

In the silence Foden knew his wife was looking at him for a reaction. He took a moment to look at her.

"Really? Good. Good."

He managed a smile and she responded by squeezing his hand strongly until he decided he needed it on the wheel.

That evening there was an unspoken contest of patience. Arabella delayed her usual habit of retiring early with a book and endured watching a football match on television. When it was ended they then watched the news headlines until she felt it was more than likely there was nothing else to delay their retirement. She said she would go up.

"You won't be long, will you, darling?"

"No. I'll just lock-up. Be up shortly."

Locking-up seemed to take time and when Foden eventually arrived in the bedroom, Arabella was sitting back on the bed, her knees pulled up to her bulging stomach and wearing a pretty, long nightdress. She smiled at her husband as she rubbed cream into her hands and arms. When he emerged from the bathroom in his pyjamas she was in the same position but had pulled the nightdress up above her knees.

"Are you all right, darling?" she asked cheerfully.

"Yes. Fine. And you?"

"Mmm! I feel much better for hoping I don't have to go

into that place any earlier than I need to."

"Yes. I agree."

He climbed onto the bed and was about to pull back the duvet when his wife reached to the bedside table and handed him the small bottle.

"What do I do with it?" His voice was hesitant.

"Just massage it into all my lower parts," she smiled.

"How do I... What is the best way?"

In answer his wife turned over, supporting herself on her elbows with her rear end in the air. She reached behind and pulled the nightdress up to her breasts.

"This would be the best way," she said.

Foden stared at her nakedness and realised he had not studied it in that situation before. His first thought was that he should take photographs of the condition and his mind was already planning the lighting. His wife looked sideways and up at him.

"Come on, darling. I don't know how long I can stay like this. Although, it is rather comfortable, I have to admit."

Foden took the stopper from the bottle and the aroma of lavender floated into his nostrils and he thought of the lavender border George had planted at Upton House.

"It smells rather nice," he said.

"Yes. I can smell it from here. Why don't you take your pyjama bottoms off; you don't want to get oil on them."

After some hesitation, Foden put down the bottle and did as she suggested, sub-consciously aware that they were embarking on a new adventure.

"Go on, Before I fall asleep," his wife told him.

He knelt behind her and began to work the oil around her bottom and inside her thighs.

"Mmm! nice," his wife murmured.

Foden got more adventurous and reached under her,

rubbing her pelvis and working down to her vagina. She murmured pleasurably as his fingers went inside, spreading the oil all around the orifice. As his penis became erect, he leaned against her and with the other hand he reached forward and fondled her breast. His wife moaned loudly and reached back to touch his genitals and penis. Foden stretched up on his knees and straddled her. His penis tried to penetrate her anus but she told him it was the wrong place. He breathlessly apologised and entered her vagina.

When he fell sideways, exhausted and satiated, Arabella eased herself off her elbows. She pulled her nightdress down then pulled the duvet over them. She kissed her husband's shoulder before turning on her side with her back to him. She reached behind and found his hand.

"That was interesting," she murmured.

Her contractions started three hours later and at eight am they drove back to the clinic. Twelve hours later Noel was born, weighing 10lbs 3 oz.

"He must be like you," Arabella told her husband. "How heavy were you?"

Foden had no idea and realised his birth had never been mentioned by his mother.

"His timekeeping isn't up to mine."

"No. But I'm sure he'll improve. We all improve with practise, don't we?"

She smiled up at him as she cuddled her baby then she caught the smile and wink from Sophie who was standing behind her husband.

The happy ending was endorsed when her sister phoned to say she thought it was a bad idea for them to stay over Christmas and that they would visit in the spring holiday instead.

Foden then wanted to cancel Justine but Arabella thought

some help for Agnes was a good idea so she would be able to enjoy Christmas too.

On Christmas Eve, Foden walked the dog to Upton House. He found it all in darkness and after an inspection he decided George had already left for the city. He left parcels containing a winter coat, two pair of jeans and two shirts on George's bed.

****

After Christmas normal relations were resumed. Arabella seemed to be happy having a new baby to look after and they were all pleased when the other two children seemed just as besotted as she was. Perhaps not unusually, she seemed in no hurry to resume sexual relations with her husband and assumed he was as content as she with the routine and time-consuming ordinariness of having a new baby. For his part, Foden was grateful that his presence was not noticed any more than his absence and that his interest in babies was not expected beyond the occasional holding and cooing,

He saw George often and their companionship grew stronger in a working and sexual relationship.

Upton House was finished with the completion of the top-floor flat and in March, Foden had put it in the hands of estate agents and in April they phoned George to say a Mr and Mrs Courtney wanted to view the one for sale.

George met them with the agent. He could see Mrs Courtney was immediately taken with the first-floor apartment and he was quick to tell them of his plans for the garden.

"So there will be a fine view from your windows in a month or two. I promise you."

461

They were both interested in the plans to dig a pond and Mr Courtney said he would like to be involved with the garden as they were renting a property temporarily and he missed his old garden. Their daughter and her husband had recently got work in the city and they were looking for a permanent home near to them.

When they had gone the agent thought they would definitely make an offer. George phoned Foden with the news. He was naturally pleased at the prospect of recouping the expense of the conversion of Upton House but subdued by George's reminder that they had to do something soon about Sandy.

The Courtney's did make an offer which was accepted and they said they would like to move in some time in May or June.

Foden arranged for a small mechanical digger to be delivered to George. He spent a month landscaping the garden and digging out the pond.

Getting the freezer out of the basement involved a set of steel rollers and an electric winch to drag it up the stairs and out onto the front porch. The digger unit was then replaced on the tractor by a fork-lift and from the porch George lifted it and took it to the rear garden where it was dropped, still with its padlock intact, into a large, deep hole and hardcore was then piled above it. The two men stood looking down at the result.

"Almost exactly one year," Foden commented. "Just after her eighteenth birthday."

George said nothing but took Foden's hand and led him away towards the house in the sunset of a bright April day.

In early June Foden found George in the garden surrounded by potted shrubs and small trees awaiting planting and being helped by Mr Courtney who knew a lot about them. They were discussing what should go where and were not always agreeing. Foden mediated.

"You seem to be very interested in the pond," he told Courtney. "If you want to help why don't you concentrate on that and let George do the rest of the garden. You can order what you like and George will get it for you."

That seemed to satisfy both parties and Foden led George away to share a beer.

They spoke of how the Courtneys had settled in and of other enquiries there had been for the rental properties. Then Foden spoke of his photography and that he was planning a surprise exhibition.

"But I need a bigger printer," he told George, which, at the time, had no particular interest to his friend, but a few weeks later it did.

"How would you like to come to Hamburg with me?" Foden asked.

George stopped what he was doing and raised his eyebrows quizzically.

"There's a photography fair there. And one of the companies I hope to buy a printer from is running a competition to select photographs to advertise their new machines. I've entered two pictures of you."

George suppressed his excitement.

"You're serious?" he said. "Is that a good idea. What if someone recognises me?"

Foden laughed. "Who's going to recognise you in Germany? Anyway, it's only a bit of fun. They'll probably only use the pictures for the fair – and that is, if they select mine. It's a trades exhibition so I doubt if anyone from Upper Stokesey will be there."

"If you think it's okay, then, fantastic. That would be

great." and he hugged Foden and waltzed him round.

"You'll need a passport. Have you got one?"

"No. I've not been abroad. Scarborough was the nearest we ever got. When is this happening?"

"Next month. I'll get the forms to apply for a passport."

The trip coincided with the visit promised at Christmas by Arabella's sister's family. Arabella was convinced it was not a coincidence but was secretly amenable as she knew her husband found her abstemious civil-servant brother-in-law hard work and as Hamburg was an almost annual business destination for him, she assumed the visit was associated with the company.

They flew out on a Wednesday afternoon and returned the following Saturday. They stayed in a small hotel off Deichstrasse, the old mercantile area of converted warehouses and residential buildings. Foden had not used the hotel before but had been taken there by a client after a business meeting. It was less public than the large hotels he had used on previous visits and had no CCTV cameras apart from those at the entrance to the underground car park and he was not surprised when the receptionist showed no interest when he booked a single room.

Having been to the city many times over the years, he was able to guide George around the many tourist areas with some authority.

"But first we're going shopping," he told George on their first morning.

They took a taxi to the Neuer Wall, the very upmarket shopping area, and Foden led him into a smart men's outfitters he seemed to know well.

"You need a suit," Foden announced and began examining the racks of ready-made, formal but lightweight materials.

"Hold on, a minute, Charles."

Foden looked at him.

"I don't feel happy about this," George told him. "I mean, I appreciate what you're doing. But I don't want to be ...."

"Kept?" Foden suggested.

"Or owned. I've never wanted something for nothing. It doesn't feel right."

Foden smiled and resisted the urge to hug him.

"George. Whenever you are able to, you can pay me back. But you can't wear shirts, vests and jeans for three days. And I can't take you to a good restaurant like that. And you need a suit for the pictures I want to take of you to get you work."

"What sort of work?"

Now Foden did take hold of his shoulders firmly and put his face close.

"My wife thinks you are beautiful. I think you are beautiful. Arabella thinks you would make a good model. So do I. You can't mess about with building work when you've got what you've got, George."

George looked at him for some time before he smiled. Then Foden patted his shoulders and turned back to the suits. George followed.

They chose a dark blue, Calvin Klein single-breasted, three shirts and a pair of black Calvin Klein slip-ons.

As they were parcelled and the labelled bag was handed to him, George's reticence was noticeable. Foden put his arm around his shoulder as they walked out.

"Don't worry, George. I know what I'm doing. You will be able to pay me back sometime."

"At those prices it will take me two years."

"No it won't. Just you wait."

They dined out that evening, George looking marvellous in his new attire – but he refused to wear a tie. They ate in a smart restaurant where Foden thought they would attract less attention, but George still got admiring looks from men and women alike as they were shown to a table.

After dinner they strolled, like most tourists, around the St. Pauli Red-Light district which amused George hugely. Then they went to bed with a bottle of good Claret.

The next day they found the exhibition. There was a digitised map inside the entrance and Foden located the stand he wanted.

It was a hot day and George had compromised by wearing his old jeans with his new shoes and a new shirt. They took some time to reach the stand, pushing through crowded isles and finding many things to take their attention. When they reached their destination they both stopped and stared. On the rear wall of the slowly revolving stand containing various photographic and printing equipment, were large prints of photographs of various subjects but the only portrait was that of George. He was naked down to his hipster jeans where Foden had cropped the picture. The background was half lit, putting a dark halo around one side of George's torso. He had half-turned and was smiling downwards as Lucky had walked in thinking it was time he had some attention. Foden had snapped the shot just at the instant of George's interest.

A female assistant spoke to them in German, and then recognised George.

"Oh, My Got!" she exclaimed. "It's you," and turned to confirm it by looking at the picture. She stepped off the revolving platform.

"It's you," she said again.

George was silent, the shock of seeing himself still on his face.

"Yes, it is," Foden answered. "This is George Fuller and I am Charles Foden. I took the picture and submitted it for exhibition. I'm flattered you chose it."

"No. It is a marvellous picture. We are very pleased."

"It shows the quality of your printers," Foden smiled. "I want to buy one."

The female was joined by a more senior colleague who invited Foden onto the stand and began discussing and demonstrating the machines. George and the sales assistant remained on the floor and George stared at himself each time the picture came into view.

"You are very popular," the girl said to him and nodded towards several people who were also looking at the pictures.

The girl attempted to hold George in conversation but had difficulty with his accent so there was a lot of repetition which was made worse by George's pre-occupation.

Foden and his guide had disappeared into an office and George was about to excuse himself and move elsewhere to escape the attention of the girl when a small man, who had been standing near to them, spoke to George.

"That is you," he smiled and pointed at the disappearing picture.

"Aye. It is,"George said.

The man held out his hand.

"I am Thomas Lieberman. I'm with the Magnox Agency here in Germany.

George took his extended hand. "Nice to meet you," he said.

"Are you American?"

"No. I'm English."

"Ah! That is good, We work with an agent in London. Sally Redfern. Perhaps you know them?"

"No. Can't say I do."

"Who are you with?"

"With?" George looked puzzled.

"Who is your agent?"

George smiled broadly.

"I don't have an agent." He turned and pointed with his thumb at the pictures. "That was just a bit of a laugh."

The man looked puzzled.

"A laugh?" he asked.

"Yeah. You know. Just a bit of fun. My friend took the picture. He's buying a printer off them."

He turned as though looking for Foden and Foden then emerged from the office. He shook hands with the salesman and stepped off the platform.

"This man thought I was with an agency," George said as Foden joined them. "Mr Lieberman."

Foden held out his hand. "Charles Foden."

"You took the picture?" the man asked.

"Yes, I did. Do you like it?"

"I like it very much. I like George very much."

"He's spoken for, I'm afraid," Foden smiled.

The man was embarrassed.

No. No. I am with Magnox; the advertising and modelling agency. I was asking your young friend who his agent was."

Foden's brain clicked into gear.

"George is freelance," he said. "He works with several people. I handle his pictures."

The man looked from Foden to George.

"That's right," George confirmed.

The man reached into a pocket and extracted an introduction card. He took out a gold pen and wrote on one then handed it to George.

"That is the the number for Sally Redfern. If you are interested, call them. I will tell them I've spoken with you."

George took the card, read it and handed it to Foden who

then put it into his top pocket.

"Thank you," George said

"Yes, thanks Mr. Lieberman. Perhaps George might call her. It was nice to meet you."

The man nodded and shook hands with everybody, including the sales girl who had been an interested but silent spectator. He looked again at George's picture as he walked away.

George looked at Foden and they suppressed their laughter. The girl was more expressive.

"That's great for you, George," she enthused. "Magnox is huge. They are in several countries in Europe."

"Really?" Foden smiled.

"Yes. You must call them."

"Perhaps we will. Thank you Frau..."

"Greta. Greta Schone."

"It was nice to meet you, Greta. And I look forward to using your machines."

They shook hands and started to walk away.

"I'm here all week," she called after them, looking at George."

George smiled and blew her a kiss.

"What do you make of all that?" George laughed as they walked away. I mean that agency bloke?"

"A great deal, George. I told you so. I think we will call this Sally Redfern when we get back. I'll have to put a portfolio together for you."

"Are you serious, Charles?"

"Very serious. We're going to make a model of you."

George didn't answer for some time.

"I don't know what to think. It's all a bit sudden, like. But thank you, Charles. For everything," he said earnestly

"No need to thank me. It was good for me too."

"I'm glad to hear it. How come?"

"I'm getting a very expensive printer for free."

George stopped and looked puzzled.

"They asked if they could use your picture to promote their new machine at their exhibitions. I gave them permission and they gave me a printer."

George reacted by hugging Foden.

"Ayee! I'm so pleased you've got something out of it Charles."

"It is good for both of us. But you've got to finish the garden before you get famous."

"Aye. That's my job. This is just a bonus."

"Let's go and celebrate. But first, I'll take you to Planton un Blumen gardens. You can get some ideas for Upland House."

Arabella hardly noticed her husband's absence as all her attention was more than accommodated by the four children, the baby and her sister and her husband until her sister asked how he was and how was his business. She had secretly been envious of Arabella having a financially successful marriage when she struggled despite her husband being a top civil-servant.

"He is well. The business seems to go from strength to strength and I don't see a lot of him, especially since he's been so tied up with Upland House. He's now got a studio over there too, which means I see even less of him."

She laughed as she spoke to emphasise her jocularity.

Her sister wanted to know about Upland House and when the development was explained to her she thought she would like to see it.

"Why would you want to do that?" her husband asked.

"It's in the country and it's near Arabella and the family."

she told him. "Isn't that what you wanted?"

She explained to Arabella they were vaguely thinking of finding somewhere in the country for holidays.

"But we don't want the hassle of having to maintain it or worry about it when we're not there. An apartment might be a good idea."

"Sharing with other people?" her husband said.

"I believe they've made a marvellous job with the flats," Arabella said quickly before her sister had time to find one of her frequent snap answers to her husband's disdain.

"Anyway. I'd like to see what they've done with the house regardless. I enjoyed visiting there when you and Charles were courting. His grandparents were very kind. You needn't come with us," she added to her husband.

"I'll phone the agents," Arabella said.

The agents apologised that all their staff were out taking people over properties.

"We're rather busy at the moment. I could make an appointment for you tomorrow."

"What about George? He can show us over," Arabella suggested.

"He's away for a few days. Visiting his mother I think."

Arabella put down the phone and her sister asked if everything was all right. Arabella's mind was back at Christmas when her husband had told her George didn't go home because his mother had remarried.

"They're busy. Everyone's out. They can't accommodate us until tomorrow."

"Don't you have a key to your own property?" her sister teased.

"I suppose we must. I'll have a look."

All the house keys were kept on a board in the kitchen but Arabella could not find any that she did not recognise. She

471

asked Agnes about the key.

"Mr Foden keeps that," Agnes laughed. "I don't think he wants anyone going to his studio."

Arabella returned to her sister.

"We could go and pick up the keys from the agent, but they're in the city," she told her.

"Don't worry, darling. It was only a thought. We'll look next time we visit." But Arabella now wanted to visit Upland House herself.

Foden and George caught an early flight home as Foden had promised he would be back by lunchtime so that his in-laws would not suspect his absence was entirely due to their visit. Both men were feeling the warmth of success, like shoppers at a January sale. Foden was still smiling inside at his achievements. both for the acknowledgement of his photographic ability and the thought of getting an expensive printer free.

George was still mentally dazed by his experiences. Even a phlegmatic Yorkshireman was not immune to the better things of life and the two days in Germany had provided several. Although his nature resisted the pleasure of being showered with gifts and determined that he would repay them, he quietly hummed at the feel of wearing a Calvin Klein suit and eating in an expensive restaurant. The rest of the visit, seeing his photograph displayed and the attention it received and the promise of a modelling career, was what numbed his brain the most and it refused to look into the future. Upland House was his only focus and he was returning with new ideas for completing the garden after his visit to the park of Planton un Blumen.

Foden's spirits remained buoyant even greeting his brother-in-law and over lunch it caused his wife to ask if the trip had secured a large contract.

"No. It wasn't entirely a business trip," he confessed. "I went to look for a new photo-printer. A company was running a competition to display their new machines and they selected one of my pictures. They want to use it for their advertising campaign and they gave me a printer for free."

His delight was not contagious; his sister-in-law did not relate to it for knowing he could afford to buy a printer and disapproved of acquisitiveness. His brother-in-law naturally hated anyone's financial success as his honours degree in economics from Cambridge had failed to produce similar results for himself, and his wife had other reasons for not sharing his enthusiasm.

"What was the photograph of?" she asked.

Foden saw the dangers but instinctively followed a bold course and maintained his joie de vivre.

"Of George," he laughed. "You were right, darling; he does make a good model."

Arabella explained to her family who George was.

"Did he go with you?"

His smile dimmed. "No, of course not. Why do you ask?"

She told him of their wanting to visit Upland House and of ringing the agents.

"They thought he had gone home. But didn't you say he didn't go home because his mother had remarried?

"I don't know where he went. I tried to persuade him at Christmas to go home but he chose to help out at a homeless charity. He's a free agent, he can do what he likes on his days off. What did you want with the agents?"

The diversion worked; his sister-in-law explained her idea of finding a country residence.

"Well, we've sold one flat. The only other larger one is on

the ground floor, but that has only got two bedrooms."

"I'd quite like to see what you've done with the place," his sister-in-law said.

"We could go over after lunch. I'll phone the house and see if George is back to let us in."

"Haven't you got a key?" his wife asked.

"Not yet. I've given one to the agents and to Richard, the architect. And, of course, George has one. I must get the one back from Richard. He won't need it any more."

He excused himself and went into the hall to phone. Fortunately George was in the ground-floor kitchen also having lunch. Foden explained the proposed visit.

"Have a look around, George. See that I haven't left any of my footprints anywhere. And check the studio; I don't think any of your photo's are lying around but do make sure. My wife thinks you went home while we were away. If she should ask, have something ready for her."

George said he would be working in the garden and keep out of the way.

The family piled into the two cars, leaving only the baby with Nanny.

On arrival Foden delayed them by explaining his plan to keep the structure of the stables and just to rip out the stalls to create a covered parking area. They found the front door to the house unlocked.

Arabella was unpleasantly surprised that the spacious marbled hall had been curtailed to expand the larger ground-floor flat to accommodate its separation into two bedrooms and was prepared to like the house less than she did before.

Foden led them first down to his studio. He switched on the lights with a touch of pride and triumph in his voice.

"This is my pride and joy. What do you think of that?"

They all thought it very smart and even Arabella too

474

seemed to be impressed.

"This is where I lose him to," she told them. "But I can see why you love it, darling. They've done a wonderful job with the old kitchen."

They started the tour at the top floor and Arabella wanted to know about the old servants quarters.

"That's where George is living."

"Does he pay rent?"

"Not while he's working for me."

"How long will he be staying?"

"He's working on the gardens now."

"What will he do when it's all finished?"

"I don't know. Become a model, probably, like you suggested. Then he could afford to rent a flat couldn't he?"

There was a slight edge to his voice.

"This George sounds fascinating," his sister-in-law said.

They ended the tour in the ground-floor flat and even Arabella had to agree they had all been well built and finished with quality.

Her sister-in-law liked the flat and even her husband showed some interest. They ended in the rear sitting-room overlooking the garden.

"Oh. My! Look what they've done with the garden," she enthused. They all stared out of the large windows.

"Is that George?"

George could be seen at the end of the garden where the excavation of the pond had been used to build two mounds for the planting of wild flowers with a path separating them. George was erecting a trellis with an arbour leading into it. Foden confirmed it was George.

"Can we go and say hello to George?"Phillipa asked and was supported by Edmund.

Foden said they could and all four children and Lucky the

dog ran out of the house and eventually appeared in the rear garden running up the paved path towards their friend. They all watched as George greeted them with hugs and Lucky jumped up at him and ran around him in excitement.

"They all seem to know George," her sister-in-law laughed but Arabella only murmured a thoughtful agreement.

George led the children to the large pond where Mr Courtney was busy planting grasses and water irises on his hands and knees.

"Well, I have to admit you have done a wonderful job, Charles," his sister-in-law said. "When the garden is finished it will be something special. Don't you agree, Arabella?"

"Yes. I think George might be right. He said this place would be worth more than ours when it was finished. ."

"He was a good investment," Foden agreed. "Would you all like to meet him?"

"No. We must get back for the baby's feed," Arabella said quickly but her sister looked disappointed. Foden opened a window and called the children, returning George's wave.

****

Foden rang the Sally Redfern modelling agency and spoke to a woman who introduced herself as Edna Fielder. She knew of George and their conversation with Mr Lieberman immediately and said she had been expecting them to be in touch. She agreed to meet George and look at the portfolio Foden had prepared.

Foden drove him to London. The agency was in two small rooms above a shop in Covent Garden and said more about the reality of the profession than about its public image. Edna Fielder seemed only to have two female assistants who regarded George with shrewd interest but blanched at his accent when he spoke.

Edna Fielder looked through his portfolio with interest and praised Foden for his photography.

"I might be able to get you some work," she told him.

Foden declined politely and explained it was only a hobby.

"So, George. Leave the folder with me and I'll be in touch."

It was a typical anti-climax to a long journey and on the drive back George had already mentally dumped modelling into a waste-bin and talked about starting the conversion of the stable block.

But three weeks later Edna Fielder called him and asked if he could be available for a shoot in London the following week.

He took the train up to the capital and stayed in a cheap hotel near Paddington. The shoot was for a new clothing catalogue and he and another man and an older woman were selected. They went for a meal and some drinks together and George learned quite a lot about the business and enjoyed the experience so that when he related it all to Foden his attempt to treat it flippantly was not successful.

"So you enjoyed it?" Foden suggested

George admitted it was not hard work and he enjoyed meeting new kinds of people.

"You'll find there are many of those," Foden smiled. "But it's good you are doing that, I feel you are a bit restricted here. You should be enjoying yourself at your age."

"I am enjoying myself. Doing the house has been marvellous. I don't think I could live somewhere like London. It's okay for a visit but it would drive me mad to be in all that noise and traffic all the time."

"You may have to if your modelling career takes off."

George made a scoffing noise.

"Come off it, Charles. It's not going to take off. Who makes a living out of modelling?"

"Quite a few people."

"Well, it's not for me. It's okay to do a bit to make some extra money but I can't see me making a life of it."

Foden didn't reply, but his mind did not leave the possibility.

Seeing George became more difficult when Arabella announced that she was determined to get fit again and lose some weight after her pregnancy.

"When you take Lucky out for his evening walk, I'll come with you," she told her husband. "In fact, why don't we both start jogging. You could do with losing some weight too."

Foden resisted looking down at his stomach but put down the glass of claret that was half-way to his lips. He was slow to find a riposte and his wife hurried on.

"If we take the path onto the Ridgeway we can run down there, which Lucky will enjoy, come out through the lower gate and back up Uplands Drive to here. That's about two miles. If we do that every evening now it's light we should be really fit by the end of the year."

Foden had run from time to time but not for a long time and the abstinence made the prospect of starting again unattractive. It was also a scheme destined to limit his visits to George to getting away from the office at lunchtime or in slack periods.

"I don't think you should get too ambitious just yet, darling. Isn't it a bit soon?"

"Nonsense. I'm perfectly all right. Thank God I didn't have to have a C-section. Then I would have suffered."

The memory of that episode sped into both their minds.

Foden recalled it with a feeling of discomfort, Arabella as a moment of enlightened curiosity.

"Right. Let's start now," Arabella said decisively. "I'll go and change."

As if to support her decision, Lucky wagged his tail at her husband and did several turns. Foden had the feeling again of being coerced and of not daring to challenge it.

They did not try to run until they were on the Ridgeway and then they stiffly shuffled their way down the slope while Lucky ran ahead and around them a hundred times, barking as if to encourage this new enterprise.

By the time they emerged at the lower gate they had loosened up sufficiently to get into a decent stride in order to tackle the now uphill route home. They entered Uplands Drive with Lucky bounding on ahead of them.

"Where's he gone?" Arabella puffed as Lucky suddenly disappeared. Her husband knew but pretended not to know. When they reached the gate to Upland House, Lucky was in the drive waiting for them.

"What's he doing?" his wife asked as Foden whistled the dog and ran on, hoping Lucky would follow. It took a while for Lucky to decide that they were not going to stop.

"How does he know to go in there?" his wife gasped.

"When I've taken him with the children at weekends George always has something for him," Foden explained.

"But you've only done that once or twice," she puffed

"Dogs don't forget."

Lucky caught up with them and thought this new game might be better than listening to his master and George humping away.

The training continued, driven by Arabella's determination, and Foden's visits to his studio were even administrated by her insistence on taking Edmund and Phillipa with him.

George was called to London on three other occasions for modelling assignments before, in the autumn, Edna Fielder told him that Magnox had a job for him in Paris.

"George, that's marvellous," Foden said enthusiastically, his confidence and judgement vindicated.

"That would be down to that meeting with Lieberman in Hamburg."

"No. It's down to you, Charles."

It was a telephone conversation and they both knew they should be hugging each other.

"George, I only took your picture. Be proud of who you are and of what you've got. If you want to blame someone, blame your father and mother for giving you those genes and that beautiful body."

"I wish he was here. I wonder what he'd think."

"He'd be pleased for you, as I am."

"I wish you were here too. Can you come to Paris with me?"

"Unfortunately not. I daren't risk it. Arabella nearly found out about Hamburg."

"Do you think she's suspicious?"

"I'm not sure. She's certainly making me aware that I spend too much time over at Upland House."

"God, Charles. I miss you."

"I miss you too. Just go to Paris and do this job then we'll see where it takes us."

"There's a lot of money in it. I can't believe it."

"Believe it. I tried to tell you."

"I know. I was scared to think it would happen."

"I know."

"I'm still scared."

"Why?"

"I don't know. I don't want us to change."

"We won't change, George. Don't worry. Remember, we're blood brothers."

"I love you, Charles."

"I love you too."

The Paris trip took a whole week to shoot stills, and film for Love Frost. The director was pleased with George and so were the executives of the company when they saw the results. They took George and the director to dinner at Maxim and the only downside was when the director kissed George at the end of the evening and felt his bottom at the same time, telling him he looked forward to working with him again.

Their separation did strange things to Foden's head which could be best explained as moments of visionary chaos. He woke in the night with a sense of fear, knowing he had been dreaming about George and Arabella and her sister and her husband who was laughing at him and pointing a finger. Then Sophie, the midwife tried to seduce Foden by opening up her smock and revealing a revolting stomach and great hanging breasts then Lucky was eating something and when he tried to take it off him he saw it was a baby.

Love Frost released their advertising campaign in Europe at the end of October. George was invited to attend the launch and begged Foden to go with him. He had told him about the director's fondness for his bottom. Foden made a joke of it and warned him it was going to be his biggest problem in the new world that was swallowing him, but inside the fear persisted.

"I can't, George. We've never had any business in France. They only buy French machines, their government secretly subsidises their farmers. I don't know what excuse I could make to Arabella. I could ask her to come with me – but that wouldn't be the same, would it?"

"I owe all this to you. I want you to share it with me."

"I know. But I'll take you to the airport and wave you off."

Foden kept his promise and drove him to the local airport which had an afternoon flight to Paris. He drove into the drop-off zone and kept the engine running. George opened the door.

"George. Wear this. Tell anyone who comes on to you that you're married."

He handed him a small box. George opened it and found a gold ring with a single diamond set into it. He put it onto his finger. It fitted perfectly. He reached into the car and kissed Foden then quickly backed out as his eyes watered. He didn't look back as he entered the concourse.

****

The physical training regime had continued but had become less regular and more selective according to the weather but Arabella's persistence had got results in that the two miles were covered in much less time and they had more breath to hold desultory conversation as they ran. It was such a conversation in which Arabella raised the subject of her husband's neglect of golf.

"You haven't played since you lost that match to Nigel Farringdon."

Foden almost shuddered at the memory.

"Are you sulking about him winning?"

"No. But now he's Captain he's even more intolerable and runs committee meetings like a military briefing."

"But you've hardly been to the club since then."

"Since the spring meeting. That was enough."

"Aren't you going back?"

"I thought I would try the new club in the city. One or two

Members are thinking of leaving to go there."

"It would be a shame to stop playing. It's much healthier than photography. You seem to be obsessed with it since you got a studio."

They trotted on in silence as Foden assimilated her remark; it was one more subtle allusion to his visits to Upland House; not quite a question, not quite a protest, but enough to put him on the defensive, ready to find excuses. It was a situation his nature did not enjoy and as if to prove it he had a vision of George in Paris, surrounded by beautiful people in beautiful clothes in a beautiful city.

"I can't play much golf in the winter can I? And these runs are going to have to stop in the dark evenings. Photography is my only escape."

Arabella recognised the anger below the surface. They had reached the house and she allowed them to get into it before she challenged him in a soft, reasonable tone.

"What do you want to escape from?"

"Who I am."

He strode into the hall and up the stairs and left Arabella wondering why he didn't know who he was. But she didn't challenge him about it again.

George arrived back on an afternoon flight so that Foden was able to meet him. They went to their quiet restaurant where George related the fascinating and chaotic experience of filming a commercial.

"We shot one scene inside the Four Seasons restaurant of the George V hotel. We had to do it early morning before they started the lunches. The story was that I was alone at a table and there was this beautiful woman in there eating with an older bloke. She was looking past him, flirting with me. I got up to leave and she pretended to go to the toilet and met me. We spoke and then I took her hand and we ran out of the hotel. We filmed again in the Luxembourg Gardens and walking along the Seine when a big limo drives up and two heavies grab her and take her into it where the bloke she was dining with slaps her. They drive away and leave me. I shrug and sit down by the Seine, then some other bird stops and talks to me."

"That's a lot about you," Foden laughed.

"Yeah. I think the film only lasts three minutes but it took four days."

"Did you have to speak?"

"Only mime. Apparently they dub it in several languages afterwards."

"Did you see the results?"

"No. We saw a few stills but the film has to be edited. The director seemed happy enough."

"The one who fancies your bum?"

"No. This was an American bloke. There seemed to be a few Americans in the crew."

"Is it an American company?"

"I don't know. I asked the Continuity girl who they were but she wasn't sure either. Who cares? They're paying well."

"But it's more than just a modelling assignment, George. It could make you a star."

George laughed but then frowned. "The commercial's for television. They said they were planning to run it in Europe for the Christmas season but not over here until next year, depending on how it sells on the Continent. Do you think that might be a problem?"

Foden thought about it.

"No. By next year no one is going to recognise you. The police operation seems to have disappeared already."

They talked generally until Foden mentioned Christmas.

"Arabella's planning to have Noel Christened on his Birthday. The whole family are coming."

"Don't worry, Charles. I'm going to the homeless centre again."

"I'd like you to be there for Noel's Birthday, but I think it would be awkward the way Arabella's behaving."

"Do you think she suspects us?"

"I don't know if it's that or she's just annoyed that I've spent so much time in the studio. But she seems to resent me going there lately."

"Why don't I move out. Then she would think I've gone away. I can afford to rent somewhere now?"

"You're my gardener. You're going to restore the old vegetable and fruit garden."

"I don't mean move away. But if you said I wasn't living at the house any more it would be interesting to see if Arabella still minded you going there."

Foden frowned.

"I can't think Arabella suspects us of anything, she wouldn't even think about that. I don't think it would make any difference if you lived somewhere else."

They ate on in silence.

"Unless you want to," Foden added.

George looked at him quizzically.

"I'd never find a place like I've got. It would cost me a fortune."

"You might soon be making a fortune."

"Naw. I'll probably not do any more for months. I'm much happier gardening."

"Are you?"

"Yeah. Honestly. I love being out there."

"You wouldn't rather be in Paris at the Four Seasons?"

"You're joking. I asked one of the waiters how much it cost

for lunch. He looked at me like I was a bad smell and said, 'More than you weel ever be able to afford.'

They both laughed. Then they went to Upland House and made love.

****

In the spring all the flats at Upland House had been taken which, when Foden mentioned the fact to Arabella she found it a reason to ask about George.

"Where's he going to live?"

"He's on the top floor; Beryl and Jack's old rooms."

"I thought they had been converted too."

"They have. George is renting the flat while he works for me."

"Why is he still working for you. I thought he was a successful model?"

Foden had decided it was better to talk about George than not to and he had related George's success in Paris, telling his wife it was all because she had said he would make a good model.

"He likes gardening. He's our gardener. He's making a marvellous job of restoring the old walled garden."

"And he's going to do that for the rest of his life?"

"I don't know about the rest of his life, but he's happy. He'd rather do that than shoot commercials in Paris."

"How strange. Is he simple in the head?"

"He thinks modelling is not a proper job."

Arabella could find no answer and continued what she was doing with a puzzled frown on her face.

They continued their running as the evenings got lighter and Foden pacified his wife by joining the new golf club where several of his city cronies had become members. He saw George mostly by visiting from the office on quiet afternoons but they had to be extra careful as Upland House was now fully occupied and even though most of the rented parts were used by working people, Mr and Mrs Courtney were always around and mostly in the garden. So much so that Foden wondered if he needed more than someone to cut the lawns twice a week.

George got a few small modelling jobs throughout the year, which meant a trip to London and staying in a cheap hotel but Edna Fielder assured him the Love Frost commercial was scheduled to launch in the UK before Christmas and he could look forward to another cheque as the first contract had only been for the European campaign. But before Christmas she had more news for him.

"George. Did you know that an American company have bought the Love Frost product?"

He told her he didn't but that the camera crew were American. She told him that was often the case anyway.

"It was an Italian product but the commercial in Europe was so successful they've sold it. Anyway, why I'm phoning you is that the new company liked what they saw and want you to shoot it again in the States."

"America?" he gasped

"Yes, America. New York to be precise. What do you say?"

"Thank you, Edna."

"Good. I'll send you a contract."

"When do they want to do this?"

"In the next few weeks."

When George informed Foden he could not hide his excitement.

"I thought you didn't like modelling," Foden reminded him

"I don't care about it. But if it means a trip to New York... Well, fantastic. I've always wanted to go to New York."

"I've been. It's noisy and busy. Like a department store on sales day."

"Be happy for me, Charles. I've been to Paris and now I'm going to New York. I love gardening but it was never going to get me there, was it?"

"No. I tried to tell you."

George hugged him.

"I know. You told me so much. You did so much. I owe you so much."

Foden noticed his help was in the past tense but said nothing. He hugged George back and told him he was pleased for him.

The contract arrived and Edna Fielder phoned two days later to ask if he'd signed it. George told her it was in the post back to her.

"Good. They want you to leave on Friday. They've sent your booking details by courier. You should have them tomorrow. Read them carefully."

"Wow! They don't waste time, do they?"

"That's something to learn, George. They do everything yesterday over there and if you're late for a shoot, you'll be out. Don't blow it. You're in the big league. Make it work."

He rang Foden with the news.

"Friday?"

"Yeah. I fly from Heathrow."

There was a prolonged silence.

"When are you coming back?"

"I don't know. They haven't said."

"Is it going to be days, weeks or months?"

"No idea."

"Didn't you ask?"

"I did. But Edna doesn't know either. "

"What did your contract say?"

488

"It didn't. It just gave a start date."

"Well, I hope you're back for Christmas."

"It's only November. Why Christmas?"

"Arabella, strangely, mentioned it. She thought you would like to come to Noel's second Birthday."

"Why?"

"I think it might be because I told Noel that you suggested his name. I didn't know Arabella was listening; I was just talking baby-talk."

"What did she say?"

"She asked me why. I told her it was when they were discussing names and you said if he was going to be born near Christmas what you would call him."

"Did she mind?"

"She seemed a bit annoyed, but said I'd better invite you to his Birthday then. I'll tell her you're going to New York instead."

"I'll probably be back in a few days. The shoot in Paris only took that long."

"They might want you to do other things."

"I've no idea what they want."

"You might want to stay on, anyway. Christmas in New York wouldn't be bad; they like to party."

"Charles, are you trying to get rid of me?"

"No. I'm being realistic. You're an international model now. The world is your workplace."

"I'm not a model. I'm a gardener. I am who I am."

"But do we ever know who we are, George?"

"Charles, don't scare me."

"How am I scaring you?"

"Reminding me. We said we'd move on."

"Sorry. Yes. We said that. You're moving on.. Good."

"You've got to move on too."

489

"I know. It will be harder without you."

"Charles. I'm only going away for a week or so."

"It already seems longer."

"Then come with me."

Foden laughed.

"Sure. I'll tell Arabella and the children."

"You've got them. I'll be alone."

"I don't think so, George. Enjoy yourself. Do you want me to take you to Heathrow?"

"No. I wouldn't like that."

"All right. I understand."

"I'll phone you again, from Heathrow."

"Better not. I've got a big customer arriving from Finland on Friday."

"Wish me luck then."

"All the luck in the world, George. And don't forget the ring."

"Love you, Charles."

When Foden light-heartedly told his wife over dinner that George thanked her but might be unable to attend Noel's Birthday because he was going to New York her reaction was not quite as pleased as he expected it to be.

"For how long?"

"He doesn't know. He's a big star in Europe apparently and now he might become a big star in America. And it's all down to you."

"I'm not the only one to think he's beautiful. Nanny thought so too."

"And apparently, you are both right. Women know best."

"I thought you were the expert on beauty."

"So I am. I took his pictures after all. Here's to George. May he conquer America."

He raised his glass of Pouilly Fuisse but the gesture was as unconvincing as his voice. Arabella drank but studied him thoughtfully over her glass.

The next morning, George had just emerged from the old kitchen garden behind the stables into the yard when a car drove in which he did not recognise. He was surprised to see Arabella Foden get out of it.

"Good morning, George."

She was dressed as though she were about to meet a friend for lunch and her smile was radiantly framed by bright lipstick.

"Mrs Foden."

"Oh, don't be so formal. Call me Arabella. After all, you are part of the family.

"That's nice of you to say so."

"You must feel that, don't you? After all, My husband, my children and even my dog seem to love you."

"Do they?"

"They must do as they've spent so much time here."

George didn't know whether to be embarrassed or defensive. He was aware of the edge in her voice.

"The children enjoyed helping me in the garden. They're lovely kids."

"Yes, they are. They're very precious to me. All my family are very precious to me."

"I can understand that."

"Can you? Do you have a family, George?"

"Only a mother."

"No siblings?"

"No."

"So you don't know what it's like to be part of a close family?"

"I think I do. I know what it's like by not having one."

"That's very perceptive. But a family is not just about feelings. It's much more than that. It's about the time it takes to make one; the sacrifices, of putting other people first, of building trust in each other. It's like building a house. You know about that. If one piece is removed the house could come tumbling down. Do you understand what I'm saying, George?"

"I think I do."

"You wouldn't want my house to come tumbling down, would you?"

"No. I wouldn't want that."

"Of course you wouldn't. You're not an unkind person. How old are you?"

"Twenty four."

"Is that all? Charles is almost twice your age. Is he a father-figure for you? I know you lost your father."

"Charles is a friend."

"Is he? Why is that? I thought you only worked for him."

"He's been very kind to me."

"In what way?"

"He gave me a job and somewhere to live."

"And a new career, apparently?"

George laughed

"That? I wouldn't call it a career."

"Wouldn't you. Why not?"

"Well, it's not a real job is it?"

"But I hear you are making lots of money from it?"

"Yes. But it won't last will it? It's just about what you look like. It's not about what you do."

"So you'd rather be a gardener – or builder. Which is it?"

"Both. I enjoy both. It's what I do. It's who I am."

Arabella regarded him shrewdly and the moment made for an awkward silence.

"Are you here to meet someone, Arabella?"

"No, George. I came to see you. I should have come sooner. I should have come often with my husband. I came to say goodbye. I hear you are leaving for New York?"

George laughed again, more in relief.

"I'm not going forever. I'll be back in a week or so."

"Will you, George."

It was not a question. Her smile had vanished like a sun into cloud and the morning seemed to suddenly get darker. Her eyes regarded him coldly and he knew she did not expect an answer.

"Why wouldn't you want to stay in New York? A young, handsome man like you. Why would you want to come back here?"

George felt the tension but tried to avoid it.

"I couldn't do that. I'd miss sausages and Yorkshire Pudding," he smiled.

"You're teasing me. What is there here for you?"

"A job. I have the kitchen garden to finish."

"You have a new job. Even if you think it won't last forever. It will certainly make you a lot more money than what you can make by gardening."

"I like gardening."

"Then garden, George. But not here."

The brutality of the dismissal showed on his face.

"My husband is vulnerable. He had a traumatic experience recently. He is still fragile..."

"I know. He told me."

"What do you know?"

"That Charles' father was in love with another man and he killed himself before Charles was born."

Her eyes dilated and the shock stretched her lipstick.

"He told you that?" she gasped.

493

"Yes." George smiled, enjoying her shock.

"Why would he tell you that?"

"Because we are friends. He needed a friend."

His eyes were equally cold and he enjoyed the anger and frustration she was unable to hide from her face.

"What sort of friend?"

"My sort of friend. The sort of friend who understood what his father did?"

"And what his father was?"

The words were almost spat at him. George thought of Katy Rose and knew why Charles had slapped her. But they were not such a shock to George and his voice was calm.

"Yes. That to."

His calmness quietened her. Her voice was almost reasonable.

"I want you to stay away from here. To stay away from my husband and from my family. I have money of my own..."

"Are you are bribing me Arabella?"

"I'm helping you. I'm helping my husband."

"Will it help him if I don't come back?"

"Yes. Because the alternative would be much worse."

"What is the alternative?"

"That you destroy my family and my husband."

She watched him considering her words.

"I don't want to do that."

"I know you don't. But that is what will happen if you come back here."

He turned his back on her, walked a few steps and then returned.

"I don't want to harm you or your children. And I don't want to harm Charles. I'll stay away."

"And never write to Charles, or speak to him?"

"That would be cruel."

"Sometimes cruelty is the best cure."

She watched him struggling to find an answer. Eventually he nodded several times.

"All right. But I don't want your money."

"Thank you, George. But I would like you to take the money. It's insurance, you see."

"Insurance?"

"In case you change your mind. I will have something to fight you with should you tell my husband about this conversation."

"Like what?"

"Like the stub of my cheque book."

"Congratulations. You've thought of everything, Arabella."

"I'm a woman. Women will do anything to protect their family."

"I knew there was something about them I didn't like. How much am I worth?"

"I thought seven thousand pounds would be enough to give you a start in America."

"Am I worth that much?"

"No. But my family is."

"You can make the cheque out to St. Luke's Homeless Fund."

"Seriously?"

"Seriously."

"I can't do that. For my purpose it has to be made out to you. You can do what you like with it when you cash it."

She used the bonnet of her car to write the cheque then handed it to him.

"Goodbye, George. I hope you do well in America."

He watched her get into the car. She waved to him as she turned it round and drove out of the yard.

George stood for some time after it had disappeared. He

put the cheque into the back pocket of his jeans and retraced his steps into the walled garden. He studied what he had done to it: weeded all the brick paths and the borders along the walls and tilled the main vegetable area. He bent down and picked up a handful of the fine soil and let it trickle through his fingers. He imagined it as it should be, with potatoes and other vegetables and the fruit trees beyond, recently laden in the autumn sun; the plums and apples and raspberries and pears bursting with colour and the insects humming among the leaves.

He wiped his sleeve across his eyes and walked through an arch into the main garden. He admired what he had created from a tired, neglected canvas. Even in the late October sun it was a scene of quiet beauty. The wild flowers would come the next summer on the mounds he had built from the pond and the pond itself looked as though it had been there forever, thanks to Adam Courtney's care. But at the pond his heart faltered and his thoughts hardened. He turned his back on the pride of his life and walked into the house, blind to anything but what lay ahead.

****

Charles Foden had expected all week to hear from George but on Friday morning he realised he was not going to.

His Finnish clients had spent all day examining machines and talking to his technical staff. He had taken them to lunch and then given them afternoon tea and then they had invited him to dinner at their hotel along with his finance director where they had eventually closed a deal for half a million pounds worth of machinery. By the time Foden got home it was eleven thirty and he expected George would then be airborne. He slept restlessly.

The next morning he phoned Edna Fielder. She did not know of George's arrangements in New York and could only give him a number for the PR company handling the Love Frost contract.

He waited three days and then found time to visit Upland House during an afternoon. He let himself in and climbed the stairs to the top floor. He found George's flat unlocked. The two rooms and a bathroom had not been fully furnished. In the living/kitchen area he saw everything was still looking new and unused and nothing of a personal nature was evident. The bedroom was similarly clean; the bed was unmade with the linen and duvet folded neatly on the foot of the bed – the bed where he and George had last made love. Then he saw the keys on the bedside table; the keys to the flat and the keys to the Daimler. He opened the drawers of the small chest. They were empty. He slid back the door of the built-in wardrobe and stepped backwards quickly. It was empty but for a blue, Calvin Klein suit. It was on a hanger but the trousers had been so hung they reached full length below the jacket as though someone had stepped out of them. Below them was a pair of Calvin Klein slip-ons and in the lapel of the jacket was pinned a single yellow rose from the garden.

Foden stared at the ensemble and tears welled into his eyes. He knew then that George was not coming back.

****

The Love Frost advertising campaign was released in the UK three weeks before Christmas. It was Edmund who first recognised George. The family had been watching a film and during the break Arabella had followed Agnes into the kitchen to get some drinks. Her husband was getting ready to take the dog for a walk.

"It's George. It's George." Edmunds's excited voice sent them scampering into the living- room.

The advertisement was nearly over. There was a long shot of a figure by the Seine and then the camera cut to the figure sitting down on the cobbles with his feet through the railings of the embankment. And then cut again to George's smiling face then panned up to a female's legs standing behind him and continued to her face, smiling down at him. George got to his feet and the girl put her face close to his. She closed her eyes as though waiting for a kiss. George just smiled then turned and walked away from her.

Edmund was excited to find that someone he knew was on television. Nanny laughed with him. Agnes was intrigued. Arabella watched her husband. Foden showed no expression.

"He was good," Arabella said.

Agnes and Nanny agreed with her.

"Didn't you think so, Charles?"

"Yes. I know he is."

"To think; you made him a star."

"No. His parents did that. I just made him believe it."

"Well, he's got a lot to thank you for," Nanny told him.

"If you saw Upland House, Nanny, you would see that I have a lot to thank him for."

"You were good for each other then."

"Yes. We were good for each other."

He called Lucky and left the house quickly.

The advertisements continued right up to Christmas. For Foden it was similar to constantly viewing old video film of someone who had died. He would have liked to have insisted they only watched the BBC where there were no advertisements but he had never shown much inclination to choose what they watched on television and now Edmund and Phillipa looked forward to seeing George whenever they were allowed to view before going to bed.

As Christmas approached, Foden secretly hoped that George would return. He rang Edna Fielder to see if she had news of him. She had. She told him, with a strong sense of disappointment, that George had left her agency for one in New York.

Her disappointment was nowhere near to the breath-stopping pain that Foden felt.

Two days before Christmas a card arrived from George. It was addressed to 'The Henderson Foden family.' It was hand-made with a photograph of two turtle doves of the sort that might decorate a Christmas tree, standing on a sprig of holly. The doves were facing each other and in the beak of one of them, as though offering it to the other, was a ring with a single diamond set into it. The handwritten words inside the card wished the family a happy Christmas with much appreciation and love from George.

Nanny thought it was very sweet when she noticed it on the mantle-piece.

Arabella feigned approval.

Foden knew it was a message of love but though it calmed the hurt of abandonment at George's silent departure it failed to explain the reason for it. That was a mystery and a hurt that would continue to haunt him for many years to come.

THE PRESENT
11

When Noel Foden entered the water his first shock was the pain it caused. He had pulled his legs upwards in an instinctive reaction to prevent his body from tipping forwards in the fifteen metre fall and he hit the surface with his feet and backside almost together and though the position saved him from injury the frictional heat burned his skin and the impact shook the whole of his body right up to his head. The second shock was that the water was much colder than the air about it and as his body continued to plummet downwards he unconsciously expected it to be like night-swimming on the south coast of England where the opposite was the case.

If he had thought about the physical details of his suicidal act before taking that course, he might have expected to keep travelling downwards to a painless expiration of life, but as force gave way to buoyancy and his body hesitated before buoyancy won the scientific debate and he began to float upwards, his mind awakened and caused an alarm which threshed his arms and legs in a state of panic that only delayed the inevitable emergence of his head into the warm night air where his mouth opened wide to protest his predicament and succeeded in tunnelling air into his deflated lungs.

The release of pressure cleared the noise and pain from his head and then the silence was oppressive, as though the experience had made him deaf.

He trod water and raised himself, turning completely around to survey – nothing. The dark blue of the sky and the sea were like one. There was no ship. There was no moon. There was – nothing. Despair seized him and his mind allowed a kaleidoscope of images to fall through his vision like a runaway film-reel until it stopped on a picture of Tracy, taking his hand and leading him off a wall and into a new world where he was reading H E Bates to an old lady.

His body had adjusted to the temperature of the water and it was not unpleasant. He swam gently in a circle but each angle was the same. There was – something. A movement. A sound. Another – and then noises; squeaks, like a chamois leather on glass and then a sound like chattering teeth and another movement, so near it washed him sideways. For a second, fear came with the thought of sharks and then he saw the shapes of the dolphins, circling him and then one would dart in and almost touch him, the wash lifting his body almost out of the water. It happened several times and then they stopped circling and swam into line and moved away.

"No," he called. "Please."

The rear dolphin turned and came up behind him and stayed and he felt it touch his back as though to nudge him forward then two other dolphins turned and went on either side of him. He kept swimming and the mammals swam beside him, making the water flume beneath and move him forward in waves of effortless pursuit of the main pod ahead, and all the time he could hear their calls like laughter in a dream. His progress became rhythmic, almost monotonous, and his mind switched off to everything except the messages to keep his arms curving forwards, clawing the water for purchase, and the twisting of his face out of the water as his arms turned his body from side to side.

There were moments when he wondered how far they were from land but he quickly shut the thoughts away, all thoughts away. He was being led by the dolphins as he had been led by Tracy. He believed in them. Stroke after stroke he swam, aware only of the sounds of the water and his friends, almost in a trance, disturbed only by the regular attendance of the dolphins making the cushioning swell that rested his body and made him smile his thanks.

When his arms moved so slowly that his mind became aware of them, he wondered if he was moving at all and they gradually flopped into the water. He trod water and then turned onto his back and thought he would just lie there and go to sleep.

A dolphin came beside him, its body touching his and then another came on the other side of him so that he was wedged between them and almost lifted completely out of the water. He didn't know whether they were moving forward or not; he just closed his eyes and smiled and when he opened them again the sky was lighter. He turned his neck and saw the line of daylight and the dolphins beneath him moved away in a chatter of sound and his body was back fully in the water. The dolphins moved around him and then one went towards the daylight and the other waited until he started to swim again and then went behind him like a herding sheepdog. He saw the rest of the pod and he swam after them and resumed the routine and realised his arms were working again and the cold before daylight urged him forward with new energy until the sun suddenly appeared in a rising ball out of the sea and he felt its warmth on his face.

They swam together until the sun was high above them and whenever he stopped swimming to rest he had two attendants quickly on either side of him. He put out his hands and touched them often and even held their dorsal fins but the skin was sharp even though they turned half sideways to allow him to get a better grip.

The sun rose and fell behind them and his rest periods had become more frequent when the chatter between the mammals became pronounced and they swam around him in increasingly fast circles so the water threw him up and down like a cork and the dolphins closed in so the maelstrom increased and his mind began to panic that they had tired of keeping him alive. And then, on the top of an upward wave, he saw the lights; tiny spots in a darkening sky. He yelled and shouted but didn't know if he made any sound because his mouth and throat had no feeling. Then the dolphins moved away and the sea calmed and he could see the lights and he swam towards them wondering where the dolphins had gone until two appeared near him and swam slowly ahead of him but taking turns to come behind and beside him and if he slowed, a nose would dip between his legs and urge him forwards.

The lights became clearer and if he raised himself above the swell of the sea he could see there was a line of them. They were small, still only dots but now much brighter in the dark of the night. He started swimming again and his companions moved beside him or behind him, occasionally dipping underneath him and raising him almost out of the water in moments of rest for his leaden arms.

He kept going blindly, relying on the dolphins to show him the way until suddenly he was again surrounded by the main pod; they circled him in decreasing circles and with increasing speed until the water gushed beneath him sending him up and down as it had before. Then he had learnt it had reason when he saw the lights and now it was sound; the sound of human voices and then a light shining towards him and the sound of an engine and just as suddenly as the melee began so it ended as the pod disappeared and a deep sense of loss stilled his body and he slid beneath the surface.

He heard the engine and the voices getting further away as he travelled downwards and then he was lifted by his crotch and thrown into the air. There was a blinding light and human shouts and the engine of the boat was cut as he fell back into the water. He reached out an arm and felt the nose of the dolphin in the palm of his hand – and then it was gone. He cried out to it but there was no sound from his swollen lips then he was jolted by the hull of a small craft and hands were gripping his arms and he was being lifted out of the water.

When his mind functioned again it was his auditory senses that were the first to work. He heard voices and thought they were speaking English but he was not able to understand the words, then he remembered that the last voices he heard had been loud and unintelligible and the memory caused a feeling of loss and stress but his brain was not yet functioning enough to tell him why. The pulses sent signals to his body and he tried to move parts of it without any feeling coming back to him to tell him whether or not he had been successful but he then heard a woman's voice and understood the words;

"I think he's come round," and he felt hands on his body as though to hold him down.

"Can you open your eyes?" a male voice asked him.

He tried but his eyelids seemed stuck together. He tried again and light entered them and he closed them tightly. He felt a damp cloth dabbing them gently and when it had stopped he opened his eyes but was blinded. He tried several times before they were able to adjust to the light.

"Hi, young feller," the man's voice said and he was able to recognise an American accent.

"Where am I?" he asked and his voice seemed a long way away.

"You're on a US navy ship," the voice responded. "An aircraft carrier to be precise. How d'ya feel?"

Noel's eyes were now functioning properly and they looked from the man's face beyond him. He saw a female in a white tunic smiling at him and he tried to smile back but had no idea whether or not the attempt was successful.

"How did I get here?" he asked and this time his voice seemed more in his head.

"That's what we want to ask you," the man said.

Feeling was returning to his body and Noel moved his head from side to side. He tried to raise himself but failed.

"Water," he said.

The woman came to his bed and lifted his head and held a cup to his lips but took it away when he had taken only a sip.

"Let's get you sitting up," the man said.

He and the female went on either side of him and lifted him and wedged him behind with pillows. He thanked them and his voice sounded normal and he had feeling in his upper body and arms. The man held his wrist to feel his pulse.

"That's good," he said. "We had to scdatc you to stabilise your body. Do you know who you are?" Noel said his name.

"Noel. Good. Do you know your surname?"

Noel's brain had difficulty in locating that memory but eventually succeeded.

"Foden. Noel Foden."

"How d'ya do. Noel. I'm Surgeon Commander Stew Nicholson and this is my assistant, Lieutenant Angie Fabrinski."

Noel said he was pleased to meet them. "How long have I been here?" he asked in a weak voice.

"You've been with us twenty six hours but it's three days since you were fished out of the sea. Can you remember what happened to you?"

Noel became anxious. "Dolphins," he said and his head moved about.

"Okay. Stay calm. Dolphins, huh? The fishermen said you were with dolphins."

"They saved me," Noel told them. "They kept me alive; showed me where to go."

"Is that right? I've heard a few dolphin tales but that sounds really interesting. Tell us about it."

Noel slowly, fitfully, recounted the moments from when he had stepped off the ship until he was picked out of the water. Stew Nicholson and Angie Fabrinski listened with interest and when he'd finished they continued to look at him trying to ascertain whether he was still feverish. It was Angie who broke the spell.

"How incredible," she said. "They really carried you and led you to the fishing boats?"

Noel just closed his eyes and smiled and when he opened them again he began to cry. Angie comforted him.

"I'll be damned," Nicholson said. "We know you went missing three days ago. There have been a few ships and choppers looking for you. So you were in the sea twenty four hours without any support," he whistled.

"I had support," Noel told him.

"Oh, yeah. The dolphins. That's an incredible story."

He told Noel he had been rescued by a local fishing boat who then called for help. A Saudi patrol vessel took him onboard and put an emergency call in to the Task Force. "The Task Force?" Noel interrupted. The Commander explained TF 150 was the international naval force to combat piracy and terrorism in the Gulf and the Arabian Sea. "We're part of the US Fifth Fleet," he said. "A chopper from one of the ships picked you up from the Saudi vessel.

They rehydrated you and treated you for hypothermia then brought you to us to check you over properly. We have all hospital facilities here. We didn't know who you were. We were too far off station to bother with the mayday alert in the Red Sea, and to be honest, the Saudis didn't think you were the same guy. Who lives in the sea for twenty four hours without a lifebelt even?"

"Where are we now?" Noel asked and was told they were east of the Gulf of Aden. The name *Aden* jarred in his head and all the memories flooded back.

"You're one hell of a lucky guy," Nicholson said but Noel then didn't feel lucky. "We've let everyone know you've been picked up so I guess your folks will have been told. Now we have to figure out a way of getting you home," the Commander said.

"I don't want to go home," Noel told them.

"Where d'ya want to go?" Nicholson asked.

"To Mumbai. I have to get to Mumbai," Noel responded. He explained he was on the way to Mumbai to work.

"And you fell overboard off a container ship?" the commander asked and still wasn't convinced when Noel confirmed it but he didn't say so.

He was given his first non-liquid food since he had gone into the water and then a stream of curious visitors, including TF 150's Group Commander, a vice admiral, all wanted to hear his story about the dolphins. Noel explained how they had raised him up to see the lights of the fishing boats and then they had done the same, causing another maelstrom when they were near the boats to attract their attention.

"And then they disappeared, all except one that stayed with me," he finished sadly.

It was a junior officer from Florida who explained the pod

wouldn't go near the fishing boats because they string nets and they don't want to get caught in them. His father was a fisherman and he knew all about dolphins and he was happy to sit with Noel and talk about them. He was also visited by a female commander who said she was a medic but he soon realised she was a psychiatrist.

"I'm all right." He told her.

"It's very hard to fall from a ship," she argued and Noel did nothing to convince her otherwise.

"Now I'm all right," he insisted.

"But you don't want to go home," she said.

"I have to go to Mumbai," he pleaded.

"Why?" she asked.

"Because that's where my life is," he answered and his face reflected his resolve.

People came and went, some took photographs of him and he began to feel more of an exhibit than a celebrity. The following day he took his first steps around the room and ate more food. His legs were weak and felt like they did after a hard, wet rugby match and a hot bath but he persevered, exercising them lying on his back, and later that day he was allowed to dress. He had been given white trousers and a shirt and a pair of white issue shoes and was taken outside by Angie Fabrinski. He held her arm as he walked along a steel corridor and into a lift.

They emerged in a hangar where aircraft were tightly packed like ferry cars and then they took another lift and walked out onto the side of the flight deck and a new world hit Noel in the face.

It was late evening and the sky was a medium blue falling indigo into the sea with red and melon streaks reflecting the sun which had then disappeared below the horizon. But everywhere there were lights, red, orange and green and some kept changing colour like traffic signals and a red one where they had emerged was flashing at them He looked along the vast flight deck and up at the enormous conning tower and at the many crew members, silhouetted, darting about performing work routines. He jumped as a hooter startled him and a Tannoyed voice issued a warning;

"Two minutes. Counting," and an electronic beep signal increased in frequency.

Angie Fabrinski took his arm and pulled him back into the low profile access point and an F 16 Seahawk dropped onto the deck above them with a scream of engines and brakes. Noel's eyes were wide and his mouth agape. Angie Fabrinski laughed.

"I never get tired of watching it," she said. "I love Navy."

Another F16 landed and Noel's eyes and mouth were still wide.

"Will I fly in one of those?" he asked excitedly.

"No. Your probable lift is coming in now. Those were the escorts."

They saw the other plane approaching. Unlike the jets which seemed to have dropped in from nowhere, the high-winged, turbo prop C-2A Greyhound winged in sedately and made a perfect conventional landing.

"What is it?" Noel asked.

Angie Fabrinski explained it was their workhorse, carrying cargo and personnel to and from land bases.

"It's got a range over one thousand miles so I guess it can get to Mumbai," she smiled.

They went back to the sick bay and Noel thanked the lieutenant for being so kind. Noel had guessed she was probably somewhere in her thirties, which to him seemed quite old, and he was surprised and concerned that he found her increasingly attractive.

"Are you married?" he asked.

"Yes. He's in the navy too. A medic."

"When do you see each other?"

"Whenever we can. We used to be on the same ship but now we sometimes meet in some port or another but we get to have leave together."

"How can you do that?

"We both love being in the navy and we both love our jobs."

"More than each other?" Noel said before he could stop himself.

Angie smiled. "How old are you Noel?" Noel told her.

"That young?" she said with surprise in her voice and she looked at him anew. "Well, love is hell, sex is great and marriage is – comforting."

"And boring?" he asked suggestively.

"Not when you're both in the navy," she laughed.

They were sitting on the bed drinking from cans of cola which Fabrinski had taken from a dispensing machine on their way below decks.

"Tell me, Noel, did you really fall off that ship?" she asked.

Noel took some time to answer by shaking his head.

"Do you want to talk about it?"

Noel physically struggled.

"Try." she coaxed.

"I want to. I should do," he said. "But I can't."

Angie put her hand on his which was pressing into the bed and gripping the blanket. "Yes, you can. You can tell me anything. There's nothing I haven't heard, believe me. We have boys coming in here who are afraid, homesick, have sexual problems, marriage problems. A ship is like any main street – so there's nothing you can tell me that is going to do anything but help you."

"I don't know where to start," he told her.

"What are you going to do in Mumbai?" Noel told her about the orphanages. "Have you been working with children?"

"No. I was at university studying politics and English."

She asked if he had finished his degree as he was so young. His voice faltered as he told her he'd dropped out. She didn't then ask the obvious question but in the silence Noel knew she was expecting him to tell her. "Something happened," he said and quickly hid his face in his hands. When Fabrinski remained silent he took his hands away and held them together as if to pray. "I was raped," he said.

"By someone at the university?"

"No. By several men."

"You were gang-raped?" Angie gasped and failed to keep astonishment from her voice.

Noel jumped off the bed, turning his head and body in different directions. "And my father killed the men who did it," he said in a loud, whining voice.

Angie reached out and took hold of his wrist and gently pulled him down onto the bed. She didn't speak. She held both his hands against his thighs in a restraining gesture but without any pressure.

"That's a lot of baggage," she said quietly when he had calmed. "Was your father arrested?"

Noel told her the police didn't know. "They were coming to Aden to question me."

"And that's why you jumped from the ship?" she asked but knew the answer before Noel nodded agreement. "That's so unfair," she said sympathetically.

"No. It was my fault."

"How can you think it was your fault?" she said.

Noel told her about his assault on Caroline. He started hesitantly, each sentence painfully assembled and in a selective order that attempted to mitigate his guilt but once he had started his self-loathing took over and he finished by saying he wished that Harry had hit him harder with the chair.

"So you see, Angie. I'm responsible for everything that happened and now my father will serve the rest of his life in prison when the police have questioned me."

"How did he kill those men?" she asked, choosing to delay talking about the rapes. Noel told her four of them were killed in an arson attack. She asked if he was there and he said he had waited for his father in a hotel.

"So you didn't actually see him do it?"

Noel looked at her impatiently. "What does that matter? I know he did it."

"It matters that you can't tell the police you know he did it," she said and the logic had obviously not occurred to Noel. "You only have to tell them what you know, not what you think you know," she explained. " Did you want your father to do what he did?" Noel said he didn't. "Then you don't have to carry his guilt around with you, Noel. Your father's an adult. He chose to do what he did."

"He did it for me," Noel protested.

"No, he didn't. He didn't ask you. He wanted to do it."

"Why?"

"I don't know. But to kill someone by arson is not an instinctive murder. It is very premeditated. I could understand it if you were a child, I would want to murder someone if they did that to my child but not if it's an adult who was raped.

"Have you got children?" Noel asked.

"No. But I know how I would feel about it if I had."

512

"You're so kind," Noel told her. "You're my third angel."

Angie laughed and leant forward and kissed his cheek.

"You're rather cute," she said. "So, who are the other two?"

Noel told her, Tracy and the dolphins.

"I know about the dolphins, I can't compete with them. But tell me about Tracy."

Noel told her how he had run from the house when he heard about the arson killings and ended up at the river. "I don't know if I was going to jump," he said. "I think I would have done."

He told her how Tracy had taken him into the home, of reading to the old people, about Claris and her interesting life and how her death had affected him and how he had agreed to go to India with Tracy.

"So that's why you must go to Mumbai?" she smiled when he had finished. "Do you love her?"

Noel said he didn't know. "How can I love someone after what I did and what those men did to me?" he cried.

"Have you told Tracy what happened to you?"

"No," Noel said miserably. "I wanted to but I just haven't been able to."

"Because you think she won't like you any more?"

"No. Just because I'm so ashamed. I hate myself. For everything."

Angie Fabrinski got up and walked away from the bed. She studied Noel for a while and he looked back at her like a wounded spaniel, waiting for a reaction from her.

"You said adults can get over that sort of thing. How?" he asked.

She walked to the door and locked it. Noel looked at her with surprise and anxiety beginning to show in his face. She walked back and stood in front of him.

"Do you feel you can't touch a woman again?" she asked.

"Yes," Noel said.

She spoke as she unbuttoned her blouse slowly.

"Noel, sex is something to enjoy. It's not love, it's not marriage and it should never, ever be enforced. There's only one rule for sex; that is, it should be enjoyable for both parties." She had opened her blouse and exposed her breasts held in a skimpy bra. "Give me your hand." She took his hand and held it to her breasts. "You see. You're not going to burn in hell. It's just a breast. My breast, and I want to share it with you." She let his hand fall and took off her blouse and undid her bra. "Now. Hold me. Gently."

Noel obeyed. He put his hands on her waist and when she eased towards him he drew her in so she was standing between his legs and her breasts pushed against his chest. Noel tightened his hold but then felt her pull away. She smiled at him.

"You see. Wasn't that easy and nice?" Noel said it was.

"Now try again and this time we'll kiss."

Noel's lips pressed hard against hers but she pulled away so their lips just touched. She did it several times before Noel stopped pressing and then her lips brushed his and pulsated against them like butterfly wings that sent his body tingling down to his feet but when she felt his trousers bulging she drew away.

She smiled at his bleary eyes and began to unbutton his shirt. Noel helped impatiently but she took his hands away and continued the process slowly and as she pushed the shirt from his shoulders her breasts went against his bare chest and Noel gripped her tightly behind.

"No." she said. "Just kiss me again and see how long you can make it last."

They made it last a long time and the messages from their

minds to their lips were only those of pleasure in experiencing the variety of sensations their cells conjointly found in each other. When Angie ended the embrace Noel fell back on the bed and smiled like a kitten.

"We'll talk," she told him. "Tell me about Tracy."

Noel didn't want to talk about Tracy right then. He wanted to take hold of her but she just smiled and pushed away his hands each time he tried to touch her and she insisted he talked.

"Tell me about the dolphins," she said. "How many were there. What colour are they. What sort of sounds did they make?"

Noel gradually answered her questions and when he had finished she found more. "Now tell me about Tracy," she insisted. "How old is she. What colour is her hair, What colour are her eyes. Why do you like her?"

He answered her questions again but then he began to talk more about her; about her parents and how she was always smiling. About her patience and how kind she had been with the elderly people in the home. They talked about the music they liked and their favourite food and then Angie climbed onto the bed and sat beside him.

"Now you can kiss me," she said.

They kissed gently and their hands explored their bodies and Angie allowed him to kiss her breasts and then her lips explored his chest and slid wetly down his body until his penis was erect. "Come in gently and rest," she told him and moved his penis into her and held him still. They lay into each other, kissing and holding and gradually moving together as though on a dance floor to a smoochy tune. The slow foxtrot became a waltz and then a quickstep and then an Argentine tango until the orchestra stopped and they lay still together without speaking.

Angie got up first and began to dress. Noel raised his head and smiled at her then laughed and fell back again on the bed.

"Get dressed and we'll go and have supper in the mess," she told him.

When they were dressed she let Noel kiss her.

"Thank you," he said.

"Now go and find Tracy and tell her everything. But never, never tell her about this."

They went to the cafeteria and lined up with their trays among various ranks who had finished their shifts. They sat at a crowded table and everyone wanted to hear about the boy who had survived in a sea for twenty four hours and they took selfies with him and shook his hand and wished him good luck. At one point he looked across and saw Angie Fabrinski watching him proudly. She smiled at him and he knew he would always remember that moment.

The next morning he was told he would be flown to Mumbai. As he followed a rating up to the flight deck there were groups of sailors whishing him good luck and the Vice Admiral and the Captain and other officers had assembled to bid him farewell. He thanked everybody and held back the tears and they laughed and slapped him on the back.

"If you ever want to join the navy, son, just let us know. We'd be glad to have you," the Vice Admiral told him.

The C-2A Greyhound trundled down the flight deck and pulled sharply away in a steep turn. It circled the aircraft carrier and Noel looked down on the most comprehensive compendium of man's technological genius ever assembled in one place, until it got ridiculously small and he could see only Angie Fabrinski's smiling face.

He looked hopefully for a sign of dolphins in the glistening sea and realised how impossible it would be to spot someone swimming in the vast arena. When they were too high to see anything but a sheet of reflected light, he closed his eyes and felt the waves and heard the calls of his angels of the sea.

THE PRESENT
12

Arabella Foden took the call from the Foreign and Commonwealth Office to tell her that her son had been pulled from the sea alive, and in one moment her life was restored, her mind, body and soul repaired. She had no breath to question the caller, and her daughter, Phillipa had to take the telephone to get further information. She was told only that Noel had been rescued by a fishing boat and transferred to a US vessel for hospitalisation. but the voice assured Phillipa that Noel was all right and the hospitalisation had been only a precautionary measure.

When Arabella had recovered sufficiently to speak she had snatched the phone off her daughter and asked how and when she could speak to her son but was told that he was in a restricted military zone and personal calls were not possible for security reasons. She was assured they would contact her again when Noel was transferred onshore.

The jubilation that then gripped the whole household was only tempered at dinner when Arabella announced that they must have a church service to give thanks for the miracle that had kept Noel alive. She would speak to the vicar and arrange a service for family and close friends.

It was her husband who failed to greet the announcement with the same enthusiasm as the women. Over dinner, he made the right noises and comments but they seemed strangely unemotional and as the two women talked excitedly his silence was noticeable, which, when Agnes had left the table for the kitchen, his wife questioned with a hint of annoyance.

"I am only concerned that it might not be appropriate to draw attention to the fact that Noel jumped from a ship in mid ocean," he responded tersely.

The possibility that Noel had deliberately jumped from the ship had not been mentioned until that moment. Arabella and her husband had not talked about Noel's disappearance as her understandable grief and anger with her husband had not been conducive to any reasonable conversation and then Phillipa's arrival had tempered any further possibility.

Phillipa had been told of Noel's sexual ordeal by her mother but there had been no mention of the consequential arson attack or of the police enquiries and certainly not of what happened between him and Caroline, so it was understandable that Phillipa would react to her father's comment.

"You think he tried to commit suicide?" she said with astonishment.

"Of course he didn't," her mother answered but her voice was not convincing.

"He told you about the dolphins," she said to her husband.

"He was probably watching them and slipped."

Her husband did not respond which made Phillipa even more suspicious. She was not a girl to be ignored or easily deceived and she persisted with her questions.

"Did he, Daddy?" she asked him.

Her father admitted it was possible and explained about the arson attack and that the police had wanted to question him about it.

Unlike her mother, Phillipa did not ignore the possibilities.

"And they think he might have been responsible?" she said with even more astonishment in her voice.

Her father said it was an obvious connection for the police to make and he had told Noel it was a routine enquiry.

"But Noel was still in a state of trauma after his experience and it's possible the police interest affected him more than it should," he explained.

Phillipa absorbed the information in silence before putting the question her mother would never have asked.

"Is it possible Noel did start the fire?"

"How can you ask that?" her mother responded. "How can you even think such a thing?"

Phillipa secretly wondered herself how she could, and her embarrassment showed.

"He was in no state to think of revenge," Foden said and the subject would have lain there except for Phillipa's active mind.

"Why Noel?" she asked when her parents had hoped she had run out of curiosity. "I mean, why was he raped like that? Have there been other cases at the university with student's being gang-raped?"

The phrase brought the image to Arabella's mind and in her physical attempts to shut it out she sprang to her feet.

"I don't want to talk about this any more," she said angrily. "Why are we discussing what happened to Noel? We should just be thanking God that he is alive. I am going to phone the vicar tomorrow and we will all pray that he is returned to us safely and when he is we will all embrace him and help him to put this awful business behind him."

She left the room almost knocking into Betsy who had been about to enter.

"Why did you have to upset her?" Foden asked and it was Phillipa's turn to get upset. Tears began to seep from her eyes and she too got up and brushed past Betsy before the tears turned into sobs.

Charles Foden continued to sit at the table as Betsy cleared it from around him. He sat much as he had sat some years before when he had decided to face Aunt Sheila over her comments about his father and Gerhardt, but now his mind failed to reach a decision as it had done then. His thoughts were eventually disturbed by a sympathetic Betsy.

"Don't worry Mr. Foden. It's been an emotional time for all of us."

Foden only nodded and continued to stare at the fine linen tablecloth. When Betsy had cleared the table and tided up she returned to the dining-room to find Foden still sitting in the same position, a glass of Port almost untouched beside him.

She stood in the doorway, unsure of what to do. "I've finished, Mr Foden. Is there anything else I can do for you?" she asked.

Foden thanked her and said there was nothing but he neither looked at her nor moved his eyes from the tablecloth, unaware that Betsy would normally take the cloth from the table. She continued to stand, hesitating.

Foden looked up at her.

"Goodnight, Betsy."

"The tablecloth..." she smiled apologetically.

"Ah, yes. Sorry." He got up and lifted the glass of Port. "Have the ladies..."

"They've both gone upstairs."

"Then I'll just finish this," he muttered and walked slowly towards the sitting-room.

He sat in an armchair and stared without seeing the other side of the room, much as he had sat and stared in his car a few days before when they had received the news of Noel's disappearance. Then his depression was understandable but now it had no obvious reason. Noel, his son, was alive when three days before they had thought he was dead. Why did he not feel the jubilation and gratitude that his wife and daughter had felt?

If his mind was less numb it might have given him answers. It might have reminded him that Noel would now be questioned about the murders of his assailants and it might have reminded him that Inspector Morrison had discovered his association with George. It might also have reminded him that, sitting in his car, he had realised who Penny Featherstone was. Penny Featherstone, whom Noel had said saw Katy Rose on Drovers' Hill which had then begun a new investigation to find her.

But his mind was numb; numb from a decision it had already made.

T he news of Noel's miraculous restoration was received with varying feelings in the police community: DS Townsend and his team greeted it with unemotional satisfaction that they could then get on with their arson investigation by arranging to interview Noel as soon as possible. The Chief Constable was genuinely happy for Charles Foden and his family.

Daphne Morrison was gratefully relieved that Noel had not died. The effect his death might have had on Caroline's mental health could have been fatal coming on top of the burden of guilt she would be suffering from her part in the arson killings and the knowledge that Penny knew of her involvement in them. And any inquiry into Caroline's affairs would severely test Penny's honesty and her loyalty to Morrison. But Noel's disappearance had given her three days to think about her investigation. She had spent much of that time with Julie Norris. The golf pro was an ideal antidote to her own introspective nature. She was pragmatic and could quickly scythe through any emotional obfuscation and she was funny too which found a response that had been buried under Morrison's professional persona.

Although she would not talk specifically about her investigation she could speak generally about it without getting into names or details which helped her review the essentials of the case, such as the pain of the Lewis family and the failure to find Katy Rose. And underneath the generalities the details became clearer and she knew what she must then do. Even if it meant handing the case to CID she had to persuade her chief they needed to search Upland House and to question Charles Foden under caution.

She knew that to attempt to do it verbally would mean an

uphill argument with her boss who had already dismissed the idea that Charles Foden could possibly be capable of setting the fire that killed four people. What then would he think of the suggestion that Charles Foden was homosexual, that he might have killed Katy Rose Lewis and attempted to kill Jenny Challis and that he buried Katy in his garden? She didn't want to have that conversation.

Julie Norris had had to stay late at the club to supervise the arrangements for a Rotary Club dinner and Morrison had said she would prepare a meal for her return. With a boeuf bourguinonne prepared and simmering gently, she cleared a part of the kitchen table and began hand-writing a report for the Chief Constable. She chose to hand-write it so that it could not get into any hands other than his; she knew she had enemies in the CID and she wanted to state her case unequivocally.

It was not a long report. It bulleted the reasons as to why she thought that Charles Foden should be questioned and why there was the need to get a search warrant for Upland House. When she had finished she put it into an envelope. She decided she had time to take it into the Station and leave it, sealed, on the Chief Constable's desk for him to see it when he got in the following morning.

****

The vicar of Stokesey was delighted that his services were needed in the middle of the week, even that his services were needed at all. At eleven am the Fodens, minus Grant who was at boarding school and Edmund who had left for Cyprus, Betsy and several friends who had been alerted by Arabella, assembled in the old church where past members of the Foden and Henderson families were buried.

Charles Foden was seated on the end of a row and next to the Henderson family chapel where, over four hundred years, members of that family, including grandfather Sir Toby, had been interred. From his seat he could see the stone commemorating his grandparent's lives and he smiled to himself as he remembered their warmth and support for him both as a child and as an adult.

'There is no love greater than that which we have for our children..." the vicar was saying. *"There is no sacrifice we would not make to maintain their happiness...'*

The words broke into Charles Foden's reverie as his mind switched quickly to his other grandparents and to his father and he saw, with a clarity of vision he was now able to withstand, the chain of events that had led from his father's association with a German prisoner of war to Gerhardt's destruction by shotgun at the hands of his grandpa as though he had witnessed it with his own eyes.

'The love within a family is the greatest bond we know and I have no doubt it was that love for you all that kept Noel alive for twenty hours in a hostile ocean and, miraculously, instead of mourning his loss as we had all prepared to do, we are here to celebrate his resurrection, for that, surely is what it is: a return to life..." The vicar rolled on, his voice coming and going in Foden's consciousness like impaired radio waves.

But the lies and deceit were less clear. He thought of Aunt Sheila and how her life had ended in all but breath the moment her father had taken Gerhardt's. He had not found a reason for his Aunt's obsession with Gerhardt's disappearance. He had assumed, and his family had not attempted to correct him, that it was because of her love for Gerhardt, but as he later discovered, Sheila knew of his father's relationship with the German. Why then was she so obsessed with finding him? She could not have known of Gerhardt's murder as she lived in the hope that he was still alive. Nor could his father have known; his letter left for his child would surely have referred to Gerhardt's death if he had known – and if he had known what his father had done. It had taken over forty years for the truth of his Grandpa's vengeance to surface. Does truth always surface?

The thought stilted his brain. How long will it take for his own lies to be revealed?

'We might ask: why has God chosen Noel to demonstrate His power...'

We might indeed, Foden agreed. We might ask why God had chosen him to meet George and to kill Katy Rose.

'...In our everyday lives, we think we know what we are doing. We think we are in control. We think the decisions we make are the right ones. We think we know who we are...'

Foden sat up quickly so that Phillipa looked at him, thinking he was about to leave.

'...But do we? Noel thought he knew what he was doing that day when he fell from the ship. No doubt he felt all was lost as he hit the sea in the dead of night. There was no hope. Nobody there to help him – or so he thought. In our darkest moments, when we can see no way into the light it is because we believe there is no light...'

"That's what Father thought." Foden told Phillipa who shushed him then looked at him curiously.

Foden's mind raced on. His father saw no way out of the dark; not because his love was denied but because of what it was; because of who he was. Because of who we are... Who are we? Who decided who we are, what we are?

'...God is everywhere, even in the wilderness of the great oceans...'

Is he? Is he here now? Was he there when I struck Katy?

Was he there when we buried her? Was he there when George threw Jenny into the stream? Perhaps he was; that was almost a miracle too. Perhaps he only operates in water..

He laughed, so that Phillipa and two other people turned and looked at him.

'...If we believe. If we look for that light in the darkness. It will be there. 'Help' Noel must have cried. 'Help' as his ship disappeared in the night..'

"Help," Foden mimicked and the whole congregation looked at him. Foden looked back at them and laughed. The vicar responded with enthusiasm.

'That's right Charles. Let us all call for help. Help. Everyone. Help'

One or two people responded and then others. The vicar, not caring that his sermon was adopting a Baptist flavour, led the chorus. *'Help. Help. Help.'*

Charles Foden looked about him bemused.

'And God answered Noel's cry as He will answer ours. Thank you, Lord for saving our dearest and showing us your strength in this little acre of your vast domain. Let us pray. Let us speak to God and feel His strength.'

As they bent forward as though God was somewhere near the floor, Foden muttered, "I never deserted you." Phillipa smiled, thinking he was speaking to God. "I never did what my father did. I only ever wanted to do the best for you all."

Phillipa looked sideways and saw her father was upright, talking into the air. She pulled at his trousers and shushed him again. He bent down and continued to address her. "I want you to understand that I had enough love for you all, not just George. Love is greater than God."

His daughter turned, her eyes larger than normal, her mouth open as if she were about to sneeze.

"Daddy," she gasped.

The Vicar recited the Lords prayer then closed the service with arms outspread as though he were about to embrace them all.

"Now, let us go and enjoy our lunch and the warmth of our friendship."

Arabella accompanied him down the aisle, followed by their friends. Phillipa and Foden were the last of the group to leave.

Near the back of the church one or two villagers were grouped respectfully together. Although not invited they had heard of Noel's escape and of the service. Arabella stopped and spoke with them, thanking them for their care and inviting them to join them for lunch. As the procession continued into the sunlight Foden, who brought up the rear, saw Tom Lewis, still sitting in a pew. He stopped next to him and Tom got to his feet and held out his hand.

"Hello, Mr Foden. My mother sends her regards. She was sorry she couldn't come; she's not very strong now."

Foden had taken his hand but had said nothing, staring at the other man in disbelief. Then he suddenly embraced Tom and held him for some moments. When he released him there were tears in his eyes. Tom smiled understandingly. Foden nodded then hurried on out of the church.

Arabella had brought her flock to a halt, waiting for her husband.

"Who was that?" she asked as he joined them.

"Tom Lewis."

"Oh!" she responded.

"Poor chap," the vicar said. "Terrible business, that. Terrible."

"Yes. I can now know something of how they must feel," Arabella said and was joined in her sympathy by several of their friends and neighbours.

"Let's have lunch," she added decisively and began to lead them towards the local pub where she had booked tables.

"I'll catch you up," her husband called.

Arabella brought the group to a halt.

"What do you mean?" she asked.

"I have to make one or two calls. Don't wait. You go ahead and order."

"Really, Charles. Can't the business do without you for a few hours?"

"Sorry. It's important."

"Then don't be long," his wife said irritably.

"He's been behaving very odd lately. I think this business has got too much for him," she told the vicar who was now looking forward to being taken to lunch, and was leading the way out of the churchyard.

"He's had an awful shock, as you all have," the vicar said.

"He's probably going to Grandpa's grave," Phillipa responded. "Shall I go after him?" but her mother told her not to bother.

At the rear of the church where the tombstones marched downwards to an uninterrupted view of the distant estuary, Foden stood in front of the graves of his grandparents and his father. The graves were side by side and a memorial stone to Aunt Sheila, who had been cremated, was on his grandparents' grave. After some minutes of unmoving reflection he suddenly addressed himself in a strong but wavering voice to his father's memorial.

"Capt'n, art thou sleepin thar below?"

He laughed at the appropriate memory of a childhood poem.

"No. Of course you are not. You are dead. You are all dead. Gone from the arrows of this world. No chance to dream or regret. No more to suffer the cruelties of other people's deficiencies. You are dead. Dead."

****

Daphne Morrison left it late to go into the office, hoping the Chief Constable had read her report before she arrived, mid-morning. After checking her desk for messages she went along the corridor and through the intersecting office where the Chief Constable's PA worked, knocked on his door and opened it far enough for her face to appear.

"Daphne. Come in."

She did so and was surprised to see Steve Jennings standing to one side of the Chief Constable's desk. He avoided her eyes so she ignored him.

"I'm sorry, sir, if it's not a good time..."

"No. It is a good time." His voice was sombre.

"I wondered if you'd had time to look at my report?"

"Yes. I did. It was a bit unbelievable..." Morrison nodded agreement. "...until Jennings here came to see me."

Morrison now looked at the sergeant who returned her look but only for a moment.

"Jennings had something very interesting for us to see."

He offered a small, worn notebook to Morrison.

"What is it?" she asked as she took it from him.

"It's Jennings' pocket book from some twenty years ago."

Morrison opened the notebook. The pages were soft and fragile and the pencilled writing inside was difficult to read.

"Try the date when Katy Rose went missing," her chief told her.

She carefully turned the pages but they easily opened at the chosen date as though it had been recently exercised.

At the top of the page, next to the date was the time; 2045 hours. Then a car registration number followed by the name,

C Foden and his address.

She looked up at Jennings but his eyes were on the ground. She read from the page,

'Mr Foden said he had come from the golf club where he is a member. He said he had played golf that morning between seven and eleven am then had gone home for lunch where he prepared photograph of Katy Lewis for police. He then returned to golf club late afternoon. He had tea then practised a few holes and was now on his way home. He had golf clubs on the rear seat of car. When I made a comment they would scratch his leather seat he explained he had his golf cart in the boot.'

Morrison looked at Jennings. "Didn't you check the boot?"

"No, he didn't," the Chief Constable told her.

Morrison looked again at Jennings who eventually met her eyes.

"We spoke about golf," he said. "I told him I went to the golf range sometimes. He asked me why I didn't play. I told him I couldn't afford any clubs. He said his grandfather had just died and I could have his."

He paused. "I was well pleased... I should have checked the boot."

"Did he give you his grandfather's clubs?" she asked. He said he had. "Do you remember what make they were?"

"Slazenger," Jennings said,

Morrison turned to her boss.

"The club with Foden's DNA on it was a Ping. So it wasn't his grandfather's."

The Chief Constable nodded. "I think this is enough with your evidence to get that search warrant," he told her.

Morrison suppressed her enthusiasm and looked sadly at Jennings.

"Steve. You should have told me."

"I should have told someone about it years ago. CID were so sure a motorist was to blame. It wasn't until you targeted the golf club and Foden that I remembered."

"I think it's almost certain that Foden had Katy's body in the boot," Morrison said.

Jennings nodded, his face screwed up .

"There's something else," he mumbled. "I think I met George with Foden. He said he was his nephew."

"When was that?"

"About the same time. They were in the village with Foden's kids."

There was a silence in which The Chief Constable and Morrison exchanged looks and Jennings kept his eyes closed.

"Well. You can take credit for keeping your notes so long," Morrison told him.

Her mobile buzzed. The Chief Constable nodded for her to answer it.

"It might be important," he said.

She saw it was a text message from Charles Foden. She read the message aloud;

'Morrison. It's Charles Foden. I have those photos of Katy Lewis you asked about. They are in my studio at Upland House, I think you know where that is. I have left the studio unlocked. And do tell Jenny Challis I am so pleased she lived. She is a remarkable girl.'

Morrison looked at her boss. He raised his eyebrows to mimic her surprise.

"We needn't bother with a warrant," he said. "He's given you permission to get in there."

"He knows who Penny is," she reminded him.

"How would he know that?"

"I don't know – unless he recognised her. Or he's putting

532

pieces together; he knows she's been helping me. I think we should get over there, sir."

"I agree. Take another officer with you. And you'd better ask DS Laxton if you can have one of his team too. It might be a crime-scene."

"Can I help?" Jennings asked weakly.

"You are suspended until we decide what to do with you," The Chief Constable told him.

In the pub, the party had seated themselves at two tables and it was only when the orders began to arrive that Arabella observed that her husband had not joined them.

"What on earth is he doing?" she asked irritably.

Phillipa said she would go and find him. As she hurried back towards the church she expected to see her father making his way towards her but when she had reached the church there was still no sign of him. She noticed the church door was ajar and wondered if the service had reawakened her father's devotions; they had been regular church goers when she was a child but had been less so in the latter years of her life. She pushed the heavy oak door and peered inside. The church was empty as they had left it.

Beginning to feel her mother's irritation she followed the path her father had taken around the church to the graveyard behind. She surveyed the scene and thought quickly how beautiful it was and was about to turn back again when she noticed that the trunk of the great yew tree seemed to be distorted. She walked towards it thinking that someone was standing behind it and was mostly hidden. She called but received no response. She continued her progress towards the tree, widening her angle of approach, and then she ran the remainder of the distance to where she had a clear view of her father heavily slumped by his neck from the tattered remnants of a bell rope.

An ambulance was summoned by Phillipa as she tried valiantly to lift her father by his ankles. He was suspended some four feet off the ground and even in her desperation she had reasoned that he must have jumped from a nearby tombstone with the rope about his neck to be so far off the ground. She kept talking to him in between talking to the emergency services but got no response and his shoes pressed into her shoulders with increasing pain.

The ambulance arrived within ten minutes with two paramedics in attendance. One lifted the other dexterously so they were able to cut the rope. They lowered Foden to the ground and loosened the strands of rope that had cut into his throat. They applied respiratory procedures as Phillipa looked on, desperately praying for God's help. But God wasn't listening and the paramedics soon declared that Charles Foden's neck was probably broken by the impact of the fall at the end of the rope and there was nothing that could be done to restore his life.

The day did not get any better for Arabella and Phillipa Foden. Another call from someone at the Foreign and Commonwealth Office informed them in a cheerful voice that Noel had chosen to be flown to Mumbai instead of returning home.

****

Morrison stopped on the floor which housed the CID. DS Laxton was keen to know what it was all about when Morrison asked for one of his detectives. She told him to talk to the Chief Constable about it as she didn't have time. He reluctantly instructed Christine West, who had interviewed Foden with Morrison after the bog-body case, to go with her. When they entered the Uniform Branch to collect a male constable they were met with a hubbub of movement; officers jumping from their desks and putting on jackets and equipment.

"What's the panic?" Morrison asked a sergeant.

"Suicide. Stokesey church."

"We'll come with you." Morrison told him.

When they arrived at the churchyard an ambulance was still there and paramedics were taking a wheeled stretcher from it and trying to clear a path through a throng of people who were dispersed along the narrow, gravel path. The officers immediately started to clear it of the onlookers. Morrison followed the stretcher party to the graveyard where the vicar was trying to comfort Arabella Foden and two of the lunch party were holding Phillipa between them. Foden's body could be seen, now covered with a blanket, lying on the grass with a paramedic guarding it. Morrison, who was the senior officer, went forward and lifted the blanket and saw that part of the rope was still around Foden's neck.

"We knew he was dead. We thought Forensics might want the rope left," the paramedic told her. The stretcher arrived and Foden was lifted onto it.

"Get statements from everyone," Morrison told the uniformed sergeant. "And secure the victim's mobile. It will be evidence."

She walked to where Arabella Foden was sobbing into her hands with Phillipa also crying next to her.

"I'm dreadfully sorry, Mrs Foden. It's an awful thing to have happened."

Arabella took her hands away and saw it was Morrison. Her sobs were replaced by a look of intense hatred and she jumped at Morrison, flailing her fists at her.

"You did this. You have persecuted him and my family."
The vicar and Phillipa restrained her."
"We're sorry. We're sorry for your loss," Morrison said.
She told the sergeant she would take one of his officers and the two of them joined Christine West who had been watching the proceedings from the sidelines.
"What do you make of that?" she asked Morrison as they walked to her car.
"He knew we were onto him. He sent me a text message. I think we'll find what we want at Upland House."
At Upland House they were met in the hall by Mrs Courtney who was on her way out. She looked and looked again at Morrison who was in uniform.
"Yes, Mrs Courtney. I am a police officer. We have Mr Foden's permission to be here."
"What is it you want?"
"Don't worry. We shan't disturb you." She turned her back in a way of dismissal and led the way to the basement door. Mrs Courtney hesitated then continued her passage out of the house.
The studio door was unlocked as Foden had promised. Morrison found a light switch and led the way down the narrow stairs. At the bottom the studio was in darkness but another switch located at the bottom of the stairs turned on all the strip and flood lighting which temporarily blinded them as they stepped into the studio. Then they each stared in awe.
The whole length of the wall facing them was covered in almost life-sized panels and each panel contained startling photographs of Katy Rose Lewis. There was Katy Rose on a swing-boat, her skirt stretching across her thighs, her hair flying and her mouth screaming; Katy Rose aiming a cotton ball; Katy Rose looking along the barrel of an air-rifle, one

eye closed and her tongue protruding from her lips in concentration; Katy Rose eating an ice-cream, looking archly sideways into the lens of the camera, her mouth pouting playfully and the cone dripping down her wrist; and Katy Rose in various close-ups, her copper-coloured curls catching the sunlight or blowing about her face, her huge blue eyes reflecting her emotions and her lips sometimes smiling, sometimes serious, sometimes questioning and sometimes unsure were always mesmerising and inviting. But the procession of joy and colour was abruptly halted by the photograph at the end of the row. It was a monochrome Katy in strange perspective; taken farther away to enclose all of her torso and her arms a little away from her body. She was wearing a flower-patterned dress, her head was back and her hair was scattered around it. She was looking straight ahead but her eyes were expressionless and her mouth was slightly open as though in surprise. The focal point of the lens was about the centre of her chest and it could only have been taken while Katy was lying on the ground with the camera held above her. The officers stopped in front of it. They knew it was significant but did not know why until Morrison found the answer.

"She's dead. It's a photograph of her body."

The room seemed suddenly to have gone cold and Christine West noticeably shivered.

"Look behind you," the constable broke the silence. The two women turned to face the opposite wall and it was only the stunning quality of the photographs of Katy that had caused them not to look at it before.

The wall was covered in similar panels of printed pictures of George. Where the black and white picture of Katy ended one wall a black and white picture of George began the other and it brought the officers to it as George had brought

Charles Foden's camera to him to take the picture.

He was half lying on the ground with his back against a tree, one leg bent upwards with an arm resting on the knee, the other leg stretched along the ground. He was smiling up at the camera and he was completely naked. The quality of film had captured the pattern of leaves that played on his body and the sharp contrasts of sunlight and shade about him. There were two other photographs of the naked George, posed in the studio, both of them reminiscent of Greek sculptures, displaying all the attributes of his beautiful body; his hair curling about his face in classical style and his eyes and mouth speaking to the camera. The other pictures progressed from George in jeans to George wearing a Calvin Klein suit and a white shirt, looking as though he were poised on the red carpet of a film premier.

The officers, especially the two female ones, were staring, open-mouthed at the photographs. "God. I'm getting wet all over," Christine West said. "So am I," the constable agreed and the laughter broke the spell George had put them under.

"But why is that first picture in black and white?" West queried.

"A good question," Morrison answered. "My guess is it was taken on Drover's Hill, as was the black and white one of Katy. Foden is telling us a story; where Katy's pictures end, George's begin. I know Foden carried his Leica camera everywhere. He would have had it with him playing golf where he met George and where Katy met them."

The theory of her suspicions were realised and she understood the graphically dramatic message Foden had left for her.

"Is that his name; George?" West asked her.

Morrison confirmed it was.

"How do you know who he is?"

538

"A long story," she told them. "Let's look for more information."

The constable had been reading a hand-written page he had taken from a table in the middle of the studio.

"I think this is a confession," he said.

Morrison took the page from him. She immediately noted it was signed, *Charles Henderson Foden*.

She read it aloud. It confessed that he alone was responsible for the arson attack '...*that cleansed the earth of those sick, abhorrent people who terrorised the weak to gratify their lust and greed...*' and stated that his son, Noel had no knowledge of what he had done. It explained that Katy Rose was angry with him because he had refused to take naked pictures to make her a Page Three model. '*We met on Drover's Hill. She saw I was taking photographs of George and got the wrong idea about us. She said I was a queer, like my father. I slapped her face, not realising I had the camera in my hand. I was dreadfully sorry for what happened and dreadfully sorry for her family. I wanted to tell them but it would have ruined my own family if I had gone to prison. The misery was already done and had to be endured.*'

It also stated that he was not responsible for the attempt on young Jenny's life; '...*sometimes desperation drives our lives where we do not want to go...*'

It ended by saying that Katy had been put respectfully to rest and hoped that '...*the forces of fate I inherited will now be stilled with my death.*'

"Well, you found her, Daphne," West told Morrison.

"Not yet. Her family have to bury her, not Foden."

The basement was locked and a notice put on the door declaring it was a crime-scene The same applied to the doors that accessed the rear gardens. Mrs Courtney made a fuss about not being allowed there and pressed for an explanation which was patiently refused by Morrison.

"I do hope you are not going to damage our lovely garden in any way," she protested.

"We'll do our best not to but we will do what we have to do," Morrison told her and declined to say that an imaging team had already been called in to survey the grounds.

The Chief Constable discussed the Foden situation with his deputy, CS Alec Faye and with DS Laxton. He brought them up to speed with Morrison's investigation which Faye praised unstintingly but Laxton could only admit 'Had uncovered unforeseen circumstances' and covered his embarrassment by raging at the failings of Steve Jennings 'which could have led us to Foden at the time'.

CS Faye reminded him that Jennings had then only been in the police force for nine months and was only twenty years of age. He declined to add that it was Laxton who led the investigation but he did say 'We all make mistakes' and the Chief Constable supported the idea by stating that Jennings' inexperience would count in his favour should there be an enquiry.

The Chief Constable said the priority then was to find Katy Rose and that he had instructed Morrison to organise an imaging search of Upland House.

"I appreciate your people will need to be involved to build a prosecution case but I want Morrison to supervise the search team and to be consulted at all stages of your investigation," he told an unhappy DS Laxton.

The imaging team scoured all areas of the gardens, including the walled kitchen garden, but failed to find anything other than three graves where the grandparents' dogs had been buried.

"The pond," Morrison announced. "The woman on the first

floor told me the pond had been dug just before they moved in and her husband helped George complete it."

"All right. We'll contact the fire services and drain it," the supervisor told her.

When a large pump was brought to the site and set into the pond it was not long before Mrs Courtney charged over the grass towards the bemused firemen.

"Stop. Stop," she yelled at them. "What are you doing. There are fish and frogs and newts in the pond."

Morrison explained they had to drain the pond as they were searching for a body.

The tenants had not been told what the reason for the police activity was and Morrison thought the mention of a body might have calmed Mrs Courtney but, in her anger, she seemed not to notice and told Morrison she would sue them for criminal damage if the wildlife were in any way harmed.

"It's sheer unwarranted vandalism," she said. "There are hundreds of fish in there. Some very expensive carp. I will ring up the newspapers and tell them what you are doing," she added and started to march towards the house.

"We'll get some aquarium experts to guide us," Morrison conceded. The last thing they needed was another media storm.

Mrs Courtney was subdued.

"It's important to keep the same water," she told them. It takes years to form the right algae to feed the fish."

Morrison sighed and wondered what the Chief Constable would have to say about the extra costs.

"All right. We'll do everything necessary to protect the environment," she promised without knowing if they could.

The aquarium provided large polypropylene tanks into which the pond water was pumped and the pump was set into a wire cage to prevent anything but water getting into it.

After two hours there was only enough water in the pond to cover the writhing mass of fish which were then lifted by hand-nets from the pond to the tanks by cursing police officers and watched by an audience of laughing firemen and other officers as the fish slithered from the nets and hands and sent unfortunate officers trying to juggle them, sprawling into the stinking water.

The pumping slowly continued until only a residue of pond silt was left. "That should be kept, as much as possible," the man from the aquarium advised. "It's an essential source of protein for them," he told the wet, unsympathetic officers who by then only liked fish served in a light batter with chips.

When the hand-bale was completed and the pond lining pulled back, a mechanical digger was brought in, which, Morrison later recalled with a sense of irony, was hired from Foden Agricultural Machinery.

The digger reached into the centre of the pond and broke through the thin veneer of concrete and began lifting the rubble carefully from under it and set it around the pond for examination. It was the next day when the digger located something that would not easily move and the operator had to drive a little way into the pond to balance the machine in order to lift the object.

The arm gradually withdrew a large oblong box covered in green and black mould which was set onto the grass and inspected by the curious officers.

"What is it?" one enquired.

"Looks like a chest freezer," another answered as he rubbed at the object with his glove.

"We'd better get Forensics here," Morrison said.

The freezer was loaded onto a trailer and taken to the laboratory where it was carefully cleaned before the padlock was then cut and the lid was lifted.

" ...*the waterproof golf club cover and the dry, confined atmosphere of the freezer provided excellent protection to slow decomposition to about twenty per cent of what might be expected by normal burial procedure. The victim was in a good state of preservation. Tissue and hair showed minimal deterioration...*"

The report from the forensic laboratory informed Morrison but a phone call from the pathologist later added, "Very similar to your bog-body, Inspector."

"...*the victim had suffered a trauma to the left Temporal Lobe, powerful enough to cause internal bleeding in that area. Indentations in the outer tissue were evidence of a round, sharp object having caused the damage, having been administered with considerable force.*"

"Might the indentations mentioned in your report match the lens housing of a small camera?" Morrison asked the pathologist after she had studied accompanying photographs. The scientist agreed it was more than likely.

"...*Extensive damage to the cerebellum and the Medulla Oblongata was evident and was probably caused by the victim falling backwards and her head striking the ground. This damage would have caused the immediate paralysis of the whole body, quickly followed by death. The evidence would suggest the blow to the left Temporal Lobe was sufficient to knock the victim over and the fall caused the fatal damage to the back of the head. There was no evidence of other injuries or of sexual activity and the victim was a virgin. The dress the victim was wearing showed no evidence of damage but there was no sign of under garments apart from a brassiere.*"

After the forensics Report had been read by the Chief Constable a wrap-up meeting was conducted by Laxton in the Incidents Room. It was concluded that Katy Rose Lewis had been killed, almost certainly by Charles Foden in Drover's Hill Woods and transported to the Foden premises and there buried.

The simple, factual detail left many questions unanswered and the assembled officers soon began firing them at DS Laxton.

"Why don't you run through everything about the case from when Penny Featherstone thought she saw Katy in the woods to when you found the body?" the Chief Constable suggested to Daphne Morrison.

It took Morrison an hour to recall the sequence of events and as she spoke she relived every moment of them. The Chief Constable had advised her not to mention the Noel Foden assault on Caroline as that would emerge in the arson inquiry being wrapped up by the other force but after some discussion and after speaking to her parents, it was decided to reveal Penny Featherstone's old identity but not her new one as the family did not want to be hounded by the media again. But Penny's extraordinary vision was too big a story to ignore and it would generate more favourable publicity for the police persistence in solving the case and offset their original failures. But the explanations did not stop the questions;

Why would Foden be taking pictures of a naked man when he was playing golf? Was George homosexual? Were he and Foden lovers? If there was no sex involved, what happened to Katy's pants? If Foden and George were lovers did his wife and family know? Is it really possible to unlock childhood memories by hypnotherapy?"

And then the questions became more hypothetical; "Is murder and suicide inherited. I mean, Foden's father committed suicide and his grandfather murdered that Gerry."

"And his son tried to commit suicide," someone else added.

"Yeah, and why did his father swap clothes with a POW to try to keep him here. Were they lovers too?"

"But why would Foden kill those other homos if he was one himself?"

The DS stopped the speculation.

"Okay. That's enough. It's useful to ask those questions because the press are going to do the same and we'll have to get our answers ready. But what we have right now is a bloody good result thanks to Inspector Morrison's persistence – and a stroke of fortune that Jenny Challis came back to Stokesey. We can now tell the Lewis' we have found Katy and let them bury her in peace."

****

Katy Rose was buried in Stokesey church. Most of the residents of Upper Stokesey and the Badgers hamlet attended but Tom Lewis requested that only Daphne Morrison and, ironically as Tom had not been informed of his failures, Steve Jennings from the police force would be welcome. The Challis family returned for the funeral and Penny cried on Daphne Morrison's shoulder.

There were too many people to get into the ancient church and the service was relayed outside. Her coffin was kept inside the church for two days before the burial and the panels of her colour photographs were displayed around the walls. Her school friends, now middle-aged with children and some with grandchildren, saw again the lively, lovely Katy as they remembered her. Her brother and mother wept continually on a private visit and their cries of Why. Why. Why, were not answered. Tom Lewis said he would put the panels around the walls of the dining area of The Badgers and it would forever be called Katy's Room.

After the service, the Challis' and Morrison went back to The Badgers for lunch . She didn't have much time to speak to Penny alone but as they hugged goodbye Penny told her that Noel Foden had got married in a Hindu ceremony.

"How do you know that?" Morrison asked.

"He wrote to Harry. He thanked him for hitting him with a chair and said it was the least he deserved."

After Penny and her parents had left, an emptiness enveloped Daphne Morrison and suppressed emotions seeped from her eyes. When she crossed the bridge over the estuary, instead of turning left towards the police station she took a right fork towards Mountfield Golf Club. Julie Norris would just have to accept she was a wet sponge and needed a drink or two.

Thank you for reading my book. I do hope you enjoyed it. If you feel you would like to comment on it, or comment about any topic regarding my work, I should be pleased to hear from you. You can reach me at:
www.penpowerwriting@gmail.com

You might also like my previous book, **Getting Tyson:** a hard-nosed crime thriller which has five-star rating.
www.amazon.com/dp/B019M4TQIG

P K Davies

Printed in Dunstable, United Kingdom

67105998R00308